I0699633

A GRAVE
NOT MADE
FOR
MOURNING

Book Cover by Seventhstar Art
Map by Caffee Cartography
Illustrations by Jan Perit Kablan

ISBN-13: 979-8-9900278-9-3
Originally published November 2025
Also available as an ebook.

*For anyone who has grieved a mother, a home,
a version of themselves*

Also by Caroline Cusanelli

A Liar's Twisted Tongue

Coming Soon

A Puppet's Broken String (February 2026)

A Note to Returning Readers

For returning readers familiar with earlier drafts or pre-release materials, you may notice a number of changes to names, nations, and terminology in the final version of this story. These adjustments were made to better reflect the internal consistency, linguistic evolution, and cultural resonance of the world.

Here's a brief summary of notable updates: Lucent is now Lyrian; Soma has become Ilyria. Lorucille is referred to as Folkara, Viridis as Eunaris, and Serpencia has been renamed Nepthara. Armanthine and Verena are now Drae and Drevia, respectively. Queen Lusia has become Queen Leiana, and Eudora is now Elowen. Kappa has also been updated to Kapha. These refinements were made to deepen clarity and immersion, ensuring the world of this story is as vivid, intentional, and cohesive as possible.

Thank you very much for coming with me on this wild ride.

— *Caroline*

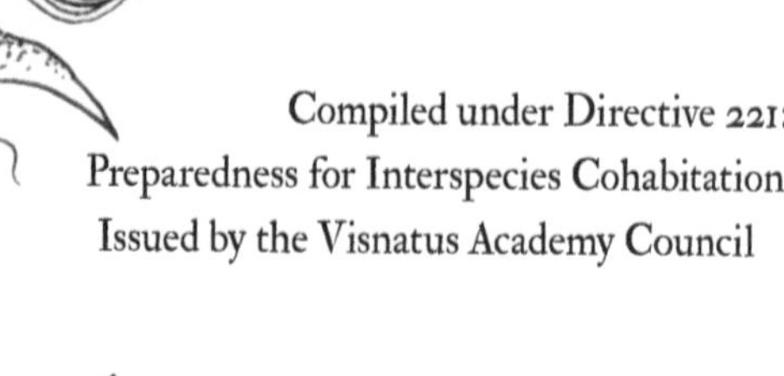

Compiled under Directive 221:
Preparedness for Interspecies Cohabitation
Issued by the Visnatus Academy Council

MAGICAL SPECIES

<u>ARCANES</u> (AHR-kayns): Classified entities of unknown origin. Referenced in unsanctioned folklore and restricted testimony. Discussion is prohibited under Ilyrian Council Order 77.

<u>LYRIANS</u> (*LEER-ee-uhns*): Descendants of the goddess Sulva and the most powerful magic-wielders in the universe. Lyrians possess a wide array of abilities—dream-walking, subconscious manipulation, shadow-wielding, and premonition—though only the most gifted command them all. They live well beyond two centuries, and are always marked by varying shades of blue eyes.

<u>FOLK</u> (*fohk*): Memory and glamour are the most common gifts among the Folk. But every Folk carries only one elemental root—and all have brown eyes.

- *Light Folk*: Disrupt electricity.
- *Air Folk*: Command the wind.
- *Fire Folk*: Can start fires, but not extinguish them.

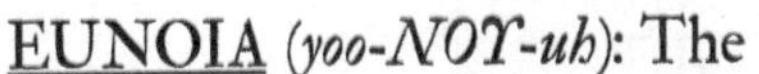

EUNOIA (*yoo-NOY-uh*): The Eunoia are bound to life itself— able to stir growth in plants, sense emotion, and seek truth. Despite their wicked ability to manipulate feelings, they are often used as healers and agriculturists. All Eunoia have varying shades of green eyes.

DRAES (*DRAYZ*): Known as the mind's creatures, Draes are the most intelligent of the magic-wielding species. They can steal mental magic from others: memory, emotion, and subconscious control. The most skilled among them can read thoughts. Their skin is nearly impenetrable and their lifespans stretching up to five hundred years. All Draes bear violet eyes.

NEPENTHES (*neh-PEN-theez*): Agile, silent, and bred for the kill, Nepenthes are considered the most dangerous magic-wielding species. With venomous fangs capable of delivering instant death, they can blend into their surroundings or pass through solid objects—powers that are banned without special permission from a Royal. With a single hiss, they can calm their prey before attacking. All Nepenthes have gray eyes.

MAGIC

<u>THE FLAME</u>: The volatile elemental magic of the Fire Folk.

<u>GLAMOUR</u>: Alters appearance of a person or object. Only Folk can cast/remove glamours.

<u>CHANNELING</u>: Temporary magical energy transfer between individuals.

<u>WARDS</u>: Mental magic defenses used by Royals and officials.

<u>BARRIERS</u>: Forcefields designed to block specific life forms.

<u>PORTAL</u>: A magical doorway allowing travel between two mirrored surfaces.

<u>RAECRIUM</u> (*RAY-kree-um*): A magical device used to project images to other raecriums.

LIMITATIONS

<u>LIFE FORCE</u>: The source of vitality, strength, and magical ability.

<u>SOUL SUCKERS</u>: Colloquial term for individuals capable of stealing another's life force. Manifestations are subject to containment and investigation.

<u>BURNOUT</u>: Overuse of magic can cause exhaustion, nosebleeds, migraines, or death. Irreversible in advanced stages.

ARTIFACTS

<u>SOUL STONES</u>: The most powerful artifacts in the universe. Each world has only one, crafted to maintain balance and keep the magic of the universe in equilibrium.

    o <u>MEMORIUM</u> (*meh-MOR-ee-um*) (Folkara): A relic of immense power over memory, weather, and glamour. The Memorium was originally a vibrant yellow, but time and overuse have dimmed it, tarnishing its brilliance into a deep, murky orange.

    o <u>STONE OF LIGHT</u> (Ilyria): Alters perception, strengthens or suppresses Lyrian abilities by providing pure light energy.

    o <u>SOUL RUBY</u> (Iris): Grants immortality or annihilates eternal souls.

HISTORICAL TERMS

<u>AA</u> (AFTER ARCANE): Current timeline. Year 1 AA marks the aftermath of the Arcanian War.

<u>BA</u> (BEFORE ARCANE): The era preceding AA. There are no surviving records of this time period.

<u>ARCANIAN WAR</u>: A universal war 1,000 years ago that lasted six months and killed 70% of the population.

<u>NEPTHARIAN WAR</u>: A conflict between Folkara and Nepthara twelve years ago. Lasted two years.

LITTALINE COMPACT: Accords protecting the alliance between Ilyria and Folkara.

IRISAN ARCHIVES: The largest library in history, destroyed during the Arcanian War.

WORLDS

ILYRIA (*ill-LEER-ee-uh*): Homeworld of the Lyrians and a military powerhouse. Ilyria thrives on alcohol, energy, fishing, technology, and control. Its government is a matrilineal absolute monarchy—power passed from mother to daughter, with little room for mercy in between.

FOLKARA (*FOHL-kah-ruh*): The homeworld of the Folk and the largest world. Its primary industries include welding, mining, livestock, and the production of luxury goods. Governed by a traditional monarchy, its wealth runs deep—but so do its divides.

EUNARIS (*yoo-NAHR-iss*): Homeworld of the Eunoia. Known for its agriculture, medicine, and the gentle magic of growth. Governed by a democratic republic, Eunaris thrives quietly—valued by all, ruled by many, and heard only when it chooses to speak.

DRAEVIA (*DRAY-vee-uh*): Homeworld of the Draes. Known for its precision industries—clothing, mining, and quarrying. Though governed by a republic in name, its representatives are chosen by Ilyria. What appears democratic is often anything but.

<u>NEPTHARA</u> (*NEP-thah-ruh*):
Homeworld of the Nepenthes. Known for its
brutal efficiency—building infrastructure,
training soldiers, and forging
weapons. Though rich in strength,
Nepthara is poor in sovereignty. It remains a
dependent territory under Ilyria's control.

<u>VISNATUS</u> (*viz-NAH-tus*): The only world where
all five magic-wielding species coexist—at least, in
theory. Visnatus exists for one purpose: to educate the
elite. It remains a dependent territory under Ilyrian control.

<u>IRIS</u> (*EYE-riss*): A dead world. Once home to a thriving
people, Iris fell during the Arcanian War, its extinction
etched into history—but not into healing.

LOCATIONS & LANDMARKS

<u>VISNATUS ACADEMY</u>: The only school open to all spe-
cies. Educates the elite in politics, power, and inheritance.

<u>LUNAR LAKE</u>: A moonlit body of water enchanted to store
magic. Located on Visnatus.

<u>THE GREAT SEA</u>: The largest and most powerful body
of water in the universe. Located on Ilyria, and energized
by its four moons.

<u>THE SEPTIC</u>: Impoverished districts of Ilyria and
Folkara.

<u>WELDING VILLAGE</u>: Fire Folk settlement in
Folkara's septic.

<u>THE SAUL</u>: A crumbling ruin from

a past war. Now a trade post and gathering point for the Welding Village.

<u>THE VOID</u>: An unverified plane said to exist outside time and regulated magic. Mention of The Void is restricted.

DEITIES

<u>SULVA</u> (*SOUL-vuh*): The Lunar Goddess. Revered as the mother of the Lyrian bloodline.

<u>AYAN</u> (*EYE-awn*): The Solar God.

<u>ZOLA</u> (*ZOY-uh*): Goddess of balance.

DEMIGODS

<u>AMUN</u> (*AY-muhn*): Descendant of Ayan. The first person to walk the universe.

<u>EIRA</u> (*EER-uh*): Daughter of Sulva. The first Lyrian.

MONSTERS

<u>FATTA SCORPION</u>: A scorpion that grows to ten times the size of an average person. Its venom does not just kill—it erases the soul. Originates from Iris.

<u>KAPHA</u> (KAH-fuh): Four-armed predator from Nepthara. Can shift between tangible and intangible states depending on its need in battle. Kills by strangulation and calms its prey with a touch.

<u>MOONARO</u> (moo-NAH-roh): A strikingly beautiful creature covered in shimmering silver fur, with antlers made of icicles. It possesses the icy power of Ilyria.

<u>PERNIPE</u> (PERN-ip): A cursed Eunoia woman who was cursed with a wicked bloodlust. Her skin was traded for bark, and her voice for melody. Only her own kind can resist her fatal song.

LORE & LIVING

<u>AIBEK</u> (*EYE-beck*): The ancestral name of Ilyria's ruling family—a lineage tied to absolute authority.

<u>CONTARINI</u> (*kon-tah-REE-nee*): The surname of the Folkara regime.

<u>MIAL</u> (*MEE-uhl*): A name half-erased. Found in forbidden texts from the Irisan Archives. No known identity—only power and implication.

<u>PENCE</u>: The universal currency.

<u>ACANSA</u> (*ah-KAHN-suh*): An elite Folk-only

school on Folkara. Admission is blood-based, not merit-based.

<u>VESI</u> (*VEH-see*): The original liquor of Ilyria.

This document was assembled at the request of the Visnatus Academy Council to assist incoming students in navigating the sociopolitical and magical complexities of the universe.

ARSON'S ALLEY
VISNATUS
LUNAR
LAKE

N
The Woods

PART 1:
THE SHELL

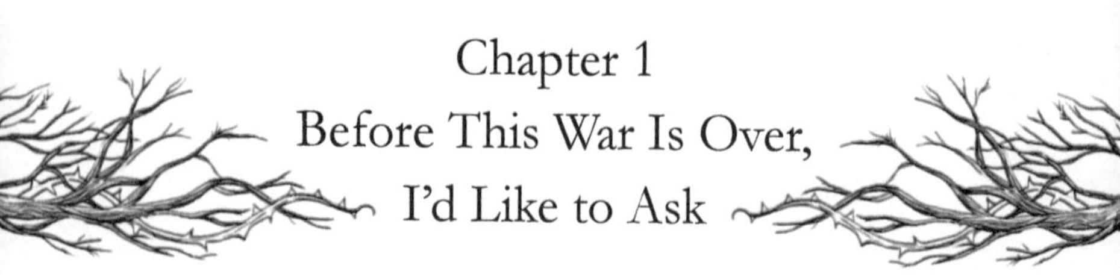

Chapter 1
Before This War Is Over,
I'd Like to Ask

The room is silent, but I hear everything.

Boredom rattles behind me like a restless foot hitting a desk leg. Over and over. Banging into my mind until I can't forget the sound. Shame slams into me from across the classroom—it's not mine, but it roots itself in my chest like it grew there. I suck in my stomach, hold my breath, make myself smaller, all for her. I do what she wants.

What she does.

Where does her feeling end, and my body begin?

The professor's irritation hammers behind my eyes. Calista's rage clings to my skin, settling beneath me like I belong to her. Lately, she feels like this all the time. There's a party in the woods tonight, meant to celebrate her engagement.

One that I know was never her choice.

My teeth grind together until I'm scared they'll shatter right out of my mouth. I want to slap the desk, throw my chair—anything to give this rage a place to go.

I want to scream. But it wouldn't be my voice.

It would be theirs.

Instead, I grip the arms of my chair, my nails digging into the cushion until I hear it rip.

The sound seems to echo through the classroom, as if this space is sacred. Holy. Even if it's far from so.

"Wendy," Calista hisses.

I look up.

The professor's face is stone. His bald head is shining. "Ms. Estridon, do you intend to participate?"

If I could explain, I would.

I am a body of water, contaminated by all that touches me.

"What was the question?" I ask, trying to separate myself from Calista's constant anger.

He sighs. "If your personality shapes your actions—and that personality is largely a product of your genetics and life experiences, both of which are mostly beyond your control—can you truly be said to have free will?"

He paces once, slowly.

"Now, let's complicate it," he says. "Add the gods. Systems above you, shaping you. Does that give you more freedom—or take it away?"

The question makes sense. It just doesn't leave room for mercy. I didn't ask for this power or choose to feel everyone inside my skin. It's the magic that isolates me. The thing that forces distance while I beg for connection.

I'd prefer free will to be a sham because I don't feel I have any in the first place.

"I'd have to ponder," I answer.

"That is the point of this class, Ms. Estridon." His tone is curt.

I sink into my seat, wishing I could disappear.

Some of my classmates scoff, and it gets stuck in my throat. Some lean in, making it impossible for me to relax.

But one person stands out from the rest. Someone with an answer they aren't ready to share; but I can feel its weight, the steadiness behind the unease. The conviction they feel for the topic.

I reach for it.

For Azaire. His emotions don't spike or sting—they root, like a tree that stands no matter the storm. And when I lean toward him, it's not just for relief; it's instinct. Like moss stretching toward a crack in the cave ceiling, desperate for light.

His calm doesn't make my palms sweat and my eyes twitch. It simply settles.

"Then no," I answer, my heart pounding like I'm prey and not a person. "If I am composed of things beyond my control, then there is no free will."

"And of the gods?" the professor goads.

"I've yet to decide."

If the gods are cruel, or just careless.

If life is punishment disguised as choice.

If the gods shaped me, then they gave me this power. They either wanted me to struggle or suffer. Or maybe they weren't paying attention at all.

But either way, they must not have liked what they made.

"It's not a decision," he says. "It's a belief. What do you believe?"

My arms shake, both from the opinions of others and my own unraveling. "I believe it's possible."

"*What* is possible, Ms. Estridon?"

"That they shape us."

"And what does that mean?"

"That… we aren't free?"

The room stings—relief, dread, judgment. Everyone's hiding behind their own answers, either thankful they're not in my position or worried they'll be next. It sets off a sequence of contradictions in my bones. Every limb reaches in a different direction, stretching me apart thoroughly.

I don't know what I am.

"You made your choice today, did you not?" the professor asks. "You chose to sit in this class, whether you knew you'd enjoy it or hate it. Why? Why do you make the choices that you do? What has shaped you?"

Shaped me? Like I'm clay in a mold.

I am.

"I'm here because I have to be," I say, choosing logic over emotion. "I'm enrolled."

"You don't have to do anything. That's a belief."

My torso tightens, unable to take in air. Calista's emotion grows heavier—not because she cares about the topic. Only because she can't let go of her future.

"There's no free will. Is that what you wish for me to say?" I ask.

"I only wish for the truth." The professor's voice is steady. But not steady enough to calm me.

The truth has never been on my side. Nothing has. Not this room of onlookers—critiquing, watching, but never feeling. Not like I do.

I fail to distinguish my feelings and choices from other peoples'. What *is* truth, in that case?

Finally, I mutter, "I don't know what that is."

"Then that's your first belief, Ms. Estridon. That your truth is unknowable. And that's a prison you built for yourself."

A cup falls from my shaking fingers.

No, not my shaking fingers.

Yes, my shaking fingers.

The glass shatters at my feet.

My fingers *are* shaking—but it isn't *my* overwhelm.

I watch myself in the mirror, green eyes glowing from the spikes of emotion around me—the other girls in the suite. It's our newest suitemate that has me acting up. Has my *magic* acting up. I've grown used to Calista and Aralia, like background noise I can tune out unless something major is happening. Most of the time, I manipulate their emotions just enough to soften the edges.

Aralia's always carried a quiet disappointment in the world, a hint of rebellion, but lately there's something different—curiosity. And I think I know why. Her new roommate, Desdemona, is a bundle of nerves. Incessant, almost whining—for as much as pure emotion can. I've never believed that people can't sense emotions, at least to some degree. So I'm guessing Aralia's sensing hers.

Calista is, as always, annoyed. She doesn't want to go tonight and celebrate her forced marriage to Lucian, though she knows the power of appearance.

I'm surprised she's in our suite, rather than getting ready with her friends. I think of walking to her room, asking her to do my eyeliner or offering her a skirt to wear. I wish I could. But that bridge sank long ago.

Instead, I do my own eyeliner and wear the skirt I used to lend her.

It was nice that she would ask. She's a princess—she could get any skirt she wanted. She may seem harsh, but a hard shell often protects a soft interior.

And I know hers.

By the time I make it to the door, ready to leave, I flinch. Unable to open it.

"Wendy," the voice in my mind says, his voice soft, delicate.

Disappointed.

"I know," I respond to the boy. That's what I call him. That's all he is.

The boy in my head.

"Come to me."

I do as he says, closing my eyes and entering the world of my mind. The four walls of my room slip away, and I fall into the woods —right beyond where the party will be.

He lies next to me in the grass.

"This is where you want to meet?" I ask him, staring into his big green eyes.

He didn't always have them. In the beginning, he was nothing but a wisp of smoke, the shadow of a person. With the years, he's taken shape, nearly growing into something real.

"You should go tonight," he answers—though, not much of an answer, admittedly.

"I don't want to." I flip onto my back, looking up at the stars and away from him, but waiting to be convinced.

"You do."

I've yet to name him. To the both of us, he's "the boy." On some days—like this one—that lack of a title makes him feel less tangible.

"If you didn't, we wouldn't be meeting here," he finishes.

Where the party is steps away.

"That was your doing."

"My doing is yours," he answers. *"You can do more than watch from the outside. That's what Ma would say."*

I sit up, dusting imaginary dirt from my leather pants and staring into the distant trees. *"When you say things like that, you make it clear that you are me."*

"You don't want me to be you?"

"I don't," I say, raising my voice the way I only can in my head. There's freedom in yelling.

I can't remember the last time I truly did.

"I disagree."

I glare at him. *"How can you disagree if you're me?"*

The boy cradles my cheeks, his palms resting beneath my chin as he lifts my face. *"Go. You cause yourself more pain by fearing it."*

I sit on the outskirts of the festivities, watching the dancing grass and bugs, feeling the sloppy students and singing stars. My classmates stand around fires with bottles of alcohol. Some dance.

It isn't long before I turn away, shunning the crowd I never joined, and walk further into the woods. I'm desperate to escape the echoing words in my mind that are not mine—despite that being the very thing I have to endure to find human connection.

It seems an impossible task. That's what I came for, and I'm already running away. I'm already weak.

There was no reason to believe anything would be different this time, but sometimes loneliness makes you do irrational things.

As I escape the crowd, my fists clench, as if holding onto something that isn't here—desperation. My feet wobble, and I almost stumble into a tree—alcohol. Someone not far from here is angry, a second is drunk, and the last is full of fear.

If this is what happens with three people, how can I face the hundreds by the bonfires?

Nearly the entire student body is out here.

I walk only far enough to take the edge off the emotion, then I drop to the ground. It's better here, away from the party, alone in the woods, but not too far inside. Any further in the woods, and I would approach the cottage. I only go there once a year, and I will not give up my future for the present.

I lie back on the grass, just like I did with the boy earlier tonight. My eyes search the sky for constellations, landing on Ma's favorite— my favorite, by inheritance. Hers are the only ones I ever look for.

The twinkling stars could dance forever, and I would lose myself in them.

However, I don't get much time tonight.

A twig snaps in the distance, and footsteps approach. My head swings away from the sky, searching for the sound. My surroundings are empty—physically. But, by the gods, do I feel whoever's nearing. Their anxiety fills my body. It doesn't disorient my mind or clog my limbs.

It's steady. It's someone who knows how to handle themselves. So careful, it's almost calming.

And I know who it is.

Quickly, I rise, running and ducking behind a tree before Azaire approaches. I hide beneath the thick bark, watching him carefully.

He sits on an unsteady rock, tipping back and forth, then pulls out a little brown journal and quill, touching the ink to the page.

My pounding heart slows, easing me into a lull as his anxiety settles slowly. Azaire takes on an entirely different emotion, something like discovery, but not so easily defined. I lean my head against the tree, drinking up the favored break from anger and fear. Still, I wait for him to leave.

I've seen Azaire almost every day for years—*felt* him every day. In Philosophy class this morning, even. He had an answer to the question of free will, one he refused to speak.

He's one of the few people I can pick out from a crowd by feeling alone.

Watching him is like being a fish out of water. All of life is, actually. Watching from the outside. Looking, but never touching. Oddly, because I could. I know what Azaire feels for me—there's no way I couldn't. It's a blessing and a curse. I'm forced to feel it.

I wonder if there would be more fun in the mystery of not knowing, or simply more misery.

As I rest my head against the tree, a nut falls crunching against the leaves and rolling in the grass. I curse the tree when Azaire calls, "Who's there?"

For a moment, I duck further behind the trunk. But if I don't come out, he will come in. He will look.

With a deep breath, I step out from my safe haven. The moment

Azaire sees me, his anxiety spikes.

"What are you doing here?" My voice trembles—too territorial.

But he doesn't think so.

Azaire holds up his notebook and shrugs, tugging at the back of his dark blue beanie. "I guess I was just following the silence."

"Okay." I duck back behind my tree, planning to go south and find some quiet on the walk back to my suite.

"Wait!" Azaire calls.

I surprise myself when I stop.

"Do you want to sit?"

Azaire's adrenaline spikes, but he's not drunk. I think he might actually be sober. I pull the tips of my gloves from each of my fingers, then back down. Over and over again while I try to make up my mind.

Up, down. Up, down. Up, down. Never off.

With a subtle nod, I whisper, "Okay."

Loneliness, I think, makes you do irrational things. It makes me sit next to Azaire on his rock as he slides his journal into his pocket. He looks at me, and I immediately look at the sky.

His anxiety is no longer steady—now, it shakes my hands. It's because of me that he feels this, and it'd be endearing if I didn't have to feel it, too. If the only way I could know how he was feeling was by the heavy thrum of his chest.

From the comfort of my mind, I reach out to him. My body trembles as I close my eyes, turning down his emotions like a rusted dial on a record player. It isn't hard; it's only a small amount of resistance, twitching in my fingertips.

Once I've calmed Azaire, my muscles relax from his lethargy. All without touching him, too.

That's something most of my kind, the Eunoia, can't do—manipulate emotion without skin-to-skin contact. It offers merit to the words I've heard my whole life: *"prodigal child," "gifted one."* But if I were to touch him, he'd die. I'd override his mind with my emotion or the emotion around me that I'm forced to contain. Truth be told, I've never found out which it is that kills.

All I know is that my touch *does* kill. I learned that the hard way, once.

And there is nothing prodigal about that.

I turn to the sky, tugging at my gloves as I watch the stars. My one comfort.

Until Azaire asks, "What are you looking at?"

I take a deep breath, contemplating if I'll answer. But this is what I came here for—company, even if I can't keep it.

"Surma," I answer, my voice quiet but the name heavy. "A constellation."

Azaire is intrigued, as if my words have painted a picture he wants to see or began a book he wants to finish.

"What's the story?" he asks.

"A sad one… They usually are." I fidget with my hands, pulling my gloves off and on, rubbing my fingers together, aimlessly searching for a way to soothe myself.

"Yeah?" he murmurs in response, and yet there's a finality to it. As if he doesn't mind the sadness I'm about to offer on a silver platter.

I chuckle bitterly beneath my breath, forcing my gaze upward, drawn to the stars that witnessed this story unfold. "Surma was the first child of the first two people—Amun and Eira. He was forced into battle against the monsters and was quickly deemed the best warrior in the universe. The people loved him. *Eira* loved him."

I pause, the words sinking like stones. I don't know why. It isn't *my* story; it's only my words. But I feel as if they're a part of me. Or maybe I'm borrowing emotion, somehow tapping into a dead woman and her motherly grief. One of the first people to ever live.

"But Eira's sister, Elysina, was bitter," I continued. "Greedy. She wanted that title for her firstborn—the power, the glory. Elysina, in her jealousy, manipulated a fatta's subconscious. And it killed Surma. But… the fatta doesn't just kill the body." I nearly shudder. "It destroys the soul, too. *Everything* about you, erased.

"Eira was devastated. She carried her son's broken body to Sulva, pleading with the lunar goddess to let Surma live on—somehow. Some *way.*" My words hang in the air, thick with the gravity of the tale. I steal a glance at Azaire, his face bathed in the light of the stars, holding his breath with me.

"Now all we have is a cluster of stars in his name," I mutter.

Azaire glances at me for a quick moment, then back at the sky without a word.

Is he going to say something? Is he contemplating? He must be. But this is the first conversation I've had in weeks, and he's not saying anything. I suppose I no longer understand how the mind works, how to communicate. It's been so long since I've had company. I've learned that emotions are different from thoughts. Thoughts tend to be linear—you can trace the rabbit's trail from point A to point B.

Emotions come in waves. You're at their mercy as much as dust is to the wind's.

So why am I upset that he isn't answering me? There's nothing more to say.

I may have taken too much of his emotion earlier, turned him into a shell of himself. In that case, I have to leave immediately, let him find his way back. He should be fine tomorrow, when he awakens from a night's worth of sleep.

I begin to stand.

His voice stops me.

"Even the most powerful of us are flawed," Azaire whispers.

He's right. Eira and Elysina, two of the most powerful Lyrians of all time, killed one another's children out of spite.

"Maybe it's the price of duality," Azaire finishes.

I nearly smile. He responded.

I wasn't expecting him to.

But I dearly wanted him to.

"You know I see it in everything," I respond, leaning my body back down against the grass. "The good and the ugly." I tug on the hairs standing up on my arms. "I'm beginning to believe that you can't have one without the other. It's kind of exhausting." I laugh.

It's the truth.

"I like the way you speak." Azaire's voice is soft, and I'm blindsided by the sentiment. That's something I've never been told, not even something in its likeness. Then again, I don't often speak to people.

"Why's that?" I ask, my voice tight.

"I—" He pauses. "I don't know. I guess you just highlight the good."

I laugh again. If only he knew.

Then Azaire says, "You understand that someone can do evil and still be good."

I shake my head. "That's not what I said."

I'm sure he's not listening to me.

"Isn't it?" he presses.

We're looking at one another now.

He's looking at *me* now.

"The good, the bad—the ugly—it's in everything," he continues, "all tangled together. You can't have one without the other, so everyone is both." Azaire adjusts his beanie, pulling at the edges like he's coaxing his thoughts from it. "You spoke of a couple losing their son, but you made sure I knew they loved him."

I watch him thoughtfully, looking for any underlying emotion. Anything that may deem him insincere. There's nothing. Nothing but a boy in front of me, being good. Nothing to show me where his dark edges lie—the ones he has to have. He told me as much, in not so many words.

"Yeah." I shrug. "That is what I said."

At least, it's one interpretation. But I prefer the way he sees it. That there is good in evil, not just evil in good. I think I'd prefer him believing that's what I meant.

"I appreciate it."

I pucker my lips, watching him while I contemplate.

"Why?" I finally ask.

"You helped me put something into perspective." He smiles, his venomous canines poking out—the reason the worlds hate the Nepenthes, his kind. I've only ever found kinship in them. A part of my body is deadly to the touch, too.

"Do you want to come back to the party with me?" He asks.

It's endearing how nervous he is. I imagine his heart hammering in his chest, hoping it's racing as fast as mine, even if it's for a different reason.

A sigh escapes me, but the longing inside of me doesn't. The desire to join him.

But people are safer at a distance.

"No."

Azaire nods softly. I can feel his disappointment in my blood, but there is no animosity. Only a small pinch of sorrow.

"I'll see you in philosophy," he responds.

I'm only subtly relieved when he gets up and walks away.

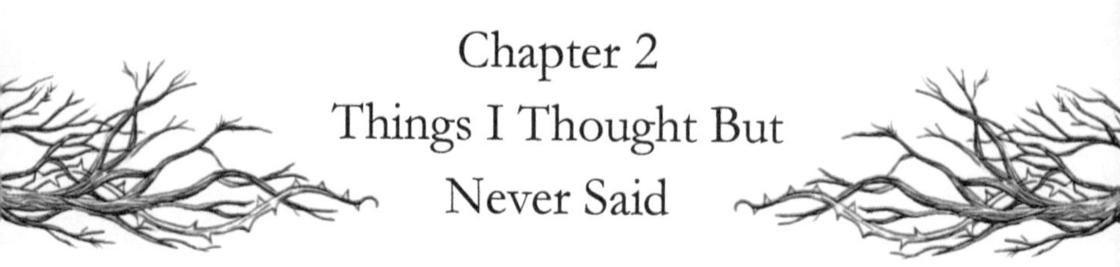

Chapter 2
Things I Thought But
Never Said

I wish the Eunoia had more control over their emotions, and not just the ability to feel them. Even in a room filled only with my kind, the air is heavy. I glance at my fellow classmates, Eunoia I've known since I was ten, who have all grown to learn about my state of being.

That I feel them all the time.

They feel violated by my presence. The masters of emotion do not wish to be read, and here I stand, doing it against even my own will.

Shame forces my head down, an attempt at invisibility I can never acquire.

Today we have volunteers coming in—people who suffered severe injuries and need healing. I think they're coming from Combat Training. This is the year my class is supposed to learn to mend fatal injuries. It's part of our training as future healers and our first time healing more than a cut or a broken bone.

But I don't want to feel all of their pain.

My heart sinks deeper when Azaire is among the crowd of injured students entering the classroom. He's scared, and I feel guilty because I want to run just so I don't have to feel his fear. I prefer his steadfastness.

Instead, I force myself to stand still, watching the wounded shuffle into the room.

All the volunteers are injured beyond the point of natural repair.

One still has a blade in his arm.

All the volunteers have gray eyes.

One is about to faint.

None of the volunteers are volunteers at all.

The room becomes a horror. All the fear, the mistreatment, the resentment, and the one girl who thinks she deserves this.

The reality of their forced hands is clear.

I stand, prepared to run, when Azaire walks to me. Scared, abused, and probably dying, he smiles at me. There's blood on his teeth. He's wobbly on his feet.

And he smiles.

I have no choice—how could there be a choice? I step toward him, holding onto his arm as I guide him to the seat next to me, before a large table. It's scattered with scalpels and herbs—every ingredient I might need to heal him. I don't know if I can.

He sits, tired and breathless. Somehow, he still chokes out, "Ms. Ferner said we're partners."

I nod, picking up his hands with my gloved ones—but I can't take pain this strong without skin-to-skin contact.

Dropping his hand and peeling my glove from my fingers, I say, "Don't worry. I won't touch you."

In response, I feel him working up something like courage. A knot forms in my gut, begging to be untied. I reach out, coaxing it out of him. Untying the knot.

"The last thing I'm worried about is you touching me," Azaire murmurs, and as I search for his gaze, it drops.

I place my attention back on my hands, raising them just over the bruises of his eyes.

It's for you, I wish to say. *I don't touch you because I want to save you.*

But my focus would be more worthwhile to him than a couple useless words.

My hands hover just above his body as I scan him, past the burning, jagged sensation that pierces through my side like a twisting knife. Past the throbbing around my eyes that intensifies with every heartbeat, as if it's splitting open my skull from the pressure. Past the razors scraping against the tender lining of my throat.

The pain is unbearable—and Azaire carried it with a smile.

I close my eyes, steadying myself. My hands hang, trembling just above his skin, refusing to make contact. The sensation is electric, the weight of his suffering like an anvil against my chest.

Shuddering, I continue to pull the pain out of him and into me. The sharpness of his agony rips me open with every breath. Every pulse of pain is a new layer of destruction.

When I stifle a gasp, Azaire reaches to grab my hands.

I yank them away before I can hurt him further.

"Hey."

My breath is ragged as I look around the room. The acute pain of Azaire has subsided, but there's a room full of it, piercing into every crack that I've carved into myself.

Cool hands reach up to my sweat-soaked face, fingers guiding me back to a gray gaze.

"Eyes on me," Azaire whispers, his voice soft like velvet.

My heart pounds as I obey, locking my gaze with his. His fingers remain steady, gripping my jaw, his thumb close to my lips. "Yeah, right here," he breathes. "That's good."

Absently, I nod, staring at him as my head spins. Dizzy from the pain.

But Azaire's pain is lessened. I've taken it. Looking into his eyes steadies me, shields me from the destruction all around.

"Thank you," I breathe, the heat radiating between us. Losing myself in the storm of his gaze, swallowed by the rain.

"Thank *you*." Azaire drops his hand, snapping me out of his trance. "You aren't supposed to take my pain."

He's right.

It's not protocol. But I couldn't imagine *not* doing it.

I shake my head subtly, raising my hands once more.

It's a shame I have to be thanked for decency. As a child, I loved the Eunoia, what we stood for. The peace Ma and Pa always upheld. But when I look at this academy, at what they've done to our message, I suddenly become ashamed I'm a part of it.

My hands freeze above the wound at his ribcage.

My eyebrows set with a heavy frown.

"Who did this to you?" I ask.

Azaire shakes his head. Blood continues to dribble from the wound in his side, and I feel it in mine.

I think my rib is bruised.

His rib.

Our rib.

"It's not important. I volunteered."

He's lying. He knows I can feel it—every Eunoia in this room can feel it.

I raise an eyebrow, looking up from his ribs.

"Really," he insists. "It's okay."

"No, it's not."

Azaire's eyes grow wide again with fear. His gaze glides across the room, and I realize I was too loud.

"You helped me." My voice is barely audible. "Let me help you."

"Heal me first." Shrugging softly, he adds, "We can talk after."

He's so gentle, so kind—too kind, too selfless. He doesn't deserve this. None of them do. A sharp prickle spreads across my hands, as though I've pressed them onto broken glass. The uncertainty creeps in. What if I can't heal him? Will anyone else even try?

"Okay." I force my doubt aside, pushing forward. I reach for the bottom of his shirt, my hands trembling slightly as I move closer. I'm careful not to touch his skin, though the proximity makes it harder to breathe. "May I?" It's a soft question, a quiet plea.

Azaire clears his throat, his eyes searching mine, vulnerable, but giving in. "Yeah—*yes.*"

The space between us closes as I tug his shirt upward, keeping my gaze on his wound. The moment my fingers brush the fabric, I take a steadying breath, just for him, which in turn is kind of for me. He's all I can feel, with my hands so close to his body and my focus on him.

More than his emotions—I can feel *him.* Every beat of his pulse, every shift of his body as he holds the shirt up. It's just the two of us in this fragile bubble now. And then, I see it. His abdomen, marred with bruises—each one a reminder of the pain he's endured. But it's the deep cut along his side that makes my breath catch. It's still bleeding, the crimson trickling down his skin.

What if I can't heal him?

I have to try.

I tug my glove back on and fill the gash with yarrow—a dried and crushed herb—stopping the bleeding and accelerating the healing.

Then I place my hand over his side. Heat from the exertion of my energy floods my palms, healing the wound. Not completely.

At least it's stopped bleeding.

I move up to his eye, my fingers throbbing as I feel the pulse of pain radiating from his skin. I sit still, all my focus on him, waiting as the swelling subsides. I rub a soft brush packed with yarrow around his bruised eye, and he inhales sharply.

I feel it in the air between us. Feel *him* in the air.

He believes in me. Not just that, he's in awe of my power. His gratitude makes me believe I can do this.

It reminds me I have to.

The boy comes to life, stirring in the depth of my mind. *"You don't have to do anything."*

I try to ignore him, gently nudging him back into the corners of my thoughts—the only place he's ever lived.

"Not now." I turn back to the real world, away from him.

When I move to Azaire's ribs, I lose confidence. This is no easy task. I feel around them, avoiding the tender areas, and I rip my hands away when I nearly touch skin, feeling the pain peak.

It hurts to breathe.

I hold my breath.

His chest constricts. He, too, is trying not to breathe.

The room seems to stop as he reaches for my hand. Something he's done before—something I want. I pull my hand away with a gasp. My breath is ragged, dizzying.

"It's okay," Azaire says. He's taking deep breaths now. It's hurting him, but he's trying to be calm. For *me*. "I believe in you."

I must look very scared for him to stop me and say that.

"You do," the boy responds to my thought.

I've always known I was easy to read. It's the first thing I remember hearing as a child—that I was so expressive, despite me never purposefully expressing myself. Always worried about being a problem, fearing someone's reaction to me. Fearing doing the wrong thing, angering, annoying, pestering someone else.

You're so expressive, Little Thorn, my family would say. I hated that nickname, and perhaps if I were a little more expressive, I could've said as much. But what people call me isn't mine to change, only mine to take, much like their feelings—and the ones they have toward *me* are the most debilitating.

Yet Azaire has only ever thought the best.

"Okay." I look away from him, then look right back. "Okay."

I rub my hands together, cracking my joints, suddenly hyper aware of the fresh air on my clammy, gloveless skin.

Another painful breath. I place my hands just above Azaire's ribs. Close my eyes. Do not make contact at any cost. Sometimes that helps me escape the world. I ask the wound to heal. And ask again. And beg. *Will* it to heal. Force the life within me to mend the life within him. My energy dwindles, escaping faster than when I mend someone's emotions.

This, in the grand scheme of things, is far more dire.

I repeat Azaire's words. *I believe in you. I believe in you. I believe in you.*

"I believe in you, too," the boy says, voice gentle.

I squeeze my eyes shut, tighter.

"Wendy?"

I don't open my eyes. "Yes?"

"You can open your eyes."

At his request, I do. Azaire's complexion has returned to his usual olive. He looks better. Still bruised, but better.

The moment I feel the smallest iota of success, the rest of the room fills me. Stab wounds, bruises, Eunoia who fear they won't heal their "volunteer."

I have to leave this room that's full of pain, of people who feel violated by my very nature.

I have to leave this room full of Nepenthes who have been deliberately hurt.

I have to leave this room.

I leave the room. The emotions are still heavy in the hall, but at least I'm away from the heart of it. I go to the garden, to the woods, to the nature. I feel Azaire follow shortly behind. I sit on the grass, and he sits next to me.

The sun shines through the tree canopy above us, casting dappled golden light across Azaire's face. The bruises are gone, leaving his skin flawless—a combination of his deep olive complexion, and the sun's warm glow. Like veined marble.

He sits inches from me. Too close, but not close enough.

No one can ever get close enough.

"Are you all right?" Azaire asks softly.

I glance at him incredulously, trying to laugh. It becomes a scoff. "You're asking *me*? You were beaten half to death."

"Yeah. I'm asking *you*."

I shake my head, muttering, "Can't Lucian do something? Why didn't he do something?"

Lucian is the prince. He must be able to stop these volunteer groups.

My comment only makes Azaire sad, and I feel guilty, all over again.

"He can't." His defeat is hopeless—like a stone in water that doesn't want to sink. It has no choice *but* to sink. "It's just life. I'm okay with it."

"You can't be."

"Yes, I can, if I want peace." There's no animosity in his tone, nor any bone of his body. "There's nothing I can do to change it, so I accept it, until maybe one day I can change it. Like when Luc is king." He smiles at the thought. It isn't a happy thought to him, though. Not completely. He is just as worried as he is relieved by the future.

Kind of like Calista.

"I don't think that's how life works," I argue.

I can't just sit around hoping that *maybe* life will get better, someday. I can't just take the pain *everyday*.

Except… that's all that I do. The only difference is that I don't have hope. I'm resigned to the fact that my life will always be this way. Always on the outside, never in.

Always alone, longing for closeness, but fearing for those who try.

"It's how mine does." Azaire shrugs. "Has to." He looks around the woods, the bright sky and trees. The willow leaves dangling over us. He's still in awe of it, despite seeing it everyday.

He looks back at me.

"Here." Azaire holds out his hands. "You can feel me, can't you?" he asks, but he already knows. Most of my classmates know my disposition. "I'll show you peace."

I look at his hands.

I don't pick them up.

He thinks I'm a normal Eunoia. The kind that needs skin-to-skin contact to truly *feel* another being.

To control their emotions.

If I were just any other Eunioa, he'd be offering up his will. I could do whatever I wished with it.

It scares me that he trusts me.

It scares me that he doesn't know what my touch means.

All I could do with my hands is kill him.

"Think of it as me repaying you."

"I-I can't touch you," I stutter through my words, scratching my forearms. "Besides, you're not indebted to me."

"You can't... touch me?" Azaire asks slowly, focusing on the wrong thing. I want to reiterate—*you are not indebted to me. I did what anyone should.* But it's not what he cares about.

"I can't touch anyone, no." I pull at the tips of my gloves.

"Why can't you?"

I look at him, and he looks at my gloves. No one else wears them. Hopefully they never have to.

My condition isn't something I would wish upon anyone.

"Too powerful," I say. It's not the whole truth, but I suppose it's a piece of it.

The last time I touched someone, they died.

The next person will, too.

"But then, you could feel if I just..." Azaire closes his eyes.

He tries hard to not try at all. Yet, slowly, it works. Suddenly, there's silence. A small gap in the noise around us. I close my eyes with him.

The world falls apart.

At first, there's nothing—the kind of nothing that's sweet. The kind of nothing I've always longed for. No emotion bombarding me, not even my own.

It's stillness.

Then I see it for what it is: *peace.*

I breathe it in like fresh mountain air. Soak it up like the sun. But with every breath, the silence around me grows, pounding in my ears. Past memories come up, begging to be relived and rehashed. Wanting me to feel the guilt, the pain, all over again.

My mom appears, dead in the ground. Her legs are swallowed by the soil, as if the ground claimed her before the burial.

I realize, startlingly, that peace is far too quiet.

The nothingness hardens into a room—four walls I built myself, with a door I locked and forgot how to open.

I walk to a wall, and I pound on the carcass. The noise echoes through the empty room. I try to scream, but the only sound I make is my flesh and bone beating against the wall.

My eyes fly open.

"Azaire!" I gasp, clutching his hand. I need him to stop, before I fall back in.

He opens his eyes wide, gasping along with me. He's in shock. First I see it. Then I *feel* it, too.

I've scared him.

"My apologies." I rush to get the words out. I glance around my surroundings. The sun glowing on the grass, the trees rustling above me. The real world that I am still a part of. I take another deep breath. "I suppose I'm not well equipped for the quiet."

Azaire's eyes hover, searching me with nothing but compassion. My gloved hand still holds his, dangerously tight.

"You can tell me about it." Azaire adds, "If you want."

I let go of his hand and pick at the leather wrapped around my fingertips, as if I could rip right through and reach skin.

It would look ridiculous if I didn't tell him why I'm like this.

I fear I would *like* to tell him why.

"I can't turn it off like the others," I say. "The empathy. Being in that room, with all the pain, it was…" I trail off, sucking my bottom lip between my teeth.

"Painful?" Azaire shrugs.

Despite the morbidity, I smile. "Yes."

"And you took even more of it for me?"

I look around, listening to the subtle music of the birds and the wind. Searching for my own version of peace. A louder one. "Good observation," I murmur.

"I do try." Azaire squeezes his eyes shut as he emphasizes each word. "Very, very hard."

I chuckle as he blinks, looking right at me. Smiling a little more, I spot a journal behind him. It's the same as the one from the party. He must've dropped it.

I reach around him, picking it up.

His anxiety spikes the moment he sees me holding it.

I quickly hand the journal to him.

"Um…" I stammer as I stand, awkwardly shifting my weight from one foot to the other. I jab a finger in the direction of the academy, avoiding eye contact. "I, uh… I'm gonna head back."

Azaire jumps to his feet. "Would you like to—" He stops mid-sentence.

I freeze, caught off guard, even though I know the direction he wants to take this. He's the only boy in this academy who has ever given me a second thought.

I would like to give him one, too.

"Like to…?" I prompt softly.

"Hang out." The words drag awkwardly. "Sometime. Maybe?"

Azaire shrugs, and I smile. He's nervous, and it's kind of endearing. For a moment, I imagine his heart is beating fast. Then I realize that mine is.

But that is exactly the problem.

"Be careful," the boy warns me, his voice echoing through my mind —and I hate that he's right.

It's better for both Azaire and me if I keep my distance. It always has been. That's why my life is the way it is.

That's why I'm alone.

That's why the boy—a figment of my own imagination—is telling me to tread carefully.

I look at the little journal in his hands and say, "It won't take away from your writing?"

Azaire tugs at his beanie, shrugging one shoulder. His eyes meet mine with hope. Longing.

"I can write anytime." He smiles.

I've never felt someone care for me this much without a reason.

It reminds me of Ma.

"Why now?"

"What do you mean?" Azaire asks.

"We've known each other for nine years. Why are you only asking me now?"

"Oh, uh…" He tugs at the back of his beanie. "Would you have liked me to find you sooner?"

My heart aches with his anxiety, and I feel frozen in my bones by my own contradictions.

No, now is the perfect time.

Yes, I've been alone so long.

No, you should've never found me.

"I'll let you know," I say. "As soon as I decide."

"That's a good sign, right? That you want to decide?"

"It's a to-be-determined." I shuffle back and forth, not daring to walk away. Not when I'm so close, even though I should be so far.

"I'll tell you what," I add. "We can watch the stars again."

I think I mean it.

I'm scared to mean it. I shuoldn't mean it.

People are safer at a distance. *I'm* safer at a distance.

I contemplate on how to leave this open ended. The best way to buy more time. "When I find you," I add."

"Okay." Azaire smiles, and I walk away with the feeling of his excitement.

Then, I feel my own. Though it's hard to notice over the pounding voice in my head telling me this is a bad, bad idea.

At the end of the day, I return to Ms. Ferner's classroom. Her dark brown curls are frizzier than usual, barely contained as she carefully imbues a bottle of herbs with her power. Her frazzled state could be on account of the harsh realities of today, though she's probably long been aware of the volunteer groups.

She looks up when I enter, gesturing toward my usual seat. I slide into it as she finishes her work.

"How was it today?" she asks, setting the bottle down.

I pick at the wood around the desk, staring at every crevice. "Difficult."

"I'd imagine." Ms. Ferner approaches, sitting next to me.

She *can* imagine, but she doesn't. This is the way of the worlds.

I drop my hands, pressing my palms flat against the wooden table. "How do you watch and do nothing?" I ask, unable to keep my voice steady.

Ms. Ferner shakes her head, as if she doesn't know what I'm referring to. "Watch what?"

"The abuse of the Nepenthes," I say, assuming that my question was obvious enough, especially for another Eunoia. She can *feel* me.

She *knows* what I'm talking about.

Her eyes find mine, severe. "You know what they did."

"One war doesn't give us the right to abuse their children—"

"Ms. Estridon," she hisses, silencing me. "*Three* battles, and against the Folk."

"Perhaps they had a reason," I press on.

"This is not the Eunoias' universe. We are here because the Lyrians decided we are *allowed* to be." Her gaze drills into mine, her voice dangerously quiet. "There is no space for revolution."

I look down, breaking eye contact when I feel her conviction. She's more emotionally grounded than me and could easily win a game of wills, despite her being *wrong*.

"I don't want a revolution," I mutter as I tug at the fingers of my gloves. "I only want people to be treated fairly."

The words hang between the four marble walls of Ms. Ferner's classroom, until finally, she cuts them down. "You like history, don't you?"

I lift a shoulder in a half-hearted shrug. "Some of it."

"Then you should know there isn't space in the universe for *fair*." She gestures to my seat. "Sit down."

I consider not doing as she asks, to take a stand. But she doesn't need to teach me magic. I'm here because *I* need her to.

So, I sit, and in that seat, I put up my shields. I envision myself surrounded by a barrier—like a blanket of green smothering me. It's meant to hold my power in, trapping a piece of me behind a mental cage of my own making.

It doesn't always work.

"Whenever you're ready, Estridon."

With her, I don't hold back. The whole point is to try and fail—to look her in the eye, tell her to feel something, and have nothing happen.

But it always works. I can always bend her emotions.

I've spent years trying to control this. Yet every time I command someone, they obey.

One day, when I finally fail—when my power is no longer stronger than my will—we'll move on to my hands and their deadly nature. I'll find a way to get rid of the gloves.

"Shields up, Estridon," she demands.

I visualize my shields, closed and locked around me. I feel my power pushing against them, clawing for freedom.

"Command me."

"You will not look away from me." I meet her gaze, my power pressing behind my words. Ms. Ferner fights, but the magic is too strong.

Even stronger than my own will.

It always works. I can always bend her emotions—anyone's emotions—no matter how hard I fight.

A tree is stronger than a piece of paper.

"Shields up, Estridon—"

"Quiet," I cut her off, and her lips seal shut.

Slowly, her pupils grow, nearly covering her entire eye.

I sigh. I failed. She is entirely under my control. A tear slides down my cheek, my bottom lip wobbling.

"You don't care for my reaction," I mutter, wiping the tear away. I don't know why I thought it'd be different, this time.

I'm always waiting for it to be different.

Ms. Ferner frowns, but she can't speak. Not yet.

Sometimes I wonder if I want to fail—if I'm scared to touch her. If I know, deep down, that I will fail that, too.

Kill her, too.

"You feel normal," I sigh. "I release you from my command."

It happens instantaneously; Ms. Ferner's green eyes return to normal. Her frustration trickles down my throat like poison—impossible to stop. I reach for them, but it's her words I'm trying to free.

The leather of my gloves is harsh against my skin. The poison only grows harsher. There's no way to rid myself of her emotion.

"You failed," she spits.

"I know."

"There's no reason you should still be unable to contain it, Wendy." My name on her lips shocks me; she hardly uses it. "You're more powerful than the rest."

"Isn't that the problem?"

"Only if you think it's one."

Ms. Ferner is always mean on the outside. It's a facade, an over-compensation. She knows she can't hide how she truly feels, how she truly cares.

Not from me.

No one can.

She wants me better. Her annoyance has become personal.

A knock at the door sounds through the room, and Ms. Ferner fumbles out of the desk just before the door creaks open.

Emotional manipulation has long been banned at Visnatus, which is why I need Ms. Ferner more than she needs me. I don't have anyone else who could help.

One day, somehow, I would like to be able to touch someone.

This is my single hope.

My heart races with the student's fear as he stands in the doorway. Something's wrong—something urgent.

"You're needed in the combat room," he says.

Someone's *hurt*. If Ms. Ferner is needed, then many people are injured, and soon, I'll be the one healing them.

It scares me.

"Wendy?" Ms. Ferner says, and I look back at her. "Return when you're able to heal a self-inflicted wound." She smiles sweetly before leaving.

Eunoia make the best liars.

Chapter 3
I Love Backwards

There's a knock at my door. One I can't ignore. Frantic worry on the other end presses into my silence like a plea.

"Wendy!" someone shouts. I think it's Lucian.

I rise, stepping toward the door and reaching for the knob. The boy in my head cuts me off, his voice slicing through my thoughts. *"Don't open the door."*

At his words, I stop—even though I have a feeling I shouldn't. *"Why not?"* I ask.

"It will be too much for you to take."

"Are you there?" Lucian calls.

My hand settles on the knob.

"Don't," the boy warns.

I push him away, and he evaporates like smoke in the wind.

Then I open the door. Two bodies stagger into my room—Lucian holding up Azaire. He's broken and battered—but worse than the bruises, he's unreachable. Completely cut off.

A blank slate.

An empty page.

Azaire—the steady boy, the peaceful man, unable to be felt.

Is he about to die? Is that what this means? Or is he already dead? It's only upon death that I've been unable to feel a person.

They were gone. There was nothing to feel.

I never saw them again.

Dead.

I can feel the boy at the edges of my mind, waiting to swoop in and tell me he was right. This *is* too much to take. It's the last thing I need to hear right now. Even the figments of my imagination don't know what's good for me.

"Oh my gods."

I don't realize I've fallen into the dresser until Lucian asks, "Can you heal him?"

Air clogs in my throat until it becomes impossible to take in. I stare at Azaire—the burns on his arms. The barely-there breath in his chest.

The empty mind. The lack of emotion.

It makes it impossible to focus on anything other than Lucian. The prince is desperate. Beneath it, he's guilty. That is the emotion I feel the most of, until slowly, the desperation dissipates, and *all* I can feel is Lucian's guilt.

I *hate* guilt.

It seeps through like gas. Poison through the cracks in my doors. The lock is not tight enough.

The knob is ever turning.

I am everyone else before I'm myself.

I focus on Azaire, searching for anything. He's not dead. He's still breathing, however little air he's taking in. Isn't that steadiness still there? Even now, with uncertainty pressing in, he's still himself, isn't he?

But there's nothing there.

"He's going to die," the boy says. *"Just like Xander."*

"Why can't I feel him?" I ask Lucian. My lip quivers, and I pull it between my teeth, needing for it to still.

Lucian's voice is a whimper. "Please."

I try to override my faculties. Deflect Lucian's guilt. Suppress the boy's words.

But nothing can keep the boy out.

He hovers like a rain cloud, waiting to be released.

"You shouldn't have opened the door," the boy tells me. *"You aren't ready to bear the pain. Not this time."*

From the corners of my eyes, I see him, as if his shadow lingers in my room. I flinch, searching for his figure, but he isn't there. He couldn't possibly be. He's trapped within the confines of my mind.

He *is* my mind.

I take a deep breath, warding against my insanity, even as I argue with myself. *"Azaire would certainly die without me."*

"He's going to die either way, love."

The words are a heavy blow. There's no other way to say it than: they hurt.

And Azaire hurts, more than I could possibly imagine. He's barely holding on to life. Taking so little breath that I can't feel him.

Even in my mind, my voice shatters as I ask, *"You don't believe in me?"*

"Do you *believe in you?"*

For a moment, I am nothing but still. Frozen as I watch Azaire, dangling in Lucian's arms—and I shift under the weight of expectation.

Of undesired outcomes.

"I have no choice," I answer, despite the boy being right. I *don't* believe. I think Azaire is going to die. I've never been able to save a soul.

But I *have* to.

I've never had the chance to try to save someone I care about. Now, I do. There's no choice, and even if there were, I wouldn't choose any different.

"Put him on the bed." I nod to Lucian as I turn away from the mess. I approach my closet, pulling out my tray of herbs, then hand Lucian a bottle of valerian root, instructing, "Put this in his nose and mouth."

It's imbued with magic and should keep Azaire unconscious, which will keep me focused in case he wakes while I work.

I hover my hands over Azaire's body—just as I had in class—feeling for the worst of it.

I can't feel any of it.

After a deep breath, my heart still does not slow.

But I won't stop trying.

I pick up his hand. It's burnt to nothing but raw skin. There must be severe nerve damage. What if I can't fix that, and he never uses his hand again?

His injury courses through my body, burning me. My hand grows sticky beneath my glove. Is it my magic, his wounds, or my worry?

Moving my attention away from Azaire, I flick through my glass jars once more, searching for a salve made of comfrey to even the burns. As soon as I locate it, I rub the brown substance into Azaire's hand. The skin sizzles.

I smile.

It *sizzles*. That means it's healing. The blood in his veins is still moving.

It's the smallest of victories, the slightest sign of lasting life, and I clutch to it, moving to the burns on his wrist, then his shoulders. The welted and raw skin slowly smooths.

I release a breath of relief, taking off my gloves. Green tendrils of energy coil around my fingers, like living vines, each one sprouting jagged thorns. I lower my hands, desperate to conceal my power from Lucian. I'm sure he's witnessed many Eunoias harness their abilities before—and none of them have thorns.

The tendrils of energy wrap around Azaire's shoulder, mending his skin as best I can. My vision begins to speck, beads of darkness overcoming me. I dig my nails into my palms, forcing myself to alertness.

For Azaire. To save a person. The only one I ever could.

My focus doesn't last. Lucian's emotions trip over themselves as they tumble with mine. If he would calm down, this would be easier. It's like class—but so much worse. His emotional stakes in Azaire's safety are higher than all the Eunoia put together when we mended the Nepenthes.

His frantic energy leaves me struggling to keep my feelings in check, much less my power. He's completely unaware of the necessity of his emotional regulation.

"*Of* your *emotional regulation,*" the boy corrects.

I don't remember him being this much of a nuisance.

It's been just the two of us for the majority of his existence, I suppose.

I extend my power toward Lucian, like a metaphysical hand reaching out to pat his head—as if he were a dog. Scratching behind his ear until he's calm, nudging his turbulent emotions into submission.

His guilt dissipates, like the tide going back to the sea. The sand quickly dries.

Finally, I can take an easy breath.

But the breath fills me with lethargy. The moment I'm alone with myself, my body tips forward, begging for rest.

I force myself to rise, gliding my finger just above Azaire's body, tracing an invisible line in the air from spine to toe. My hands hang loosely for a moment before they drop, heavy and unceremonious.

Nothing like the skilled healer I'm supposed to become.

I shove my fingers into my palm—pulling blood, forcing myself to feel the liquid of life beneath my nails. Then, I raise my hands. The light green energy springs from me. The essence of life, healing him. The essence of life, sucking from me—like a thirsty syringe in my bones, slurping up my marrow.

But as I'm depleted, Azaire comes alive.

Fresh skin blossoms over his burns, stitching itself back together like a flower blooming in reverse.

I've fixed him. I've healed him. He will not die.

He'll be fine.

For a moment, I feel proud.

It doesn't last, though, because Lucian's guilt fills me to the brim. I drown in his emotions, submerged in a sea of regret that wraps around me like suffocating liquid, dragging me deeper into its depths.

Worse than that, when I look to Azaire, searching for solace, he's still vacant.

It must be—has to be—the valerian root. It's likely knocked him out far past the barriers of slumber. Lucian may have given him too much.

I hold onto that idea. It's easier than any other.

I'm not sure I could handle any other. I'm drained—like an old rag, twisted and wrung dry. It took everything I had to mend his skin, and I don't know if I have enough left to fix his mind. He is thoroughly used up, worn out, like a shirt with too many holes or a pair of pants torn down the middle, falling apart at the seams.

A needle and thread won't fix this.

It will take days of sleep for him to heal from the mental damage alone.

After I've done the best I can manage, I tug my gloves back on and say, "It'll be a few days."

But I've *done* it; I've healed him physically. His mind is silent, but he's *alive.*

Lucian says nothing. After all I've done, a bit of anger pricks at me.

I deserve more than silence, don't I?

"What happened?" I ask.

Lucian's guilt floods back to the surface, a wind that cannot be tamed, despite me doing my best to repress it.

"It's not safe to talk here." He looks away. As if he knows that eye contact will heighten my power, and he doesn't want me to find the truth.

Raising an eyebrow—that no one will notice—I ask, "Then where?"

"Past the barrier. By the coast."

Past the barrier. He says it cooly, as if the barrier is there for no reason.

But we're within that barrier for a *reason.* It's our safety net. It's what keeps the bad things out.

I glance at Azaire. Maybe the bad things have already gotten in.

"You're growing perceptive, Little Thorn," the boy says mockingly.

I shake him away.

"Fine," I mutter as I walk to the door.

Lucian remains behind me, hesitant to leave Azaire. He's filled with a mix of guilt and a protective urge, and it gives me pause.

I catch Lucian's gaze and try to free myself from his emotion: "He'll be safe here."

Lucian nods subtly, understanding. When I open the door, he follows.

We walk to the shore, the turquoise tide calm as it rushes past my feet. But when I face Lucian, his hesitancy hits me. Whatever he has to share, he isn't sure how to tell me.

No, he's not sure he *wants* to tell me, yet he knows he has to.

I open my mouth as if I have something of my own to proclaim. But at my sides, my fingers twist and curl, weaving through the air, pulling the truth from him—unraveling a seam, each thread loosening and slipping free, until the shirt is nothing but bare strands.

"They're back," Lucian says with a sigh. The intensity behind his words knocks into me. My fingers still. "The monsters are attacking again, and it coincides with recent revelations of the Arcanes."

I step back instinctively, my gaze darting to the woods just beyond the rocky coast. The barrier—it's right there. I could flee to safety in a heartbeat, disappearing into the protective shield before anything could catch me.

But I know there's more he has to say.

"The monsters are attacking, and you're taking me beyond the barrier?" I ask, incredulous.

"There's none in Visnatus." He wants me to calm down.

"That could change at any minute!"

"I can take care of it if anything happens," Lucian tries to assure me. But he doesn't believe it himself. The guilt clings to his skin like sticky sap in tangled hair.

"Why are you involving me in this?" I ask. I don't want to think about monsters anymore. But I fear this is as important as Lucian believes. Monster attacks *are* important.

The boy hums to life in my mind, always watching. *"Or, might I add, important to you."*

"Someone was taken by the Arcanes," Lucian answers. "I tracked down the one person who might be aware of a detail I'm missing." He pauses, again, weighing his options.

I feel like a hangnail, dangling on a thread of skin, waiting for whatever information he may or may not reveal to me. Will it tear me off or stitch me up?

"Your mother was involved," he finishes.

I freeze. My blood thickens to sludge, heavy and slow. My legs turn to dust, barely holding me upright. It's a struggle just to stay standing. All I can do is cling to whatever remains of myself, trying to keep it all together.

"You shouldn't have opened that door," the boy says—as if he's prophetic. As if he foresaw this moment long before I did.

"Go on," I mutter to Lucian.

"Eighteen years ago, a woman faked her death. Supposedly, your mother knows why. We were told to find her."

I pick viciously at the fingers of my glove. "Was she the one taken by the Arcanes?"

"Yes." The remaining words hang uncomfortably on the tip of his tongue, like a stubborn spice that lingers long after the meal. He's not proud that he told me anything at all. A man who wishes to handle everything on his own. Something I know well.

But I do not find kinship in it.

"What was her name?" I demand.

"Isa Althenia."

The name rings like the bell of my childhood door—a familiar sound I can barely recall.

When I don't answer, Lucian grows weary. He needs my help, yet he doesn't want me involved. It's nice to know I am not the only one who is a paradox. It still fails to make me feel less alone.

"Because you are alone," the boy says. *"But you need not be lonely. That's why I'm here."*

I glare at Lucian, confused as to how I feel. Grateful that he's brought me a piece of my ma? Angry that he didn't want to share it with me?

"Next time, don't be vague about matters regarding my mom," I say. "But you were sent on a fool's errand."

"How so?" The worry seeps into more than Lucian's tone. It's in his tongue, his skin, and in turn, it's in mine.

I straighten myself, *prepare* myself. These are words I hardly say. Words I don't wish to carry as truth.

But it's the truth, and denial won't change a thing.

"My mom is dead."

Chapter 4
The Beginning of
the End

ONE YEAR AGO

I enter Ms. Ferner's room for our usual training. I'm not prepared—I rarely am. I worry about what will happen on the day that she pushes me too far, demands that I command her to do something more than feel angry or sad.

Worried for the day that I commit another atrocity.

But as I open the door, Ms. Ferner isn't what I see. It's blonde hair tied in a neat braid down a girl's back, and shaking hands standing where Ms. Ferner ought to be.

"Calista," I greet her.

We've shared a suite for years, and I hardly know her. But she's a Folk. There's no reason she should be in here, where they teach the Eunoia.

Then I notice the blood seeping through her blue academy uniform. The shaking breath in my chest, mimicking hers.

I step forward, throwing my bag on the nearest chair. "I can help."

Calista opens her mouth, but her lips quiver, and no words escape. When she realizes the state she's in—in front of me, no less—she grows embarrassed.

Then, tentatively, she nods.

Carefully, I guide Calista to a desk. *It's only a little cut,* I tell myself. It isn't deadly—it isn't beyond my control.

It's only a little blood.

Calista takes off her academy jacket, revealing the gaping wound in her forearm. Nearly to the bone. I almost faint—but I think it's her dizziness. Now, I understand why she won't speak.

She's worried she'll bleed out.

I rise, running to Ms. Ferner's stash of herbs and quickly rubbing some into Calista's wound. She bites back a scream, and the ball lodges in my throat, begging for release.

Carefully, I take off a glove, healing her wound until I'm sure I'm going to pass out, too. When I finish, I slump back in the chair, my head falling back. I'm suspended in a moment of exhaustion. The weight of her wound has drained me.

It's silent—nothing but ragged breaths—for a long while.

Finally, Calista says, "Thank you."

I pull myself upright, but Calista is staring at her arm, pinching the stitched skin.

"What happened?" My voice is barely a breath.

She glares at me. "You have no right to ask."

Her tone is angry. Her emotions, not so much.

I raise an eyebrow, holding her gaze, but I don't respond. I pick up my bag and start toward the door.

"My apologies," Calista calls once I've nearly reached the exit.

Glancing over my shoulder, a faint smile tugs at my lips. "That's a new one."

"So are people walking away from me."

"Well, I'm going to"—I gesture toward the door—"unless you want to talk."

I know she does; I'm only giving her a way out.

"It's my magic," she says. "Life has been difficult recently and…"

She raises her hand, her fingers poised and elegant—her magic not so. The ball of energy forms in her palm, turbulent. She's an Air Folk —controller of wind. Those energy balls should be clear, pristine, but hers is nearly gray, as if the wind won't cease in her control.

"The emotion, it's… hard to manage." Calista stares absently into the ball of air.

I sit at a desk, multiple feet away from her.

Worry hits me—her worry that I'm scared of her. I am, but not for the reason she thinks. If she were to lose control of her magic, I could subdue her with a word.

It's something else I'm scared of. Something she wouldn't guess.

"That's how you cut your skin to the bone?" I ask.

Calista tilts her head to the side, but she finds my question amusing. Her little sphere of gray wind isn't going to gash flesh.

She rolls her eyes as she says, "I shattered the skylight in the training room." Then she looks away. "I came to Ms. Ferner because the healers of Visnatus report to my family. My mistake... they could deem me unfit for the crown."

Her words are bitter; she fears not getting the crown.

"I can help," I say. She narrows her eyes, skeptical. "My magic is turbulent, too. That's why *I'm* here."

"Says the *life bringer*," she hisses, as if it's an insult. "What can't you do? Make a tree sing?"

"It's what I *can* do, actually."

Calista continues to glare, her gaze falling to my hands. Realization sparks, as if she's never noticed my gloves. Even after eight years of knowing one another. Even after years of sharing a suite.

Every other Eunoia *needs* physical touch to bend emotion.

But not me.

She leans back, smiling. "You control people."

"Scared yet?" I glance down.

But I don't feel her retreat. Her interest only grows. I start to hope —foolishly—that this is the beginning. That I'll make a friend, have a person to talk to. Spend time with.

I try not to focus on the impossible.

Until Calista says, "The opposite."

And she means it.

Chapter 5
When I'm Done Dying

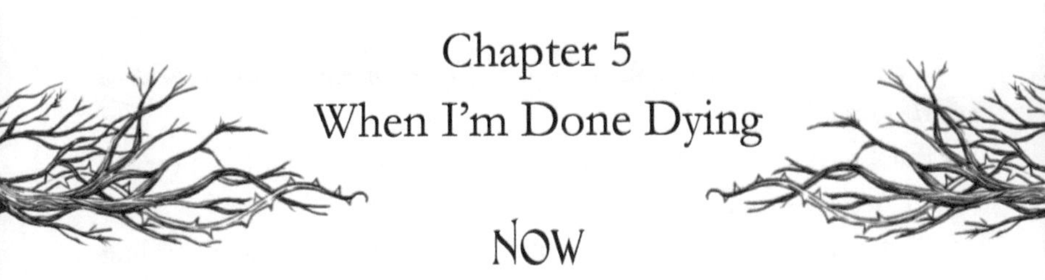

NOW

I wake on the floor, a pillow resting on top of my back. The door to my room is made of a precious stone from my home world, Eunaris. It's supposed to block mental magics from passing through: in my case, emotions. It works for other Eunoia. It doesn't always work for me.

I nearly pulled out my hair last night. Ever since Desdemona arrived, it's been harder than usual to adjust. A new feeling in such close proximity takes a bit of time to get used to, and she's the worst of them all.

She's in constant, budding fear. Emotion is worse when it's suppressed—even more so when you fear the emotion itself, and Desdemona does.

I toss the pillow, one I'd wrapped around my head in a foolish attempt to silence something beyond the mind, onto the bed. Then, I rise to my feet. Normally, I'd tidy my room, but the last few days have taken a different course than the usual.

I grab my bag and race out of my suite, straight to Azaire. I check on him everyday—heal him everyday. Sometimes for only a few minutes. I *try* to make it only a few minutes. Though, I tend to stay longer, hoping to see the wiggle of a finger, the twitch of an eye.

I've yet to see him awake.

Resting beside him on the bed, I begin to take my gloves off. My bare hands hover over his body, and today, I beg my magic to reach him—to rouse him.

"So sentimental." The boy takes my attention. *"The human body is so*

frail. Easy to break. So very difficult to fix. This will only end when it breaks you."

"*Are you suggesting I* don't *save him?*" I ask the boy out of anger, the green tendrils gushing from my fingertips with the influx of feeling. I pull my hands back, not wanting to deposit anger into Azaire's broken being.

"*Not at all,*" he echoes in my mind. "*Your conscience is far too feeble to withstand that.*"

But I'm not doing this for my conscience. I'm doing this because Azaire deserves to live.

"*I'm going to save him,*" I say with finality and go back to healing Azaire, proving a point to my own mind.

The green light wrapping around my hands and Azaire fills the room. I try to mend him on a level deeper than the body. I try to reach his mind. To fix it.

It's tiring, but in the mornings after a night's rest, I have enough energy to spend. This healing doesn't hurt, not like when I repair physical wounds. It's different. Exhuasting. The coma that's taken Azaire lures me in, and I fight it.

It's a difficult task, and it takes focus, but somehow, it feels like his mind guides me through the worst of it. Today, as my eyes begin to flutter shut, energy rushes through my veins, filling my head.

It isn't mine. I wonder if it's Azaire's. If maybe he's waking up, or can somehow feel me and hopes to help.

It's a kind thought—which is not something my mind often offers me—but it's unlikely.

When I'm finished, I sit at the foot of his bed. I watch—his chest rising and falling in shallow rhythm. I feel nothing from him, as usual. And I contemplate, reaching for what isn't there.

First and foremost, I make sure he isn't in pain.

"Wake up, Azaire," I find myself whispering, maybe to him, maybe to myself. "Please, wake up."

His eyelashes flutter, and I sit up straighter, waiting for more. At first, nothing happens. Then, I feel a prickle in my hands. Something moving beneath my skin.

Him.

As if heeding my command, his eyes slowly flicker open. A smile breaks over his face like sunlight.

"Okay," he mumbles, groggy, looking up at me in awe. "But only because you asked."

I never knew I was worthy of such surprise.

"He could be the one," the boy says. "Or just another one. You're better off not knowing. Either way, it ends the same."

I meet Azaire's gaze, trying to see his eyes instead of the boy, who's lingering nearby in my mind. But I can't ignore the boy.

I can't ignore him because he's right.

It always ends the same.

"It's fair to see you awake."

"Yeah, I like seeing you awake, too," Azaire mumbles, scratching his forehead, beneath his beanie.

Heat rises to my cheeks, and I take a deep breath. I don't want to feel this, or what will happen if I let this go further. Because the boy is right: whatever this is, it ends in pain.

And I am better off not knowing that pain.

Every day I've come here, I've lived with the suffocating fear that I *can't* save Azaire. And even if I did this time, I know one day I won't. One day I'll be too late, too weak, too feisty, maybe even too strong.

Maybe it will be me *staying* to fight that gets him killed—like my mom.

Maybe it will be me touching him—like Xander.

"Azaire..." I trail off as I look away.

"Bad news first," he says. When I glance back at him, he smiles again, but his heart isn't in this one. "I try to end things on a positive note."

"I don't..." I shake my head, biting my wobbling lip. "I don't think I have good news."

Azaire's eyebrows knit together, his mouth falling. "Oh."

"We have to end here," I mutter, the words shrinking in my throat.

All the joy seeps from his very marrow and, in turn, from my own, leaving me in grayscale.

"Why?" He sounds as sad as he feels.

I lick my lips, stuttering. "I-I don't know how to do this—"

Azaire cuts me off. "Can you look at me?"

Only now do I realize I'm looking at a willow tree in the garden.

More specifically, a single leaf on the tree. At the lighter shade of green that marks its veins.

I look at him to ease his desperation. It makes mine worse.

"Did something happen while I was unconscious?" Azaire asks. He really wants to know, to fix it.

I can't let that happen.

"It's not that." Looking him in the eyes is killing me, but I endure the steady slaughter. "It was my mistake."

"Mistakes are still your choices," the boy says. *"You get to make them, and you're making the proper choice now."*

"Okay," Azaire answers.

The way I feel—whether it's Azaire or me—isn't good. It scarcely is. Emotions are fickle, even the okay ones are easily demolished. The not so okay ones tend to get worse with time.

I would like to say something more—I have something more to say. Alas, my vocal cords have frozen.

I rise, turning to the door and prepared to walk through it.

Until a hand catches my wrist, oddly strong for a boy who could've been on his death bed this morning.

He would have been, if it weren't for me.

I turn to face Azaire, and he meets my gaze. His mouth hangs slightly open, eyes wide. His skin nearly brushes my own—but my long sleeve stops him.

"Don't go," he says.

I know he doesn't need my healing. This is about a yearning.

Still, I ask, "Do you need me to stay for something?"

"No," he murmurs, tugging me closer to his bed. "Just don't go."

I look down—at his hand on my glove, nearly touching my skin—and all I can do is numbly nod.

"Okay."

When Azaire's fallen back to sleep, I feel bad for leaving. But I don't turn around. There's something I need to do, something I've put off so I could heal Azaire. For days, I've ignored the flooding thoughts each time the tide brought them in. Ma, the monsters and Arcanes, the woman who was taken to The Void: everything Lucian told me but couldn't explain.

Today, I'll get answers.

I go straight to my suite, resting my hand on the mirror in my bedroom and visualizing my old home on Eunaris. Portals are the only means we have of traveling between worlds, but they're not without danger. You need time, patience, and clarity of mind to open a portal properly. If you don't, you could get stuck between the mirrors—between worlds—and no one knows what happens after that.

There's only one mirror in each town on Eunaris—one way to portal in and out. And I haven't been in years. I concentrate on the sensory details: the groaning wood, the sweet scent of flowers, the view from the community garden—rolling mountains, roaming animals, and ranging greens.

The mirror vibrates beneath my hand, the glass rippling like water as an image of my hometown begins to replace my reflection. It stretches to match my height, and with a steady breath, I step through.

The moment I cross, the air shifts, thick with the warmth of the place. I'm immediately engulfed by the heady scent of orange blossoms and violets—Ma's favorites. It could turn cloying with the memories, if I let it. But I have to hold on to what's left.

The community mirror is just past the gardens, and I walk through them to make it home. It's a graveyard of memories. Only, all the good ones have withered away into the one. I hold my breath, shunning the scent.

The home where my brothers and father reside is small compared to what we have at Visnatus Academy, but it looks as I remember. Everything is made of dark wood: the kitchen, the tables, the chairs, and stairs.

I feel sick to my stomach at the sight. All the memories it holds. The last time I set foot in this house, Ma's body was split in two. Dismembered, never to be put together again. The gore covers my eyes, coating the world in thick, iron-scented red.

As I double over, refraining from puking, I know that this is entirely my own feeling—the grief, nausea, and guilt—untainted by anyone around me.

It's rare to feel anything that's entirely my own.

I step into the house, the dark green couch and wooden table luck-ily empty. I run through, making a beeline for the steps, and tip-toeing around the one that always creaks. Trying hard not to alert anyone of my presence. Praying no one can sense it.

Pa is here—I can feel him in his room—but no one else.

I stop. Despite all that happened, his dead wife and missing daugh-ter, he feels nearly the same. He was always the rock in our home, and Ma was the muse. She was who we went to for a laugh, but he was who we wanted for a cry. Steady in the mind, solid in his form.

Ma was a free spirit, nearly like the air—try to grab her, and she slips right through your fingers.

I can feel her here, too, but I'm not sure if it's magic or habit.

I continue up the stairs.

Down the hall, the door to Ma's study is left wide open. I freeze, checking my perimeter to make sure no one is around, in case I was wrong in my prior assessment. In case the one time my power would be of use to me, it's decided to turn off.

But the house is, as I knew, completely empty. I move forward, into her study.

The room is frozen in time, untouched, as if Ma has only just stepped out and not left us entirely.

Not been dead the last five years.

Papers lie scattered across her desk, collecting dust. The books on the shelf across the room are leaning, their spines curling, the covers fraying like forgotten things, slowly decaying without the careful hands Ma used to give them.

The room is a time capsule.

I understand why; it was where she spent all her time. The family can come to the door, close their eyes, and pretend she's still sitting here. Zola knows I would've done it thousands of times if I ever vis-ited my old home.

But this is no longer home. It feels like I've broken in—like a new family lives here, and I couldn't let go, so I've forced my way in to get one last glimpse.

What am I doing? I'm unsure what I'm looking—hoping—for. One last piece of Ma, left in the ruckage, untattered by the new family that replaced the one I once had?

But I remember the name—Isa Althenia. I can almost put a face to it. A piece of Ma. One last shard to dig into my skin.

One last way to pull blood, to prove her memory.

Could anything of importance be left in Ma's work, all the philosophy books she wrote that only the Eunoia agree with?

I step toward the bookshelf, then stop.

There's a lump in my throat. If I looked in a mirror, I'm sure I'd see something lodged there. Like a snake swallowing its prey. I don't know if I am the snake or the mouse. Nor do I know which is worse—*their* pain, or my own.

Because this is all mine.

The worst part of the room is that it still smells like Ma: violets and freshly chopped wood. Is this the best part for my brothers? My father? That they still get to smell her?

I move away from the bookshelf, starting with the pile of papers on her desk. As I run my fingers along each page, I imagine Ma doing the same. I imagine my hand in hers. Her ghost sitting in the chair beside me.

It's not very long before I notice a similarity between the pages: some are stamped with the seal of Folkara.

But there's no reason Ma would have anything from Folkara. The worlds don't often share with each other—least of all the monarchies. Not unless it's with someone in their service.

I shuffle through the papers faster. Some are signed by King Easton and Queen Melody—the rulers of Folkara.

It must be a mistake. It has to be. Except, they're all addressed to her. *Willow Estridon* written in shining ink, making the hope of doubt nearly impossible.

There's no reason she would—

Yet the reality of what I've found hits me like an axe to wood.

She worked for the kingdom. That's the only explanation. My mother, a philosopher and Eunoia, worked for the Folk. It seems impossible. Yet I can't deny the logic of this. She managed to secure my enrollment at Visnatus, an academy built for future leaders.

She *had* to have ties with the current ones.

I'm halfway through the pile on her desk when it dawns on me: I need something more personal. There will be nothing about Isa in government papers. Stepping back to her bookcase, I'm prepared to look for a journal... Only to stop short, my hands inching toward the books but never touching. I don't understand why at first. Maybe there's a magical barrier, stopping me.

Until the boy comes to life in my mind, saying, *"You're looking for the final words she penned."*

That's why I didn't start with the bookshelf and why I can't touch it now.

I feared this would be too much.

I try to swat at him, like he's a persistent fly. But he says, "I'm not here to annoy you," and I understand. "Close your eyes. Join me."

The offer is a tempting one, and I take it. I have enough mercy upon myself to place the two of us back at Visnatus Academy, in the garden. I can hardly bear the grief of Ma's study in the real world—I don't know if I could handle it in my mind.

The sun shines over the boy and me, the colors around us spiraling lazily. As if painted of water color instead of reality. Yet reality weighs heavily on me. My body still stands in my hometown, where everything tastes of bile and blood.

"This is hard for you," the boy says, staring at me from a foot away. His features are more muddled than usual. No part of him is easily defined, like a smeared piece of art.

He is dark, even in the light.

"Yes."

"I know, love. It wasn't a question." He steps closer, his movements like water flowing downstream. Then, he folds me into an embrace.

Years ago, when I discovered him in my mind, his presence and touch felt strange. Over time, our embraces have become the only I receive.

The sun shines in my eyes.

"Things like this can be healing," he murmurs into my hair, his voice weaving with the wind. A tear slides down my cheek. *"Since she died, you've only avoided her. Sometimes you must let things in."*

"I miss her," I sob, leaning into the boy.

"You always will."

"I don't want her to be gone."

"These are the things we cannot change." I clutch him tighter, and he

continues, *"There is something in the bookcase, I can feel it. Find it."*

Slowly, his touch dissolves from under me, his edges softening like a shadow met by the sun. I clutch onto him tighter as he slips away.

Then, my eyes open, leaving me standing before the bookcase in Ma's suite. Alone.

But the boy left me with a parting gift.

I follow his instruction, scanning the spines. I assume I'm looking for Ma's classic leather-bound journals, something that looks battered enough to be my age.

Something she penned her thoughts in.

Instead, my eyes stop on a philosophy book: *The Mendacity of Good and Evil.* I glide a finger down the rough spine, feeling every crease and indentation, stopping just over the author's name. This copy is attributed to Marto, but I know it was written by Shenlin. As I pick up the book, something foreign comes to life.

This is what the boy pointed out. What I pointed out to myself. I felt it the moment I stepped into the room. It was pestering in the back of my mind. But something off isn't always so easily defined, like trying to recognize a wrong note in a song you've never heard.

Until it sticks out.

This room is the song—the book the wrong note. It doesn't feel like Ma.

It feels like magic.

A glamour. Folk magic, which means a Folk hid it. It adds weight to my theory that she was working with Folkara.

But I don't know *why.*

I slip the book into my bag, though I can't be sure it's truly a book beneath the glamour.

With the bag clutched close, I step out of the room and avoid the creaking floorboard on the stairs once more.

My eyes land on the table, where my father sits alone. Watching him now, I realize I misread him earlier—when all I had were echoes through the walls.

He is not the same. There's a grief in him, heavy and hollow, like the pit in my own chest—something he's holding back with all he has, trying not to be swallowed whole.

And it's all because of me. I've done this to him, and now I've broken into his home, taking away his last scrap of relief.

Before he can see me, I press myself against the wall on the stairs —as if I could disappear into the wood forever.

"Terran?" he calls.

It's been five years. He can't see me, not like this. It's been five long years of knowing they were better off without me. I can't bombard him with my presence.

Yet, there is no way to get back to Visnatus other than the community mirror.

There is no way to hide if he chooses to feel.

I have no choice.

I step into view.

Our eyes meet for the first time in five years. Tears slide past mine.

"Wendy," Pa remarks in awe.

There's a bright feeling.

It's the rising sun, but the day only lasts so long. No matter what, night will come again, overshadowing the sun.

In the end, only his blame will remain—resting solely on me.

As it should.

Pa's eyes turn glassy as he walks toward me, wrapping his arms around me. "My sweet Wendy."

It's been so long. I haven't heard my name spoken like this… in so long.

I wish I could hug him back. It's the first hug I've had since Ma died. But I'm as stiff as a board, scared my movements might scare him away faster. Like I'm a wolf, and he's a rabbit.

This warm feeling he holds—that I am holding—will not last.

It's only the rising sun.

"Has something happened?" Pa asks, the same cadence to his tone as before, back when I knew him.

Yet his feelings are still conflicted. I understand. I am his daughter and his wife's killer. He blames me as I blame myself, yet loves me as I never will.

I wonder if he knows of the things I learned today. Why Ma worked for Folkara, or why a woman she used to know was taken by the Arcanes.

"No. Nothing's happened." Then, "I missed you."

I choke back a tear. One falls down his cheek.

"And I've missed you, Little Thorn."

I've always hated that nickname. *Little Thorn.* But he means it. He missed me. I am his daughter, after all.

And his wife's killer.

"Will you be staying?" Pa asks.

I hate that he has hope. That despite it all—the guilt he gives me, the grief I gift him—he still wants me here.

He wants to torture me—for me to torture him.

That is all my presence is good for.

That is the game people play.

I bite my bottom lip, shifting the weight between my feet and angling my body toward the door. "It's probably best I get back to the academy." Tears well in my eyes.

"Are you sure?" Pa asks, his tone timid. "The boys would love to see you."

The saddest part is he believes it. There's scarcely a chance my brothers will want to see the person who stole their mother from them.

I glance at the door, my escape, the only exit in this house. It's so close, just a few steps away.

So why does it feel so far?

"I have a lot of work to do," I manage to say.

"I see." Pa doesn't mean it, and he knows I can feel that. "Will we see you soon?"

"Yes." The lie is sharp and bitter, and he feels the sting. The ache of his disappointment resonates inside me, but I force myself to turn toward the door, whispering, "I really have to go."

Pa frowns. He lost his wife and his daughter on the same day. He's feeling it all right now, all over again. Death is what he remembers when he sees me, the death I feel every time I walk through the garden in this town.

That's why I stay away.

I leave before he answers, each step heavier than the last. Overgrown roots and mushrooms blur beneath my feet. Ma's death lingers in my chest as I race through the garden. I still feel it; I feel it all.

I think I feel it everyday.

My hand shoots up the moment I reach the community mirror, opening a portal to the one place I reserve for a special day. Today is not that day, but I got the the small cottage in the woods, just beyond the academy's barrier. A place where I can be alone.

A place I used to be alone with Ma.

The trees of the academy woods aren't as lush as the ones at home. I've always known it, but knowing something isn't the same as living it. After my first trip home in years, I'm reminded of how sparse these trees feel despite their abundance.

I walk along the cobblestone path, its stones split and uneven, veins of green mold creeping between the cracks. Tufts of grass push through where time has softened the edges. The path leads to the chipped, purple door of the cottage.

This is one of the few quiet places in my world. Yet, despite my constant longing for escape, there never is any. Because the moment I am alone, it is not a relief. These are the few moments I feel *myself*. Never enough time to heal, only enough time to open the wound and watch it bleed.

But sometimes I like the shade of red.

I drag myself inside, past the old, rotting kitchen. Past the purple stools and up the colorful steps.

Most of the second story is consumed by the top of a tree bursting through the floor. The ground is covered in decaying leaves from seasons past.

Behind the branches stands a stained-glass window of a woman dressed in leaves and branches. Grass and flowers grow from the top of her head like hair. Ma used to think it was Zola. I never thought the goddess of balance would look like a Eunoia.

Now, I tell myself it is. If only because it's a way to hold onto Ma. I pretend like I can hear her voice or laughter when I told her I thought the woman looked like Atlas—the first pernipe.

A monster? Ma asked, her voice full, luxurious.

Before, I had said. *When she was beautiful.*

Ma kissed my head then and said something under her breath. For many years I've tried to remember what it was. But with every try, the memory has only withered more.

I have only withered more.

Some people heal with time.

I've only fallen apart.

I curl into a ball on the floor. How I hate it. I will always be alone. I will always be destined to solitude. There is no changing that. There is no fix. How can I live among others when I'll always feel them? When I am always bound to disappoint them? I can't feel it again. I won't.

I want to cry, but it's as if I'm no longer composed of water and now made of ice. Nothing flows. When it comes to finally being alone, I'm out of emotion to spend. But it's still there, omnipresent. The boulder in my chest, the weight to my step, the crumbling in my bones.

No escape.

The birds chirp outside the house, a discombobulated sound to match my confusion.

There's something outside.

I rise, wanting to lash out—kill anything in sight. Out the window, a bird is perched in the tree. I run toward it, arm stretched back and prepared to pull the poor thing apart.

It's an uncontrollable bloodlust guiding me. A hatred. But it isn't mine. And as I reach for the bird, I see the monster below.

A pernipe.

The very creature that killed my mother. I see this moment as a gift—a way to succeed where I once failed.

I stand, traveling down the colorful step and onto the broken path outside. Then, beneath the setting sun and the trembling trees, I wait.

The boy comes to life in my mind. I feel his warmth, his warning. *"Do not fight, my love.* Run. *You have nothing to prove."*

I nearly hiss when I answer, *"I have* everything *to prove."*

The pernipe sees me, but I see Ma. Her legs sinking into the floor, becoming roots. When she finally died, those roots turned back to legs. They were still stuck in the ground, disconnected from her body.

That's what I see when I raise my hand. Not the pernipe, but the sentient tree shaped like a woman, with green eyes and leaves instead of hair.

I see what one of them did to Ma.

Grabbing a branch from the tree's trunk, I shudder at the sharp pain that radiates from the plant. But I hold the branch like a weapon, sending the tree an apology. When I feel its acceptance, I charge, every step sharp with the need to succeed.

I hit the pernipe—the once beautiful woman whose skin has been turned to bark—again and again. The pernipe strikes back. A hundred times stronger than I ever could.

I fly through the air, the impact brutal. The last time this happened, I lost consciousness and woke to the sight of my dead mother. This time, my back slams into a tree. The wind is knocked out of me, and I collapse to the ground.

But this time, I will do what I never could.

I raise my hand, summoning another branch. When it snaps free from the tree and floats in midair, it feels as though I've torn my own arm off. A cry of pain escapes me as I hurl the branch at the pernipe.

She falls. I stand. I reach for her life, doing what I never could. Instead of mending it, the way we're taught to do, I crumble it, like a discarded piece of paper in my hand. I force her into submission, lifelessness.

It's as if I'm crushing my own insides, stomping on my own lungs, suffocating myself. But it's no more painful than healing something.

It's exactly the same, and I push forward.

Reversely, I feel her life, buzzing my hand—coursing through my veins, like alcohol, like fire. It hurts, it burns, I want it to stop.

I like it.

I pick up the branch I'd thrown at her, standing over the monster. I hit her until each of her branches fall off. I hit her until she has no means of fighting back.

And then I reach down, shoving my fingers into her eye sockets, the bark softening—as if to flesh—at my touch.

One by one, I rip her eyes out—the only way to kill a pernipe.

I do what I couldn't when it mattered.

It doesn't seem so hard now.

It doesn't seem nearly as important, either.

Chapter 6
What's a Life Without
the Consequences?

It's almost a relief, returning to the academy and letting other people's chaos drown out my own. The moment I step on campus, it all crashes into me: their stress, their love, their woes. Adrenaline writhes against my muscles, pushing through my skin itself. I itch to move, run, do anything.

But I'm exhausted.

I collapse into bed, the weight of the day dragging me under.

The sleep is hardly restful.

When I wake, I search for Lucian, finding him in the combat room. He fights with Yuki, but when his eyes meet mine, they're smug. Every drop of him is. He thinks he convinced me to be here, to do what I've already done.

I swallow my annoyance. The arrogance he must possess to think there's anything he could do to pique my interest in *my* dead mother.

As I glare past him, my eyes snag on the armory in the back of the room, left open. With swords, shields, and a pair of twin blades with green and gray stones embedded into the hilt.

They're gorgeous. I could see myself using them, fighting the way Lucian fights Yuki.

I could have used them against the pernipe.

Perhaps I would, if I were allowed in Combat Training.

Lucian approaches, sheathing his sword. He's out of breath and sweaty as he asks, "What did you find?"

I don't look away from the blades in the armory. I want them for myself. Would anyone notice if they were gone? There's so many.

"Not here." Before I can stop myself, I add, "Are those all the weapons?"

"Not even close. Why do you ask?"

"No reason."

I wonder what other weapons would call to me. I can still feel the pernipe's life buzzing in my hands, taking power back from the thing that deemed me powerless. I don't know how long I'll hold this feeling in my fingers, but I like it. It's a reminder that I can save myself. That maybe, just maybe, I can save the next person.

"Let's go," I mutter.

I follow as Lucian walks through the academy halls, ducking my head as students pass. They're already suffocating me; I fear what eye contact would do right now.

When Lucian approaches the academy exit, I grab his arm.

I open my mouth, choking on other people's words before I can get out my own: "We can't go past the barrier."

"What happened?"

I don't answer at first. Not because I don't want to. There's a part of him that already knows. A certainty stirring in his question.

Perhaps he's making an incorrect assumption. Perhaps he's keeping things from me. Whichever it is, I anticipate that he will share his secrets when I share mine—that's what a decent person would do.

I'm not sure I believe that Lucian is a decent person.

Every second I remain silent, his suspicion simmers beneath the surface, and I can't help but wonder how much he truly understands.

Has he learned something about my ma?

"A pernipe attacked me," I spit out. "I killed it."

His eyes widen, and I'm delighted by his shock and sudden appraisal. He looks at me as if I've changed before his eyes—a delicate seed has sprouted into a ferocious thorn.

I think I'd like the worlds to feel this way about me—to see me as strong. It's no secret that the Eunoia are regarded as weak. As if the balance and peace we accomplish is not a worthy cause for life.

I disagree with that. But I don't think I believe there's *never* a reason to fight—unlike most of the Eunoia.

There's a time and a place for it, the way there was today with the pernipe. Even if every Eunoia would have run, I'm glad I stayed to fight.

"All right," Lucian says with a nod, the hint of a smile curving his lips. "I have another location."

We walk through the halls once more, stopping at Lucian's suite. When he calls for Azaire, I stay silent.

Azaire exits, glancing at me and searching for some kind of connection. I can't give him any, and he quickly understands, looking away.

The emotions of the two boys are abundantly clear. One is confused but hungry. Insatiably so. He believes knowledge will fill a pit within his soul. The other feels quiet. *Azaire* feels quiet. I like that. I cling to that, and my heart finally slows. It's been beating like a lone leaf trembling in the wind for days now.

We walk upstairs to the Royal floor. As far as I know, it's never used. I stifle a sneeze as I sit, running a finger along the table, collecting a pile of dust and revealing the dark wood beneath.

"I found this in my mom's study." I pull the book from my bag. "It's glamoured."

"How do you know?" Lucian asks.

"For one, this book is written by Shenlin, not Marto. Second, it doesn't feel like my ma or anything else in her study."

Holding it feels like carnage incarnate. I don't know how else to describe it.

"Can I see it?" Azaire asks me.

"Yes." I quickly hand him the book, avoiding his fingers.

Azaire examines it. I try not to examine him. It looks so natural in his hand. He's always the shyest kid in class, perhaps second to me. But when he says, "They didn't get the book right," I have the feeling he could answer any question asked of him.

"Whoever glamoured it was in a hurry," I add, but it's only a guess. "Whatever it is was valuable enough to not warrant destruction."

"Or it was indestructible," Lucian says.

"Why wouldn't they just take it?" I ask. It's an open-ended question. I don't expect him to answer.

But Azaire does not disappoint. He mutters, "Things are best hidden in plain sight," and hands me the book.

I smother the smile that creeps up my lips.

"There's more." I clear my throat.

Something is hidden beneath this book. Potentially something dangerous. Whatever is beneath these fake pages could be horrific.

Unlike Lucian, I don't want to draw people in with false pretenses.

"Whatever this is, I think it came from Folkara," I tell them.

The air in the room goes still. I glance between the boys, waiting for their reply. But when Azaire and Lucian look at one another, I know immediately: *there's something they're not telling me.*

About *my* mother.

My *dead* mother.

How dare they hide that from me?

"You hide, too," the boy says.

I rub my knuckles into the sockets of my eyes. *"That's not what this is about."*

"You're free to hide, my love. I like you better to myself."

"May I see the book?" Lucian asks.

I rip my hand from my face, begrudgingly handing it over.

"Why do you think it came from Folkara?" Azaire's voice is gentle.

I don't feel gentle when I look at him. I feel like I'm being lied to.

"You are," the boy reminds me.

"I can force the truth if I have to," I remind *him.*

"But would it feel truly earned, then?"

"I found papers," I mutter to the room. The boy is right, but not entirely. I won't find out anything about Ma if I can't compromise. "All stamped with Folkara's crest and signed by King Easton and Queen Melody."

Azaire and Lucian glance at one another *again.* If it wasn't clear before, it's clear now.

They know something more.

"Tell me," I demand.

Azaire's gaze meets mine, and he doesn't hesitate. "Folkara is making a Weapon."

A Weapon? They must be wrong—they must have misunderstood. Or *I've* misunderstood. Ma would never… she would *never.*

Weapons have been outlawed for centuries. And for good reason. They're powered by *people*—our life force. They steal our magic and potentially our lives if taken too far. In a similar vein, if the life force is strong enough, there's no telling what a Weapon could do. Destroy every world. Possibly the entire universe. One nearly did in the Arcanian War. That's *why* they're outlawed.

But I feel the dread coming from Azaire, and that doesn't manifest without truth. Without *knowing*.

There really is a Weapon, isn't there?

"You've seen it?" I ask, and guilt curdles in my gut like month old milk. I could nearly puke. *Lucian* could nearly puke—and it puts together the pieces for me. "That's where you came from? When Azaire was half-dead."

Lucian avoids my gaze. "Yes."

"You lied to me." Anger floods through me like lava ripping through cracked stone. This is about *my* mother.

"You would've known if I'd lied," Lucian says, so smugly I'd like to shake him. To curse him. *So very funny, asshole.* As if my being able to pinpoint lies is a parlor trick. As if my power is a pleasantry and not a plague.

"At what point does omitting the truth become a lie?" I ask him, trying my very best not to sneer. Wondering if I'm failing.

Sure that I am.

Words from a past life haunt me. *You're so expressive, Little Thorn.* Because feeling others' emotions is not nearly enough to torment someone. The gods had to make sure I couldn't hide my own, either.

"When you're intentionally hiding something," Azaire says.

My heart flutters. I look at him momentarily. Give him a small smile.

Grow angry with myself for feeling gentleness in his gaze.

I don't want to look away, but when tears prickle at my eyes, I look forward and bite my lip.

That's exactly what Ma would say.

Ma the philosopher—not the weapon builder.

"Yes," Lucian sighs. "I lied."

"I told you not to be vague about my mother," I scold while trying not to scold. Trying not to lose my head. But there's no adverse reaction. Lucian understands the outburst. Azaire does, too.

Does he know?

Did Lucian tell him about Ma?

"Did he tell you?" I snap, accidentally, at Azaire.

"Tell me what?"

"I didn't tell him." Lucian's words almost make his intentions seem sincere. But I can feel the deceit beneath. It wasn't sympathy or respect that convinced him to hold my secret.

"Tell me what?" Azaire asks again.

My heart aches for him. He's being roped into this, I know it. Lucian's will is strong, cold and sharp like edged steel. Azaire's is a caterpillar in a cocoon, waiting for his wings to grow.

I shove the book in my bag. "My mom's dead," I answer without looking at Azaire. I'm not prepared for his sympathy.

I think it would break me.

I think gentleness is the one thing I don't know how to handle.

I think it would be my undoing.

Everyone else walks around with armor on their hearts and knuckles. Always so ready to punch, hoping the blow will land twice as hard as the ones they've received. But not Azaire. A part of me thinks he should. A part of me thinks ferocity is strength.

Another part doesn't know either side of that coin.

"Whoever gave you her name likely didn't even know that this was in her study," I continue. "And if they did, they didn't think you'd find it." I look at Azaire. Someone has to tell him. "They sent you on a fool's errand." I twist toward the exit, my hand on the knob as I say, "I'm going to get the glamour stripped."

"Allow me," Lucian interrupts. "I'll take it to Calista."

I pull my bag closer in case Lucian reaches for it—I wouldn't put it past him.

"I can do it."

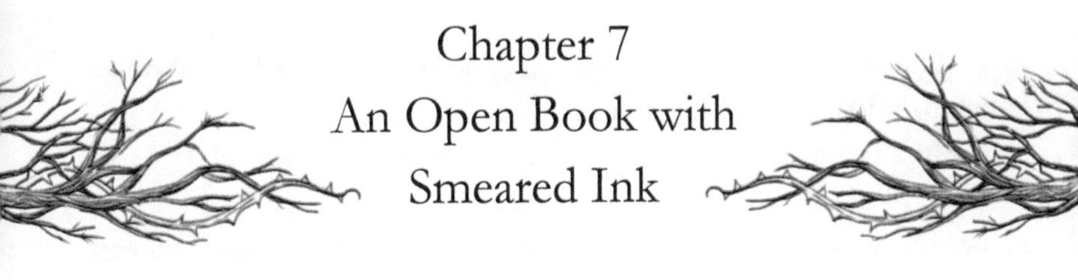

Chapter 7
An Open Book with
Smeared Ink

I wait until Desdemona and Aralia have left the suite, then I plant my feet on the floor, walking to Calista's door.

Aside from Desdemona, Calista is the most difficult to be around. Turbulence is her emotion, always on the verge of a freak out. Whereas Desdemona is scared, acting like it's anger.

Fear is the worst emotion.

Something about those words wake the boy up. He says, *"What will you do if she does not agree?"*

I exhale, closing my eyes and following him into the realm of my mind. Today, it's dark here. Shadows overcast every object, blurring the edges. But the boy who stands before me is entirely material. His features are far from smudged: he is fully fleshed out. His sculpted nose is like Azaire's and his hair is like Lucian's—though in the darkness, it almost looks blue.

I meet his gaze. *"I don't know what I'll do."*

"Yes, you do." A smile spreads across his full lips. *"If you do not want to know, that is one thing. But you cannot pretend you do not."*

I know what he's insinuating, and I shake my head. *"I wouldn't control someone's emotions. That isn't who I am."*

"My love," he murmurs. *"What do you think I am?"*

When I hear Calista's door swing open, my eyes flutter open. She stands before me, rolling her eyes as she glances up to meet my gaze. Her long golden hair hangs down her body, which she doesn't often allow. Most girls in Visnatus have their hair braided at all times. It's proper.

"What do you want?" Calista asks. She sounds annoyed, but I know she's not. We have our history.

"I need you to strip a glamour." I hold her gaze, making sure she knows this is important. "From something that belonged to my mom."

She presses her lips together, nodding as she runs a hand through her hair. Reluctantly, she mutters, "Come in."

It's been nearly a year since I was in her room. It looks different—more plain. She's taken down the art and stripped the room of the personality it once held. Now it's beige walls, beige bedding, and new beige furniture.

Different.

"Make this quick," Calista demands.

But she cares; I feel it, her warmth in my chest. It's the only reason I'm able to hand her the book. To show her the view that was once my ma's.

Calista examines the book, flipping it around in her hands. Then she looks at me, her doubt tearing at my chest. Clutching my heart. It's the same fear of inadequacy she's always had. Though it feels stronger than ever before.

"The glamour's strong," Calista says. "I don't know that I'll be able to lift it."

"You're stronger than you think," I remind her. It feels like I could almost slip back in time. Into my body, mind, and soul from a year ago. Those measly months of friendship.

Calista takes a deep, shaking breath. Then she closes her eyes. I try to look away so I don't have to feel the claws of her doubt. But this moment means too much. My gaze is important.

There's a softness in her, trying to dull the sharp edge of fear. Two sides of her—tenderness and terror—wrestling for control. She's trying to believe in herself, and it's working.

Her exhales come out unsteady. Her head begins to tilt.

Then it happens.

The book in her hands dissolves into yellow light, lifting off her palms, suspended in midair. It flickers—book, then something smaller—back and forth, like a glitch in the universe.

She's about to do it—get me answers, tell me why Ma had materials from Folkara. If she was involved in the Weapon and its conception.

Then the book falls, the light subsides, and nothing more happens.

"Did you—"

"No," Calista cuts me off, running her fingers through loose hair. "Just give me time."

"You almost had it." My tone is gentle.

"Do not speak calmly of what you know nothing about!" Her head snaps up, eyes dark with frustration before she collapses on her bed.

"Get out."

"Calista—" I start, but a sudden gust of wind sweeps through the room, silencing me. The furniture trembles. The windows groan in their frames. My breath catches, but Calista doesn't look at me. She stares at the floor, her gaze distant as her irises glow yellow.

As she steadies her breathing, the wind slow fades, retreating with her anger.

"I'll work on it." Her voice is strained.

"Thank you." I step toward the door, my words feeling inadequate.

I don't think I should leave. I wouldn't have a year ago. But Calista doesn't want me here, so I exit, shutting myself in my room.

Sitting on my bed, I focus on the plants on my windowsill, at the leaves spilling from their pots. As much as I try to focus on their life, the tension leaks from me, tears clinging to my eyes.

So I close them.

I'm still on my bed, still in my room—only now, I'm not alone. The boy is next to me.

His presence steadies me as he pulls me close to him, his hand stroking my back.

"You haven't gotten a dress yet," he whispers. A kind way to divert my attention, but it doesn't work.

"What if Calista can't lift the glamour? What if I never find out what Ma was involved in?"

His fingers glide along my shoulders. *"You know Calista is powerful. Give her time."*

Calista doesn't need time. With a word, I could change her mind.

Make her *want* to lift the glamour. More than that—make her believe she can.

Isn't that the easiest way to get something done?

I shake my head at the boy. *"Maybe time isn't what she needs."*

I don't realize how the words sound until they've left my lips. Instantly, I hope he didn't hear. But even if I hadn't said it, he would've known. He *is* me.

"I thought that wasn't you," the boy whispers.

"It isn't." The words are unconvincing to even myself, so how could I convince him? I wipe my cheeks, even though there are no tears. I was crying in real life, not in my mind. *"It will be a last resort."*

"If it's a resort at all, it's a part of you."

I turn to face him, and with a flick of my finger, his image dissipates like smoke. Sitting alone in the room of my mind, I sigh.

Chapter 8
Buried in My Mind

ONE YEAR AGO

In the Elemental Magic classroom, Calista stands alone at the center, sunlight pouring through the newly repaired skylight above her. Between her hands, she holds a yellow ball of light, larger than the one she showed me the day we became friends. But like then, it isn't transparent. The air churns inside relentlessly, creating a tornado, rather than the bubble of pristine air it should be. The edges of the sphere begin to ripple and shift, distorting to an uneven oval.

I try to breathe, not wanting Calista to think she's scaring me. As I clutch the rose amulet at my chest, I think of Ma and her words. The rose is an amulet of protection. So, when emotions become too tangled around me, I hold onto it, searching for safety.

With a scream from Calista, the ball pops, and the wind rushes through the large room. I'm slammed against the wall—that's thankfully padded, for reasons like these.

My hair blows in my face, filling my mouth. I turn my head against the brute of her power, watching as Calista crashes to her knees. When the wind subsides, I rush to her.

Her usually perfect braided hair is a mess, loose strands sticking out from every stitch. It falls down her back, looking like it'd be better undone.

"What is it?" I sit next to her.

"Do not act as if you don't feel it." Calista stifles the cries between her sharp words.

"You're sad and angry," I say—an understatement. "But I'm not asking what you feel; I'm asking why you feel it."

Calista lifts her head, a sheen of tears over her brown eyes. "It's Lilac… She won't even look at me anymore. I broke her heart, and I can never tell her why."

A few times now, she confided in me. She had a relationship with Lilac, and her parents—the King and Queen of Folkara—forced her to end it.

"Lilac could keep the secret," I say, and as I'm about to continue, Calista cuts me off.

"My mother would kill me if it ever came out." She stares at the ceiling, plugging her nose and clamping a hand over her mouth as she cries. She always does. *Sorrow should be suffered in silence*, Calista says.

I believe those are her mother's words.

"But you told me your secret," I whisper.

"That's different."

She doesn't need to elaborate.

I know why it's different. If I were to betray her trust, and her secret came out, she could say I manipulated her emotions. I am the easiest scapegoat, the only person she could safely be honest with.

It would be simple to turn the tables on me.

It's the only reason she could have a friendship with me.

"It wasn't only that Mother denied my feelings for Lilac," Calista whispers. "It's something worse—" She chokes once more on her sobs.

As she reaches to plug her nose, I grab her wrist, stopping her. "Cry, Calista. It's okay to cry."

My words give her pause for a moment. Then her head crashes onto my shoulder. I release her wrist, holding her back as she cries into my shirt, dampening the fabric.

"Mother told me—" She hiccups. "She told me that I am to marry Lucian, and Lilac is to marry Kai." The sobs echo through the room. "There is everything standing against Lilac and me, and if I am to utter these words to Lilac before our parents announce them… I could lose what little I have."

I hold onto Calista. I have no words. Her sobs burn in my throat and ache in my stomach. I wish there was something more I could do with this awful power. Something other than saying, *I know*. But it seems that's all I'm good for.

"I need you." Calista forces herself up. The tears continue to stream as she sits straight. "I need you to take away my love."

I shake my head, and Calista picks up my gloved hand.

"Look me in the eye, and force me to stop feeling this way," she demands.

"Calista… No. I can't do that." Gently, I tug my hand away.

As I stare at her, I think of what she is asking me to do. If I do this, there's no telling if I could undo it. Would Calista ever want me to?

But it isn't the immortality of the decision that makes me hesitate.

It's the danger. If I do one thing incorrectly, I don't know what will happen.

My compulsion could kill her, the same way my touch would.

I am a carnivorous plant. I will eat whatever comes near.

"Think about it," she begs. "Please."

"Okay." I force the words out. "I'll think on it."

Chapter 9
The Sweetest Torture

NOW

This time when I go to Lucian and Azaire, I don't have a plan. Do I tell them Calista can't remove the glamour, or wait like she asked? Maybe I could get the book to Lucian and let him find his own Folk to deal with it, like he wants. It's not that I don't trust Calista, it's that the boy was right.

If manipulating her emotions is a resort at all, it's a part of me.

And I already know I'm willing to do it.

But it seems it won't be an issue for now. When I knock, Azaire opens the door. Without Lucian.

"Hey." His voice bubbles through my chest like foam.

I stand at the door, right at the threshold, awkwardly balancing at the precipice of the exit. "I um… I'm working on removing the glamour from the book."

Azaire nods, words lodged in his throat. He wants to talk to me. I have nothing I'm willing to share. Nothing to help him understand my decision.

Telling him I'm saving us both the pain is not often what one hears when they are starting a relationship.

"We should wait for Lucian," Azaire says at last.

"Yeah," is all I manage. The rest of my vocabulary gets caught in the spaces between the alphabet.

"He appreciates your help more than he shares," Azaire tells me, and he means it.

"I'm not doing it for him," I say, and Azaire shifts, tugging on his beanie. "I'm doing it for me."

Lucian's hungry for answers—I might be starving.

Azaire nods, then after a moment, he says, "I love Lucian, more than anyone. But if you didn't want to be here, I'd tell you to run."

"That is what someone who cares would say," the boy murmurs to me.

"I can feel that he cares."

"Would you like to do anything about it?" the boy asks, but he doesn't sound happy. He sounds curious.

He feels scared.

"Then why are you here?" I ask. "What's in it for you?"

Azaire shrugs. "Lucian's quick to go to extremes."

"Why are *you* here?" I repeat the question, taking the opportunity to step fully past the threshold.

He glances at me, standing in his suite, as if he wasn't sure I ever would again. Finally, he says, "Because I want to help the worlds."

He truly means it. That's the most baffling part.

I've never felt such selflessness in my life.

"The way things are isn't right," Azaire finishes.

I agree, to an extent. As much as I know this life is wrong, I don't know what could be right.

So, I ask, "What is right?"

"I don't know yet. But I'd like to." He smiles a little, meeting my gaze. *"That's* why I'm here."

I smile a little, too, turning to leave.

"Wendy?" Azaire whispers, his voice barely a breath, but what he's about to say is going to be dangerous.

I glance back at him.

"When you dance at the ball tonight…" He pauses. "Think of me. And I'll be right there, thinking of you."

I smile, nodding once, even if I can't verbally agree.

As I step out of his suite, the boy asks, *"Do you like him?"*

"Yes," I answer.

A girl twirls by in her silver dress. Another with blue. I do nothing more than watch.

My gaze catches on the girl in the gold, sticking out like a candle in the dark: Desdemona. Always scared. Perpetually steeped in fear, like a tea bag drowning in water. It's hard to be around her. If I didn't feel everyone, I think always being scared would be the worst fate.

Especially when you're in denial of it.

She thinks she's angry.

More partners pass, dancing and smiling. Two things I'm forbidden from. These fundraisers are mandatory to attend, but I am not allowed to interact. The faculty sees my power much like I do: a disease. There is no cure, but the gloves contain it, to an extent.

They mask the symptoms. They do not cure the sickness.

If I were to dance, someone could still touch the skin of my wrist on accident. Though, touching my wrist wouldn't be quite as damning. Eunoias' hands are the conduits of our power. My sitting out is a precaution. There may be ways to fight compulsion—but not mine.

Mine is certain compliance.

Whether or not someone touches me, I could command their minds, which is exactly what they're afraid of.

The gloves are meant to hold me in place, but I sit willingly in my cage.

"I *could touch your wrist,*" the boy whispers from my mind, his voice low and dangerous, as if he's trying to tempt me.

Suddenly desperate for company, I close my eyes. The boy stands before me. His hair is brighter in the ballroom, shining like twilight. He reaches for my hand but touches my wrist with a mischievous smile.

"*See?*" he says. "*I can touch you.*"

"*I see.*" A subtle frown shapes my lips. "*But you're not real.*"

"*I am very real, and* you *are very beautiful.*" The boy picks up my hand and bows. "*A dance, my love?*"

I look past him at the empty ballroom. Before I entered the landscape of my mind, this vast room was full of people. Now, the moonlight shines in at odd degrees, not truly illuminating anything. It's more akin to a streak of silver on a canvas.

"*It's too empty,*" I say, pressing my lips together. "*Too depressing.*"

The boy smirks, raising a hand and snapping his fingers. The people return, though their faces morph and blur. I can't get a good look at any of them, but I try.

"Stop," the boy says, reaching out and grabbing my chin. He gently guides my gaze back to his. *"You focus on everyone else too often. Let tonight be for us. You haven't even told me the color of your dress."*

He takes a long stride to the left, and I follow. My dress billows around my legs as he spins me through the room.

When we finally slow, I ask, *"Told you? Can't you see it?"*

The boy looks down at my gown, shaking his head. *"My world is black and white, until you paint the picture."*

Confused, I nod. I've had him in my mind for years, how could I have not known this?

"It's silver," I tell him as our dance finds its rhythm again—his hand steady at the small of my back, mine resting lightly in his.

His eyes trace the gown, lingering longer this time. *"It suits you."*

"It isn't meant to."

It's the color of Ilyria—there isn't a choice as to whether or not I like it.

The boy leans in, his breath warm against my cheek, just enough to unsettle the air between us. *"Perhaps that's the trouble,"* he murmurs. *"Even that which you never wanted finds a way to belong to you."*

"I could think of many," I say, my voice quieter now, colored by the ache of memory.

"Don't offend me, my love."

"Not you. You know I'm happy to have you."

The boy smirks, but there is nothing content about his gaze. He stares at me like he's losing me and wants to see me thoroughly before I go.

Then he speaks again, quietly.

"Are you happy to be here tonight?"

The people around us continue to dance, but there is no noise. No bustle. Just marionettes with porcelain smiles.

"No," I answer honestly.

"Why not?"

"Because I can't do anything."

He lifts my hand and spins me, his fingers grazing my palm. The silver of my dress swirls around me. When I've finished, he draws me back in, steadying me with both hands. This time, his smile is more earnest, a toothy grin. There's a light in his eyes again, like I've given it back to him.

And without meaning to, I smile back.

"We're doing something right now," he murmurs. *"Aren't we?"*

"Yes, but—"

He cuts me off with a gentle tug, pulling me closer to him. *"But what? Can you not be content in your own mind?"*

He leads with long strides, and I follow, willingly. The brush of his thumb against mine, the pressure of his hand at my waist—I feel all of it. And I enjoy it.

I enjoy doing the things that I only ever get to watch—even if it's in my mind.

Yet, I still shake my head and say, *"No, not really."*

"I know that's not true," he says. *"I've held you in my arms, and you have smiled."*

I roll my eyes, making sure he can see. *"Okay, so perhaps I can be content. But I cannot be satisfied."*

He slows the dance—barely. Enough to draw me in closer.

His lips brush the edge of a smile.

"I do not satisfy you?" the boy asks.

I laugh, thinking it must be a joke. But when I meet his gaze again, I see that I missed the mark. *"I don't see how—"*

"Then make me physical."

My feet stop moving under me. The boy tries to tug us back into the dance, but I am much stronger. We are in my mind, after all. I don't budge.

"What?" I shudder.

Have I misheard him?

The boy frowns. I don't see how he could be upset; he must have known this would be my reaction.

"You say I am not real, but I am very real." He raises a hand, the edges of his fingers blurring like the people dancing around us. *"What I am not is tangible."*

I stare at him, open-mouthed. I wish I could close it, but even in my mind, I am the expressive Little Thorn.

"I don't have the ability to do something like that," I say.

"You can, my love," the boy says. *"The things they've always said about you —prodigal daughter, most powerful—those things are true things. You could bring

I don't give myself a moment to think. I open my eyes, escaping. But even as I watch the real ballroom, the clear people and the true noise, I can feel the boy in my head. I've spent years with him as my only companion. Have I taken it too far?

Is it possible for this figment of my imagination to grow attached to me?

I contemplate going back to the boy, asking him these questions myself. But I need to think. Making him tangible would defeat the purpose. If he were real, I wouldn't be able to handle his companionship.

Would I?

As if I'm lost at sea and he is the lifeline, my eyes drift toward Azaire. He's back to dancing with his fair share of girls. Or, I suppose, he's been doing that the entire time. I'm the one who left.

There are girls I've never seen, girls I've seen a million times, and none I've ever spoken to.

I was older than the others when I enrolled at Visnatus—ten years old. Most of the kids already had their cliques, and I had no interest in being in any. I had no interest in company. Company was a burden back then, before I grew up and realized intimacy was something I craved and could never have.

Now I am here, sitting in a corner amongst the rulers of our worlds. No one pays any attention to me. I think I prefer it this way because if they did, then the question would arise: What is wrong with her?

I don't need anybody answering for me.

Azaire looks at me, looking at him. I shake my head, quickly looking down. Irrationally hoping that he saw nothing. Oddly wondering what the boy in my head is thinking.

I'm staring at the glowing marble floor, at my silver shoes to match my silver dress for the silver ball. The silver chandeliers reflect through the room, and the moonlight reflects in from the wall of windows behind me.

I sit at the very edge of the tables set for the rulers. Entirely alone, suffocated in this room.

Sometimes it feels like someone is holding my head under the water, forcing me to choke in the liquid. Then I realize it's my own hand keeping me under. That there's no one to blame.

As soon as I fully dive into that emotion, another crashes over me —fear. The desperate kind.

My eyes flicker, darting nervously, my muscles taut, hands clenching like I'm about to fight.

Someone is looking at another person—recognition edged with panic. They're clinging to the hope that what they're seeing isn't real, that it's a trick of the light. But beneath that hope is a bitter dread: part of them always knew.

I glance around the room, trying to pinpoint this sensation. It's as if my powers are a radar, guiding me right to the Queen of Ilyria. She stares into the ballroom, through the dancing bodies, but I can't see who she looks for.

Shaking her away, I try to take a sip of air without breathing in something else. Fear like smoke, love like poison.

Then a hand reaches in front of me and a knee settles by my foot.

Looking down, I see it's Azaire who kneels before me. I avoid his gaze as I ask, "Don't you have a partner?"

"No one that could compare to you."

I shake my head, but I'm secretly smiling at the words. "I'm not supposed to dance with anyone," I tell him. "In case I touch them."

"Wendy," he breathes from the depths of that bow, "I told you once, I was never afraid of your touch."

The boy watches me. Dangerously, he longs, the same way I long to take Azaire's hand.

I do exactly that, my intentions blurred. Do I wish to pull away from the boy's yearning, or pull closer to Azaire?

It must be for Azaire. When he rises, his fingers curl tenderly around mine, making my pulse quicken.

Together, we walk to the dance floor, his hand settling on my waist. Then I'm looking up, into his eyes, and I know this is real—the way he feels and my desire to reciprocate it without fear.

This dance is nothing like the one in my mind with the boy. The faces around us hold steady, unchanging. Moonlight spills over the gowns, soft and silver, and the marble beneath my feet is cool and solid—real.

But most importantly, Azaire's hand is real. Really holding mine.

"You know I could make you," I say, and Azaire gives me a quizzical look. "Fear my touch. Or love me, or hate me. I could make you feel anything. That's why you're not supposed to touch me."

"I wouldn't mind." His anxiety always spikes when he speaks to me. But it's not like others. It's heady, going to my brain like a drug, the same way alcohol heats blood. "It'd be a privilege if you felt enough for me to even consider doing such a thing."

"Even if it was out of hate?" I ask. *Hate for myself,* I don't say.

"Yes," he says softly, and suddenly I become hyper aware of his hands on my body. So close to skin. "I've spent most of my life watching you notice other people. I want to be one of them, in any way."

I know he does; I've always known. I've always felt him, *noticed* him, as he puts it.

I try not to stutter as I say, "Most of the time I'm noticing out of annoyance."

Or jealousy. Jealousy that people can find friendship, can care for one another, can touch each other. Any number of things.

It's with that in mind—my true desire—that I decide to add, "But I always noticed you. In a different way. I liked that you were quiet."

Azaire smiles, then looks down, shaking his head. His heart thumps like a rabbit chased by a snake.

My hands shake in turn.

"That's a first," he whispers.

"I mean it," I say, glancing at his face, willing him to look at me. When he does, our eyes collide. I swallow the lump in my throat and add, "I *like* it."

His gaze shifts, searching mine—equal parts longing and something softer, almost desperate.

I hold his hand a little tighter, feeling the warmth of his skin beneath my palm. His grip tightens in return, answering my silent question without words.

He won't let me go.

"You know… at first, I liked that you saw people," Azaire whispers. "I thought you'd see the things I couldn't show. Until one day, I saw you dancing in the woods. It was like discovering a new star.

When I saw you alone, I finally saw *you*. I'd had a crush on you for years and then there you were, this new person. No longer focusing on everything, just dancing in the silence. Exactly what I wanted—for the things I couldn't show to be seen, I saw in you, and I just… I could've watched you dance forever. 'Till the end of days."

His words—and the raw earnestness behind them—catch me off-guard. A flicker of something electric traces up my spine.

I think I remember that day.

I knew he was there. I always know when someone is there. But it's different with him. I don't want to run from him as much as I want to run from the others.

"You wanted to watch silly old me?" I laugh.

"Want to," he says. "I *want* to watch you. Not that you're silly. I think you're just shy of perfect." He smiles, and I can feel it in my marrow, vibrating my bones.

"Not perfect?" I whisper, half-joking, half-hoping.

"I like to think I have a keen eye for character."

"It's not the scar on my lip?" I laugh—the first time I've *ever* laughed about my scar.

Azaire draws closer, his gaze tracing the curve of my lips. "I love the scar on your lip," he murmurs, his voice low, almost reverent. Like this moment between us is glass, and he's scared to shatter it. "It's your mark—a story you have to tell." He pauses, his gaze meeting mine. "I love your eyes—not just any green, but the kind that belongs to the wildest places in the worlds."

Slowly, his hand rises up my waist, and I hold my breath as he continues, "I love your nose. Your freckles…they're like constellations. And your smile. *Gods*, I love your smile. If the world was ending, and I could ask for one thing to see before it all went away, it would be that smile."

I stare at him, silent a moment. How could he mean all this? How can I listen to his declarations, knowing without a doubt he means them, and still wonder?

How could I have ever run from this boy? I *have* to, and I will after this. But I don't *want* to.

At a loss for words, I ask, "You think my smile is worth that?"

Azaire nods. "Rarer than gold."

"Because I'm standoffish?" I ask, really laughing. I wouldn't be surprised if everyone at this academy thought so.

"Because it's *real*," he says.

His hand moves from my waist up to my face. Before he can settle it where I know he will, I flinch away.

Looking down, I shake my head. "You can't touch me."

"Okay." Azaire lowers his hand.

"Really," I say. "No one can." I look up to see Ms. Ferner staring at me. I drop both my hands and step back, nearly running into another couple. I mutter my apologies, then look back at Azaire. "I'm not supposed to be dancing."

I try to walk away. *Try* because Azaire's hand is still on my waist, and he spins me back into him, holding me close.

Our chests touch.

"But I'm fine," he whispers. "More than fine. You can feel me, can't you?"

I nod. "Yes."

"Then feel me." His eyes don't move away from mine as he lifts his fingers back to my face. Right before making contact, he says, "Feel my heart leap out of my chest at the mere thought of being skin to skin with you."

I grab his wrist, for the first time ever being thankful for the gloves. But I feel it, I do. His heart leaping. His longing.

"I want to be touched as much as you want to touch me," I mutter, dropping his wrist and using his momentary shock to slide out of his grasp. "But I don't want to hurt anyone else."

Though I fear being in close proximity to me will be enough to ruin him.

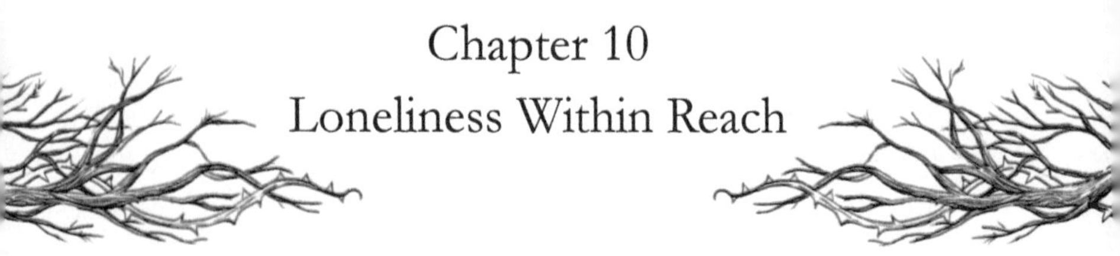

Chapter 10
Loneliness Within Reach

Keeping my distance proves impossible.

Azaire is brought to class once more, his presence commanding despite the fresh wound along his cheek. He weaves between the long tables—strewn with herbs and vials—until he reaches me.

His cut isn't as severe as the last time, but it's enough to draw a stark line across his otherwise flawless skin. The room falls into a tense hush as we prepare for today's lesson: working on aesthetic healing.

It's important, Ms. Ferner said before the Nepenthes arrived, *for Royals and government officials. They must always appear strong—unmarked.*

My task is to restore Azaire's skin, erasing the evidence of pain without leaving a trace. If I fail, that wound will become a permanent reminder of this moment. A record of how the universe chews him up and spits him out at its leisure etched into his face forever.

In some cruel way, it's a mirror of me. The scar along my chin holds the memory of Ma.

Only his memory wouldn't be a death—it would be the moment that the academy took him, doing what they pleased with his body.

Azaire rests in the stool beside me, the jars on the wooden table rattling as he scoots closer.

Despite everything, I can tell something's changed between us. As he sits, his gaze lingers longer. His hands hover just above my skin—as if he heeds my warnings but aches to defy them.

In turn, I do the same.

I clear my throat, scooting closer. Because I have to heal him—not because I long for his nearness.

But I do.

The room isn't as bad today. The pain around me is bearable. None of the wounds inflicted upon the Nepenthes are deadly. They're merely for aesthetics.

This time.

I grind the gotu kola into a fine powder, adding just enough water to form a thick, greenish paste. With careful fingers, I coat Azaire's wound, hoping to erase the memory of the cut before it has time to settle into a scar.

With every stroke, my hands tremble more.

"It's okay," Azaire whispers, his smile creasing his skin. "There's no way I'm dying this time. It's just a little cut."

As I pull my hand away, my glove is coated in red. "And just a little blood," I mutter.

I wipe off my gloves, raising my hands again.

Azaire gently catches my wrists. His grasp stills my trembling.

His eyes meet mine. "Feel me, not everyone else."

For a moment, I stumble. My hand stays in the air. My wrist stays in his hand, my skin just beneath my shirt sleeve. My head tilts to the side, staring at him in awe.

"I always feel you." I hardly realize the words are coming out. "It's what I was telling you at the ball." I shake my head, trying to shake the words from me, but they come out anyhow.

Expressive Little Thorn.

"In philosophy…" I trail off. "You always have something to say, but you never do."

Azaire shrugs with a smile, then lets go of my hand. It returns to my side, denying the part of me that wishes he held on.

"I'm just holding my insights close," he jokes. "I can't have someone in class stealing my ideas."

I smile, a small laugh escaping me. "Steal your ideas?" I ask, still smiling. "So you want to be a philosopher?"

Azaire nods. "I do."

"My mom is a philosopher," I say, before I realize that those aren't the right words.

They aren't the truth.

Ma *was* a philosopher.

"I can tell," he says.

I swallow my sorrow, narrowing my eyes at him.

"You can *tell?*"

Once more, he shrugs. "It's in you, the nature of pondering. You question what you see—it's the best way to learn."

"That's what you do, isn't it?" I ask, though I'm sure I've felt it before.

Azaire tugs at his beanie, growing shy. I've all but forgotten about the gash on his cheek—and he has, too.

"I guess," he murmurs as I unbutton one of my gloves. Instantly, green vines of light wrap around my fingers, as if my magic is waiting to jump out.

I raise my hand to his face, healing the wound left on him by the faculty of this academy.

"Tell me," I whisper, "what you were thinking about the free will question?"

Azaire stares at me blankly.

"I felt you in class," I add.

He nods, his shoulders deflating. His posture sinks just slightly. It makes it easier to heal his skin without touching.

"Promise you won't steal my mighty insights?" he asks.

A joke.

It's been so long since someone joked with me.

"Oh, I couldn't possibly promise that. What if I get rich off your mind?"

"Then it'd be a fair trade," he replies. "I'm already getting rich off yours."

I laugh under my breath, soaking in the sensation. I've missed it, the lightness. I've only ever felt its residue these last few years.

But right now, this smiling, this laughter—it feels like I'm glowing.

"Go on then." I lower my hands. "Make it a fair trade."

Azaire rolls his eyes playfully, clearing his throat mockingly—the same way our professor does.

I would never think this boy was being tortured by the academy he attends.

His voice is wholly serious when he says, "I think our professor misunderstood the question. It's not about free will, but something grander, a piece of a soul, the nature of a person, beyond the experiences that shape them."

A piece of us, unblemished. A piece that *stays* unblemished.

Something in me that is not destroyed by the events of my life.

"So, if there's something beyond our nature and experiences," I ask, "wouldn't that fit into the professor's argument about the gods? Something predetermined?"

"It might be from the gods." Azaire shrugs. "And it might not. I only think that we carry something with us into this universe. We're not blank slates, waiting to be filled by nature and nurture. There's just… something else."

"I, for one, cannot wait to get rich off that idea."

"You wish," Azaire laughs.

I drag my fingers across my lips, like a zipper.

"So, what do you think, Estridon?"

"I think free will scares me," I say, the words slipping past me. Yet I'm glad to speak them aloud. To finally share my mind and be the expressive Little Thorn I was born to be. "I prefer it to be some weird, grand design or a total accident, rather than thinking that I orchestrated it."

"Yeah," Azaire whispers. "I understand."

Calista is awake—I can feel her. I sit on the couch in the common area, allowing the fullness of her emotion in.

To be sure I'm there in the event she can strip the glamour.

But Calista doesn't seem to have made any progress.

The boy in my mind asking me to make him human reminds me of Calista asking me to steal her love for Lilac. On the surface, they sound like things that shouldn't be done. But with the boy—how could I hurt him if he is simply me?

How could he hurt me?

It could be my best hope of true companionship.

"We can take it slow. Start with something small."

I don't like how tempting his offer is, but still, I say, *"I'll think on it."*

I rise, knocking on Calista's door frame. She sits huddled in the corner, the book sprawled open on her bed.

"I can't do it," she sighs. "I can never do anything right."

If it were a year ago, I would sit with her. Try to console her. She might not want me near her anymore, though.

I keep my distance.

"You're too far in your head," I say. "You can't think your way through magic. You have to feel it—"

"I don't need lessons from *you!*" Calista shouts.

I think of sitting. Staying and helping. But I feel people drawing near. Injured and worried, on the hunt for something.

Lucian.

Instead of staying, I escape to my room. Minutes later, a knock sounds on my door. Pain is on the other side of it.

How many times will he come to me, on the verge of death?

I open the door, and my eyes immediately fall on Lucian. He feels… like a corpse. As if a dead body is rotting inside of him. I stare at him, searching for that reeking emotion.

He looks all but normal.

"What happened to you?" I ask, barely audible.

Lucian clears his throat, stuttering as he says, "Desdemona needs your help."

My gaze shifts to the girl in his arms. I'd hardly felt her through Lucian's torment. Shaking my head, I try to understand what happened to him. But instead, the pain from Desdemona's broken body slowly takes over.

The pain is in my shoulder, but also not. It seems further than that, like fire in my bloodstream.

"What happened to her?"

"Dislocated shoulder," Lucian answers.

It isn't the full answer, yet I wince, understanding the pain that seeps through my shirt like blood.

"Okay." I nod, turning to get my herbs and leaving the suite.

I stay a few paces behind them as we walk through the academy, Lucian carrying Desdemona in his arms. She nuzzles her head into his shoulder.

And Lucian *cares*. It emanates from him like smoke from a bonfire. It reeks so strongly, I could never miss it.

It clings to me.

It's hard seeing that even someone as calloused as Lucian can care for a person. Even someone as scared as Desdemona can reciprocate. I must be the most wounded of us all, because I don't know that I could ever be on either end. That is why I stay a few paces behind as we walk. It is why I watch from afar.

It's the best I can do.

I think of the boy. If he were tangible, would he hold me like this? His voice fills my mind, *"I would hold you however you wished me to."*

"You make a compelling offer."

We make it to the Royals' room, and Lucian lowers Desdemona on the couch. I watch, pretending I'm not, as he tucks her hair behind her ear. Their eyes meet, and my heart picks up its pace.

There's familiarity and fear in their gazes, but more than that, adoration. They hide from it, yet neither can deny it.

They are a seesaw, as one comes down, the other goes up. A dance, a game, and it's one I want.

I shake my head, rushing to their side to do what I came to. Lucian breathes heavily beside me, not because he's tired, but because he's worried.

He doesn't know what he'll do if something happens to her.

I'd like to leave soon. People-watching is fun in spurts, but it grows weary over time, and I can only take so much.

Lucian has filled Desdemona's wound with shadows, keeping her from bleeding out. For a moment, I only look. Wondering if someone would do that for me.

"Can you?" I finally ask, turning to Lucian, and he waves a hand. The shadows pour to the ground, regrouping with the rest scattered around the corners of the room.

I dip my gloved finger in valerian root powder and place it under Desdemona's nose, telling her to inhale. With fleeting peace, Desdemona slips out of consciousness.

Working quickly, I begin to mend the flesh around the stab wound. Then I move to the burns. Nothing I do helps to cease the pain or refurbish the skin.

"How did she get the burns?" I ask, threads of green magic flowing from my bare palms… and doing nothing.

"There must have been poison on the blade."

It doesn't feel like a poison, but there's no other plausible explanation. There's a burn around the stab wound and on her palm. I try harder to heal her, but the ashen flesh continues to reject my power.

The sensation seeps into me, like water corroding metal, slowly burning through my skin.

Shaking my head, I say, "I can't fix it."

Lucian's worry grows louder. In between the cracks of emotion, I can only feel how much he cares.

"Try again," he says.

"I *am* trying!" I snap, dropping my hands.

I stare at Desdemona, reaching for the peace of her unconsciousness. All I can feel is Lucian.

"Apologies," I mutter. "Just—can we talk about something else? I need you to get your mind off her."

"My mind off of her?"

"Yes." I sigh. "Your emotion for her—it's too much stress for me to take at once."

Lucian quiets, his confusion palpable. He might not know exactly what he feels for her. Yet, whatever they are, he can't ignore them. Not now. Even as he tries. It helps, for a moment. But soon that bottle will crack.

"The glamour," he says softly, tapping his foot in a steady rhythm. "How's it going?"

When I pop Desdemona's bone back into place, she jolts up, about to scream. I cover her mouth before the sound can escape.

My mouth opens involuntarily, desperate to let out the cry for her.

"Calista's working on it," I answer before turning to Desdemona. "It's all right." I hold her cheek gently with my gloved hand. "You can rest."

Lucian doesn't continue to ask questions. His focus goes back to Desdemona, aching in my chest. That plus the death within him is unbearable. I feel it manifest physically in my back, making it hard to stand upright without pain.

After several moments, I ask, "What's that about?"

"What's what about?"

He knows what I'm asking. His feelings around Desdemona linger, but the ones around the death inside of him increase.

"That feeling."

"Is she out?" Lucian tilts his head toward Desdemona.

She isn't, not entirely. But slowly, she loses consciousness. Her lethargy could pull me down with her.

"Yes," I answer. "Now, are you going to tell me what happened to you?"

Lucian shakes his head, looking away from Desdemona. To the ground. He doesn't want to answer.

It's bad.

It's worse than bad. The sorrow—it makes me wonder if I've misjudged him.

"You don't feel the same," I add.

When Lucian says, "I'm not the same," I know that there has been a misjudgment on my end. Though I'm not sure where. "But what matters now is Desdemona. Then the book."

"She'll be fine." I nod.

Lucian's gaze slowly makes its way back to Desdemona. It lingers there lazily, as if he is looking but not seeing. As though he is in a trance and cannot shift out of it.

As though he wishes he never looked in the first place.

"Yeah," he says at last. "She will."

He means it with full sincerity.

He will make sure of it.

Chapter 11
Losing by Your Side

Turn the corner and I'm at Azaire's window. Knock on the window and he will answer. But I don't knock, I stare. I contemplate. I know how easy it would be to leave.

But when I see Azaire writing at his desk, I know that I'm not ready to walk away.

There's precision in his emotion as his pen glides along the page. Something that's almost calculated, mathematical. It's specific and expressive. There is no other way to describe it but *him*.

And I fall into it—silently descending the endless well.

"There is still time to run," the boy tells me, his words a rope, pulling me back up. He's right—I want to run. I almost listen.

But this is a trial. This doesn't have to mean anything.

The smoke of Lucian's care still clings to me, the scent wafting with every breath. *I want that, too. I want what everyone else has.* So I plant my feet.

But fear overcomes me—I *can't* have what everyone else has, and I don't need the boy to tell me. I already know why.

Before I have the chance to give in to fear, to *run*, Azaire looks up from his black journal. His gaze meets mine, and he smiles.

Turning around is no longer an option.

As he opens his window, his smile grows. "What a surprise."

The sound of his voice lifts something in me.

"A happy one, I hope?"

Azaire narrows his eyes, teasing. "Horrifically scary, actually."

I bite my lip, taking a small step back from the window. "Then I better be on my way, huh?"

Before I can move, his hand flashes out—fast and certain—catching my wrist. I look up, breath caught, meeting his gaze.

"Leaving," he murmurs, "would be more horrific."

I can't help but smile.

"This is all it takes to woo you?" the boy taunts. *"I could do this in my sleep."*

"Then you should try it sometime."

Azaire releases my hand, and I step closer. "What are you writing?"

I'm trying to distract myself from the boy. It took a lot of guts for me to walk here today, especially with the boy berating me, telling me what a bad idea this is.

I already know.

But, for once, I don't want to face this day alone.

Azaire blushes, sliding a book over his notebook. "Nothing."

It isn't nothing—the opposite, actually. But he doesn't want to share with me, and there are a million things I don't want to share with him. So I leave it be, extending a hand through the window, over his desk and into his room.

"Coming?"

Azaire doesn't hesitate before slipping his hand into mine. My longing and fear mix in equal measures. I've spent years running from this very moment, yet here it is.

It's found me.

I pull him out of the window, both of us laughing when his feet catch on the sill, and I tug him closer, barely managing to steady him.

His hands grip my waist, fingers digging into the fabric of my shirt. It's the same way he held me at the dance—only this time, there's an undeniable intensity in his touch, as if now he knows it's welcome.

For a breathless moment, we're standing so close I can feel the rapid beat of his heart against mine. His eyes drop to my lips, and a surge of heat pulses through me, desire coiling like a serpent. Every part of me is drawn to him, every nerve humming with need, my skin burning where his hands rest.

I've always wondered if my first time touching a person again would be a kiss.

I can feel his body against mine, every inch of him. I can feel his gaze on my lips, every moment of desire.

It's the culmination of years of stolen glances, yet in the face of it, we both close our eyes.

Neither of us acts.

I'm the first to pull away, because that's how it has to be.

I can look.

I can never touch.

We walk through the woods, the sun peeking through the trees. It's mostly silent, the tension teeming between us, like the calm before the storm.

As if we both know that this is as inevitable as the rain.

That *we* are inevitable.

Azaire is wondering where we're going—I don't want to explain before I have to. It's not a bad surprise, but it's not for him either.

This is for me.

This is my dream.

To live this day with someone else. Someone who cares.

It's been a long time since I had that.

We clamber over the rocks and weave through the bushes until a small cedar cottage emerges into view.

Azaire glances at me, his dark brows lifting in surprise—as if he can't believe I brought him here. As if he already knows what this means to me.

I could almost believe that *he* is feeling *my* emotions.

The last time I was here, I killed for the first time—tore the eyes out of a pernipe. I try not to let that memory taint my sanctuary as I step through the door.

Inside, the cottage is covered in dust and cobwebs. A thick layer of grime coats every surface, like always. The purple chairs and cushions are decaying with time, and the kitchen is something from the past— only one counter with a wooden mortar and pestle, and a big black iron pot on the floor.

It might be a part of the reason I enjoyed this cottage so much through the years. The world would change, but this stayed the same: dusty, old, and decayed.

The remnants of a world long forgotten. No one has lived in this part of Visnatus since the Arcanian War, before the academy opened. This cottage is, at least, a thousand years old. But it still stands, despite its neglect. Despite its loneliness.

It gives me hope.

"Upstairs is the best part," I say, making my way to the stairs.

Every step is a different color—an array of dark blues, purples, yellows, greens, and reds.

Azaire likes the second floor, too. A tree has pushed through the home, its trunk breaking through the floor and its branches spreading wide. He steps forward, brushing his fingers against the leaves as the sunlight filters through the stained-glass window. The colors dapple his brown skin in shades of green, blue, and purple.

"What is this place?"

Branches and leaves crunch beneath my feet as I step into the room, moving away from the staircase.

"A very old home," I answer. "Before the Arcanian War there were villages on this land. This is the last cottage standing." Pausing, I gently touch the stained glass. "I come on this day every year." I run my fingers along the rough edges of the window. "I used to come with Ma."

I wasn't allowed to return home to Eunaris on Ma's birthday, so she would visit me for the afternoon.

We loved this room.

Today is the first in years that there was a possibility of not being alone here. It was selfishness that led me to drag Azaire along.

I stare out the window, past the trees and into the woods. Sometimes, if I squint just right, it blurs into something familiar—my hometown. A place I once considered the safest in the worlds. I can almost see Ma and me, gathering wildflowers in the fields. She used to cover one eye with a violet and smile at me, an image so vivid it felt straight out of a painting.

Ma was beautiful. Full cheeks with freckles and elegant emerald eyes. People used to tell me I was her spitting image. I hope I am.

I don't realize I'm touching the scar along my chin until Azaire says, "I'm sorry."

My hand falls away as I look back at him. "You aren't supposed to say that."

We don't say *I'm sorry* at the academy. It's improper. We say *my apologies*, and we don't mean it, either.

Azaire chuckles softly. "I'm the farthest thing from elite here."

"Yeah?" I smile. "Maybe that's why I like you."

"You…" Azaire steps forward, lips twisting into a grin. "*Like* me?" His voice lilts with teasing curiosity.

I shove an arm into his shoulder, laughing, then bite my lip to hold it in. "Don't get all smug on me now."

"*My apologies.*" He smiles. "I just like hearing it."

Turning from him, I move toward the gap in the wall where the balcony used to be. I sit on the ledge, legs dangling, the ground far beneath my feet.

Azaire's soft voice fills the room. "Thank you."

He feels like love and gratitude. I don't understand why, but I like it. The sun is in my chest, feeding the flowers.

"For what?" I ask, staring at my legs kicking in the air.

Azaire sits beside me, his hands resting on the floor, a breath from mine.

"For showing me."

"It's not a big deal." I shake my head.

"It is," he says, with so much sympathy that I long to pull away. Hide my face, because I don't deserve it.

I am the reason I sit here alone every year.

"You don't have to keep people out," Azaire whispers. "I did it for a long time, too, until I finally realized that this life is meant to be enjoyed, no matter how many of those moments are fleeting."

He says it, but he does not mean it. Not all of it. Behind his words, there is a twinge of guilt. *That* is the feeling I can't help but cling to, because it is the very thing I fear.

My gaze drifts beyond the treetops into a blue oblivion. My voice stays soft. "You don't understand the circumstances."

There's a lapse of silence as Azaire contemplates. I fall into his feeling, using it as a crutch, a way to carry my own.

"I lost my parents, too," he says.

My head shoots up, but Azaire is looking down. I look down, too, seeing my dead mother on the ground. I rub my eyes, wondering what

Azaire sees.

He knows this pain of mine—understands it. I study the planes of his face, the lines creasing in his forehead as he furrows his eyebrows.

"Do you… want to talk?"

It's as if the cracks in Azaire's shell fortify and send spikes through my walls. I don't want him to tell me if he isn't ready. I'm about to say as much when he mutters, "All I remember is someone taking me to Visnatus in the aftermath."

I feel his pain, a guilt-ridden agony like my own. But he doesn't harp on it, doesn't tug the splinter out just to shove it right back into his skin.

Azaire's gaze shifts to mine. "I don't want to make you feel this," he says.

I realize his walls closed not because he didn't want to tell me, but because he wants to spare me the pain.

It's the most thoughtful thing anyone has ever done for me.

It makes me feel guilty—drawing him in, knowing I can't give him everything. I can't give him *me*. He will only ever get pieces, crumbs of a meal, and it doesn't seem fair.

With a single shrug, I try to give him all I can from my half-empty cup. "You don't have to be alone in feeling it."

Azaire looks away, back into that blue oblivion. "I don't mind it, really. People have their problems, and you have yours. Sometimes you meet someone who has a chance of understanding, but most people don't." Then he adds, "I think I prefer it alone."

His words sound like my own. I could almost get used to him speaking my mind. If there's anyone in this universe who has the chance of understanding me, I think it would be Azaire.

Selfishly, I hope he feels the same.

Selflessly, I hope he finds someone else.

Alone is the one place I could sit without the burden of others. The one place I could reside without the added weight of someone else's pain.

It's the only place I can be myself, where I can feel my grief without someone telling me it's wrong. I never wanted to open myself to the criticism—I've always known I was wrong. That I'm a burden.

I don't need someone's words to tell me so, nor their emotions.

Meeting Azaire's gaze—heightening his emotion within me—I decide to give him all of me, even if only for a fleeting moment.

"Feel it," I tell him as I reach for his hand. "I'll be right there with you."

"I want to try," I whisper to the boy as I enter my room.

Seeing Desdemona and Lucian, being with Azaire today, it stirred something within me—the aching emptiness I can never forget. A gap that is always growing, no matter how much I try to ignore it.

The boy is the safest way to fill it—to quiet the emptiness that lingers beneath my surface, if only for a moment.

He sits before me, cross-legged on my bed, his posture unbothered, but his gaze is intent. He watches me with the kind of attention that makes me feel like I'm the only thing in the world.

I suppose in his world, I am.

"I don't know I can do it, but—"

"Don't you dare underestimate yourself, Wendy Estridon." His voice may be low, but it still carries conviction. He rises to his feet and takes my hands in his.

My gloveless hands.

His skin is the only warmth I've felt in years. His thumb grazes over my knuckles, tracing circles, as if he's grounding me.

"You are power incarnate. You are everything."

"Yeah," I mutter, looking down. The boy knows exactly why I disdain such a title. My power was revered my entire life—but it was never useful.

"Tell me why you want this," he says. *"What is it that's changed?"*

I meet his gaze at last, his dark green eyes piercing through me as if he's searching for something I haven't said yet. It's a charade; he already knows.

"You know what happened." The words are thick in my throat.

"Yet I ache to hear it, spoken from your lips."

"Being close to people… it only reminds me of what I can't have. And for the first time ever, there's a way to have it."

"To have me?" His voice is barely a breath, teasing, but there's

something more beneath it. Something raw, something vulnerable.

"Yes."

"You can always have me, my love," the boy murmurs. *"Morning, noon, or night. In life or in death… I am yours for the taking."*

"Yes, well"—I pull my hands away from his—*"I need power to do that."*

The boy's plump lips turn up at the corners, as if he knew it would come to this and was simply waiting for me to say the words.

"Go to the garden, and I'll be there waiting."

I open my eyes, the boy disappearing from my room, the ground now steady beneath my feet. Real—exactly as the boy will be, if I succeed.

It seems insane, but the more I think about it, the less wrong it feels. I'm different from the others—my power is stronger, deadlier, more self-destructive. The best path for me might be him.

I rise, walking to the academy garden with a silent determination. When I stand by the bushes and beneath the sparse trees, I close my eyes once more.

At first, I don't see the boy. Then, my back meets his chest, and I gasp. Deftly, his fingers settle under my wrist, drawing my arm upward. His fingers glide up my arm, stopping at my shoulder where he wraps my hair behind my ear.

His lips brush my skin as he whispers, *"All the power you need… is already within you. Find it."*

I shiver, followed by a deep breath as his fingers brush against my shoulder.

I can do this—for him.

"No," he mutters. *"Not for me. All I do is for you."*

"Then for me." I revise my thoughts.

"For you," he agrees, guiding my arm out before me, my hand reaching for a tree just to my left.

I can feel the tree, the budding life within it. It's steady, solid.

"Life," the boy murmurs, *"is everywhere, in everything. It is in abundance all around you, and it is your power. You can never run out."*

A single finger glides down my bare neck, over my spine, and rests at the small of my back. He holds me roughly, propping me up.

"Once you tap into it, nothing can stop you." His lips graze the shell of

my ear. *"You could save anyone."*

I take the tree's steady, unwavering strength, and I shape it. I bend it, and as I do, I feel the tree gives way to my will. Its branches stretch downward, pressing into the world like outstretched arms, until the roots break through the soil.

It is mine.

But I might also be its.

A single thorn emerges from my wrist—from the inside out—and blood drips to the floor. I inhale sharply. It's a pain I should be used to. My magic has always ricocheted, hurting me in the most unexpected ways: tearing my skin apart, killing my friends.

I turn to the boy, and he holds the back of my head. *"It's all right, my love."* He turns my gaze back to the tree. *"Your magic will soothe with time and power. Continue."*

With every movement of the tree, another thorn breaks through my skin. A strangled cry escapes me until eventually, I have to open my eyes and return to the real world.

When I do, the boy disappears from behind me. But even in reality, the tree is alive, walking where I order it.

The thorns continue to grow, ripping me open from the inside out. A pit expands in my stomach, tearing through like a black hole, swallowing all it can find until, finally, I release the tree, clutching my torso.

The tree stills, its roots growing back.

But I don't still.

I weaken.

My legs give out. I crash against the floor. Then I puke.

Words drift from a distance, echoing as though we're on opposite ends of the same tunnel. *"Tap into the life,"* the boy says.

I pass out.

Chapter 12
The People with Power

ONE YEAR AGO

Beneath the canopy of trees, Calista and I sit in the woods. She lies on her back, gazing up at the sun. I pluck a blade of grass from the ground and make it grow back, twice as tall.

"Azaire was looking at you again today," Calista says, smiling as she turns her head toward me.

"He's always looking." The grass pushes up, tickling my palm.

Calista flips onto her stomach, meeting my gaze. "My apologies." She laughs. "I should have said *you* were looking at him again today."

A laugh escapes me. If I were a normal person, I think this would be a moment for a playful push. But I've long since learned to keep my hands to myself. "Yeah."

"Quite the vocabulary, Wendy."

I shrug. "You already know everything."

What am I supposed to say? That Azaire was my friend before Ma died and I retreated from the world? That he was my friend before I created the boy and lost my mind?

Not that Calista knows about the boy—or that anyone ever will.

Calista rolls her eyes, lying down on her back. "You're a poor gossiper."

I'm bad at talking, period.

Bitterly, I think about how I'm not Fleur or Eleanora or any number of her other friends. She'd prefer any of them to me.

"Are we ditching second period, too?" I ask when I find the strength to speak.

"Up to you."

Calista didn't want to go to her first class. I didn't want to go to any class. I never do, truthfully. If I could live in a cave, I might.

"It's Lilac, right?" I ask.

She picks at the polish on her nails and looks up at me. Her eyes say it all: *you already know.* Her mouth says something different.

"It's everyone," she sighs, dropping her head in the grass.

"Yeah… Me too."

"It's settled then," Calista says. "We avoid the world together."

"Isn't that what we've been doing all these months?"

Calista smirks, but I can't smile back.

"You know you could just go back," I say. "All your friends, Fleur and Eleanora, even Aralia—they'd take you back."

She pushes herself up, tilting her head as she meets my gaze, sun shining on her face. "And how do you feel about them?"

I drag my bottom lip between my teeth. "It isn't about me."

Calista pulls a joint out of her pocket. Holding it between her lips, she lights the end of it. She uses her ring finger to scratch her eye, gracefully blowing the smoke before saying, "They'll know something is wrong."

Hm. I kind of wanted her to say something about me, as opposed to herself. Something about our friendship.

But I suppose that is what drew us together—loneliness. Calista's is shiny and new; mine has been rusting away for years.

She hands me the joint. I don't often use intoxicants—secondhand emotion is enough. But sometimes it's easy to smoke with Calista.

The drugs ease her out.

Calista's doubt subsides, and she asks, "Do you want me to go back to them?"

"No," I answer. "I'd rather not lose you."

Her finger touches my glove as I hand her the joint.

She stares at the smoke, and I don't think I'll like what she says next. "Is that why you won't take my love away? You're scared you'd lose me if you did?"

It's the subject I feared. One I don't want to talk about.

"Calista…" I sigh. "You know that's not why—"

"I don't know that."

I fold further into myself, eyes on the grass. Pulling the blades out and growing them back. Tug of war.

"If I took that kind of emotion from you, there would be a gap that needed to be filled," I finally answer. "Like a black hole, whatever comes close would be sucked right into you."

It's not entirely that. Not to me. I've never manipulated emotions before, only ever turned them down for my own peace of mind.

The truth is, I'm not entirely sure *what* would happen.

I wouldn't have to touch her, like the rest of the Eunoia would. It wouldn't be a *repeat* of Xander—not exactly.

But either way, my power is dangerous. I've known it my whole life, even before I killed Xander.

We were playing tag on a cliff in Eunaris when I understood the extent of my danger. We were laughing, our feet slipping on the sharp rocks as we raced around. I'd caught him finally, and Xander kept laughing. He never bothered to care about losing.

But then something went wrong.

I must have left my hand on his shoulder for too long. I must have made a mistake.

A gasp escaped him—perhaps his final exhale—before his eyes rolled to the back of his head. His pupils vanished, replaced by white. His legs gave way, and he fell to the ground. The second half of his body dangled off the cliff, his hands hanging limp at his sides, not reaching for safety. He couldn't.

Xander was convulsing.

I lunged forward, reaching for him. My fingers were inches from his wrist, a breath from pulling him back.

Then he twitched, slipping away like water.

Xander rolled off the cliff.

I watched as his body disappeared over the edge. Then I fell to the ground, and my head started bleeding. It felt as if I hit rock after rock.

As if *I'd* tumbled down a cliff.

When my parents found me, I was crying and nearly unconscious.

I said, *There's so much blood.*

Little Thorn, Pa said, *you aren't bleeding.*

The pain subsided in that moment, replaced by worry. It was later that I put it together; it was Ma and Pa's worry I felt. It stopped me from reliving the pain of Xander's death.

A few days after, his body washed up on the shore, his skull cracked open.

They said the tide ran him into a rock.

But the green of his eyes was gone, replaced by nothing but white. No one had an explanation. And no one knew what I'd done.

At least, no one said it.

I always suspected Ma knew. She'd seen the look in my eyes, the way I flinched whenever anyone mentioned Xander. She never said a word, but I think that's why she pushed so hard to get me into Visnatus Academy. Maybe she thought they could fix me, that they could stop what happened to Xander from happening again.

Calista rolls her eyes, and her secondhand smoke stings as I take a deep breath.

"Maybe then it'd be a boy," she says, responding to my concerns about her loving the next person who comes close.

"Calista—"

"Father tells me it's because I am to marry Lucian," Calista says hastily. "But I know that if Lilac weren't a girl, he'd have no problem with the fling. Gods, even if I were married, I could probably have male consorts."

My homeworld, Eunaris, never had any qualms with sexuality. It was a question of what you like, never a fuss, as simple as whether you preferred sweet or salty. As a Eunoia at Visnatus, I'm familiar with her worlds' customs. We're here to serve Ilyria and Folkara.

"When you're queen, couldn't you do it anyway?" I ask.

Calista scoffs, an emotionless laugh. "The crown is an invisible cage," she remarks. "I am held in place by public scrutiny."

"Couldn't you change it?"

"The only people who believe in change are those without power."

<h1 style="text-align:center">Chapter 13
The Burden of
Unspoken Truths</h1>

NOW

"Wendy? Wendy!" a voice calls from the distance.

Or is it beside me?

A body picks me up, holds me. It is flesh. It is real. The skin is warm, the blood pumping.

But in my mind, all I see is the boy.

"Oh gods, Wendy, wake up!" the boy screams—but it isn't his voice.

It's Azaire's.

Blood flows from the wounds along my arms. All the thorns breaking through. The boy rests his hands atop them.

I jerk up, eyes opening, breath ragged. I scan the world, searching for a bit of reality to hold onto.

All I can feel is the panic coursing through my chest. Like an intoxicating warmth, and it hurts.

It burns.

"Wendy," the person with me says. He holds me. "Wendy, you're okay."

My head is cradled against a chest. Hands wrap around my hair. A chin settles there, pressing softly. Breath brushes through my scalp.

Gently, we rock back and forth together.

And slowly, in this person's arms, the world comes back to me. I recognize the scent—the sweet edges of Azaire. The metallic essence of blood.

The thorns are pushing through the skin of my arms. I feel them beneath my clothes. There is no comfortable way to sit. No way to run from the excruciating nature of my power.

No way to bring the boy back without causing myself pain.

"No," the boy replies to my thoughts, his words echoing in my mind. *"Remember what I told you. Power is life, and life is all around."*

Azaire pulls back from me. He holds my cheeks in his hands, my hair scrunching beneath his grasp.

I realize I'm sitting between his legs—as close to a person as I've been in years.

"I'm fine," I whisper.

But I don't move.

"You weren't—" Azaire takes a breath. "I thought you weren't breathing."

I raise an eyebrow, but I stare at him in awe. In awe at his relief that I'm alive. In awe of his caring.

Of his being.

Of his beauty.

"I suppose I'm stronger than I look," I say.

"And aren't I glad about it."

He pulls me back into him without warning.

It feels good in his arms. Like a cold night at home, when Pa would build a fire and the whole family would sit around its warmth.

His heart hammers against me. It's the small residue of his fear for my potential death.

I never thought anyone would care if I were to go.

There's no one else around. No other group with Azaire, worried about the girl lying on the ground, possibly dead. There's no other person who cares.

"I don't understand." I lean into him more. "How did you notice me?"

No one else did.

Azaire leans back slowly, staring at me in disbelief. He feels that way too, as if I've asked an outrageous question.

"Wendy," he sighs. "I always notice you."

I shake my head, my gaze falling, unwilling to meet his.

If he's always noticed, then he must know that I feel the same. That it terrifies me.

"I don't deserve it," I say.

"You don't have to do that."

"Do what?"

"Be strong. You don't have to carry it all alone. You're allowed to give in."

My heart falters as I meet his gaze, slow and searching, my bottom lip caught between my teeth. My mind caught between uncertainty and longing. "You don't understand what giving in means for me."

"The only way I'll know," he mutters, picking up my hand, holding my arm that's riddled with thorns, "is if you show me."

His fingers curl around mine, lifting my hand to his chest, where I feel his heart beating steadily beneath his skin.

I think he's going to pull me close, and this time instead of holding me, he'll kiss me. A kiss that feels long delayed.

That doesn't happen.

His brows furrow, his gaze lingering at my wrist—at the thorns peeking out where my sleeve cuts off. Then, he murmurs, "What is this?"

I jerk my arm back, panic rising.

"Did someone do this to you?" The question slips from his lips, laced with horror.

"No," I say, my eyes avoiding his. "Of course not."

But his gaze sharpens, the gentleness replaced by something darker. He thinks I'm lying. Quite perceptive, because I *am* hiding.

"Who?" The word lands between us, and I have no answer. At first, I can't read him, can't place the shift in his demeanor. But when he asks again, voice trembling—"Who did this to you?"—I realize what I couldn't place is anger.

I've never felt Azaire angry.

And it reminds me of Lucian, standing vigil over an unconscious Desdemona, transfixed upon her. At that moment, I knew Lucian would do anything to keep Desdemona safe.

In this moment, I realize that Azaire feels the same about me. It's the same fierce devotion.

Without thinking, I move closer, my gloved hand gently cupping his cheek. He sucks in a deep, uneven breath as I lift his face to mine.

But he still won't meet my gaze.

"Azaire," I whisper, "look at me." His eyes finally lift, the gray in them crashing like tumultuous tides. Roaring like relentless thunder. Churning like swirling storms.

"Who, Wendy?" he mutters, his voice deep, dark—dangerous.

Something I've never heard from him before.

"What would you do to them?" I ask, my heart pounding. "If I told you, what would you do?"

Azaire shakes his head, as if he's warding off his own thoughts. "Something I'm not proud of…"

"*I* did it, Azaire." My voice breaks. "I did it to myself."

The anger in his gaze cracks like lightning. "Why?"

"Because I'm tired of being alone." My words ache like a knife to the chest. "I thought I could change it. But I was wrong."

His head still sways, lips parted slightly as he looks at me. His gaze is a painting, a paradox, blending concern and adoration in a way that feels impossibly tender.

"You have me," he murmurs at last. "Whenever you want, whatever you need, I'm there."

His hand rests gently over mine, the heat of his skin searing through my glove, a promise in the press of his touch. He traces the edge of the leather with his thumb, as if memorizing every detail of me, down to my fingertips.

"Nothing, Wendy," he continues, "not your magic, not even a death sentence, will ever scare me away from you."

For a heartbeat, I forget how to breathe. The world narrows to the warmth of his hand over mine, the conviction in his voice, the raw honesty in his eyes. Something in me unknots. And for the first time in forever, I let myself believe in someone.

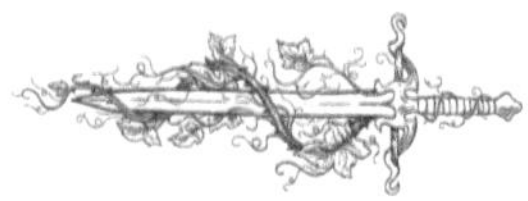

In my room, I peel off my long sleeve and sit on the edge of the bed, breath shallow, heart pounding. One by one, I pull the thorns from my skin—jagged little things, buried deep. I wince with each tug, the pain sharp, precise, and awfully familiar. Each thorn clinks softly against the floor before I toss it out the window, as if the night can swallow what I no longer want to carry.

Blood wells up in thin, stinging trails. I press an old shirt against the worst of it, the fabric already stained from past wounds.

It isn't the first time I've done this.

It certainly won't be the last.

When I've finished, and my skin is free of magic, I stand before Calista's door, contemplating. My hands and their nefarious ways. My *power*. The boy knew it would come to this before I did.

I told him that wasn't who I am.

It *isn't* who I am. This is only a desperate time, a desperate measure. I stand at the door, tugging at the fingers of my glove as Calista appears.

"I told you I'd come to you when I finished," she sighs.

First, I look past her shoulder, spotting the book on her desk. The glamour is still in place. She hasn't succeeded.

Second, I set my hands on her shoulders, forcing her to meet my gaze.

"You're not upset or confused that I'm touching you," I instruct before she can retaliate.

Her pupils widen, her mind becoming pliant.

"You believe in your power." My voice drops instinctually. "You know you can lift the glamour. I'm going to move my hand, and you are going to let me inside your room. Do you understand?"

Calista stills. A wave of dread washes over me. I'm terrified I've done something irreversible—overwritten her mind with emotion. Destroyed her brain.

Then, absently, she nods.

I jerk my hands back, relieved as Calista's eyes refocus, her usual resolve slowly fading into a confidence. She opens her door, and I step inside. The first thing she does is step toward the desk, picking up the book.

I watch Calista carefully. She weighs the book in her hands, flipping it back and forth.

"You can do it."

From across the room, she glances up at me, eyes sharp. "I know."

She rests the book in her hands, palms open. Her face is an empty canvas—blank, serene, almost devoid of emotion. There's no tension, no hint of anticipation or expectation. Calista *knows* she's going to succeed—because I *told* her to.

As with every time before, a bright, golden light spills over the book, casting warm halos across the room. Its edges flicker like a flame. Slowly, the book lifts from her hands, suspended in the air as it shimmers between solid and spectral—less an object, more an idea in motion, a blur of possibility.

This book could be anything. A map. A memory. A warning. I hold my breath on the precipice of revelation, my heart thudding with the weight of what I might learn—what Ma knew, what she carried, what she kept hidden.

Then, clarity. The image sharpens in an instant, as though I've put on glasses. And from the golden haze, a single sheet of paper flutters down, spiraling delicately through the air before coming to rest at my feet.

Someone went through all the trouble of a permanent glamour for a piece of parchment?

I reach for the paper, but Calista snatches it before I can. I sit back, allowing her to bring the page to her gaze. If this page came from Folkara, she has the best chance of knowing what it is.

Breath catches in my chest as I feel for every shift of her emotion. If this were the usual Calista, she would be excited to have completed the spell. With the borrowed confidence, she feels nothing.

This was the expected outcome, after all.

Yet, as her eyes peruse the page, the feeling of uneasy betrayal fills me.

The unshakable confidence I lent her has broken.

Calista's voice trembles as she meets my gaze. "You're working with him." The pain in her eyes—the pain in mine—feels like someone is taking a burning knife to a healed wound. "You said this was your mom's!"

"Calista," I say, reaching out—not just with my voice, but with my energy, desperate to tether her unraveling emotions before they slip completely out of reach. But I'm too slow.

She's already moving, hands trembling as she grabs the paper. And then—she tears it.

"No!" I lunge forward as the first harsh rip begins to sound.

Only, the paper doesn't tear. It doesn't even budge.

The parchment holds firm, utterly untouched, as if reality itself refuses her rage. She stares down, stunned.

Then her fury slams into me like a wave, threatening to drown me. I reach into that storm and strip the emotion from her—stealing it, subduing it, swallowing it down into myself until the air stills.

"Don't do that!" Calista shouts, knowing well what it feels like to have her emotion stolen by me.

I release my hold on her at once.

"It's not what you think," I say gently, raising my hands, signaling to her that I've ceased using my power.

"So you're *not* working with Lucian?"

"What's on the paper?" I ask, deflecting, as I take a step back.

Calista frowns. "You know."

I shake my head. "I don't."

"A Weapon." Her tone is harsh, laced with venom.

My face falls. My body almost does too. Why would Ma have anything to do with the Weapon? Ma, a Eunoia, the very last of us who would help create a Weapon of destruction. Ma, who believes in peace and healing and learning, never destroying.

Ma.

I manage a meek whisper. "You're lying."

I feel ready to pounce when she smiles. *Pounce.* I've never thought of violence the way I'm thinking of it now—as something I'm willing to partake in.

Calista's eyebrow raises. "Fun, isn't it? Finding out who your parents really are." She shoves the piece of paper into my chest with enough force to knock the wind out of me. "Get out."

For a moment, all I do is stand here, trying to catch my breath. A Weapon and Ma? It doesn't seem possible.

"Did you not hear me?" Calista shouts. "Get out!"

My heart races with the need to explain, but I know Calista. No explanation is ever enough for her.

My mouth opens anyways, just before I turn, leaving her room and taking the paper with me. When I'm safe and alone, I lean against my door, looking at the page.

Design No. 27.

My breath catches as I realize what this is—the blueprint of the Weapon.

It looks more like a jumble of random parts. Arrows point from one messy bit of metal to another, connecting them to a big, ugly lump that's supposed to be the Weapon. I have no clue what any of this means—there's no real order, just scribbled lines and strange shapes that don't make sense. It's like someone threw a bunch of ideas onto paper and hoped it would come together, but it's hard to tell if it even can.

Or maybe I'm just hoping it *can't.* Because this is too much. I could almost believe Ma wasn't involved, despite this blueprint being found in her study. I could almost believe this was all a farce.

Except for the date at the very bottom of the page. A date when she was supposed to destroy this blueprint. A date, two days before Ma died. The impact of realization hits me, and I fall.

A secret Weapon. A blueprint meant to be destroyed—but now indestructible. A rogue monster attacking Ma and me.

Ma went against Folkara's wishes. For some reason, she preserved this page, and the kingdom killed her for it. Calista's parents killed her. All for a Weapon.

A small note in the margins reads, *Do not power on Folkara.* But by that logic, it'd be okay to power anywhere else. It'd be okay to kill anyone else, just not the Folk. Not the best of us.

By that logic, it meant that if they were to *test* this Weapon, they'd be testing it against innocents.

How could Ma help with something like this?

The emotional distance I tried to keep cracks, sucking me in. I am skin-to-skin with Lucian, mind-to-mind with his iron will. Because now I *have* to know what the Weapon is for.

Because now I'm willing to go further than even he might be.

Without a second thought, I rest my hand on the mirror, opening a portal to my old house. I move through the garden of my hometown, ignoring the spot stained by Ma's last breath. The house creaks beneath careful footsteps as I slip inside, climbing the steps to Ma's study.

I stare at the bookcase. For half a second, I see the spines, but my vision quickly blurs. A feeling so strong it steals my sight. A hatred that could boil my blood.

There's no need to look to know who stands behind me, framed in the doorway like a shadow I can't shake. As I turn to face him, I have to hold back his anger in my bones—keep myself from tearing my hair out.

My brother Terran, my brother who I haven't seen in five years, stands a few feet away from me. I try to meet his eyes.

The second I do, I feel the pang in my heart.

In *his* heart.

I am nothing.

I've imagined this reunion a thousand times over. I would tell him how profusely sorry I am. Not only for failing to save Ma, but for disappearing. For everything before and everything after. I would beg for forgiveness.

But now, faced with reality, I am frozen.

Words I said to Calista once upon a time play in my mind.

I feel like if I wait, just enough, that the right time will find me, Calista said.

She was talking about Lilac. That's what falling in love does—it makes you cross-eyed. The world away from that person becomes a blur.

Or so I've felt through others.

There is never a right time, I told her, thinking about my family. *You make the time and hope it's right.*

My words ring true. There will never be a right time to face them. I'll never be ready.

Terran steps into the room and closes the door. Looking at him sometimes feels like looking at myself. The same freckles around our noses and cheeks, the same green eyes—Ma's green eyes—the same small nose and big mouth. Only, his isn't marked by a scar, solidifying the day he failed.

The day I let my mother die.

"You're not welcome here," Terran says, his voice shaking on the precipice of fury.

My stomach tightens. I focus on him, that hatred, that blame. An invisible pipe between us deposits it into me. At what point does it become my own?

My silence doesn't seem to be welcomed, either.

"What are you doing here?" he asks me. "I've heard about the monster attacks on Visnatus. Do you have something to do with those, too?"

I know what he's doing. Possibly better than he does. I can *feel* his desire for my response. He wants me to lash out—because *he* wants to lash out.

He wants to punish me, but he will never know that my guilt is punishment enough.

I want to rip the thorns that stitch my lips shut. If only they weren't metaphorical. If only there was such a simple way to reclaim my voice as pulling thorns from my skin.

Terran doesn't stop—he has no idea what I'm feeling. Unlike me, he has to *try* to sense emotion, to even brush against them. But he never tries. I'd know if he did.

"Dad will tell you he loves you," Terran spits. "Jasper and Cassius will tell you they miss you. But it will always be a falsehood in their hearts, even if they tell themselves they believe it in their minds."

I'm finally able to croak a measly two words. "I know."

"No, you don't. You killed the love of dad's life. You killed your brothers' mother." His voice cracks as he shouts, "*My* mom! They can play at forgiveness, but they will never win."

"I know, Terran," I say, this time a hint louder.

"Don't come back here." He turns to the door.

There's more to this than you think, I want to say. I want to say anything that could tempt him to listen. Perhaps even forgive me. The only thing stopping me is the fear of what he'd do if I planted those seeds of revenge in his mind. Because I don't know what I'll do in the end if I am to find out that Folkara orchestrated Ma's death.

So I let the door slam.

I decide to save him from himself, while preparing to throw myself to the sharks.

Terran and I were never close. There were few times that we got on. Times when I would see him laughing, face to face and not from afar. Times that I cherish, because that's all I have left to hold onto.

My love for my family.

It's why I've stayed away.

If it had been someone else that killed Ma, I wouldn't want them around.

So I'll make myself scarce as quickly as possible.

I begin to really look at the books. I don't know what to look for. If there *is* anything in here regarding the weapon, it'd be glamoured like the last. But I don't know if I can hope for such a sloppy mistake again.

After too long of staring, I go to Ma's desk, daring myself to sit in her chair. It smells just like her, almost feels like her. I close my eyes, visiting the boy. But he's not here.

In my mind, I'm standing before her desk, instead of behind it. Here, Ma is sitting in her chair. Her hand reaches out to me, her skin resting on mine.

"Is this what you need?" she asks, but I shake my head—I know it's the boy.

"I need something that no one can give me," I reply. *"I need to be normal. I need to be able to touch someone. I need to stop being suffocated by other people's inner voices."*

Ma nods. *"Only you can give yourself what you need. Only you can find your meaning of peace."*

"It's not the meaning of peace I'm looking for. It's fucking peace!" I pull my hand away, turning around.

The bookcase blurs as I lay my eyes on it. There are no titles on the spines, not in my mind, just dark colors splotching together.

"Don't try to tell me what she would say," I sigh, staring at the blob of books. *"Just be the boy."*

I turn back, and Ma is gone. Only the boy sits before me now.

I miss her instantly. I didn't think I would—I thought I'd understand it's only an illusion. But suddenly my mind is screaming: *come back.*

"I'm sorry, my love," the boy says. *"I thought it'd be helpful."*

"To speak as the woman I killed?"

The boy flinches, his features squishing in anguish, as if I've said something far worse than the truth.

"You did not kill her, Little Thorn." His voice is soft—much too soft

for the lament written on his lips.

"You're the only person in this house that believes that." I turn away, just to turn right back. *"If you know what Ma would say so well, riddle me this: whether accidental or not, if my actions led to a death, does that make me the one who killed them?"*

The boy opens his mouth, but he does not speak.

"Did I kill her?" I repeat.

"It's more complicated than that—"

"What would a philosopher say?" I ask. *"What would* Ma *say?"*

When he doesn't answer, when he doesn't tell me, *"No, you did not kill her,"* I open my eyes, escaping my mind. Tears flow from me in the real world.

My head crashes against the desk—the desk that still reeks of her, the room that clings to the echo of her presence—and I break. Each tear slices through me like it's ripping me in half, each tear like my mother's blood, coating my cheeks, filling my mouth with salty sin. I cry until my throat is raw, until my chest feels like it's caving in. I cry until I can't breathe, until my ribs bruise under the weight of it.

Guilt or grief, I can't decide.

Either way, it's agonizing.

Chapter 14
Anything but What
I've Become

After an eternity, the tears subside, as if I've cried myself dry. If I were a world, my inhabitants would die of thirst. I'm dying, my head limp against the wooden desk.

I only twitch when the boy's voice curls through my mind like smoke.

"I cannot answer the question for you. It would be too easily dismissed. You must find the answer yourself. That is what a philosopher would say."

With my head now facing the window, I don't move for hours. I watch as the sun sets, as the sky turns from bright blue to navy to black.

I watch as the stars come out from hiding, twinkling in the dark. For just a second, I see Ma, shining on me in this darkness. I think of all the stories, all the people who were laid to rest in the sky. All the constellations, all their gory stories and heartbreaks, and I think of her. She showed me all of them.

She must have known, in some way, that her death would follow the pattern of those stories: gory, egregious, gut-wrenching. But she went on anyway. She found the strength for it all.

I only wish for half of it, only a piece of her—but I will never get that if I give up now, when I'm so close to her.

My hands press firmly into the wooden desk as I force myself to rise. It feels like stepping back from the brink, like I am rising from death. It would be so easy to sit here and wither. But I don't.

I rise.

The same way Ma did a million times.

Because I have something to do—whether I clear her name in my conscience alone or find justice before the masses, I have something to do.

I dare myself to open her desk drawers. Inside, pens, scattered pages, and small, worn books crowd together. The papers are filled with philosophical scribbles, their words heavy with thought. But when I touch them, the stack crumbles in my hands, disintegrating into a fine dust that slips through my fingers and vanishes before my eyes. Beneath, leather-bound books lie waiting, their covers etched with the marks of time.

Each one is homemade. Journals upon journals, carefully hidden, Ma's secrets pressed between the pages.

I look at the door to the study. Closed.

Opening the first journal, I flip through the pages, reverently touching the edge of each one. I peruse every word Ma penned. Soaking in the scribbled sentences, learning her mind in a way I never thought possible.

There's nothing about a weapon, but Isa's name comes up a few times, and I pass a picture of Ma at my age.

She looks so much like Terran and me.

She's with a Folk in a home I recognize. The woman's hair is dark brown, highlighted by the sun. I *know* this woman in the faintest of ways. A distant, foggy memory.

Beneath the photograph reads: *Willow and Isa.*

Isa. The memories return to me now. I don't know how they hadn't before. I heard Ma say that name a thousand times before. Ma and I would visit her when I was a child, and I'd play with Isa's daughter, but we stopped visiting before I could grow.

Certainly, Ma had a connection to the woman taken by the Arcanes. It opens a million doors, connects very few pieces.

As I open the second journal, it feels like an overstepping of boundaries. By the third, it feels a little less intrusive. Ma writes about her parents a lot. They wanted her to be a gentle, tame, and kind Eunoia.

For her to be like all the rest.

A healer, a helper, always second—never best.

The entries grow in intensity.

The further along I go the less these sound like Ma. The sentences get shorter, hastier.

Angrier.

With every page, she talks more about being a fighter. Proving herself. Ma, the *philosopher*. These are someone else's journals—not the woman who raised me.

Then I find a particularly peculiar passage.

She wrote this a year before I was born.

She made the Weapon to defeat the Arcanes.

It all makes sense—she was doing something *good*, and the Arcanes took her friend as a result. The Royals killed *her*.

Ma might have been more volatile than I remembered, but it was for a good reason. She still wanted to help. She had to.

This is why I picked up my broken pieces—this is why I always have. There is more for me to do, more for me to prove.

I continue searching her journals, looking for something to tell me about the Weapon. Is this the birth of it?

There is nothing more. Ma continues to talk about proving, proving, proving herself.

Until…

I reach for the rest of the journals. The entries end around the time of my birth. I rip out the pages of the entries that matter, knowing I might need them, and shove them in my bag.

As I rise from Ma's chair, I feel her hands on mine, then I feel them release me. As if she's telling me I'm going the right way.

I look back once more at the dust-cluttered pages scattered on her desk and my tears that have soaked through, and I know I won't be coming to this room again.

Behind me, I leave the door to the study open as I step into the hall, but instead of turning right to the staircase, I turn left, toward my room.

My silent steps do not echo through the wooden hall, but they feel weighted in my mind. Each step a compulsion. I am not choosing this, I am following a trail of the past.

I take a breath as I stand before the cedar door.

It still smells the same.

Like childhood.

I push it open.

To my surprise, not a thing has moved. The small bed with green sheets sits in the far corner. The porcupine Ma crocheted sits by my pillows, and the light shines in through the window the same way it had years ago.

Just like Ma's study, my room is frozen in time.

I step back, tears pressing against the barrier, desperate to break free. But when I finally let them through, there's nothing left—no more to spill, no more to cry out. Just emptiness.

I stand in silence at the precipice of the door.

The doors to the closet across from it sit open, slightly ajar, and my old, handmade clothes peek out. Clothing I made with Ma. Ma who dreamed of being a warrior. Ma who made a Weapon.

I find the strength to step inside, grabbing a cardigan from the closet—one of her hand-me-downs—and holding it like a teddy bear.

I figured my childhood was expunged. My family had four years to fix this room, to erase me, and they've done nothing.

They've preserved me the same way they preserved Ma.

Whispered words jolt through me: "You're back."

I drop the cardigan and turn, knowing it's Pa before I see him.

"Yes," I say, looking down, away from his smiling face. "It's my inadequacy, showing up as such."

"Such a silly thing to say," he mutters. "*Inadequacy.* What are they teaching you at that school?" He smiles, but I remain sullen.

His words are a reminder of how far apart we are.

How far I am from the girl who lived in this room.

Pa clears his throat, dropping his smile. "We're always happy to see you."

But in my mind, Terran's words follow: *It will always be a falsehood.*

I smile without teeth.

"You'll be staying this time?"

Despite him asking, I don't know if there is any answer other than, "Yes." I pause. "For a meal. I have to get back for an assignment."

"Of course." Pa smiles and wraps his arm around my back.

I recoil at first, before settling into his embrace. His feelings are tricky, like a spider web that gets stuck on your fingers, and you have to pull and pull to get it off, but you never seem to be able to rid yourself of it entirely.

That's how he blames me.

That's how he loves me.

Yet he kept my room intact, as if he wanted to keep me intact, in some way, too.

We walk down to the dining room in silence. Dad doesn't want to scare me away. He thinks that's what he did the last time I came. I want to tell him that I was never running from him, but the words die in my throat.

I sit at the table, and he brings plate after plate of Eunoian dishes. Rowan berries, breads, forsagga cheeses. Pitchers of wines and teas. Nothing seems less appetizing.

The last time I ate a meal like this, Ma was alive.

There is no escaping her death here. It's everywhere. In Visnatus, sometimes I get to remember her as she was.

Her skin not grayed.

Her eyes not glossed over.

Her legs attached to her hips.

Here, she's just dead.

I understand Terran, his hatred for me. If our roles were reversed, I'm not sure I'd act differently. It makes me feel guilty for being here. Intruding on the little peace my family is managing to find.

But they kept my room.

Pa looks at me, and I smile—for him.

"It's okay to feel," he says.

I look away as my smile fades.

Don't do that, I want to say. *Don't read my feelings the way I am forced to read yours.*

I understand why others feel violated by me. It *is* a violation.

Pa sits beside me, reaching for my hand. His fingers never touch mine. He pulls his hand back, thinking *better* of it. I wish touching me felt easier, that it wasn't so tangled in hesitation. Wasn't something to think better of.

"Pardon me." He clears his throat as he stands.

I try to distract him—and myself—from the overwhelming feeling sucking the air from the room. "Where are Cassius and Jasper?" I ask.

We never eat without the six of us.

Five... *five* of us.

Four.

There's only four of them now.

"Cassius is with his partner, and Jasper's working," Pa answers, the steady rhythm of his knife chopping through vegetables echoing against the wood.

Life never stops moving.

I froze on the day Ma died, my life stunted, but they continued to move forward. If grief is a race, I lost by a landslide.

I choose not to dwell on it. I think of Jasper, my youngest brother. He trained his whole life to be a healer. I can't believe he graduated before me.

"When did Jasper graduate?" I ask. The small amount of excitement I feel for him crumbles under the overbearing weight that settles in my chest.

"He didn't," Pa mutters. "He works at blue beam."

I shake my head. "But he was going to be a *healer.*" A great one at that. He could patch me up with more ease than growing berries.

"He enjoys the farm," Pa says, filling another plate with food.

That's not right. He went to the best school in our hometown. Everyone always saw me as the special child, the prodigal daughter, but that's how I saw Jasper. Steadfast, reliable, powerful. He was the one who deserved the spot at Visnatus. He deserves more than to be an agronomist.

"Why didn't he graduate?" I mutter, almost to myself.

Pa turns to me, shrugging with a frown tugging at his lips. "Healing's not as urgent here as it is in the other worlds. But agriculture? That's what matters."

Because our world supplies the rest. Jasper isn't a healer because I took his spot at the academy. I eat the food he grows; I heal the elites that he should be healing.

I killed his mother, and I stole his dream.

I don't even *want* to be a healer.

"Will they be back soon?" I ask, taking deep breaths as Pa turns away, his attention fixing on the food once more. I ignore how eager I am for an escape, in case Pa reads me again.

"Jasper, yes. Cassius is hard to determine. Sometimes he's home late."

"Do you wait for him?" I ask, regarding the meal.

Pa meets my gaze, nodding once. "Always."

I watch a firefly hover around the berries on the table. I breathe in the familiar smell of the wood. All of the wood in Visnatus is finished; it doesn't have a scent anymore.

The minutes of silence pass by with the fireflies buzzing wings.

"What has been bringing you about?" Pa asks.

He sits next to me, his hands folding together over the wooden table. I'm not sure how to answer his question. If I tell a lie, he will know. If I tell the truth, I don't know what he'll think.

But he might have answers.

At this point, I'd do anything for them.

"Did you know Ma worked for Folkara?"

Pa picks at the loose wood on the table. "Yes," he answers slowly. Cautiously.

I begin to feel constricted in my clothes, in the seat.

Claustrophobic in my body.

"Do you know what she did for them?"

He continues picking at the table. "She occasionally helped them decipher their prophecies, sometimes the stars," he answers. He *lies*.

My skin feels as if it is stretching too tight over my bones. He knows more than he lets on.

"What about Isa?" I pull at my gloves. "She worked for Folkara too—"

His palm meets the table with a loud *thump*. "We do not speak of her, Wendolyn."

Pa's face grows red, as if the mention of Isa is too much for him to swallow. He's choking on it.

But there is something more. His fear is growing through me, the pit in my stomach becoming a tree. For the first time, I think there may be an answer to find.

"And Freyr?" I ask, feeling him come undone. The spider web of emotions unraveling itself.

"*Wendolyn.*"

"Do you know what Ma was involved in?" I ask once more, my voice shaking with the growing volume.

Finally, Pa meets my gaze. "Do *you*?" The fear isn't just in his voice or in my bones anymore; it's written in his eyes.

Written like all the things I've learned, left for me to find in her journal.

"I think I do," I answer. Pa reads me, searching for the truth.

He finds it.

He knows I do not lie.

"Let it go." His jaw tightens.

"I don't believe that's what she would want," I whisper.

Ma would want me to uncover what Folkara has planned for the Weapon. She'd want me to stop something with any propensity for destruction. I *know* her.

Knew her.

Pa's voice is as soft as mine now. "Willow would never want you involved in this."

"That's not true."

"You can't do what she could've done. Drop it."

The words land like arrows in my chest.

Never once has anyone told me I can't do something. They've only ever pushed me to do *more*.

I'm left in a state of shock, and before I can fight for further answers, Jasper walks in.

His green eyes light up when he looks at me. He reeks of what could only be defined as nostalgia.

Jasper opens his arms, the way he used to, expecting me to get up and run into them. It's been so long. I'm so far from that girl he knew. But I run anyway, crashing into him. At first, I stiffen in his arms, despite their familiarity. Then I force myself to sink.

He spins me, and it's easy to pretend I am anything but what I've become, for a moment.

"My favorite sister has returned!" Jasper says as he sets me down. He's so happy. In turn, I get to feel that smile. His warmth.

"My favorite youngest brother." I try to smile. But even with the warmth of his excitement, Pa's worry boils in the background.

"How long are you here for?" The remnants of soil and magic waft off Jasper, lingering in the air.

"For a meal," I say, suddenly feeling guilty.

Jasper only smiles. His hair is the lightest of the four of us kids, and he doesn't have freckles the way Terran and I do.

He carries the least of Ma in appearance. But I always thought he had her spirit.

He can make anything fun.

"Cassius should be back soon," Jasper says, looking into the living area. "Is Terran home?"

I don't answer, and Jasper looks at Pa, still sitting at the dining table.

"He is," Pa says.

Jasper looks between us, his smile faltering. He feels the animosity—and other leftover emotions—that lingers between us. No one says anything more.

When Jasper nods, I see how much he's started to look like Pa. The same lean build, the same creases in his chin when he frowns, the same dimples. But it's the smile that stops me. A smile I haven't seen since Ma died.

It hits me how much I've missed. Years have passed, lives have moved on, and I wasn't there to see any of it. They weren't there to see mine, either.

It's been a sorry excuse for a life, anyhow.

I can only hope Jasper continues to carry what Ma did—a way to keep things light, even while bearing the heaviness.

Then Terran enters the room, every inch my opposite, yet still a twin in appearance. His gaze meets mine, a scowl already etched into his face. He looks like the angry little kid he once was when his eyes narrow.

When Cassiues joins us, we sit around the table and begin the meal, but Pa doesn't look at me. Terran continues to scowl. Jasper tries to include me in conversation, and Cassius smiles sometimes, but I keep my head down more often than not.

Every time Pa looks up, I feel full of sorrow.

I can more than imagine why.

Chapter 15
Maybe Paper Is Painless

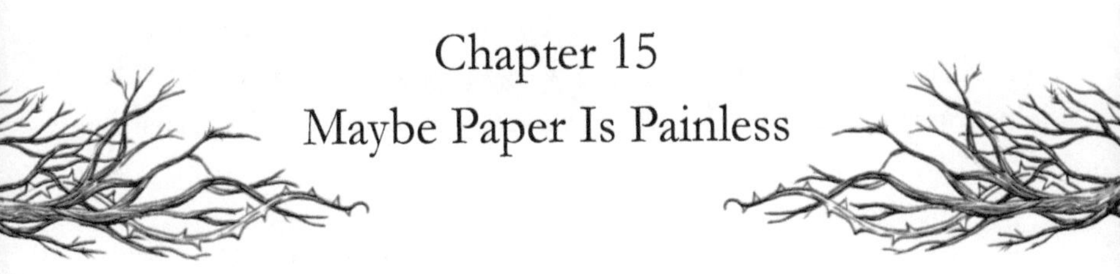

The first thing I do when I return to Visnatus is search for Lucian. For better or worse, we're kin now. Kindred spirits. What he wants, I need. What he needs, I want.

He is my partner, by proxy of a forced hand. Shackles of the past tie us together.

But when I reach his suite, I only find Azaire.

I guess it's his suite, too.

It doesn't seem right to look him in the eye—not after I've let myself trust him. If I look at him now, I might tell him the truth. I might put him in danger.

I look right past him, asking, "Where's Lucian?" My voice is close to shattering. My mind is close to shaking its way out of my body.

I only wish to keep Azaire out of this, if I can manage it.

"What is it?" He reaches for my gloved hand. Stilling me. Forcing me to look into his eyes while tears stream down mine.

"Would you rather tell him than me?" the boy asks.

In my mind, I roll my eyes. *"You know I'd tell you anything."*

I can feel the boy smile. *"Yes. And I'd listen to anything, so long as it's your voice I'm hearing."*

His words writhe with romance, but I shake him away. I have a real person in front of me. A real person who meets my gaze.

"Something no one's brave enough to admit," I whisper the words I've carried for so long. "It's my fault she died."

My family won't admit it, but they all think it. I *feel* them think it, every time.

Strong child, chosen one, most powerful failure.

Maybe they immortalized my room so they could remember who I used to be, instead of what I became the day Ma died.

Azaire doesn't respond—not verbally. But his thumb, resting gently on my hand, traces a soft stroke over mine. All while his eyes become a storm of emotion. Too much, too powerful, and I make the mistake of not looking away. My grief sets a forest aflame. Like watching my childhood home burn down and realizing I lit the match.

It's *his*.

The anger I feel at his emotion is irrational.

What happened to peace? I want to scream. *Where did that go?*

"What is it?" I manage to ask him.

For once, Azaire is the one to look away from me. "I didn't mean for you to feel that," he mutters, dropping my hand.

I laugh, but it is no more than a breathy scoff. "I feel it all."

"I know."

"I wish you didn't."

"I'm glad I do." His stormy eyes meet mine again. He tries to smile, then he shrugs. He works to balance his emotions, sliding along the scale until they settle. "I like knowing you."

My form deflates as I release a deep breath. I lose track of time in his eyes, in his emotions that are overflowing like the rivers when it rains.

I feel guilty for ever wanting to bring the boy to life when a real one stands before me.

"Tell me what I felt."

What is your grief, Azaire?

Why do I know it so well?

Azaire shrugs, shoving his hands inside his pockets, cheeks reddening. "How about I tell you when you tell me?"

I pull my lip between my teeth, nodding. It's fair. I'm cryptic. If he's going to share with me, he deserves the same in return. But I'm not ready.

"Fair," I say.

We both know I won't tell him, not right now, and Azaire takes the opportunity to say, "Lucian isn't here. He's training."

I glance toward Azaire's room, although I don't need to. I can already feel it, someone's presence, and it's not Kai.

"Yuki is here," I state—Lucian's training partner. Is Azaire lying to me?

No. I'd know it. And he wouldn't smile like that. It quickly lights up his whole face. He's intrigued that I could tell Yuki was here, though not surprised.

"Lucian's training with Desdemona," he clarifies.

"Oh."

I sit on the couch, taking a deep breath. Azaire lowers himself beside me, his knee brushing mine.

It's devastating to shudder at the smallest of touches. But I am devastated. I glance at Azaire, who seems to know exactly what's churning inside me. Who feels it too.

And I wonder if I'll ever be able to have it—love, connection, companionship. If I'll forever be trapped behind the bars of my own making. Or, more adequately, my power's making.

I wonder if bringing the boy to life, even with the pain it would cause, is the best thing for me. Even if my body is overtaken by thorns, even if it rips me apart. But that kind of thinking is an even deeper devastation than staring at Azaire—a boy I know I could love —and choosing to run instead.

I stand. I think about telling Azaire that I care for him. That I'm running *for* him. That I'm a mess that he need not tangle himself in. That I don't want him caught in the danger I'm running toward.

Instead, I leave. Like a thousand times before.

The next day when I beckon Lucian, he tries to get Azaire, and I freeze. *No.* This weapon is more dangerous than a few Fire Folk welders. It got my mother killed. It's related to the most ambiguous evil our universe knows—the Arcanes.

I think of Azaire's will, his flightless wings to Lucian's steel.

He can't be involved.

It's why I ran.

"No," I say. I wish I was shocked by the pleading tone that comes out of me. "It's not safe."

You're so expressive, Little Thorn.

"Is this a romantic thing or an argument?" Lucian teases. The worst part is that he's pleased with himself. Thinks of himself as funny, and not smug. "I suppose they'd both stem from romance—"

"Neither." I reach into my bag, pulling out the piece of parchment that Calista tried to tear. I hold it up, waiting for Lucian's curiosity to grow and his arrogance to subside. "But you'll want to see this."

His eyebrows rise, a small smile curving his lips as he contemplates what the paper could be.

When he walks in the direction of the Royals' floor, I follow, and when we sit at the dusty table, I slide the paper across the surface. Lucian looks at what Calista tried to tear.

He looks at the weapon—and he is so uninterested.

It angers me.

He wanted me to do this. *He* pulled me into this.

But Ma is what made me stay. It is not entirely fair of me to put the blame onto Lucian.

I snatch the paper away from him, making the motion to tear it—showing him what Calista showed me. But he feels *nothing* at the thought of me destroying the one thing we know about this Weapon.

I want to shake him and scream.

I take a deep breath. "You were right." I set the paper back on the table. "They glamoured the blueprint because they couldn't destroy it. My mother must have tampered with it, and the Royals retaliated."

I choke back my tears as best I can manage. Lucian looks at me—*really* looks at me this time. He's finally interested in what I have to say.

"Retaliated?" he asks. "How?"

Pointing at the bottom of the page, I say, "The destroy-by date? Two days before a monster killed my mother—monsters that hadn't attacked for centuries."

Lucian looks up, his gaze locking with mine, and it's like being hit by the pernipe that killed Ma. He knows what it is to lose a parent, I realize. He carries the ache in the shape of his heart, the creaking of his bones. The hollow space it leaves between the two. He knows the world can rip everything from you without mercy.

That's how I've misjudged him.

He knows how it feels to have people more powerful than him

take everything he has.

He knows what it is to lose it all.

But I don't understand how.

Have we been walking side by side this entire time?

Slowly, Lucian asks, "That's why you don't want Azaire involved?"

He's walking down the same path as me. His emotions close to my own.

For the first time, we're perfectly aligned. He wants to protect Azaire. So do I.

But Lucian's selfish—I can feel that. If Azaire could help him get further, I have no doubts he would use him as a stepping stone.

Desdemona doesn't know what she's getting into with him. I'm more than convinced he would stop at nothing to get what he truly wants. And sadly, for the people he lures toward him, it's never them.

Though, with Desdemona, there was something else from him. Something I could have detected even without the power of empathy. His want for her is different—between a stepping stone and something more.

Only time will tell.

"I care about him, Lucian. More than I should," I say, forcing the feeling into him as the words leave my lips.

My fingers buzz with power beneath my gloves, twitching like live wire. Lucian doesn't realize what I'm doing, but he knows the weight of what I'm saying. He doesn't realize that the weight in his chest is mine, but he feels it all the same.

"If something happens to him…"

"I meant what I said, Azaire can handle himself. As for caring about him, go for it. He's not only the strongest person I know, he's the most moral." Lucian's words only reveal one thing.

He doesn't get it.

He doesn't understand that morals aren't good in this world. Morals got Ma killed. Morals are a double-edged sword.

As tortured as this prince seems, he's still sitting on a pedestal above the rest of us. He's still in line for a throne.

When you're so high above, it's hard to understand below—no matter what woes that power has bestowed upon you.

Lucian grabs the paper again, but he still doesn't care enough. I wait, hoping he'll come to his senses. The Weapon could destroy much more than we imagine. As a Eunoia, I'm not allowed in War Strategy, and as such, I have no idea what a Weapon could do. But Lucian *does*, and still I have to beg him to care about lives other than his own.

"I was there when my mom died."

His sudden understanding makes me soften and sick at the same time. He thinks I'm *confiding* in him.

I sort of am.

"I'm the strongest in my family. *Magically*," I clarify. "I should've saved her, but I didn't. No one ever said it, but I felt their blame. I still do."

Lucian *still* doesn't get it.

I continue, "I'm telling you this because... if I get close to Azaire and something happens to him... I already know how that feels." I look up, meeting his eyes to make sure he understands. "And I fear morality will become a weakness."

I almost despise the honesty in my words.

"I know. But he has us. We'll protect him."

I placate Lucian, saying, "You're a fair friend."

"He's more than a friend. He's my family."

"Well then you're fair family to have."

"He's better than I ever was," Lucian says. At least he knows that. "He'll take you, too, Wendy."

I know Azaire will. The problem is that wanting me is a cause for concern.

I do nothing but hurt the ones I love.

"You can't hurt me," the boy says, his voice low and buzzing in my brain. *"I like the pain when you're the one who inflicts it."*

I sit silently with his words. I don't think I love him.

"But you will," he replies in my mind.

I don't answer. Instead, I stare at Lucian, waiting for his response. He cares about many things, he's full of ambition, but not for this Weapon. Not yet.

Perhaps I should have taken a different approach.

"There's something more," I whisper. "Isa, the woman who was taken, I remember her."

Lucian sits up straighter. His heart beats a little harder. His blood tingles in my veins.

Finally, he's interested, asking, "You knew her?"

I pull my bottom lip between my teeth before I say, "Not well, but we used to visit her…"

This is harder to share than I believed it would be. I remember Isa vividly—more vividly than I imagined. I suppose seeing her photograph pinned the image of her to my mind. The sunspots on her skin. Her hair that seemed to have a million different shades of brown.

And the little girl I used to play with. For the life of me, I can't remember her name. Just her smile.

"I was trying to figure out why Ma would be involved in something like this," I say, entirely forthcoming. So much so that it's hard to look Lucian in the eye. It's easier to look away. "She kept journals. Over and over, she wrote the names 'Isa, Freyr, and *Weapon*.'"

Lucian stares at me, clearly understanding the implications I'm suggesting. "You think they built the Weapon?"

I've got him like a fish on a hook, now. The only problem is that I'm becoming the sea, and not the rod.

It shouldn't bother me how little he seems to care about anything other than the Weapon—that's what I wanted. But he is the first person I've told any of this to, and he couldn't care less.

"Originally, yes," I say. My next words are what I hope to be the truth—what I *have* to believe. "They thought they were doing something good. In her journals, Ma said the Arcanes returned and killed two little girls—Marbella and Annabetha. She wanted to make a weapon to stop them."

I pull my bag closer to me, thinking about Ma's journals inside. They're proof that she wasn't a regular, *good* Eunoia.

They're proof that maybe she didn't want to make the Weapon for something good.

As Lucian thinks over what I've said, I listen to the silent spikes of his emotion. The rising adrenaline and the up and down capriciousness of humanity. He's trying to decide what to feel, and I want to help him along. But I fear I already did too much to his emotional state in a short period.

He picks up the blueprint once more. That feeling of selfishness—the part of him that would step over anything and anyone to get to the end—intensifies.

But this time, it's regarding the Weapon.

Excitement warms me.

"It's missing something," he mutters. "There isn't a power source."

I narrow my eyes. "What do you mean?"

His gaze stays glued to the blueprint. "Weapons like these don't function on their own. They need magic to fuel them."

He looks up, waiting for my response. But I don't have one. A chill runs through me.

"*Our* magic?" I ask, frowning.

"Yes," he replies, looking back at the blueprint. "It would need a generator to amplify the power. That much magic would likely kill someone."

Quick to respond, I shake my head. "My mom wouldn't do something like that."

But I don't know if that's true anymore—not after what I read in her journals.

The room falls silent, eerily so as I ponder what Ma would and wouldn't do. Would she kill a person to power a Weapon against the Arcanes? To become the warrior she longed for the world to see her as?

I fear the answer isn't what I thought it would be.

I fear I will only learn who Ma was after death.

Finally, Lucian speaks, voice low. "You're probably right."

His lie dangles in the air, the haze of uncertainty clouding everything. But one thing becomes clear amidst the fog: he doesn't know what my mother would do, either.

Which means I know her as well as a stranger.

Chapter 16
Show Me Your Scars
So I Can Forget
Mine

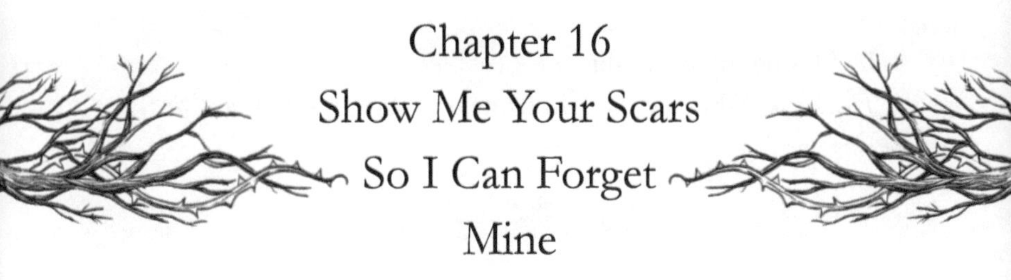

Most of my time has been spent trying to understand Ma. Countless times, I've reread the three journal entries I stole from her study. The ink is etched into the back of my eyelids. Closing my eyes always brings her vision—her words, her form, her presence.

The boy's presence fills my mind, like fog at the top of a mountain.

"You're torturing yourself."

"What if I deserve it?" I retort. *"I should have seen it sooner..."*

"You don't have to see anything."

I close my eyes, reaching for the boy. Even in the realm of my mind, I'm still clutching Ma's journal entries. I hold onto them tightly, as if they might be swept away by the wind, and my nails dig into my palm with the strength of my grip.

"This is proof," I say. *"It's proof that she* would *use a person to power that weapon, even if it kills them. It's proof that I was wrong about Ma my entire life."*

The boy stands up from my bed, walking toward me with tentative steps. He reaches for my cheek, but I flinch, and he slowly lowers his hand, frowning.

Taking a soft step back, he nods. Though he exists only in my mind, I start to sense him as I do others. I think he's afraid of losing me to this.

"What you have is a glimpse of her mind when she was eighteen. It isn't proof, it's an idea, a journal. It's the impulsive inklings of a teenager, immortalized by a pen." His tone is soft, gentle. It's hard to reconcile that he's a part of me—I'm never this gentle with myself.

I step past him, falling onto my bed. *"I just don't know what to believe anymore."*

Am I losing myself to this?

"That's good," the boy says, sitting next to me. *"It means you'll find something new."*

I go far into the woods—far enough that I don't have to feel anyone. There are the trees, and there is quiet.

It's all I want.

It's all I hope for.

I sit in the grass, running my hands through the blades and sipping the silence.

It could be peace—until the pain hits.

I reach for my torso, trying to staunch the blood. But there is no blood. Not mine, at least.

I rise, searching for the sensation. I hardly last a second until I feel it again—claws digging into my gut. I crash to my knees, collapsing against the sharp rock. But the borrowed pain is far worse than the bruise and blood.

The terror shrivels my insides more than the gut-curdling scream. On shaking legs, I stand, walking toward the fear, the pain, the hollow ache in my chest. It's beyond the protective barrier but I go anyway, unaware of my own insanity.

Each step brings another emotion. A cry escapes my choked throat, a feeling of remorse. A deep devastation.

But I can't find anything.

The ground begins to shake. Heavy footsteps approach. Could there be an army out here? Nothing else would rock the world with such strength.

My limbs hang heavy, longing to fall to the floor as exhaustion overwhelms me. Then, a monster races by. A towering beast, limping.

Exhausted.

Its bright eyes meet mine, gray fur glinting in the sun, as it passes by me.

The pain in my torso makes sense as I set my gaze on the monster's blood soaked claws.

It attacked someone.

If I could, I would run to them. They're likely bleeding out—dying. But between that and the monster's ache, it takes all I have left to stay on my feet.

I stumble through the woods. My body twitches. My head swims with sensation, none of it my own. I fall against a tree, harsh bark biting into me. My fingers tighten around the wood, splintering my skin. The pain is nothing, now. There's too much in its way. I pull myself up.

And I fall again.

I cry, not understanding why.

Force myself to my feet.

Hardly can stand.

Walk, then fall, and walk again.

Until, at last, I spot Lucian.

My legs give out, dropping me before the scene of the crime.

He is the pit in my stomach, the knife in my chest.

I've never felt more distraught in someone else's life.

He picks someone up, and I spot the blood—the girl's stomach is slashed open. Ivory bone shines beneath her torn skin. Lucian tucks her closer to his chest.

It's Lilac, his sister, his torment. I'm surprised her guts are not spilling out.

They're barely being held in.

First, I cry. For everyone else.

Then, I lean over and puke, unaware if it's on account of the gore or the emotion churning in my stomach.

It's difficult to pull myself back up.

Lucian runs, leaving Aralia in his wake, kneeling over the puddle of blood. I try to leave, but Aralia turns.

"Please don't leave me," she says. "Don't leave me alone."

I freeze. Friendship has never been my forte.

I've known Aralia for years. She's my suitemate. I've scarcely talked to her.

I clutch onto the scraps I know.

"You two were friends," I say, talking about Lilac. The girl gowned in gore. "Weren't you?"

I know the truth perfectly well.

Calista's version of it.

Aralia's stomach pumps up and down until the tears win the fight, then she chokes on her cries the way I think I might if I was in a similar position.

"Yes," she sobs.

I sigh over what I have to do, then I walk to her despite my reluctance. I put my arm around her torso and get her to her feet while she sobs. We have to get within the barrier. I don't know what hurt Lilac, but I can't risk it hurting Aralia.

I can't risk not being able to save another person.

I've known Aralia since I was ten. When we became teenagers, she left for two years—to the all Folk academy, Acansa—then came back to the suite like nothing happened. We never talked much. I wonder if we should have.

My hands run along Aralia's dark, untamed hair, smoothing down the wisps. "She's going to be all right," I say.

People find comfort in lies, even when they know how untruthful they are.

Even when they are aware how little the other person knows.

I do not have a clue what will happen to Lilac.

Aralia knows that.

She sucks in strange, gargled breaths as I pull us beyond the barrier. I head to the academy, but Aralia stops me, asking, "Can we sit?"

I nod, setting her on the ground. We sit for a long while, and I try to get a clear read on her emotions.

I can't—she's a jumbled mess.

Sitting in the silence is worse than awkward; it's debilitating. With every breath, I feel the pain in her lungs, the grief in her ribs.

But I know the Eunoia; I know how we are trained. The healers here will do everything to save Lilac. She's the princess of Ilyria, and they don't have a choice.

After a bit, Aralia's lips wobble as she asks, "Can you say some-thing?"

I look up, meeting her gaze with shock. "Like what?"

"Something surprising."

I stare at her. I don't have many surprising facts in my arsenal, nor do I have an abundance of social skills. I say the one thing I can think of: "I'm a virgin."

Aralia laughs for half a second. Then she cries. Her tears are fol-lowed with: "I said surprising."

I narrow my eyes at her. I'm not sure why I feel offended. "Why is that not surprising?"

"You don't talk," she says, "let alone get laid." Moments pass us by before she asks, "What's it like on Eunaris?"

My home world. The world where Ma was killed.

But that isn't what Aralia is asking. She's only searching for a dis-traction—and somehow, it's working for her. She's able to center her-self when she's focusing on something other than herself.

"Are you worth more pence if you're a virgin?" Aralia says, crack-ing it like a joke—though unease edges her words.

Or… is it mine?

"That's not how Folkara works," I say, though it comes out like a question.

"Not anymore." She swallows, shudders, then shrugs. "How does Eunaris?"

"They don't teach you?" I ask. They teach us about Folkara. I fig-ured the Folk would learn the other worlds' customs. They govern over them, after all.

"Not really."

If they're not teaching the Folk about us, what are they doing?

"We're all equal," I say, and she raises her eyebrows. "I mean, ob-viously not equal to the Folk and the Lyrians, but amongst each other there's no hierarchy."

Aralia wipes her tears. "So why the fuck did you come here?"

I shrug, pulling at my gloves. "My mom."

"She made a mistake."

I sink inside of myself, wishing I could shrink in further. Leave the shell of me behind and never return again. As always, this person across from me is oblivious to how their words make me feel.

"What's your deal?" Aralia asks. "Why do you never talk?"

"Is this helping?" My tone is a bit too harsh. "Talking about me?"

"Yes." Aralia crosses her arms over her chest, and a feeling I know like no other fills me. It's almost comforting, her hesitancy. It feels like my own.

"What's worse?" I ask, meaning the question genuinely. "Never talking, or not knowing how to talk about yourself?"

Me or you?

Aralia looks into my eyes, and with more casualness than the two words deserve, says, "Fuck you."

The playful nature in which she meant it almost makes me smile.

Or perhaps I did smile, because Aralia smiles back.

"The former sounds worse," she answers. "I'd rather nobody know me than be lonely."

I give her a sidelong glance. "Isn't that what loneliness means?"

Aralia shrugs, answering, "Only when you're alone." I must have a knack for getting people to tell me odd little details about themselves, because she follows with, "The two people who knew the most about me left."

Half of that is a lie. The lie makes her feel better.

I know what the lie is, but only because of Calista. She stopped talking to Lilac and Aralia after her parents found out about Lilac. After that, Aralia did the same.

Calista hates that they're all alone now.

She was forced to leave Lilac, but she wishes that Aralia and Lilac still had each another.

Or, she did.

"Me too," I say, to be of comfort. But she isn't talking about death.

"I'm tired of this conversation." Aralia leans back.

I can still see the pieces of Calista in her. It's hard to rid yourself of someone you loved. They stay, long after they're gone, in the same way that dead things decay. They turn to fuel, soil, food.

They become your world.

"Do you want to go back to the suite?" I ask.

"No." She stares into the sun. "Tell me something surprising."

I said all I could about me. So, I reach for something else. "The Collianth Cycles are getting shorter, and Lyrian scientists predict that our universe will implode on itself in five million years."

"I said surprising, not existential," Aralia drawls.

"I killed a boy when I was ten."

The words weren't supposed to come out. It was a little test. It was what I thought of when she asked the question the first time. But I knew I'd never say it. I only wanted to place it on the tip of my tongue and see how quickly I could swallow it.

But I didn't.

I spit it.

"Shit," Aralia mutters.

"Yeah," I say, "shit."

"You're choosing him over me?" the boy asks while I enter my room.

I stand in front of the mirror, unclasping the rose from around my neck. The necklace Ma gave me when I first left for Visnatus—a charm of protection.

"Answer me," the boy begs.

"I am not choosing anyone."

"Don't you understand the sanity I've offered to you? Who do you think you would be without my companionship?"

"Maybe not a loser who talks to herself." It's the kind of thing I'd only ever say to him. My inside voice.

He nearly chuckles. *"You would have lost your mind by now, Little Thorn."*

I close my eyes, turning to him quickly. Today, everything is oddly sharp in my mental landscape. The boy looks more material than shadow, and the world looks more acrylic than watercolor.

"You only call me that when you're angry!" I shout. *"Why are you angry that I want to help someone?"*

"Because you want more than to help him!" the boy yells, his eyes widening as he steps forward. *"You* want *him."*

"Why does that matter?"

"Because I want you!*"* The boy collapses on my bed. It bounces with

his weight—as if this is real.

As if this is all real.

I cover my mouth with my gloved hands.

How did it come to this? I must be misreading something. My mind hasn't *fallen* for me. That isn't possible.

"I knew it would come to this." His voice drops to a murmur. *"You haven't even named me."*

"Tell me your name if you want a name," I sigh, gently sitting next to him. The boy does not answer, and I place a hand on his knee. *"I love you—but not in the way you want me to. In the way a broken leg loves a crutch. You can't be angry with me for talking to people. You must want more for me than that."*

The boy shakes his head, dark hair falling from its place. *"I'm not angry,"* he says. *"I'm scared."*

"What are you scared of?"

He looks up with tears in his beautiful eyes, shaking his head as he mutters, *"That we will go through it again."*

I sigh as I stare at him.

I'm scared of this, too.

"I'm older now," I say, despite not entirely believing in my words. *"I can protect them this time."*

"But how can you know?" he asks.

Images of my mother grab me by the neck, and they don't let me go. She tells me to run, and I plant my feet, then I'm thrown by the pernipe when I should have fought. I wake up to Ma, dead.

Images of Xander grab my hair and pull me down. I touch him when I shouldn't—before knowing so much. He falls into the water, off a cliff, onto rocks. I feel the wound in my head.

I nearly black out.

When the memories shake me loose, I look away, toward the window, and I lift my hand from the boy's knee. He grabs it back greedily, kissing my knuckles.

"Don't go to him," he murmurs. *"I would be him for you, if you only asked."* A tear slips from him, landing on my hand.

"I love you."

"No," the boy says. *"Don't say it—don't say it without meaning it."* I shake my head, and he grasps my chin, pulling me back to him. *"I am*

clay in your hands. I am yours to mold. Tell me what you want me to be, and I will be that for you."

This time, I reach out and pick up his hand. *"I want you to believe in me. I want you to know that I can protect someone this time—that no one else will die because of me."*

The boy sighs as he says, *"But that isn't true. It is law that everybody will die."*

I hold up the rose pendant. *"That's why I'll give him this."*

I'm at the door to Azaire's suite, my hand hovering over the knocker, the rose amulet clutched in the other. I just have to give it to him and leave. That's all.

I'll shield him the only way I can—with Ma's pendant, her protection meant for me now resting with him. Because, if I'm truthful, I agree with the boy.

I only wish he didn't agree with me.

So I knock.

No answer. As I turn away, a sigh of relief escapes me, and I realize I was hoping this would be the case. I wanted only to prove I was brave, but to ultimately go back to safety.

I didn't intend to break any boundaries.

But Azaire *is* inside—I can feel him. He's the only one here.

He must be avoiding me. Though, I don't feel any of the telltale signs that tend to accompany avoidance.

I stand, pulling at my gloves. It's only a necklace. It's only a means of protection. It's only a moment, a second of my life.

My hand moves of its own accord, pressing into the door and pushing it open.

"Hello?" I call into the suite, stepping cautiously down the three marble stairs.

The layout mirrors ours exactly—only reversed. The small kitchen sits at the opposite end, and the couch and tables face the wrong direction, as if everything's been spun around.

"Azaire?" I call again.

There's a calming buzz, the sound of running water. He must be in the shower.

I sit on the unfamiliar couch, nerves prickling beneath my skin. Close my eyes and focus on the feel of him. Warm. Familiar. It's comforting. For a moment.

Then the bathroom door clicks open.

I jolt to my feet, the amulet clutched tightly in my hand. I brace myself to speak—to give it to him and leave. But then he steps out. In nothing but a towel.

No beanie.

No hair.

"Shit!" Azaire mutters, and that easy feeling is sucked out of me. He pulls the towel from his waist and covers his head. Then he runs into his room.

The door slams.

I am frozen solid. The blood does not move in my veins. I should leave but I cannot move, as if I've been turned to stone. Azaire doesn't want me here. He's confused and angry and in so much pain. In grief.

The match is falling from his hand again.

The house is burning down.

From behind the door of his room, he says, "Did you…" I can't turn toward the closed door. "Did you see?"

Where everyone else has hair, he has snakes. A mane of them.

He is petrified, cripplingly so. It's left me frozen, the intake of all his emotion. More than anyone else does.

This isn't good.

The last time I felt another's emotions so strongly, Ma was dead and Terran looked at me with more than his usual disdain.

I'd felt his true hatred for me.

The last time I felt another's emotions so strongly, someone died.

Azaire steps in front of me, a beanie covering his head—his eyes impossibly full of emotion.

"Wendy?"

I open my mouth, but nothing comes out. He grabs my upper arms and shakes me a bit. "Are you all right?"

"Y-yes," I finally manage, my voice stunted. "Yes, I'm all right."

He lets me go. His hand runs down the length of his face, dragging his features with it. I hate that Aeliana and Persiphis comes to mind. A constellation, an old story, one that ends in blood like all the others. I should have turned around when I had the chance. Never indulged in a conversation with him.

I should have listened to the boy.

I want to take it all back.

I want to erase the story I've started.

"I regretfully apologize for showing up this way," I mutter, walking to the door with my head down.

"Don't," Azaire says, and I halt. "Please don't talk to me like that."

"I'll see you in Philosophy?"

"Wendy, please," he whispers, and I almost cry for him.

The burning house scorches me; the match in his hand suffocates me. This feeling of his that I think I understand strangles me.

This feeling of his. This feeling of mine.

It's all the same.

I finally turn to him. "What is it?" Look into his eyes. "What are you feeling?"

Azaire glances down, pulling the beanie over his forehead. "You shouldn't have to…"

"What?"

"When I saw you I…" He runs his hand over his face once more. "I thought you were dead—and I knew I killed you." There is something more that he is not saying. It sits beneath his words.

"You didn't," I try to say gleefully, but my voice is a traitor.

Azaire shakes his head. "I don't know why."

"I'm glad I'm not dead." I step closer.

"You don't know how much it means to me that you're not."

"Have you…" I trail off, trying to tame my words. "You've killed someone before?"

He looks at me, and I don't need an answer to know his. There's pain in his eyes, tension in his gaze.

His overwhelming guilt becomes me.

"As have I," I say quickly, meaning for him to know that he isn't alone. "Power and adolescence don't exactly go together."

Subtly, he nods. "Yeah."

I'm pulling at the fingers of my glove, trying to bring myself to say it. The reason I came here, the reason I fought so dearly with myself.

I want him to have it.

"Um…" My fingers close tighter around the amulet. "I wanted to give you something." My voice sounds shaky, unsure.

"Are you sure?" the boy asks.

I ignore him.

"Okay." Azaire smiles a little, fangs poking against his bottom lip. Dark eyebrows falling over his face, chiseled from marble.

I understand now why that is. As if his appearance has taken on his power.

I've heard fleetingly of what those snakes beneath his beanie do— they turn people to stone. There is no reason for me to be standing here, alive, right now.

And yet, I am.

As if the universe knew I had to give this boy the rose.

I release my grip, holding my palm open. The rose amulet made an indentation in my glove, I'd clutched it so tightly.

"It will protect you," I say before I've even told him what it is. I'm terrible at communicating. Azaire has shown me that more than any-one.

Because he's the only one I've tried to talk to.

"Um… Just wear it. Always." I pick up his hand and place the rose in it. "Okay?"

"Okay." His smile is small. I think he's a little amused. Emotions are such a pointless commotion.

I stutter as I speak, "I-I'm gonna go."

"Wait." Azaire steps forward, frantic. His hand twitches at his side, as though he wants to reach for me but thinks better of it.

I'm waiting again, and he's trying to steady himself.

"I have something to say."

My—*his*—hands are shaking. Trembling.

I nod.

"I don't know what this is between us," he starts, his voice catch-ing as he continues, "but it'd take more than a loss of sight to deny it." His lips pull into an uncertain smile. "I *see* you—everything you don't show. And I want *you*, Wendy Estridon. I want your hesitancy. I want your caution. I want your heart. I even want your fear. I think I want you more than I've ever wanted anything in my life."

I stand still, uncertain how to continue. How to move forward, now that this boy before me has articulated exactly how I feel.

Now that he's taken the words from my tongue and wrapped them in a bow.

"But why now?" I ask. "Why all of a sudden?"

"It isn't all of a sudden, Wendy," Azaire breathes. "You know that." He swallows hard, the words fighting to escape, his vulnerability so pure it's almost painful. "I'm not asking for anything you're not ready for. But I want you to know this: I'll wait. I'll wait for you, no matter what. But you should know, every part of me is already yours. I've been yours, this entire time. Since before the night in the woods. Since before the day you healed me in class. It's been since the day I met you eight years ago. *This*"—he steps closer—"this was never sudden."

Tears sting my eyes. "That's the truth?" I ask. I know it is.

"The truth, truth." He laughs, and his entire face goes red. Blood red. He looks down at the ground for a moment, then back up at me.

"I think I want you, too." My gaze drops, unable to meet his. "It just doesn't work like that for me."

"*Good,*" the boy interrupts—condoning.

"What if I promise you, right now, that I will be the one who is hurt by you?" Azaire says it with such optimism. He says it, and he means it. "Whatever happens, I take the blunt end. Wherever this goes, I swallow the worst of it."

My frown is heavy to hold as I say, "That's actually what I'm afraid of."

"Then how about I promise no one gets hurt?"

"We both know that's not possible…"

Azaire takes a step closer, the air shifting with his anticipation. His hand brushes against mine, uncertain before he picks it up. And oh gods, do I feel it. His warmth, his certainty, his heartbeat echoing in my own.

I feel it all.

"Then how about we swim the lake when we get to it?"

He really means it, really cares. Really *wants* this. Wants me, for whatever reason. The feeling overtakes me while he stands a foot away from me, blushing like a *rose*, not blood.

"All I want is for us to get to it," he mutters.

I step towards him, without meaning to.

I pull his lips to mine, without meaning to.

And I enjoy his kiss, without ever meaning to.

"Bad," the boy says. *"Lips on lips on happiness, that can all be taken away with one, small, fragile moment of pain."*

PART 2:
THE FISSURE

Chapter 17
Everything I Want

Calista ignores her impulses, fighting to keep her eyes locked anywhere but on me.

We sit at the top of the tiered classroom, with a direct view of the board. But that isn't what I focus on. Across the room, Azaire is looking at me—I can feel him.

"Calista?" I whisper again, intending to apologize—for the Weapon, the blueprint—all the ways she believes I've deceived her. But she keeps staring ahead.

So, I stare ahead as well, though my mind drifts.

Azaire's been stealing glances momentarily. I'd been focused on Calista, but now that it's been confirmed she is content to ignore me, I meet his gaze, searching for solace. He smiles. That's enough for me to get through the rest of class.

By the end, Azaire is waiting for me at the door, his silhouette framed by the afternoon light. Without a word, his fingers curl around mine, warm and steady beneath the barrier of my glove. How I wish this fabric didn't separate us—that I could feel the pulse of his skin against mine.

How I wish to have what I can never have.

It's only human to want it.

We step away from the crowded hallway, drifting in the opposite direction of my next class. The world feels quieter here, the noise of school fading behind us.

I glance up at him, voice tentative, "Where are we going?"

He looks at me, smiling. "It's a beautiful day today."

"Okay," I say with a soft laugh, falling beside him as we slip out of the academy halls and into the garden.

The sun presses warmly against my face, bright and high in the sky —an uncommon gift during the school day. Usually, I'm trapped behind classroom windows, watching the world move without me.

I close my eyes against the light, savoring the warmth, trusting Azaire to lead me wherever we're going.

He moves with ease; I don't stumble over rocks or trees. The path is smooth, and for a moment, there's nothing but him.

When his movements stop, I peek my eyes open. Ahead, the lunar lake stretches out, its surface rippling softly in the breeze, silver flecks dancing across the water.

At our feet lies a carefully placed blanket. My heart skips as I take in the spread before me. Native berries, slow-roasted meats, sauces infused with Eunoian herbs—the flavors of my homeworld, brought here by him, for me.

Azaire leans close, his breath warm against my ear. "In case you're homesick."

I stare in shock, shaking my head. "How did you—"

"Eudora has a soft spot for me," he says—the head chef of the school, who is also a Eunoia. That's how he got all this food.

I sink onto the picnic blanket, the soft fabric folding beneath me. With careful hands, I start assembling a wrap—stacking tender slices of slow-roasted meat with sweet, bursting berries. The scents mingle—smoky, woodsy, and just a hint of something wild.

When I pass the wrap to Azaire, he smiles softly and says, "It's for you."

"I'll make another one." I pick up his hand, dropping the food in his palm. "I want you to try it."

He looks down at the wrap in his hand, then back to me. As I nod, he lifts the food to his mouth. I follow just after him.

It isn't long until most of the food is gone. I've missed it. I hardly ate when I visited home last. I didn't have the stomach for it.

"Next time, I'll have to get you Neptharian foods," I offer—food from his homeworld. He's probably homesick, too.

Azaire chuckles, but it's devoid of humor. "This is far better than anything I grew up with."

I glance at him, raising an eyebrow. "You don't have a favorite dish?"

Warmth blossoms in his chest, as if he's calling the sun into him. "There's a soup—cured cattle, dried rosemary, powdered pumpkin seed, all mixed with water. My mom would make it when we had the ingredients." He frowns and avoids meeting my eyes. His gaze is distant, far off, as if looking into a memory. "It's war food, probably impossible to find now." He shakes his head, meeting my gaze once more. "It wasn't any good, anyhow. I think it's the memory that I like."

I scoot closer to him, taking off my academy jacket beneath the warm sun. "My mom used to make those wraps." I rest my head on his shoulder, right in the crook of his neck. "It's the first time I've had one in years, too."

I decide I'll give to him what he gave to me: a piece of his mother, gifted in flavor. I'll find those rare ingredients and make that soup, the same way he found Ma's ingredients.

Before this, I hadn't known his mom was dead. It isn't uncommon to have a dead parent here. Most of the students have parents who are either high-ranking in the military or government. Those with military parents are often the ones who end up orphaned. If their parents weren't the muscle, they were likely high up in the government— which made them prime targets for torture. While there are fewer casualties among them, they still exist; though the fighting mostly stopped after the end of the Neptharian War, it hasn't completely gone away.

Azaire's gaze shifts, landing on the scars that mar my arms. I can feel the question coming before it leaves his lips. For a moment, I think about reaching for my jacket, hoping to close off the conversation before it goes any further.

But I don't want to.

"What happened?"

I meet his eyes, not sure how to answer. Little light marks cover my skin, remnants of the thorns that have grown there over time— thorns I've pulled out, each one leaving a trace. Little reminders of the things I cannot have.

"Power and adolescence," I whisper. "When I was a kid, my magic was… turbulent."

Not that the thorns don't still grow today. They're just fewer and farther between.

The words linger, but I don't explain further. I don't think I have to. I think Azaire knows exactly what I mean.

The first time my magic materialized, it came in thorns. They poked through my skin, from the inside out. Ma ripped each one out with tweezers. The only thing I really remember is the pain.

The blood that dripped at my feet.

Azaire lifts my hand, slowly at first. Reverently. Like he's trying to gauge if I'll pull away. Like he's waiting for permission. I feel a sudden flutter of vulnerability rise in my chest. Then a flicker of doubt.

Should I pull back? Shield myself?

I don't.

He lowers his lips, brushing across my scars. Tingles shoot up my spine. But I don't pull my hand away. Instead, I keep my eyes on him, searching for a sign, a pause, a retreat.

But I realize: I don't want him to stop.

Azaire's lips trail higher, moving from my arm to my neck, kissing what I never thought anyone could touch.

My eyes close softly, surrendering to the deadly game. Tentatively testing the edges of what I believed was forever out of reach. It's not just his lips on my skin—it's his presence in my heart that makes this a risk.

And here I am, willingly throwing myself to chance.

A smile spreads across my face, and I *want* Azaire to see it.

A moan escapes me, and I *want* Azaire to hear it.

"I would kiss every inch of your skin," he breathes, his lips barely grazing mine as they trail slowly, deliberately, until they settle just behind my ear. "A thousand times over. Just to hear you again."

Warmth bubbles in my stomach at his words—at his want. It's so rare to hear Azaire like this, and I want to hear more.

I turn my head, just enough to meet his eyes, and the feeling intensifies. I glance down at his lips, then back at his eyes.

The silence hones in until there's nothing in the world but us.

"No one is stopping you."

His smile is small, almost fragile—but I can feel the rapid thrum of his heartbeat beneath. His thumb tracing a path across my cheek.

The touch is soft—too soft to be casual.

"Then show me," he murmurs, the words moving through me. "Where are your scars?"

I don't pull away, even if instinct is telling me I should. Everything else is telling me to lean in.

"Everywhere."

Azaire's gaze sharpens, and I can feel the weight of it as his thumb moves across my cheek. I can't help but grip his hand, but I don't pull him closer.

"Power doesn't care about where it hits," I add, the words coming out colder than I meant.

"No. It doesn't," he agrees quietly.

I lean in, drawn to him despite the truth of my words and all the scars I have to prove it. My lips find the edge of his wrist first, kissing up the length of his arm—the same way he had touched me.

"Hey," he breathes, his voice rough. "That's not fair."

I press my lips against the hollow of his neck, meeting his eyes. Against his skin, I murmur, "What isn't?"

"I don't have any scars."

I kiss one more time. Then another. "Maybe I just like kissing you."

Azaire's smile doesn't fade, but there's something in the way he looks at me—a look I don't need empathy to decipher.

It's desire that deepens his gaze.

"Then," he says, his voice low, "I couldn't possibly stop you."

"You're making a mistake, Wendy," the boy tells me the moment I enter the confines of my room.

I slam the door shut behind me, trying to block out every emotion but my own.

I *know* I'm making a mistake—I could feel it when I first kissed Azaire.

I don't need my mind to scream at me.

This is a mistake I'm choosing to make.

"It's just for a little bit," I say as I lean against my door. *"I only need a*

little companionship, to recharge."

"That is not how these things go."

I pull my bottom lip between my teeth, shaking my head, although no one can see. Against my better judgment, I close my eyes.

On my bed, the boy is lying leisurely—despite his voice sounding anything but calm, prior to now.

"Lie with me."

Once more, I shake my head. *"I know what you think this is—"*

"Wendy," the boy breathes. "Please. *Just lie with me."*

I stare at him for a moment, trying to think of a better excuse.

"Don't make me beg," he says. *"Because I will."*

The moments pass, and his desperation grows. It presses into me as if he were a person.

In the end, I walk to my bed. I lie with my back touching the boy's chest, and his arm wraps around me.

"I choose him—"

"Shh," the boy cuts me off. *"Allow me to hold you without the crushing restraints of a world beyond me. Let us just be here."*

I nod against his chest, leaning into him deeper. His breath pushes through my hair like the wind, and I hold him tighter. For better or worse, this is the single person who has been by my side for years.

For better or worse, his arms are my comfort.

After a while, the boy says, *"Given your past, do you feel safe to be with him?"*

"Yes." I struggle to lie to myself, and the boy must know it too. *"He's strong."*

"Strength is not power," he warns.

I look him in the eyes, the dark green swirling until it's a muddied brown, and I clarify, *"He's powerful."*

Chapter 18
A Halo Wrapped
Around My Neck

Azaire and I lie in his bed, his fingers wrapping around my gloves. He wants to take them off—it isn't the first time I've felt it.

If the boy were around, I know what he'd say.

Don't you dare.

But after the last night I spent with him, he hasn't come back. Not even as a ghost in my head, a conscience of my thoughts. He disappeared with one last goodbye: *"It is too painful to see you with him. Please return when the inevitable happens."*

I've been ignoring that goodbye. He told me he was clay for me to mold, yet struggles to believe in me. There's no way to reconcile that your brain thinks you can't find love, so I don't try to.

It's been a week with Azaire, of feeling almost close enough to touch him. Seven nights of indulging in one another's pasts and futures.

Or lack of them.

It's easy to see that neither of us know what we're going to do next. And tonight, in his arms, the Weapon comes up, as it tends to.

"We wait for Lucian," I say, hoping Azaire will let it go, that I can take care of this on my own. "He's the person best equipped to find answers."

Azaire's eyes and fingers remain on my gloves. "I can't do nothing. Not when I know it's happening."

Whispered words slip past my lips. "I don't know how I'd feel if

Ma weren't involved." Something about the lack of eye contact and the dark room makes me feel safe enough to tell the truth.

His fingers trace over mine—over the leather. "Yeah." He nods absentmindedly. "I get it." His eyes shift to mine. "Why can I kiss you but not hold your hand?"

"Oh," I sigh. Facing the dark ceiling, I hope that avoiding his silhouette might make it easier to just get on with it. It doesn't. "Is Yuki coming back anytime soon?" I ask instead.

It feels like even my bones are frowning.

"Yeah, but not for a few hours."

"Okay."

Our hands are the conduits for our magic, everything we Eunoia channel goes in and out through them. Though any skin-to-skin contact with me is tricky. If I say the wrong thing, if there's any small accident, the other person can't deny me.

They are at my mercy. That's what happens when you're powerful, I've been told.

You lose control.

And I don't want to tell Azaire the mental strain it takes to kiss him. How much work I put in to maintaining my shields—keeping my power in and protecting him. I don't want to tell him why I wear the gloves.

Yet I feel that he deserves something from me. Some kind of an answer.

"When I was five, I felt someone's emotions for the first time." I try not to sound like I'm struggling to say the words. "My brother, Terran. I'd accidentally wrapped him in tendrils." *With thorns*, I don't say. Some truths are too bitter. "He was only a little more afraid of me than he was disgusted."

Azaire's fingers freeze on top of mine. But he doesn't feel like he automatically understands me, and for that, I'm grateful. I don't quite know what he thinks—but I feel like I can tell him more.

He reaches up, holding my cheek in his hand. There's just enough moonlight coming in through the windows to see his eyes. It's the kind of look that makes me wonder what he's seeing, even though I can feel him.

"Gods, you're making this hard," I breathe, leaning my head further into his hand.

"What?" He smiles. Fangs and all.

"Keeping my distance."

"Well," he says, and I can feel the heat of his face in my own cheeks, "I never hoped it would be easy."

It never was. Can I communicate with my eyes? If I can, that's what they're saying.

"Can I..." I trail off. "Can I tell you something?"

Azaire tucks a strand of my hair behind my ear, the tips of his fingers grazing my cheek. "Anything."

"You know what I said? About power and adolescence not mixing well..."

Azaire nods.

"Before I came to this school, I had a friend—Xander. I made the mistake of touching him." I pull my bottom lip between my teeth. "His was the first funeral I ever attended."

Azaire opens his mouth, but I shake my head, moving closer. Our noses nearly touch, and my voice is barely audible.

"After my mom died, I lost hope. I believed I was cursed—that anyone who cared about me would end up hurt. I pulled away from the world, became a ghost among the living. And from that loneliness..." I pause, voice thinning. Then, "Something inside me made him. The boy, I call him." A soft, self-conscious laugh escapes, cracked by tears. "I know it sounds strange. But ever since you and I got together... he's been gone. Like he was never real. I don't know whether to thank you or blame you for that—but I needed you to know. Someone had to know."

Azaire nods, as if it isn't the most insane thing he's ever heard. It must be.

Yet he seems to understand, somehow.

"Loss is never easy," he says softly. "Give me your pain, Wendy Estridon. I can handle it." He picks up my hand, his grip steady. Far steadier than I am. "I can carry it."

I shake my head, staring at his hand in mine. "You don't think I'm crazy?"

"Not at all. I've hurt people the same way... with my snakes. It's no surprise your mind would try to protect you. If I'm honest, I think

I would've done better with a friend like that, too."

The weight of his words shifts my gaze to the side, unsettling something deep inside me. I can't say I agree with Azaire—not fully. I'm not sure if the boy is just a coping mechanism. For the first time, I wonder if I believe he's something more.

If I truly believe he's real, even without a body of flesh and bone.

I stop at the kitchen, sitting on the stool as I wait for Eudora, the academy chef, to appear. When she emerges, I meet her gaze. She's always stood out—Eunoia are rare at the academy, and hers is one of the few familiar faces.

Her dark hair is always in a tight bun, never the traditional braid like the others. Her skin is a warm, rich brown; her eyes a vivid green that borders on turquoise—much lighter than anyone in my family.

"Hi Eudora," I greet her.

"What do ya need, Wendy?"

I blink, brow furrowing. We've never spoken before; hearing my name in her voice stops me cold.

"How do you know my name?"

"I took notice of you," Eudora says, her voice flamboyant. "And I remember your mother. One of the first kind faces I knew when I first got this job."

A stone scrapes down my throat and crashes into my chest, making it hard to breathe.

Ma. As a teenager. It doesn't seem possible. It feels like she should have been a graceful adult her entire life.

But then again, her journals say otherwise.

I guess I can't tie her past self to the woman I knew. I guess that's what I'm struggling to understand.

"Can you…" I clear my throat. "Can you tell me about her?"

"Quiet," Eudora answers instantly, the single word lingering. Until she says with a shrug, "Like you. But beneath it she had big dreams, ambition. You're her spitting image these days—that's how I remembered your name. I looked at you and thought *Willow.* And every time, I corrected myself, *Wendy.*" She says our names like we're glorious—

something to be revered. Not a fallen mother and a failing daughter.

Shaking my head, I try to take the compliment, wishing I saw Ma when I looked in the mirror. But beyond that, I'm focused on her dreams. Her ambition.

Did others see what she hid in paper?

"Wh-what—" I clear my throat. "What kind of dreams did she have?"

Is there more than what she left in her journals?

Eudora's voice is gentle. "I remember she fought to get into Combat Training. She was the only Eunoia in the history of the academy to do so. The old headmaster thought she had spirit."

"What else?" I ask quickly, urgently. Pleading for someone to tell me what I should already know—the details I've forgotten, the moments I never knew I missed. Buried deeper than any journal, scattered like dust in the wind.

Praying that some of it clings beneath Eudora's nails.

"I don't know much, honey," she sighs. "Last I heard, she got in a lot of trouble with the kingdoms, was forced out of the academy and punished. But that isn't happy talk. What else can I do for ya?"

I open my mouth. No words come out.

Ma's relationship with Folkara—with King Easton and Queen Melody, every document signed by them—it was a *punishment*.

Is that why Pa is scared for me to push further? Does he fear the sins of the mother will fall to the daughter?

"I—" My words catch in my throat. I shake my head, loosening my tongue and warming my vocal chords. "I wanted to know if you could get me something from Nepthara?"

"What do ya need, hon?"

"Cured cattle, dried rosemary, and powdered pumpkin seed."

Eudora leans to the side, placing a hand on her hip as she assesses me. "It'll take some time."

For once, I feel like it's in my favor.

With a smile, I say, "Take all the time you need."

Without any warning, Lucian's completely disappeared. It's been weeks, and I'm scared he's forgetting about the Weapon altogether.

Azaire has brought up the boy a few times, in moments of deep conversation, and despite the boy's disappearance, I can almost feel him recoil inside of me. As if the boy believes it to be a betrayal that I've told another of his existence.

The view from Azaire's window has become familiar. The willow tree always blows in the wind. Its branches are nearly empty of leaves, nature shedding its skin for another revival after the winter season.

Like the bare tree, we've lost all leads on the Weapon.

Azaire's next move is to break into the kingdom of Folkara.

Would it be so wrong to strip away his emotion? To *force* him to let go of the Weapon?

It would be, I know it. It would take something from him I love—his selflessness. More than that, his unwavering belief in something better.

But wouldn't it be for his own good? If he goes to Folkara—if he touches the Weapon at all—he'll likely die. He's a Nepenthe, and as much as I wish I could ignore what that means, as much as I wish I didn't burn with anger every time I remember, it marks him as scum in the eyes of our universe.

And I always burn for it.

"What is it?" Azaire asks.

Sitting on the edge of his bed and catching my breath, I turn to face him. "What?"

"You've been staring out the window, at the willow tree." He presses his lips together. "You do that when you're avoiding something."

I pull my bottom lip between my teeth. I thought I was on track to find the Weapon and do something. For Ma. For the universe.

Today the goal has never felt so far.

It feels worse than far. It feels like it's falling into Azaire's lap—the last thing I ever wanted.

Other than my family, I've never had someone sense my emotions. And, to a lesser extent, that's exactly what Azaire's done—he's gotten to know me well enough to know when something is wrong.

I'm avoiding the conversation I'm desperate to have. That I think we might have to break into Folkara, no matter how bad the plan is.

That I don't think *he* should be the one to do it.

I should be, if Lucian isn't around. He and I have the most riding on this. Not Azaire. He's an innocent bystander, pulled in because he cares about us.

And by Zola, does he care. I feel it every day. It settles deep in my bones, down to the marrow. I've been running from it since the night of the party.

Now I'm forcing myself to sink.

Everytime I try to run, I tie boulders to my feet.

"We can't keep waiting around for him," I say, stepping closer to Azaire, toward his desk.

I'm right.

We can't.

It leaves our options limited.

"He'll come back to himself," Azaire says.

His worry and slight disbelief shakes me. Maybe Lucian is too far gone.

"I know." I say it for his sake. "What we don't know is when."

He reaches for my hand, and instinct has me ready to pull away.

I don't.

"What do you want to do?" he asks, pulling me toward his chair.

I stand between his legs and squeeze his hand. "Go to Folkara."

It was always the contingency plan we hoped we wouldn't need.

Azaire nods—*misunderstands*. "Whenever you want."

"Not you." My eyes widen, but I hold his gaze, feeling every ounce of his shock. "I'm going to do it. Alone."

He loosens his grip on my hand slightly—subconsciously—and shakes his head. "It doesn't make sense," he says. "I can scale and morph through the walls, get in and out."

"And if you're caught?" I ask. It'll be worse than what's already happening to him at the academy—all the volunteer groups, all the pointless pain. The government of Folkara, the *Royals*, will have no problem killing a Nepenthe. We both know it.

"Wendy that's…" he trails off. "It's kind of exactly what I was made to do."

"You were made to bring yourself to the brink of death every time your friends need something?" My mouth flips upside down, inside out.

Azaire shakes his head a bit. "That wasn't—that was once."

"And this could be twice," I say firmly. He frowns, matching my expression. "I'll do it," I add decisively.

"Wendy—"

My chest tightens. "I'll be fine. At least they won't kill me." I shrug. "It's not like it's Ilyria."

I'm not actually sure one kingdom is any better than the other. Not anymore.

"Wendy," he says again. But he doesn't continue.

His unspoken words choke me.

"Say it," I demand, recoiling at the strength in my voice. I begin to shake my head, to mutter my apologies.

But Azaire picks up my hands, rubbing circles into them, softening my edges. His frown is heavy, his emotions dreary. But his voice is soft. "Who says they won't kill you?"

I have to look away, unable to meet his gaze. There's only one thing left to say—one undeniable truth. I could lie, but I'm learning there's no point in lying to Azaire.

I push it out, ripping a petal from a rose. Pricking my finger on the thorn.

"I don't care if they do."

Aziare takes a—disapproving—breath and I can't help but pull my hands from his. His mouth opens, and I cut him off.

"At least I'll die doing something important."

"Your *life* is important!" Azaire shouts.

"And you'd be willing to risk it if it was yours!" I retaliate.

It's been so long since I've screamed. My vocal chords rub together like sandpaper.

A fight rises in me—half his, and half mine.

But it only makes me stronger.

I slowly reach my hand to his shoulder, planning to hold him down. Make sure he can't look away from me, should he try. "I have Calista's favor," I tell him. It's not the truth, but he doesn't know. "I'll be fine."

My hand is inches away from him.

"If Queen Melody or King Easton caught you, she couldn't stop it," Azaire argues.

I know he's right. Calista couldn't stop her parents.

"If anyone gets close, I wouldn't even have to touch them to change their minds," I remind him.

I'm dangerous. More than anyone would expect from a Eunoia.

Once I look into someone's eyes, my words are the only truth. I'm more powerful than the rest of my people. More deadly.

Others can control emotions. I demand them.

My fingers hum beneath the gloves. I feel the terrifying force prickling beneath my skin—my very nature. I could take over the world, person by person, meld their minds to one.

Mend them to my will.

Carefully, I rest my hands on Azaire's cheeks, forcing his gaze to meet mine before he can realize what I'm doing.

The saddest part is, he doesn't even suspect it.

It gives me a momentary pause. He sees me so purely, believes in me so completely. I'm going to crush that faith like a bug. But for just one more second, I want to linger in his purity—the innocence I'm about to strip from myself, a burden he will never know.

For one last second, I breathe in his fresh air.

Then I light the match.

"You don't want to go to Folkara. But you support me going." My voice takes on a terribly intoxicating tone. His emotion bends to me like clay—the way the boy should have. The way Azaire never should.

But this is for Ma.

"You understand the risks," I whisper, "but you believe in me more."

I watch him, feeling a piece of my heart chip away—like a fragment breaking off a fragile vase. I can glue this small shard back, but the scar will never fully disappear.

I'm taking something from myself: his integrity.

Watching closely, I wait for his mind to change—wondering if maybe I've failed. Maybe because his snakes didn't kill me, my power won't be enough to control him. Maybe I can take it back. Maybe he can see what I did, then see beyond it, understand me more deeply than before. Maybe he'll *understand* what this means to me, and together, we can find a way forward.

The hope in me shatters as Azaire nods, his expression unreadable, as if the weight of my power has numbed him. I can't bear to hold his gaze any longer, so I turn away. Out of the corner of my eye, I see him shake his head, the fog in his eyes clearing as he forces himself back into focus.

"Before you do this, I have to ask…" His words trail off, and he tugs on the sides of his beanie. "Can I… can I hold you?"

I don't know if that hurts or helps my cause.

"My hands?" I shake my head. I don't deserve to be asked. "I'm sorry it's—"

"Not possible?" he answers for me. He's gotten awfully good at reading me. But not good enough to know what I've done to him.

Surprisingly, Azaire reaches to his beanie. He takes a deep breath. My blood spikes, my heart beats. Thorns rise from his emotion, just beneath my skin, daring to emerge.

With one movement, he pulls the beanie from his head, as if he's laying himself bare for me.

Green and gray snakes hiss around his face, their tongues flicking in and out, their scales shimmering in the light. As they meet my gaze, even they are surprised I am still made of flesh.

I watch in awe.

Azaire's eyes are alight, the brightest color I've ever seen. They could pierce through any darkness, even my own.

He looks at me like I'm the only thing that matters—the center of his world, the home he never knew he needed.

He looks at me like he loves me.

I fear he feels it, too.

I want to look away, but I already know that no matter how I try, I'll never be able to again.

I am his.

But I've already proven that there is no worse fate than being mine.

"It's not possible for someone to survive my snakes either." Azaire's voice barely carries.

Aeliana and Persiphis.

The constellation. One of Ma's favorites.

It's not fair to hold onto that now, after what I've done. It's not fair to hope.

Yet, I look down, staring at my gloves.

I think: *What if?*

I say, "These kinds of things never end well."

It's stupid to think like that—to wonder.

Aeliana was a Eunoia with a power no one else had, either.

It's stupid to think like that. I don't deserve to be touched after what I've done to him.

"You're the only one who's seen me and hasn't died. It's fair to reason I'll be the same for you," Azaire says with a shrug and a voice full of heart.

As I flex my fingers, I know how deeply I long to hold him close. To hold him and never let go.

To wrap my hands so tightly around him that he leaves indents in my skin.

It could kill him.

But it isn't fear for his life that gives me pause. It's fear for mine.

I am not worthy of a touch, after all I've done. And I've only proved this tonight. I've killed and manipulated…

But I look at his cobalt blue beanie. The thing that protects others from him.

And I look at my brown leather gloves. The thing that protects others from *me*.

But not well enough to protect him.

We're eerily similar, the two of us. I fear it means more bad than good.

He's my venus fly trap. Or, more accurately, I might be his.

"Have you ever heard of Aeliana and Persiphis?" I ask, my voice hesitant. "It's kind of a misleading name, actually, because the constellation has three figures: Aeliana, Persiphis, and Heili." I swallow hard, my nerves catching up with me. "Do you know the story?"

Azaire shakes his head, watching me intently.

"Aeliana had this power—or curse, depending on what you believe. Everyone she met fell in love with her instantly. Except Persiphis. With him, it was different. Their love grew slowly, naturally. But before they realized it, three princes were already fighting for Aeliana. Heili, the prince of Folkara, won her hand. But when Heili saw her love for Persiphis…" I falter, my heart pounding. "Heili decided to kill him.

"Their fight was brutal. Heili almost won—until Aeliana stepped between them. She took the blow meant for Persiphis and died. Heili lost her forever, and Persiphis lived the rest of his life alone."

It's proof there are no good endings to this story.

Azaire doesn't say anything at first, just studies me in that way of his, gaze sharp and unwavering.

"I love your mind," he says finally, his voice soft. "The way you connect stories to the world—but that's only one. Maybe ours, and maybe not. We'll never know if we don't try."

"Maybe we shouldn't." My voice trembles. "What if this whole thing was a cosmic mistake? What if we were supposed to stay away from each other all along, like I thought?"

He tilts his head, his expression thoughtful. "And what if it's the opposite? What if we're Zola's way of finding balance? Putting together two people with a similar predisposition?" he counters.

"That's not—" I start to protest, but he cuts me off gently.

"I'm not saying that's what this is. My point is, there are an infinite number of 'what if's.' If you let them stop you from making a decision, then you're only going to imprison yourself. Whether you built the cage or not, it's still a cage." His lips curve into a small, almost shy smile. "You've been trying to stop yourself from falling for me this whole time. Because of your past or your powers, but I love you, Wendy."

He laughs and tears form in his eyes. He's realizing this for himself, right now, right here. Am I, too? Or did I already know?

"Wendy Estridon, I'm in love with you." I open my mouth, and he puts a finger to my lips. "Don't say anything, not unless it's a confession, because I'm about to do something, and I don't want to let my what if's stop me."

I close my mouth.

I'm trying to let the sensation of air leaving my chest pass. It only grows more intense.

He loves me. I feel the same.

If I'm capable of doing to someone I love what I did to him, then what does love truly mean for me?

Azaire holds his journal in his shaking hand, opening to a random page. The journal that he's feared me touching every time I held it.

The journal that holds all of him.

I don't deserve it.

"Read it," he says, handing the open journal to me.

I've never read something he's written before.

Slowly, I unfold the page, looking at him as I do. Waiting for him to change his mind and tear it back.

He doesn't, and I care too much to do it myself.

The guilt of overtaking his emotions, his mind, presses down on me like water—like I'm suffocating for air—until I finally catch the words on the page.

I know that change is inevitable, that there is nothing constant in life. But when I look into her eyes, I don't believe it. What I do believe is that, more than anything, she and I will break those odds.

Azaire stutters. "I-I have more, it's just—"

Suddenly, everything sharpens into one overwhelming moment. Into the ache in my chest and the tears threatening to spill.

I scoot closer to him.

This time, when I kiss him, all I can feel is *me*. My love, my heart, my feelings. My hands drape around his neck and my fingers reach up his head. They graze over his snakes, and he shudders.

Maybe it's the way he softens me with his touch and opens my closed borders, but he's seeped into me like rain in the cracks of an orchard.

I lean my forehead against his, our noses forming the ghost of a touch. I put my hand on his chest.

"I want to feel you the way you feel me," he murmurs.

I won't hurt him.

I can't.

I kiss him again, until my lips burn. Then I force myself to take off my glove. Only one.

I can control it—the thing that's always controlled me.

I can do this.

"The moment it becomes too much, say something," I tell him.

"You could never be too much."

I bite my lip, nodding. Then I place my hand on his cheek, shutting my eyes. My shields fall into place; I block anything from coming out.

I feel him, fast and slow, until I see that he's showing me something through his emotions. Love, like I've never felt before. Making my hands tingle and my heart flutter.

I feel safe.

Safety I don't deserve.

So I open my eyes. Azaire is smiling softly at me. Only then do I realize his hand is resting on mine—his skin pressing gently, both above and below.

He's all around me.

"You're beautiful."

I shake my head.

"No," he says. "You are the most beautiful thing I've ever had the good will to feel."

My brow furrows.

Azaire picks up my hand, kissing it again and again.

He says he doesn't know what he did to deserve me.

I ache.

"What did you feel?" I watch his face carefully, staring back and forth between both his eyes, searching.

He kisses me again.

"You," he says. A smile. A shrug. "I think." He raises one free hand and wiggles his fingers. "Look at that. Not dead."

"Not dead," I whisper.

I can touch someone.

Chapter 19
Too Much Skin in
the Game

The next morning, I walk fast through the halls, heart pounding, the memory of Azaire burning just beneath my skin. I'd like to tell someone—I'd like to scream it from the rooftops.

I can touch someone.

Yet I still watch my feet as I walk.

With each step, I refrain from meeting gazes. With each step, I think of the horrible thing I've done.

I can touch someone, but not much has changed besides that. I suppose that's life, a series of small changes until one day you wake up, and nothing is what it used to be.

All I hope is one day it happens to me.

I'm okay with that. I'm more than okay with that. This is the only small change in the last five years that I've been excited for.

That I've enjoyed in any regard.

I'd scream it, if I thought I could scream.

For now, I will whisper—and I will never utter a word of what I did to Azaire.

It's a promise I make to myself as the whole world goes white.

The light is blinding, searing my vision until there's no up or down, no hallway or floor beneath me. I see nothing. I say nothing. But from my mouth, words spill like rain, torn from a part of me I didn't know was there. The sound is muffled and monotone. Distant. As if I'm underwater, drenched in the rain drops.

Words tear through my lungs, anyhow.

"Time fractures with the stone.

The one who leaves returns alone.

When the cracks in the universe divide,

love will be your demise."

My throat constricts. The air leaves my lungs. The world freezes. Infinite cold. My family stands. Spiders crawl from their mouths. Their eyes go white. Their dead bodies fall.

Azaire is on top.

Eerily, slowly, his head turns to me.

"Stop this," his corpse croaks.

Then the image burns, the ash falling away with the rest of the ruins. I am left looking at Desdemona, who stares back in shock.

I'm not breathing.

Or is she not breathing?

I'm not sure anymore.

I run.

Is this real?

Was Azaire real? Has this all been a—

"A prophecy," the boy interrupts me, making his first appearance in ages. The relief feels like a lullaby Ma used to sing, gentle but haunting, and I don't know if I love or hate it. *"I could have helped."*

"How could you have helped?" The question scrapes through me, breathless even in my mind. My feet strike the floor over and over, the rhythm relentless, turning into a song I can't stop playing.

"I felt it coming. I could have prepared you for this feeling."

The corridors stretch endlessly ahead, but I can't outrun Desdemona. Fear drips from her like sweat in a way that tells me I will never feel the end of it—of her. As if I feel her very soul, her life. I turn every corner, and I still can't escape it.

Or is this fear mine?

I can't rid the bitter taste from the back of my throat. I can't rid the horror from my head. All I can do is race through the halls.

Until I spot Calista far ahead of me. I run to her, grabbing her shoulders and pulling her toward me.

Calista stares up at me with horror, retreating before she recognizes me.

She shakes her head, confused. "Wendy—"

"We need to talk."

Calista releases a deep exhale, falling back into herself. Then, she looks past me.

"Now," I demand.

Calista smiles, rolling her eyes as she laughs. "All right."

She finds no humor in it. None at all.

She's scared and putting on a facade. Her laugh is a distraction. She's smart enough to know that laughing won't stop me from feeling her terror. Yet she does it anyway.

I pull her through the halls to the first uninhabited place I see—a classroom. We sit against a window, the sun shining on our backs.

My—*their*—emotions scream at me from just beyond the threshold. Everything, everywhere, all at once, no matter what, always. I feel every foot step, every breath. Every tug of a sleeve, every shifted shirt.

All of it, all at once—all that is theirs becoming mine.

There is no escaping it. There is hardly relief. At least there's relief at all.

There wasn't before Azaire.

On top of everything from afar, Calista is scared, too. Was it her fear that pierced through me, and not Desdemona's? I can't tell anything apart anymore.

The world is blurry, but it must be my eyes.

"Wendy?" Calista's words echo through the vast room.

I see the world for the first time since I sat. The classroom is dim, the only light from the sun through the curtains. Rows of escalating seats extend before us.

"What is it?" she asks.

Shaking my head, I prepare to tell her, a mirror to what we did a year ago. She came to me because I was the only escape route, the only person she could confide in without fearing what would happen if I broke that trust.

Like then, she is the only person who won't share what I say now.

"You can't tell anyone." I speak fast. "Especially Lucian."

This can't get back to Azaire. Not if what I felt means anything.

Not if the prophecy is true.

Calista folds her arms over her chest. Defensively, she says, "I don't tell Lucian anything."

I don't care for her resistance. I need to say something, tell someone.

"There was a prophecy." I watch as her features turn in shock. It's the reaction I expected. She'll do anything now to hear the truth. "Before I tell you more, you have to give me your word."

"What is the prophecy?" she demands, disguised as a question.

"This is important."

She doesn't want to give me her word, for obvious reasons. Once she does, there is no taking it back. Offering a favor, or their word, for a Royal is far different than a regular citizen. They are forced to uphold it, against their will.

It's a magic, of sorts.

Calista rolls her eyes as she contemplates. I can almost feel the mechanics of her brain wiring.

"*Fine*," she breathes. "I give you my word, Wendy Estridon, that I will not repeat what you say to Lucian Aibek." She raises her eyebrows, as if saying, *go on*.

"Or Azaire Wenejad."

Calista scowls, reluctantly adding, "Or Azaire Wenejad."

I sigh, leaning against the wall. "I don't know how to explain it."

Nor do I want to.

"Figure it out," she huffs. "I didn't offer my favor for nothing."

I expected no less from Calista. I find my words.

"It felt like the end…" My throat tightens. "Of everything." My eyes sting with tears, and I swipe them away with the back of my hand.

I recite the prophecy with a shudder, then say, "The first line—time fractures with the stone. Maybe we can stop it."

"Whose prophecy?" Calista asks, her voice casual as she examines her nails—but her emotions are reeling. She's scared, confused, and already calculating her next move.

I'm sure I've trusted the right person. Cunning is practically a synonym for Calista.

Reaching out, I grab her hand, pulling it from her gaze. I lock eyes with her, my voice steady. "You can't hide from me, Calista."

She yanks her hand back, her glare darting to my gloved one like it's something vile. "That's precisely why I stay away."

It's not a lie, there's just more to the story.

But I already know the name of the chapters.

"It was Desdemona's prophecy."

Calista's eyes widen as a small smile pulls at her lips. There's a moment of smug righteousness. Then she tips her head back and laughs. It's not fake, only embellished.

"Oh my gods!" she exclaims, returning her head to its natural position. Beneath her smugness, there's that familiar feeling of inadequacy creeping back into her.

"Her necklace," she finishes, as if it's the obvious conclusion.

My voice is tinged with skepticism as I ask, "What necklace?"

Calista places a hand on her chest, her fingers lightly brushing the fabric. "She wears it…" Her words drop to a whisper as two silhouettes pass the window in the door. Her eyes flick toward them, waiting until they're out of sight before she speaks again. "She wears it under her shirt. A memor, I think."

"No." I shake my head, the prophecy persistently playing inside of me. "It's more than that."

"More than a precious stone?" Her eyes narrow to slits, and her tone drips with mockery.

"It's enough to shatter time…"

Realization slams into me like a pernipe. My breath catches.

Shatter *time*. Memories. Folk magic. A necklace that looks like a memor, worn by Desdemona, the girl whose prophecy will shatter time.

"It's the Memorium," I mutter, my heart slamming against my ribs.

Calista doesn't agree, not one bit.

Each world has one Soul Stone, and the Memorium is from her world, Folkara. It's been missing for ages—not public information, but something I've learned through Calista's complaining. It's said to have powers of glamour, elemental magic, and, more importantly, *memories*.

It can take, or it can give.

It can shatter time.

And the Royals of Folkara want it back desperately.

"Think about it," I say quickly, my mind racing. "How long has the

Memorium been missing?"

"Centuries." Her breath trembles, and mine mirrors hers. "Why would Desdemona have it?"

"To fracture time?" I suggest.

Desdemona isn't just tied to the prophecy.

She could be its catalyst.

Calista huffs, her determination breaking through the fear. "Then we take her necklace," she decides. "And *if* it's the Memorium, I take it home."

Hastily, I agree.

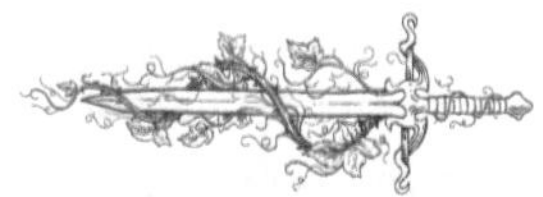

Telling Lucian about the prophecy could help. He's the closest to Desdemona. He's publicly shunned her. He must know something more.

But I won't put Azaire in that kind of trouble—not when the end could be so near.

I won't undo the reason I stole his emotions.

Going to Folkara is a long shot—but I will go. Because, in a way without words, I promised Azaire I would. I promised to carry his belief when I stole a fraction of it.

But before I go to Folkara, I go to the last place that might still have some answers.

I go home.

This time, when I pass by the meadow where Ma was killed, I don't feel it. I feel everything else.

I feel Desdemona.

Like she's under my skin, unraveling me, digging into my core. I know it's her. Or, at the very least, it's her prophecy pressing against me, begging to be seen.

To be answered.

Today, it's unlikely I'll get those answers. Instead, I'm pressing on for the Weapon. This time, completely alone. I won't share what I find with Azaire, and Lucian hardly seems to care these days.

That's fine. Alone is what I know. It's how I've always survived. I've carried every discovery we've made so far, like boulders across a mountain. I'll keep doing so.

I have to.

I knock on the open door to my old home, calling inside, "Pa?"

He appears, smiling, though his weariness betrays him. "Wendy."

He opens the door wider, inviting me inside, but the tension between us lingers. He still carries the residue of our last meeting, and so do I.

What a shame. What a *freeing* shame.

There is no reason to tread carefully.

I enter my old home, the wooden floor groaning with every step I take, as if this house can tell my presence will only bring pain. That I will only rip open old floor boards—old wounds.

I agree with the house's prediction, as if it's a sentient being. As such, I don't waste time.

"Isa and Freyr," I say, staring up at my father. "I need to know what you know."

The words are out. They cannot be unspoken. All the times he told me to let it go, he failed.

Pa rubs the bridge of his nose with a heavy sigh. "This? Again?"

"Yes, again," I reply, my voice firm.

This *always*.

"It isn't your problem," he mutters. His words are barely audible, yet they're heavy enough to hit.

My feet move back before my brain can catch up, disbelief crashing in. *Not my problem?* Who *is* he? My chest tightens, and my hand twitches, ready to jab a finger at him, to scold him for his indifference. But I stop.

I use my words, the way I always have.

"If I know, then it *is* my problem," I say. "You taught me that. *Ma* taught me that. If you know there is evil to come, and you don't stop it, then you are allowing it."

My eyebrows furrow as I watch him carefully.

He shakes his head, not looking at me—not allowing me to meet his eyes. I would feel too much. I would *control* him, he must think.

How little of me he must think.

And yet he knows I'm right. It's the most basic of philosophy—of Ma's lifework. Or what I thought was her lifework.

If we don't stop Folkara, if we don't stop this Weapon, we become complicit.

But he doesn't care—not nearly enough. It feels like I'm talking to Lucian again. It feels like this entire universe only cares about themselves.

But this is my *dad.*

He has to be better than this.

He has to be my pa, who held me in his arms as a child. Pa, who kissed my scars. Pa, who picked me up when I fell.

Whoever is standing in front of me now looks just like him, but he does not feel like him.

So I offer him the same treatment I offered Lucian. I give him pieces of information, praying that it will be enough to clean his lenses.

"Ilyria is involved."

He tenses, and I work hard to keep from following.

It doesn't work. My muscles tighten from heel to spine.

He wasn't aware. Was Ma?

Ilyria is cold. Ruthless. From the outside, we're expected to believe that Folkara runs the show. That Folkara aids the lesser planets, and Ilyria aids themselves. That Ilyria had no skin in the Neptharian War. No say in the treatment of the Nepthenes. But Pa knows what I have learned, what Ma must have learned at Visnatus as well—that Ilyria is the true tyrant.

Folkara has, and always will be, second to Ilyria.

I know Pa—I *feel* him. He wants to keep the peace. He longs for tranquility, like most Eunoia.

That's why he doesn't say a word. He doesn't have a good word to say.

It's a mistake. A Weapon is the opposite of peace.

I think of Azaire, of his gentle hands and strong heart. *He* wants peace too, but he wouldn't forsake the worlds to get it. He wants peace, and he knows that in order to obtain it, one nation cannot have a Weapon capable of destroying the rest.

I meet Pa's gaze, narrowing my eyes. "When did peace become complicity?"

"This isn't complicity—"

I cut him off. "On some level, it is. Ilyria and Folkara have a Weapon that Ma helped build. When does that *not* become, in some way, our responsibility?"

"If Willow were alive, it'd still be hers!" he shouts, his voice cracking as he finally lets go of the reins he's held so tightly, releasing all the control he's struggled to maintain.

The blame—still clinging to him, still faulting me for Ma's death—leaks out, like sap from a tree, tangling in my hair. It isn't as heavy as the weighted guilt I carry, but it's still too much to bear.

Every bone, every muscle, every *cell* in my body collapses. *They can play at forgiveness, but they will never win.* Those were Terran's words, and this is them in action—the final battle. This is when I lose. Because it's all about him—the blame. And it's all about me—the guilt.

We both can feel each other.

What a feeling for a sore soul.

I force myself to stand taller, pulling myself together despite the weight of it all. "And what was she doing to stop this?" I ask. "What's going to happen when Ilyria and Folkara can power the Weapon?"

"It's not our problem," Pa says again, his voice tight with frustration.

I've never felt him so angry, never seen his face so slick with sweat.

I've never been so disappointed in a parent.

"It will be. Tomorrow, next year—at some point they're going to use it." I point a finger in his direction. "If you don't stop it, then you're condoning murder. *Genocide.*"

He doesn't answer, but his eyes hollow, sharp with spite. Is he thinking of Ma or Xander? The murder *I* committed, not him. The accusation fills his eyes before he can even speak. I respond before he can give it a voice.

"I was ten!" I shout. Tears well in my eyes. "If I had any idea what would've happened"—my sobs catch in my throat—"I would've never…"

I would've never touched Xander.

Pa stumbles back, shaking his head. "I would *never.*" His voice shakes. "I would never use that against you."

But he thought it—and we both know it.

He steps forward, wrapping his arms around my shoulders. I sink into him, into the comfort I've missed for so long. I miss him.

Minutes pass—minutes of crying, of being held.

Then he speaks, his voice soft but steady. "Take off your gloves."

I pull back slightly, startled, ready to ask what he means, but before I can, he adds, "I need to see what this means to you."

"But you don't have to touch me." I shake my head. "All you need is eye contact."

He gently cradles my cheek, smiling, though the sadness is evident in his eyes. "We aren't all as powerful as you."

I stutter, my words catching. "But I-I can't—I can't touch you—"

"I'm your father, Wendy." His tone is warm, despite the tension. "Of course you can."

All I hear is that he's *listening*.

If he sees what this means to me—beyond words, beyond explanations—maybe he will understand. Maybe he will *help*.

I pop the button of my gloves, and Pa steps back, nodding. If he sees for himself, he might answer, finally answer. I pull the left glove from my palm.

He's older; he must be stronger. He's my *father*. I am half of him—his power is half of mine. He must know how to deflect.

I pull the right glove from my palm.

Still, I steady my shields around myself, trapping the beast inside me behind bars. Holding my magic back as much as I can.

And I hold out my hands.

Pa grabs them, closes his eyes, and for a moment I only feel… me. For a moment I see it, my goal for the Weapon and all the ways it isn't altruistic. All the ways it's just a little girl calling out for her mom, one last time. A last plea to remember her.

Then it all goes away.

Stripped like the pigment of fabric, bleached by the sun.

I open my eyes, realizing now I'd closed them. He's doing to me what I swore never to do to others. A vow I've broken, and now my empty promises are being repaid.

My hands struggle to break free from his grip.

"Pa." My voice shakes. "Don't. Please don't." I keep tugging, but he won't let go.

He won't let go.

I can't let go.

Don't make me let go.

"I'm sorry, Little Thorn." He meets my gaze. "But from here on out, you feel nothing concerning the Weapon, or your mother's involvement."

He drops my hand.

For a second, I'm angry. Blood boiling.

And then I can't remember why I didn't want to let go.

I can't remember how I felt at all.

The world is a haze, as if a cloud has settled before my eyes. Blankly, I stare at Pa. He hugs me, asking, "How do you feel?"

My gaze drifts past his shoulder, settling on the ashen wood stacked in the fireplace, behind the green couch.

"Nothing," I tell him.

It's not the right answer, but it's the only answer I can figure out.

"You are missing a piece of yourself, but I am still here," the boy says, as if he could feel how lost I've become. As if he wants to be my map.

"What's happened?" I ask him.

"It is time for us to move on."

The walk through my hometown is a daze, like walking through a cloud, but somehow the water clings to me, making each step heavy. Pa leaves me at the community mirror, and I portal back to the academy. It feels like there should be something more I want to do.

I walk to Azaire's room and knock on the door until he opens it. He thinks something is wrong—can *tell* something is wrong—but I don't know what's wrong. Yuki sits on his bed, and I look past him, crashing into Azaire's arms. His body holds me up. I'm this tired?

Azaire pulls away slowly, holding onto my face. My cheeks are in his hands, and his eyes search mine as he asks, "Wendy?"

I feel like a blank slate, waiting to be filled.

"Can you keep holding me?"

Instantly, he pulls me back into his arms. His chin rests on the top of my head, and his hands weave through my hair, gently brushing back and forth. Softly, he kisses the top of my head, and I wrap my arms around his back, pulling him closer.

"Pa took it from me," I say against his chest. "I think I should feel... *something.* Anything. Mad, maybe."

"What did he take?" Azaire's breath tangles in my hair.

"My emotion."

This time, I pull away. I hold onto Azaire's elbows. He's my feet, my oxygen, my gravity. He's why I'm standing here, upright.

Is this how I really feel about him?

I take it all in—the nothingness around me. Perhaps it's a symptom of my getting used to the lack of what I once felt so deeply. I did feel deeply, didn't I?

I can't remember how I felt.

But I remember Azaire. I remember this feeling in my chest, in a different way. I remember how it felt in *his* chest.

This is how it feels in mine?

Like everything.

Like I love him.

"Wendy," the boy warns.

I nearly heed the boy's warning until Azaire snaps me out of it: "He didn't take you."

I let go of his elbow to touch his cheek.

"No one could ever take you," he whispers.

My thumb brushes over his jaw, to his lips. It lingers there.

Azaire looks me in the eye as he calls, "Yuki?"

"Yep." A moment later, Yuki walks past me, and the door closes, leaving Azaire and me alone in the room.

We sit on the bed, and my head falls into Azaire's lap. I look up at him. The room seems brighter than usual. Something feels different.

"I think you're it for me," I whisper. My hand reaches back up to his face.

Then the fear settles in.

The first thing after love.

Fear is the opposite of love. Or it's love intensified. You love someone so much, and it turns to fear.

What if I lose him, like Ma?

What if I hurt him, like Xander?

What if he hurts me, like my brother Terran? Like Pa? Like the universe?

Azaire's hand is on my cheek. His eyes are sparkling. "I think you're everything for me." He smiles. "Not think. Know."

"I know it," I say. "I'm scared because I know it."

He holds my hand in his. "It's all right. There's nothing to be scared of."

"There's everything to fear."

I sit up abruptly. Is this what I felt for Ma, the Weapon, before my father took it from me? This fear? Is this what replaced it? My hands are shaking. I'm shaking.

I love you becomes I'm scared of losing you becomes I've lost you.

"Wendy? Just hold me. Okay?" Azaire reaches for me.

I take off my gloves for the second time today. I put my hands on Azaire. Hold him. I can do that. I can hold him.

I hold him. He is tangible tranquility.

He is peace when I'm in peril. I feel him. All I feel is him.

He is the love I've found in limbo.

There is no need for the boy when I have Azaire.

I breathe him in, every second that I get this touch. He's all I want, all I need. How couldn't I see it sooner? How much time did I waste in fear?

But Azaire's not scared. For once, I'm not either.

My heart beats a little faster. It feels more like a hum. A high. *I love you.*

I dare myself to say it, to spit it out.

I open my eyes again, and he opens his.

Before I can say a thing, Azaire asks, "What happened?"

It's a strange thing to lose feelings. I remember they were once there, yet I cannot feel what they were. I cannot even feel their absence. Something is missing, I'm aware of it, yet I am not searching for the thing gone.

"My dad made me forget my feelings about the Weapon," I admit. *Weapon.* It sounds silly now—like a play on words. I lick my lips and look at the willow tree out his window. "I remember begging him not to, and now I can't remember why I cared at all."

"It's okay." Azaire nods through his disappointment. "That's okay."

"It's not," I say in realization. "Not to you... You want to save people."

I want him to let go of the Weapon, too. He's in a direct line of danger because of it.

He glances down at me, where I rest on his chest. "I want them to have the chance to save themselves."

"All I want is you. You're the only thing I can remember feeling."

My face is in his hands again. His eyes race through mine, searching. "You have more than me, Wendy," he breathes. "Don't let him take it from you."

The sharp pricking of déjà vu peels away at me. It's Azaire's.

But something else is mine…

Prophecy. Desdemona. Calista. Stone.

The end of everything.

Something beyond the Weapon, and perhaps worse.

That's what I have. That's what's there. It's all I can remember feeling. But it still feels faint. Even Ma.

Even her memory.

"The Weapon is gone," I tell him. "I'm never going to care about it again, not the way I used to." And I can't tell him what's left—can't put him in more danger.

"That's all right. Lucian and I will take care of it."

I don't care—I don't *want* him to.

I say, "Okay."

Chapter 20
I Didn't, I Just Wish
I Did

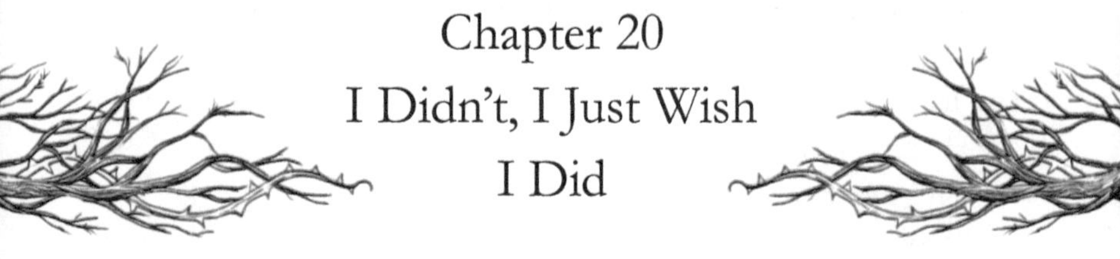

ONE YEAR AGO

We pass Lilac in the hall. She casts her eyes downward, her shoulder tensing. Calista falls into herself, retreating behind a wall of silence. The quiet between them stretches, as if the smallest word might shatter everything, until Lilac is out of sight, and nothing has changed.

There is never a day Calista sees her and is not broken by it. There is never a time the truth does not weigh on her, like an ant trapped beneath a fallen tree.

The hardest part is Lilac feels the same. She carries the same love, but both are kept apart by Royal duties and miscommunications.

If I had someone who loved me the way they love one another, I would do anything I could to be with them. Or I think I would.

I'd like to believe I would.

I turn to Calista, whose gaze remains fixed ahead.

I've thought about it a thousand times over—taking Calista's love away. I've thought of the opposite, too—telling her to give her love back to Lilac. It's on my mind quite often because it's always on hers. I am always feeling the loss of love.

But not in a way as severe as what Calista wants me to do.

I've never *taken* emotion—not permanently, not to that extent. I'm not sure I could, but I'm sure I don't want to. The only person I've manipulated is Ms. Ferner. She's grown better at resisting my power, but I'm still stronger.

I can make her mad, I can make her sad. I can make her punch holes in the wall and scream like a banshee.

I never enjoy a second of it. But I understand why I do it. I understand what usefulness it will one day serve Ilyria and Folkara—the two remaining kingdoms.

Maybe this could be a test. I've never met someone with a stronger will than Calista.

She could be the first person to resist me.

"I'll do it."

Calista's head snaps toward me. Her eyes widen—and I feel it, the sudden surge of hope rising in her chest. It's warm at first, but beneath it runs a chill, sharp as ice. She's glad to let go. Relief floods through her. But underneath that, she's terrified. She doesn't want to want this. Not really. Not yet.

I'll be doing her a favor.

Without a word, she grabs my wrist, pulling me into the nearest empty room.

The door slams shut behind us. The desks are vacant, and the lights are off. The hope that Calista felt moments ago dwindles into fear. What will she be without her love?

We stand in silence as Calista stares at nothing.

But I worry someone will walk into this room before we're finished. Subtly, I do what other Eunoia can only accomplish with a touch. I reach out to her, pushing past her anxiety, gently probing her thoughts, urging her to speak what she's thinking.

"Will I... will I grieve her?" Calista finally asks.

The question stuns me. Is she not already grieving Lilac?

"I don't know." I shake my head. "Probably not."

If I were to do what she asked of me, I don't think she'd feel anything.

I'm not sure I will.

Calista pulls her hands farther from me. She still thinks I need skin-to-skin contact to control her—like all Eunoia do. I've never given her a reason to believe otherwise.

"Will I remember how I felt before we fell in love?" she asks quickly, panicking. "All the years before?"

I look down, staring at my shoes, as if they can answer the questions for me. "They don't teach us about emotional manipulation. It isn't legal here."

"What if I'm not ready?"

"You're scared out of your mind," I tell her, and she hates that I can read her. "But you're hopeful. I don't know why for either."

Calista steps back, sitting at one of the empty desks. Her hands shake against the surface as she holds the wood tightly.

"I don't want to leave Lilac alone in this feeling. I thought I was ready to forget, to let go. But I love her too much to be that selfish." She shakes her head as she looks up at me. "I can't do it, not unless you take her feelings, too."

Her gaze finds mine as I settle into the desk beside her. "You know I can't do that if she doesn't want me to."

"But it'd be better for all of us," Calista says in a rush. "We're being forced to marry each other's *brothers* for gods' sake! There is no point in maintaining our love when it will only break us."

Her desperation cracks her resolve. Her body slowly crumples over the desk. She won't beg me, because she feels she is above it. But she wants to.

She wants to cry and plead.

Slowly, I put my shields back up—the ones I've been practicing with Ms. Ferner. I've hardly mastered them.

They're a fail-safe. Ms. Ferner fears I could override someone's mind even *without* touching them—that I could kill with a verbal command and eye contact.

The shields are meant to contain me. To keep my powers behind their walls.

My gloved fingers brush her shoulder. "Let me try to help you first."

Calista shakes her head, hesitant, but her gaze meets mine. It's all I need to convince her of anything I please.

Anything at all.

"Do you want this?" I ask.

"Yes."

With her gaze locked on mine, I say, "Tell Lilac how you feel."

I know what this will cost me. I'll lose Calista. If she returns to Lilac and her old friends, I'll be forgotten, a memory of a girl she used to know.

But I've felt her heartbreak everyday. I've felt Lilac's confusion, and this is the one thing I can do to change that.

Calista gasps, choking on a breath as she tries to look away—but can't.

She's too late. Her mind is already mine to mold. I don't need to say anything more to convince her, but I do.

"You want to try to find a way to make your love work." I release her shoulders.

Her eyes flash green for an instant before returning to their usual brown. Her pupils are still wide. She'll need time to adjust, before she realizes what I've done. But for now, Calista exhales, settling back into herself.

And that's it.

Chapter 21
Hills to Die On

Now

The thought of going to class leaves me hollow. Most thoughts do now, without what I once held so deeply.

Sometimes there is a weight in my hands, but when I look, I'm not carrying anything.

Somehow, in some way, I worry this is what Azaire feels. I didn't take from him like Pa took from me, but I'm the reason he no longer wants to go to Folkara.

I took something from him, however small.

It doesn't feel so bad. The Weapon is inconsequential.

As time passes, I begin to remember what the weight in my arms is. I remember I'm carrying something new, something to get used to.

The prophecy.

When I visit the kitchen for breakfast, there's a new kind of emotion in me.

Deadlier than hope, but almost its kin.

Then Eudora gives me a sneaky smile.

I step toward her, resting my elbows on the counter. With a smile back, I ask, "You got it?"

"Of course I got it," she replies, her tone playful. With a groan, she bends down beneath the counter, then stands up holding a brown bag. "It was mighty hard, but I found everything you asked for."

"Oh, Eudora," I breathe, grabbing the bag when she offers it to me. "Thank you so much."

"It's a nice thing you're doing. Whatever Nepenthe it's for, I doubt they felt any kindness since they got here. This isn't a universe built for them."

I sigh. "It doesn't seem like it's a universe built for anyone."

Eudora smirks. "Only the richest Lyrians and Folk get the good stuff." Her tone is light, but her expression turns serious as she continues, "The rest of us get mud."

"Scraps," I add.

"Shit," she finishes.

"Yeah," I agree, "Shit."

Anger fills me—a budding desire to do something impossible.

I swallow it.

"Thanks again." I hold up the bag.

"A little kindness goes a long way." Eudora smiles. "Thank *you*. It's your generation that's going to mend our relationship with the Nepenthes."

I nod, offering Eudora one last smile before I leave the kitchen.

I don't go to class. Instead, I find myself retreating back to Azaire's room. He's still tangled in bed.

His eyes lift to meet mine the moment I enter.

There's something in the way he looks at me—something I could sense, even if I didn't already feel it.

He looks at me like I am relief incarnate. As if every time I leave, he's scared I'll be gone forever.

Then he smiles. An irreplaceable grin.

I feel it in my heart.

"I'm back," I whisper.

"I wish you never left."

I set my bag by the door—with the soup ingredients. I decide to save them for the right time. Maybe I'll surprise Azaire between classes, the way he did with me. Instead of the lunar lake, I'll take him into the woods, to the place where we met during the party.

Then I climb into his bed, falling on my stomach before burying my head into Azaire's chest.

"Me too," I mutter. "I wish I could stay here forever. I like your arms."

"My arms like you."

"Oh really?"

"You're their favorite thing to hold."

I laugh, and it's ridiculous. "Oh, shut up."

Azaire's hand rests on my cheek, his thumb scraping against my skin. "I'm not kidding. You're my favorite thing in this universe."

I shake my head. "Don't lie to me."

I'm afraid he isn't.

"Wendy Estridon." His voice drops low, my name a caress on his lips. "I know you better than that."

My breath catches in my throat. "And I know you aren't lying."

He touches his nose to mine. "I know."

I move forward, filling the gap between us and resting my lips on his. The kiss is gentle, the way he always is at first. As if, even after all this time together, he's still trying to know me.

In every sense. Every flavor, every way.

As if he could find the answers in my lips—learn me inside out.

His hands graze down the sides of my body, resting on my hips. His grip turns firm, and he pulls me against him. We are chest-to-chest.

We are skin-to-skin.

I wrap a leg over his, pulling him even closer.

He holds my hip tighter.

I hold his face.

"Azaire Wenejad." I trace his jaw. "You are my favorite thing, too."

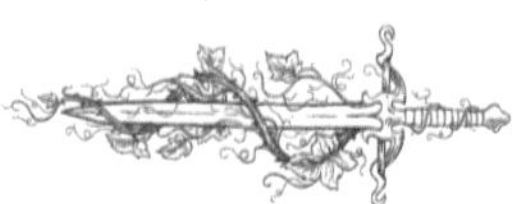

We lie in bed for most of the morning. I'm content to stay here forever, but Azaire rises, putting on his academy uniform.

"You already missed first period," I say. "Why not go for double?"

My smile quickly fades. The humor quickly stanched from my bones.

With his back turned to me, Azaire says, "I… have to go to Ms. Ferner's class."

I jolt upright. "Again?"

He turns to me, nodding with a quiet sadness in his eyes. "Someone has to make you a healer."

I rise to my feet. "Mending intentionally harmed people is not the definition of a healer."

A small smile tugs at his lips. "There's that mind of yours."

"No. We're not going."

"You might not be," Azaire sighs. "But I have to." He throws his bag across his shoulder.

Taking one long stride toward him, I grab the bag's strap.

"Why? Why don't we do something—take a stand?"

"A stand with one person isn't much of one at all."

"But—"

"It'd just be rebellion—not revolution," he says, reaching for my hand.

He holds it tightly. His touch stills my shaking head. All my disagreement suddenly understands him. He'll get there, I know he will. He'll change the world.

But not today.

"I don't want you to be there." His thumb strokes the back of my hand. "To have to feel it—"

"I don't want to risk someone hurting you *more*." I turn and grab my academy coat.

"I can take it."

"I can't," I say, grabbing his hand once more and walking to the door.

Together, we walk to class, and when I see Ms. Ferner, it's hard not to give her the evil eye. This isn't her fault. These volunteer groups aren't her doing. But she's complicit.

That's half the evil.

She tells the class we'll be hiking beyond the school's garden, searching for poisonous herbs. It's a double lesson—identifying plants and learning to heal poison.

The Nepenthes have to ingest what we find.

When she's done, the class and the "volunteers" quickly rise, filing out the door and beginning the hike. Some of the students chat as we walk, but I can't find any words.

It's only the Eunoia who speak.

The Nepenthes are all dejected, for obvious reasons.

We're far in the woods now, and as I pass a poisonous hemlock, I avert my gaze. Whatever I collect, I'll have to give to Azaire. With every step and every student who picks their poison, I pretend not to see anything.

But Azaire's eyes rest somewhere in the distance, over my shoulder and past the foliage.

I watch him intently. He's determined. There's something he wants to do, and he's going to do it. It's a nice feeling from him. Uncommon.

But I invite it.

He is the person I enjoy feeling the most.

Azaire walks past me, and for a silent moment, I hope he isn't reaching for a plant of his choosing. I'm sure he knows what I'm doing—delaying the inevitable—and I don't want him to feel that he *has* to do this. Even though he does.

When Azaire returns, he stands inches from my face. His eyes hold a softness that rivals the harshness of the day. Slowly, he reaches out and tucks my hair behind my ear, then gently places a delicate stem there. The nature brushes against my skin, and his closeness warms me.

"What is it?" I ask with a laugh, letting out a breath of relief. We only have a few more minutes before I have to harm him.

Azaire meets my gaze, his own glistening, bright, hopeful. As if he doesn't even mind the poisoning, so long as he gets to do it with me.

"A violet," he murmurs. "It brings out your eyes."

For a moment, I falter. And when I recover my motor functions, I raise a hand to my ear, pulling the flower away from my skin. I hold it between my gloved fingers, twisting the stem and looking at the pollen.

I see Ma in the flower. The way she'd cover one of her eyes with a violet, just like this one, then tuck it behind my ear with a kiss on my forehead.

I smell her as I hold it close to my nose.

Glancing up at Azaire, my eyebrows knit together—tears close to spilling.

"How did you know?" I ask, my voice barely above a whisper.

He smiles but shakes his head. "Know what?"

I choke on my words, the feeling tightening in my chest. There's no reason he would know that this is Ma's flower. It's just one example of how Azaire understands me like no one else can.

"Violets were my ma's favorite," I finally manage to say.

His shoulders lift slightly, like he's trying to give me space. "I didn't know." There's a soft sadness in his tone that makes me feel like maybe he *does* know, in some way.

Not about the flowers—but about this feeling.

"My mistake." My voice drops, and I shrink back slightly. Have I crossed an invisible line? Am I overbearing, have I said too much?

The quiet between us is heavy.

But Azaire doesn't think so.

"No," he says. "It isn't a mistake at all." A soft pause, then, "How did she die?"

His eyes meet mine with an earnestness that makes my chest tighten. Every word he speaks is laden with patience. He genuinely wants to know, wants to help.

Azaire knows that there are no easy deaths—not for kids like us. No neat, simple stories. Oddly, he wants to make me feel less alone in this moment.

"I'm sorry," he blurts out when I don't answer, his tone soft with regret. "If you don't want to tell me—"

"She was killed." My gaze moves on the ground, unable to meet his eyes. "By a pernipe. I should have saved her, but I-I couldn't."

Azaire stops walking, and the group around us passes by. So many of the Eunoia twist their poisonous herbs between their fingers, as if they're nothing more than pretty flowers.

As we stand still, Azaire searches for something to say that will adequately display his sorrow. I can already feel it rolling off him like the mist from a wave, as if he's trying to carry a part of the burden with me.

"It's okay," I mutter, shaking my head. "It's been a long time, so…"

Azaire gently takes my hand, and I nearly choke. It's strange how fully he seems to understand. "The loss never goes away."

"Yeah," I choke out. "But some days are easier to pretend than others."

He stands there, understanding and holding my hand. Hands that —in a few moments from now—will feed him poison and be forced to heal him.

"You know it's not your fault, right?"

I pull my hand away, and my fingers suddenly feel cold without his touch. "I don't see the relevance."

"You said you tried to save her but couldn't." Azaire's voice drops even lower, as though he's treading carefully through my pain. "I'm asking, do you think that it was your fault?"

I open my mouth, expecting words to come out. All that escapes me is a small gasp. I stare at him, confused, because he feels as if he is speaking of fact and not fiction. As if he *knows*.

But he wasn't there when Ma died. He wasn't a stubborn fourteen-year-old who thought he could fight. His mother didn't take the blow that ended her life to save him.

Then, Azaire adds, "It's normal to have survivor's guilt—"

"I don't *have* survivor's guilt," I spit, the words sharper than I mean them to be. "I just have guilt."

Once the words have left my mouth, I catch my breath. The truth of it lingers, worse so the intention.

I didn't mean for the words to come out so harshly.

I didn't mean for them to come out at all.

But Azaire doesn't back away from my sting. Instead, he whispers, "I know what it's like—"

"How could you possibly know what it's like for me?" I cut him off, the words burning more than just my tongue. They burn Azaire, too. Because *I* know what it's like for him—I know what it's like for everybody.

But nobody knows what it's like for me.

Quickly, Azaire grabs my hand, pulling me aside from the group— some of whom are staring back at us. All of whom are judging.

From the back of the line, Ms. Ferner meets my gaze, a dangerous glint in hers.

"I don't need a lesson in grief." My free fingers absently twirl the stem of the violet as I stare at my retreating classmates.

Azaire's voice is quiet, steady, wholly consoling. "I'm not giving you one."

"Fair." I don't look at him. Unprepared to feel the fullness of him.

But I have no choice when his next words slip past his lips and into my ears.

"I killed my parents."

At first, everything inside me stops. I want to step back, to put distance between us, to run from the weight of those words. My body tenses, every instinct screaming at me to retreat.

But there it is—the childhood home burning and the match in my hand. In *his* hand.

I don't step back. I can't. I know Azaire well enough to know there's more. A reason he's telling me this.

I ask the same question he asked me. "How?"

All Azaire does is point at his beanie.

I take a deep breath.

His snakes—that *I* can see—killed his parents.

"They grew fast," he mutters. It takes me by surprise, how willing he is to share this story. "Out of nowhere, really. Um… One day, during the Neptharian War, my mom, she came to check on me and turned to stone. I screamed." He shrugs. "I shouldn't have. Dad came in." He breathes. "Then he died, too."

"Oh my gods." A chill runs over my skin. "How did you—how old were you?"

"I barely survived." He answers the question I was too scared to ask. "I was six. I was alone an entire day before the soldiers—the Folk —came rushing in. They looked at me, and they all died, too. After that I wrote a note on the door. It said, '*Hungry. I keep turning them to stone, but I need food.*' Those words never left my mind. I think they were the first I ever wrote… But the next group of soldiers thought it was a joke, and they came in with swords ready. The next time… I left the note *on* the stone bodies.

"The soldiers threw me a rag to wrap around my head. I'd nearly starved to death by that point, I think my body started consuming itself to survive. I don't even remember how I wrapped the rag.

"The soldiers carried me out, brought me to Ilyria first, I think. They decided that my power was too *dangerous* to be left in the wild. They brought me to Visnatus."

I shake my head, but he continues.

"Everyone has their shit, Wendy. But things like this… they're not our fault. I didn't know my snakes would kill; you didn't know a pernipe was coming."

Saying anything in the wake of his tragedy feels wrong. Despite wanting to argue against him—that maybe I didn't know the pernipe was coming, but I should have *stopped* it—I take his hand, and I put the violet inside of it.

Azaire shakes his head. "It's for you."

"I want you to have it." I close his hand around the flower. "I want you to have a piece of the kindness you offer me."

Azaire pauses, his eyes lingering on the flower, then meeting mine. "It isn't kindness." His eyes soften, his breath catching for a moment. "It's love."

"Wendy!" my classmate calls.

I clear my throat, trying to look into Azaire's eyes for as long as I can before I glance up. The girl holds a white flower between her fingers. The hemlock I avoided earlier. One of the deadliest plants in the woods. "I have extra for you."

The worst part is that she thinks she's helping.

I try to speak, but all I do is stutter. "Um…" I clear my throat. "Can you hold it, for a moment? It's hard to clean the hemlock residue from my gloves." I hold up my hands with a shrug.

She nods, walking back toward the group of students.

Azaire and I follow, and the moment I step between the people sitting on the ground, their judgements fill me. They've already made assumptions about Azaire and me, and there's more than a touch of contempt.

My classmate hands the hemlock to Azaire—hands the *abuse* to the *victim*—and thinks nothing of it. He smiles at her, as if she's done him a favor.

She thinks she has.

I sit with Azaire, unbuttoning my gloves. My hands shake with fear. I didn't want it to come to this. I don't want to feed the boy I love poison.

As I peel the gloves from my hands, my breath shudders.

"Hey." Azaire wraps both of his hands over mine. "Eyes on me, remember?"

I look away from our hands, at him.

"That's good," he says.

I take a deep breath, nodding, and he releases my hands. I'm still shaking as Azaire drops the hemlock in the mortar. I raise the pestle, crushing the plant and mixing it with water.

Gently, I hold my hand under Azaire's chin and let the poison drip down his throat.

As we walk back to academy, Azaire healed—but perhaps not healthy —and next to me, Ms. Ferner steps beside me.

"We need to talk," she says ominously.

I glance at her, slowing down my pace to meet hers, but she continues to look ahead. I glance at my feet, keeping my head down with every step.

She doesn't leave my side.

There are many things Ms. Ferner might want to say to me. We used to see each other every day, but now there's a distance between us. A gap where familiarity used to live.

Ms. Ferner has nearly slowed to a complete stop, and Azaire meets my gaze. I nod, gesturing toward the academy, and he walks with the rest of the class. They all quickly disappear between the walls.

Neither of us says a thing for a while. We walk at a snail's pace to the building, until Ms. Ferner tries to fill the gap between us.

"You were quick today," she says.

I was.

I healed Azaire before the poison even made him puke—far more than any of my classmates can say.

It's hardly a compliment, but that's how Ms. Ferner gives them. "Thanks."

Her tone turns sharp. "I saw him touch you."

I take a breath, my torso stiffening. *That's* what this is about, and she clearly doesn't want to waste time.

"How?" Ms. Ferner asks.

I shake my head, the truth catching in my throat. There's no point in lying. She'd recognize it immediately. "I don't know."

Ms. Ferner glances over her shoulder, her eyes narrowing with suspicion. "Did you do something to him?"

"*Do* something to him?" I repeat her question with incredulity. "Wh-what could I possibly do to be able to touch him?"

The question stirs through my mind. What did I *do* to him. Can I not have this one thing? This one relief from my life? Do I have to be controlling or manipulating because of my magic?

Can I not touch a person and be touched in return?

"I don't know," Ms. Ferner says sternly. "That's why I'm asking you."

My voice is more broken than I intend as I say, "I did nothing to him."

Ms. Ferner stares at me, silent. My panic picks up, my breathing following closely behind. I'm staring at the academy, so close and somehow still too far, as she says, "I have to alert the academy."

I stop in my tracks, turning in her direction.

Tell the academy? She must know what that will mean for Azaire —what they'll do to him.

"Don't," I whisper. "Please, don't."

"Ms. Estridon—"

"He's already one of their guineapigs. You *know* that. You'll only make it worse."

Ms. Ferner doesn't answer me; she only stares. I take a step closer, not sure what I'm going to do but knowing I need to be prepared.

"We've spent a lot of time together," I remind her. "On some level, you care for me. I feel it. And I care for him. You can't—" My breath shakes. "Please don't do this to him."

For a moment, Ms. Ferner looks truly saddened, but I can feel, deep down, that my words haven't changed her mind.

I take another step closer.

"You have unusual powers, Wendy," she reprimands. "The best way to make strides forward is to study them."

I meet her gaze, one final time, one last bout of begging. "Please."

Her face remains stiff. Her mind unchanged.

My hands find her shoulders before I realize I've moved. It's when my nails dig into her skin, pulling blood and keeping her in place, that I know my intentions.

"You want to stand still."

Her eyes glaze over, as if for a moment, she's gone entirely blind.

She freezes, still as a statue.

There's only one thing I can think to command. One set of words that will keep Azaire safe—no matter how much they hurt, no matter the cost. She was my mentor, my only guide for so long. The one who showed me my magic, the one who truly cared enough to help.

I cared for her in the same way she cared for me. Stubborn and unwilling.

But I tear that all away.

"You don't care about my powers." I breathe deeply, trying to steady myself amidst the shift in her emotion.

Her interest in my magic drains away—her interest in me. It's hard to stand, losing what has been a constant for so long.

She's always cared—perhaps more than I once knew because the absence of it makes me hollow.

I've lost Ma, Pa, and now her.

It shatters me to pieces, watching as she lets me go against her will.

Ms. Ferner's eyes stay open wide as I let go of her shoulders. For a moment, I wonder if I've killed her—overrode her mind the way she feared I someday would. Then, I slip away, moving quickly back toward the academy.

Chapter 22
The Best I Never Had

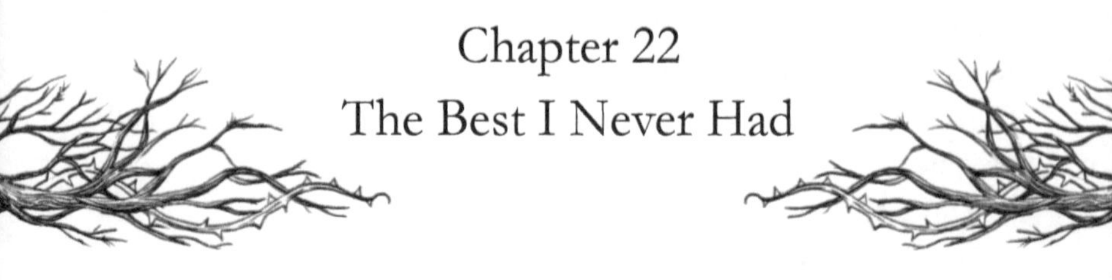

I shouldn't have done it. I shouldn't have done it. I shouldn't have done it.

What if I killed her or did some other irreparable damage?

But… what if the same thing happened to Azaire because of her? What if I *saved* him?

I go to Azaire's next class. Perhaps it's guilt, or maybe I need a kind hand, but I wait at the door until he sees me. Immediately, he rises. He doesn't even think twice before walking to me.

When he approaches, I wrap my arms around him. I want to tell him what I did to Ms. Ferner. Yet when he asks, "What's wrong?" those words don't slip out of me.

"I was worried about you," I say instead. "The poison."

I grip his neck tighter, unsure why I'm lying.

"I'm okay." His breath slips through my hair.

I pull back, holding his waist as I look up at him. "Can we go back to your suite?"

He answers instantly, his eyes never leaving mine. "Of course."

We walk together, hands intertwined. My thoughts race past Ms. Ferner. Is she okay? Should I be alerting someone that she might be hurt?

When the door to Azaire's room closes, I press my lips to his. His hand rises up the back of my neck, his fingers tangling in my hair before both hands cup my jaw. His forehead rests against mine, and slowly, he pulls away.

"I'm okay," he whispers again.

"So am I."

I grab the back of his neck, pulling him to me. All I want is to lose myself in his touch—the only touch.

Azaire kisses me back, ravenously, indulgently. For once, he isn't gentle, as if he understands that gentleness is the last thing I want.

Greedily, I reach my hands up the back of his neck, tugging his beanie off. He gasps, worried for a moment——a trained reaction.

Then he settles down.

I watch him. Watch his snakes, watch him in his fullness. I *want* to see him.

Slowly, he trails the backs of his hands down my arms. Stopping at my wrists, he unbuttons my gloves with reverence. As if he's unshrouding a constellation. A deity in the sky, pulling down the stars.

His fingers linger, outlining the shape of my hand. He glances up at me, eyes searching—for permission, for understanding.

I offer it to him. I want him—the same way he wants me. The way I've never been allowed to have anyone. And yet happily, wholeheartedly, he gives himself to me, everything he has. Knowing my past, knowing my story, it doesn't stop him.

I want to return the favor.

The gloves slide off completely.

It's rare to feel the air on my skin—the same way it's rare for him to feel it on his snakes.

He lifts my hand to his mouth, eyes never leaving mine, and kisses my fingers one by one.

Every finger that's capable of killing meets his lips.

Then his hands rise, settling on my waist. With urgency, he tugs me back into him. My lips fall on his with a deep sigh. I trail kisses down his neck, stopping at the hem of his shirt. I reach for it, tugging it over his head.

Azaire looks at me like I've done something impossible.

Then his hands come to the bottom of my shirt, tearing it from my body, too.

Both of us take a step back, my eyes searching every inch of him. Him seeing all of me.

When I look up, his gaze meets mine. Slowly, I reach behind my back, unclasping my bra and letting it fall to the floor.

Something in his gaze shifts. He closes the distance between us in a single step, one arm slipping around my back, holding me upright as he leans in. My spine arches as his mouth finds mine.

Ungracefully, I fumble with the button of his pants, failing to undo them multiple times. Azaire leans back, his gaze soft as our laughter mingles.

Then, softly, he asks, "Are you sure?"

I nod. "Positive."

I pull his lips back to mine as he unbuttons his pants.

There's a knock on Azaire's door, and I ignore it, blissfully ignorant in his arms.

He holds me tighter, pulling my back against his chest, and I lean into it—as much as I can.

But Desdemona's feelings grate at my skin, tearing me apart. *Desperation.*

"Wendy?" Her voice is muffled through the door, and I sit up.

Azaire's hand rests on my thigh as I wrap his jacket around my torso. "One moment!" I call through the door.

"Is that Desdemona?" Azaire asks.

"Yeah," I say, a little breathless, while I tug my pants over my hips. "I think."

I know.

"Okay." The word is light on his tongue, but it lands heavy in my chest.

The surface is calm, almost careless, but beneath it, I feel the pull. He feels he owes her something.

I turn to him, meeting his gaze. "What is it?"

"Lucian," is all he says at first. "He thinks she's connected to the monster attacks."

I narrow my eyes at Azaire. "What do *you* think?"

He shrugs. "I think Lucian is intelligent but sometimes shortsighted."

"Sounds about right." I nod, leaning down and kissing his cheek. "I'll see you tomorrow?"

Azaire smiles, nodding once. "Tomorrow."

Then I'm out the door.

Desdemona stands at the entrance to Azaire's room, ready to knock again when I walk past her.

"Follow me," I mutter, walking fast.

Her mentioning the prophecy in front of anyone in this suite is a risk I can't take.

This is between me, her, and Calista.

Desdemona follows, her fear trailing close behind. But beneath it, something else pulses. It flickers at the edge of my senses, a close hum, like a bee brushing past my ear. It crawls over my skin but remains just out of reach.

I lead her to my favorite corner of the garden, tucked between the academy's outer walls and the edge of the woods. It's a mostly desolate place. In all my years at the academy, I've never seen another student here.

There are no windows on these academy walls—no prying eyes from the inside can peek out. In the center, the statue of Zola stands, a scale balanced in one hand while the roots of a tree coil around her other arm, anchoring her to nature.

It's quiet here. Secluded. Grounded. All the reasons this corner feels like mine.

I sit, and Desdemona mimics my movements, looking at me expectantly.

I already know what she wants.

The memory of the prophecy rushes through me like ice trapped beneath my skin, in my veins. I shudder. It either belongs to Desdemona, or she is the catalyst that will make it happen. Either way, the end of the universe will be on her hands.

Unless I can stop it.

I hold my hand behind my back, trying to fight the idea. Torn between resistance and resolve.

The thought is dark in my mind. Like a cloud, coming to take away the sun.

Still, I unbutton my gloves. Slowly, at first, like I'm hoping hesitation will stop me.

A part of me knew. From the moment I channeled the prophecy, I felt it settle in my bones like a verdict. This is the way to stop it.

The only way.

All paths must end with her blood on my hands.

"So much for fighting," the boy mutters.

"What do you want?" I ask, my tone gentle. There's only so much I can feel guilty for, and I won't add being mean to the boy to the list today.

"I want to make you whole." I ignore him, and he adds, *"You think accidental death stings, but deliberate killing stains."*

I wipe him away like an ink blot. He only smears, sitting at the corners of my mind, watching.

I pull my gloves completely off, knowing he can see.

"I felt something when I channeled it," I tell Desdemona, referring to her prophecy. The reason she wanted to speak to me. "I can share it with you."

I hold out my bare hands.

She's severely undereducated.

She takes hold of my hands immediately.

If I were any other Eunoia, this would be enough to control her emotion. But for me, this is enough to kill.

I don't blame her. She's from the septic. She doesn't know any better. She likely has no idea what the Eunoia can do. What *I* can do.

Perhaps I'll cut the prophecy down before it grows roots.

All I have to do is hold her. If I wanted, I could push my emotions into Desdemona. It would be more than enough to fry her brain, like I did to Xander.

It's his memory that holds me back—the little bit of Xander that lives in the boy. He keeps me from deliberately killing Desdemona.

Instead, I wait for my touch to take its natural course.

Her skin on mine, her feeling this prophecy in its entirety, it has to be enough to kill her. It should be.

I begin to share the prophecy with her.

The first part is mind-splitting agony—becoming someone else involuntarily. Perhaps it's what Xander felt when my emotions overrode his own. The next part is agonizing loneliness—not much different from my past four years.

It's the end that feels like the end. *When the cracks in the universe di-*

vide. Death, so much of it. How it felt when Ma died, times thousands.

I wait for the breath to escape Desdemona—for her to keel over.

It never comes.

She pulls her hands from mine when the prophecy ends, alive and well. One part of me breathes a sigh of relief. The other feels like it was a job not well done.

"Don't take this path," the boy warns. *"It's stained in black."*

"What the fuck was that?" Desdemona's voice trembles, her hands held out before her, shaking more violently than mine.

"Your prophecy." My gaze follows the natural curve of her collarbone. Beneath her shirt, the faint outline of a necklace presses against her skin—just like Calista said.

The bee buzzing in my ear intensifies, as if it's turned human and started screaming.

"It's what I felt when I channeled it," I say, voice low as I fixate on that necklace.

There's something off about it. About her. The agony, the fear, everything she always feels is twisted beneath the surface, tangled with that necklace. It's as if a shard of her pain is lodged there, buried in the stone.

Her claws start to flex as I focus on the necklace. Her fear makes sense now. The stone isn't just a trinket—it's a cage holding pieces of her soul. The lines between her and that necklace blur until I don't know where one ends and the other begins.

But the stone has to be the Memorium, and something bad has happened to it. Something has broken.

It feels like darkness incarnate.

"And you can just pull up that feeling, whenever you want? Give it to someone else?" Desdemona asks, and I glance up, meeting her gaze.

It's a confusing sight at first. I swear I'd seen a million images of her in that necklace—but it was only feeling that I saw.

I take a breath, remembering what she asked.

Sharing emotion is the least of what I can do. But I don't say that. Truthfully, I'm slightly in awe that she survived. I frown at the thought. I didn't do enough.

I could've done so much worse.

But what if I don't have to kill *her?* What if the darkness lies in that necklace?

"Pretty much," I answer.

Desdemona frowns. "You *feel* it?"

"I just did."

Remorse. She feels remorse.

She feels remorse for me trying to kill her.

I quickly brush the thought aside. Maybe there's a reason I failed.

"I'm sorry," Desdemona croaks.

The strangest thing is that she *means* it. Her sorrow buds in my chest, yet I prefer it over her fear. It's an easier emotion to swallow.

"I'm surprised you weren't found out sooner," I say, and I truly mean it. She speaks like someone from the septic. "No one here says sorry."

Desdemona raises an eyebrow. "Well, I am."

"She's one of the firsts," the boy says. *"One of the firsts, and you tried to kill her."*

"Shut up."

"You need me."

"It's fine," I tell Desdemona. The boy is right, as he usually is. The guilt is already here. "I've felt worse."

Desdemona's mouth opens slightly, her eyebrows jumping up her forehead. "What could be worse than that?"

Ma flashes before my eyes, half of her body in the ground.

"The real thing," I say my voice far—numb. I glance at Desdemona's necklace once more, searching for any way to change the topic. "What stone do you wear?"

For a moment, Desdemona stares at me. Her eyes narrow, angry. As if all the progress I just made, all the remorse she felt, is being wiped away with every word that comes out of my mouth.

"It was my mom's," Desdemona says. It's not a lie. Nor is it the whole truth. There's something she's not saying.

"Why do you wear it under your shirt?"

I feel her sorrow dissipate. So quickly, too.

"To keep it safe." Desdemona's hand reaches for the outline, anger emanating from her movement. "It's the last piece I have of her."

Not a lie, not the whole truth. She's smarter than I thought.

"Is it the Memorium?"

Desdemona smiles, somehow finding humor in this. "You do know I'm from the septic, right?"

"Answer the question." Pressure builds behind my eyes. Power surges into my hands.

"No, it's not the Memorium."

Desdemona laughs a little, and she's not scared of the threat of my glowing eyes—my magic. I could pull the truth from her with a thought. Is it possible she's not hiding anything? The theory would hold weight if it weren't for the power that builds in her. A tide reaching for the shore.

It feels different than an ordinary Fire Folk. Hot enough that the feeling alone could burn me if I let myself dive into it.

"We don't get to keep the precious stones; we only mine them," she spits with an edge to her tone. A clench to her jaw.

"The Memorium is a Soul Stone."

Desdemona sneers as she replies, "All the more reason I can't get my grubby hands on it."

Gods, I've annoyed her.

The pressure behind my eyes begins to burn—*her* burn, her power pressing against me. As if she wants to fight me for the crime of being annoying.

Desdemona stands, turning to walk away as she says, "Thanks for showing me the rest of the prophecy."

But she's not very thankful. How could she be?

It's awful.

Facing the academy, she stops midstep, turning to look into the woods. Fear floods her veins like air—lethally.

"What is it?" I ask.

Desdemona doesn't turn toward me. Her gaze remains fixed on the distant trees, waiting for something to emerge.

I sit up. What could she possibly be waiting for?

"You should go," she mutters.

The mental strain is equivalent to a sword fight. She's sparring with something in the woods—something I can't feel or see—and she's desperate for me not to sense it.

Her desperation goes to waste.

The trees rustle, and I flinch. Dark gray shadows cast upon the leaves.

"What's out there?"

"Nothing," she lies.

"It's certainly something, I can *feel* you."

With her gaze settled in the distance, Desdemona shakes her head.

For good reason, too. Because a dark gray cloud of smoke hovers towards us.

Chapter 23
Queen Takes Queen

I'm watching Desdemona; she's watching the monster drift toward us. A giant creature with four elongated limbs and a tail dragging along the ground. Its body billows like smoke, flickering between transparency and solidity—unreal, then real. It towers over Desdemona by at least two heads, staring down at her with unreadable intent.

If there was somebody I *could* tell this to, they'd never believe me. Because I swear to the gods, Desdemona is communicating with the monster. Her eyes are locked with its hollow, swirling gaze—somewhere beneath the darkness it's shrouded in—as though she's listening to some silent, unspeakable sound.

The kapha reaches for her, its movements slow, almost tender, like it's afraid to startle her.

Like they're on the same team.

There's no way I can fight both a Fire Folk *and* a kapha.

I take a deep breath, calling to the nearest tree. I feel the thorns pricking through my skin; the very possibility of them haunts me. I push past the sharp sting of fear, reaching for the tree with an arm that exists only in my mind—and stretching it far beyond my shoulder would ever let it go.

The air hums, wrapping itself around my senses as my feet solidify beneath me. The power is overwhelming, grounding me, rooting me so deep into the world. I've become part of the very trunk itself. With a heavy sweep of my arm, the branches surge forward, curling tightly around the kapha's four arms.

With a tired heart, I summon another tree, its bark groaning as it twists upward from the ground. It's a lethargic thing, the branches stretching wide after being rooted down for so long—like it's no different than a child waking from a long night's rest. My limbs feel nimble, as if I, too, have been stationary for centuries. But despite its groans of protest, the tree heeds my commands. Branches wind around the monster's torso, pulling tighter than the last, holding the kapha still.

Then, almost instinctively, another one of my trees begins to stretch toward Desdemona. I hesitate—I haven't decided what I'll do with her yet.

Before I can, Desdemona turns to face me.

"Thanks," she mutters, breathing heavily as the kapha wails behind her. Its loose limbs yank and twist against the bark of my tree, but they don't break. Not yet. The tree holds steadily onto life.

Though I fear the monster is getting close. The breakage brews in my bones. The carnage curls in my stomach.

The pain of the tree I brought to life.

"We need to drain its blood," I say, hoping—praying—that killing the kapha is truly what Desdemona intends.

To my relief, she nods. I can't shake the worry that it's just for show.

"Go to Leiholan," she tells me.

For a moment, my worries fade, replaced by a rush of excitement at the thought of stepping into the combat room.

But that excitement is fleeting.

Behind Desdemona, I hear it—the sickening crack. The kapha breaks through the barrier of bark, its smoke-like limbs tearing free. I feel the tree's agony as if it's my own, a sharp, jagged pain ripping me apart.

Like a knife plunging in my stomach and yanking down, tearing my torso in two.

The kapha charges, legs dangling above the ground as four arms reach toward me. Its movements are faster now, more focused, and yet again I wonder: what does it want?

Because it didn't attack Desdemona. It talked to her.

"Go!" she shouts.

I run, nearly tripping on overgrown roots. The pain of the tree buds in my torso. But my curiosity for Desdemona is more ferocious than any ache.

Once I turn the corner, I lean against the academy wall, waiting for the pain to pass, but more importantly, searching for an answer.

I close my eyes, my gaze swiveling behind my eyelids. There are so many emotions, materializing as spots of light, overtaking the darkness. But one is certain: Desdemona feels a familiarity with this creature—an interest in the monster.

When I open my eyes, I stare into the garden before me. The kapha has no intention to hunt me—it hardly remembers my existence. The only question now is: do I *want* to go back there? If the kapha isn't going to hurt Desdemona, then she doesn't need me.

But I don't *know* it isn't going to hurt her.

And yet, if it does, that's a problem solved—a prophecy avoided.

If it doesn't, and she survives this, then I may never know what the kapha wants from her.

The garden blurs into a watercolor mess. I think I understand why. Despite my attempts at murder, I know if Desdemona dies out there, I will be guilty.

I will be complicit.

It's the answer I asked of the boy not that long ago. It shouldn't matter, but it means the entire world to me.

If my actions lead to a death, does that make me the killer?

Yes.

Yes, yes, yes.

It would.

It does.

I want to know what the kapha wants.

I want to hold onto some idea of innocence, I think.

Running again, my shoes skid on the marble floor when I reach the academy. As I enter the combat room, Leiholan sits in the corner drinking, and my eyes land on the display of weapons in the back.

His eyes meet mine—confused, but not overly so.

"Kapha." I heave a breath. "We need help."

Leiholan nods like it's a secret language only he understands. He runs to the back of the room, immediately alert, as if he has been waiting for someone to tell him they need him.

He searches the armory in seconds, the movements a blur of superspeed.

"Where?" he asks, grabbing a rusted blade—old. It must have the type of metal needed to kill a kapha. Every monster can be killed only one way, lest their magic bring them back to life.

"Zola's circle."

Leiholan sheathes the blade, grabs me around the back, and races toward the fountain. We're there in seconds, and what I see is not what I expected.

Desdemona is *touching* the kapha. I look to Leiholan, searching for a companion in my suspicion. He, like everyone else, is oddly protective of this girl.

My stomach churns with power as I pull another tree from the ground, its roots growing into legs. The tree moves like a sentient being toward the monster. Its roots shift and creak with a life of their own. It takes every ounce of my strength to keep it upright, alive, and moving.

My heart races. The trees pulse beating inside of me.

Blood drips down my arm, passing over my glove and to the floor, as thorns break through my skin.

My knees wobble, my core gives in. Fatigue feels like dying.

As best as I can, I listen to the kapha. My hands stretch before me, aiming for something I can't reach. I don't understand what I reach for or why I do it.

I know only that there is no other option.

This feeling—one that isn't mine—distracts me from my magic, the life of the tree. The kapha longs for something, but the longing does not belong to it. This is artificially placed, as if this monster is doing a greater monster's dirty work.

For just a moment, I think of Desdemona. Speaking to it. Touching it.

A greater monster.

There's a hum of sound—Desdemona and Leiholan speak. My tree keeps the kapha from killing them.

Desdemona couldn't be the monster—not unless this entire fight is a show.

Each time I push against the kapha, it feels like I'm betraying my-self, as if its motives are replacing mine.

Put down your hands, Wendy.

Reach with me, Wendy.

The monster speaks to me through emotion.

The humming in my brain blurs my mind, making it impossible to hear Desdemona and Leiholan. They're planning something. Leiholan will fight, and Desdemona will not, I'm guessing, by the way they feel.

Leiholan brandishes the sword.

No! I nearly shout. *Don't kill me! I need something.*

I try to fight, to pull myself into reality. To release the kapha and read Desdemona. What is she doing here? The monster?

Why is her prophecy the one that will end us all?

But someone is ripping my organs out. First my lungs—I can't breathe. Next my kidney—I'm going to puke.

Finally my heart—I fall to the floor.

Glancing down, I see my body fully intact.

But my tree has died.

I am dying.

I claw at the floor, my nails digging past the grass and seeping into the cool soil. The sensation wakes me up, but not nearly enough. I push further into the world, begging for something else—any other feeling to hold onto. There is only failure and fear.

From the ground, I watch helplessly as the kapha strangles Lei-holan in its arms. Desdemona throws knives at its limbs. When she manages to cut one off, another wraps around Leiholan's leg. I reach for mine, feeling his breaking bones.

The kapha drags Leiholan across the ground and into its chest. Limbs wrapping him like a blanket, before the Combat teacher disap-pears entirely.

Devastation weakens my heart.

Desdemona fears he will die.

Soil sinks deeper under my nails. Then, the monster wraps two long arms around Desdemona, coiling her within its body until she's completely disappeared, like prey being swallowed by a snake.

I take a deep breath, fighting myself to rise. Begging myself to resist before the monster captures me, too.

And suddenly, I feel bliss. Oh, sweet, glorious bliss.

For a moment, I breathe deeply, sinking into the sensation, letting it wash over me. I lie on my back and stare up at the sky, a smile tugging at my lips, as if the world itself has paused to gift me this moment.

I smile while Desdemona suffocates. I'm ready to leave, to give in, to go out. This is bliss—to be able to die.

But I'm not the one dying.

I'm not the one surrendering.

Desdemona is.

The kapha subdues its prey, weaving its will over Desdemona, coaxing her into a false peace, so she doesn't struggle in her final moments.

To make the kill easier.

Conversely, that very peace fills me. Offers a break from these aching bones. My bloody thorns. For the first time in this entire fight, I take a deep breath—I finally have the mind to.

I rise from the ground.

It's the kapha's own magic that will be the reason for its death.

And I feel a sick sweetness in being the one who gets to dole it.

My feet press into the world like roots. My arms extend, and trees shoot up from the ground beside me. As if I am the wielder of life itself. The thorns push out from every inch of skin; they coat my arms, my legs and hands, down my spine. The blood trickles, from neck to shoulder, but the pain is nothing against this peace.

My trees pull on the kapha's arms, forcing them apart. Desdemona falls first. Then, the sword tumbles beside an unconscious Leiholan.

My heart races as if I'm running from the monster itself, all while I pull it apart. Two trees hold onto the kapha, keeping it down.

Quickly, I pick up the sword.

I lift it over my head.

And as I sink the blade into the kapha's chest, I understand Ma for the first time.

There is something glorious about the kill.

I am more than a mender.

I am stronger than a murder.

I am the very giving and taking of life.

I carve the blade down the kapha's body. Blood sprays on my face. Organs spill on my feet. The sight, the feeling, it's too powerful. I don't know what I do next, only that when I'm done, the sword is buried to the hilt. The blade sticks through the other end of the monster.

But the kapha isn't dead. In its last moments, that dark swirling gaze meets mine. It sees through me, understands me. It knows what I am.

Because it does to me what I do to others.

With a final, twisted flourish, the kapha reaches out, and it controls its prey.

The agony of the monster's last moments are transmitted into me, a thousand times over. The dread of death, sharp and suffocating, pulses through my veins. It's as if I'm drowning in it, the weight of its terror crushing me from the inside out.

I fall to the floor, trying to catch my guts before they spill.

Trying to stop my mind from calling out: *Desdemona.*

The kapha wants her help—her *saving.*

Slowly, oh so slowly, the kapha takes its last breath, and with it, it finally releases me. My head crashes to the floor. Have I cracked my skull open against the packed soil?

My vision swims, the world blurring as I sink into it—unable to escape, unable to breathe.

Desdemona's cries fill the air around me, singing me to sleep. I can't do anything more. I have nothing more to give. She shouts, cries. I look at her holding a very near dead Leiholan, and I wonder: *Who are you, Desdemona?*

I realize, too late, that she's looking at me, asking for something. Her hands are in front of me for the taking. For a moment, I stay silent, staring at her flesh.

Then I peel off my glove and, while wondering what she is expecting me to do with her hands, I hold them. An idea blossoms in my mind.

I meet her gaze, her pliant pupils.

"You will answer my questions, but they do not mean anything to you," I say. "You will not wish to recall these questions. Do you understand?"

Desdemona's eyes gloss over, glazed. Her will, gone. A blank slate for the taking.

"I will answer, and I won't care."

I look at Leiholan, fully aware that he could bleed out while I get my answers.

But one man's life isn't worth a universe. If this is how I can save us all, I would let him die. I would let anyone die.

"That isn't true," the boy interrupts.

Immediately, I think he's right. My eyes drift down to Leiholan's missing leg. It's too similar to Ma.

It's too similar.

"What did the kapha want?" I ask Desdemona quickly.

Her mouth opens and from it comes a string of words, similar to the prophecy. "'For you, pain awaits. Free me and accept. Your fire draws you closer to my home.' That's what it told me, but what it wants, I didn't understand."

"*Told* you?"

"Yes, it spoke to me," she answers.

"But you are not its controller?" I clarify.

"No."

"Who is?"

"I don't know."

Something else ties them together. But as Leiholan groans, I *know* the boy was right. I won't be the death of him. Though, I hardly have the energy to hold my body, let alone save a life.

I twist to Desdemona. "Give me your energy."

Desdemona closes her eyes, doing as I ask.

She channels her power to me, moving through my body like a line of fire. I nearly cry out in pain as my blood heats, sure that there are boils forming on my skin.

Desdemona's hands fall from my grasp, and in the blink of an eye, she regains control of her consciousness. Without a word, we pick up Leiholan, carrying him to the infirmary. His blood splashes down my ankle, but I hardly recognize the feeling.

My mind is occupied with the monsters, the prophecy, everything but the blood smearing on my hands.

We hand Leiholan off to the healers—each Eunoia looking at my blood stained clothes in shock, then acceptance.

They think all I did was save Leiholan.

They do not know I killed a monster.

Why is the first more acceptable than the latter, when *killing* the monster is *how* I saved him?

The second I can, I leave, weakly stumbling through the halls.

"Come to me," the boy says. If the circumstances were only slightly different, I would ignore him.

But he took too much from me today.

I crash against the marble walls, my back cracking against the pressure. I slide down, closing my eyes. The boy is in front of me in the hallway, but the walls are muddy. Instead of beige marble, they're dark brown blobs, nearly black.

Like a child painted the landscape.

Rising, I grab the collar of the boy's shirt. It's looser than usual, like the shirt isn't a real shirt at all. I release it, shoving him into the wall and holding my forearm to his chest.

"You're the reason Desdemona is still breathing!" I scream.

He is not fazed by my violence. How could he be? He is a figment of my imagination. This scene is not real.

It never was.

"If I cannot be a person, I will be your conscience."

"I have a conscience!" Much too large of a conscience.

"What would you have done if Desdemona died? Could you have beaten the kapha on your own? The very peace the kapha bestowed upon her in death is the reason you could continue the fight."

I don't answer.

"And what of Leiholan?" the boy asks. *"You said you'd allow one man to die to save the universe, and that's almost what happened. For one simple reason: he was there."*

Shaking my head, I take a step back as a tear falls from my eye. Only, in my mind, the tear does not tumble down my cheek. It moves before me, creating a bubble between me and the boy. Smudging the already blurry lines of the make believe.

The very manifestation of my unease.

"Don't."

"I don't have to. You know what being close to Azaire will do." The boy

reaches a hand to my cheek. *"It's what happens to everyone who gets too close."*

The words—my own words—haunt me. Leiholan was there, and because of that, he almost died. Because *I* brought him there, he almost met his end. For the simple reason that he was in my presence.

The same way that Azaire is bound to be in my presence one day. One bad day is enough to end it all. Just like Ma. Just like Xander.

For a moment, I lean into the boy's touch. I feel at home with him, and in the midst of this storm, all I need is four walls of comfort.

A roof of relief.

"Everyone but me." The boy touches his forehead to mine, his thumb stroking my cheek as our noses brush. Our eyes meet. His voice is tender. *"It's always been you and me."*

I nod against him, and he doesn't move. He just holds me close. *"I know."*

"Do it," the boy responds, his voice wholly consoling. There isn't an ounce of animosity. *"Do what you must with him before you come to me."*

I shake my head, feeling his nose against mine for one final second before opening my eyes. I force myself away from the marble wall, walking down the hallway once more as the tears tangle in my eyelashes, blurring my vision.

In the corner of my mind, I think, *I'm not going to come to you.*

And I wonder if he can hear such an obvious lie.

Chapter 24
There Is The Worst, and Then There Is More

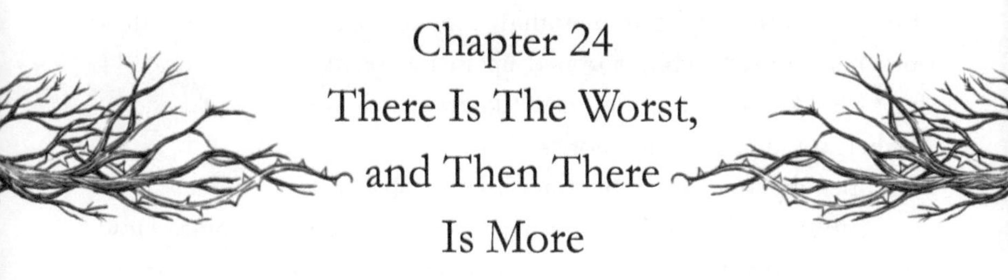

ONE YEAR AGO

Calista barges into my room without warning, but it's no surprise. Her anxiety has been buzzing through the suite. The door slams shut and I look up, taking a few deep breaths to steady myself. Her nerves tickle me, the hair on my arms rising.

She cracks her knuckles, the sound like snapping bones as she paces my room. I watch from my desk. Words sputter from her mouth, but they aren't cohesive.

Then she sighs, stopping in her tracks. "I told Lilac."

I sit up, trying to act surprised. "That's great," I say, but my voice shakes—something is wrong.

"It *was* great," Calista corrects me, flopping onto my bed. She stares at the ceiling absentmindedly. "It was great."

Something went very, very wrong. I back away, without meaning to. Guilt steals me, but I try to return myself. I don't know the circumstances yet.

This might not be my fault.

But I know—I feel the panic, the sadness, the rage.

She tips her head toward me, her eyes stinging with tears. "Our parents found out... *Again*. This time, Mother didn't let us off easily."

Quickly, she wipes the tears from her cheek.

"Do you want to talk?" I rise from my desk and sit next to her.

"No," she sighs. "*Yes.*" She shakes her head. "It would be pointless."

"Emotions aren't pointless." I worry she hears the pity in my voice.

"Maybe not to someone who wields them." Calista's voice is flat. "But to the rest of us, they're nothing more than a nuisance." She flips onto her stomach, chin propped up in her palm, eyes far away. "I don't even know why I told Lilac. I knew exactly how it would end—Mother would take her memories."

I open my mouth to reply, but nothing comes out.

I swallow a shaky breath, anxiety creeping up my spine. How quickly will she start piecing things together? A part of her *has* to know what I've done; it's still there, buried. She's a Folk, a being who controls memories. If she wanted to find it, she could.

When I find the courage, I ask, "Wh–what did your mother do?"

Though, I'm not sure I want to know—to feel any more responsible.

Calista scoffs a humorless laugh. "She made Lilac believe I left her horribly."

Her gaze moves, distant, and her body goes cold, chilling in my veins, as if the words themselves drained the life from her. She shuts herself off from the world like a tourniquet, cutting off the pain before it can reach her.

"Instead of me telling her the truth…" Calista trails off, her voice breaking. "I told her a lie. In Lilac's memory, I told her I never loved her." She sighs, a long, tired exhale. "Gods, if you could feel her... My heart shattered in that moment, but I can't even begin to imagine what it did to hers."

I sit back, eyes widening even as I don't mean them to. I wanted to do something good.

Didn't I?

I forced Calista to tell Lilac the truth because I felt what they were missing without the other. Wasn't my intention entirely unselfish? How could good intentions turn so sour?

"Calista," I breathe. "I'm… I'm so sorry."

She sits up abruptly, her posture straightening as she brushes off my apologies. "I'm not common swine," she hisses, her voice laced with authority. "Don't use such language with me."

"Calista—"

"*Don't.*" She turns sharply in my direction. This time, her eyes lock onto mine, a piercing gaze. She studies me for a moment too long, then, beneath her breath, mutters, "What is happening with you?"

"N-nothing," I stammer. "I just—I feel bad."

"Normally you're like a chameleon. But not today." She lies back on the bed, a sneer curling at the corner of her lips. "It's strange."

I turn away, staring out the window and into the academy garden. I want to tell her—to come out and say it.

I wanted you to have love, and instead, I have made you lose it.

Though my desire to say that isn't entirely for her. It's for my own guilt, my own grief, the weight I've piled onto the tower of my mind. I need to unload it, to ease the pressure before it crushes me.

I plan to do it, but as I begin to say, "Calista," the words freeze in my throat. I regret it instantly.

But it's too late. She's already waiting, expecting something.

"What?" she asks, sitting up with a sharp tilt of her head.

I open my mouth. Once more, nothing comes out. Like I've lost myself somewhere between the words I'm not saying.

Calista's eyes narrow, her mouth opening slightly as the mechanisms of her mind crank. I begin to shake my head—to try to explain myself—as I feel her putting together the pieces I failed to share.

Silent and steady betrayal pumps from my heart to my bloodstream. The rapid thumping in my chest is on the cusp of a heart attack.

"Oh my gods." Her voice catches. I try to shake my head, but she cuts me off. "This was you."

I bite my bottom lip, rising to my feet and walking slowly around the edge of the bed toward her. "Calista—"

She scoots back, drawing in a shaking breath, like death rattling in her chest.

"It really was." Her eyes widen as the truth unfolds in front of her. The page I tried to crumple irons out, but the creases made will never be reversed.

Calista wasn't *sure* it was me. My response has confirmed her suspicion.

"No." I shake my head, panic rising. "It wasn't like that—"

"You made me tell her." Calista's voice is sharp and accusing. Her irises glow an unsettling yellow. She pins me with her gaze as she says, "Did you think I wouldn't remember? You may have power, Estridon, but I have memory."

My throat tightens, and the walls close in. I shake my head again, tears forming with fear—the fear of losing yet another person by my own hand.

"I thought I was helping." My voice is raw with regret.

She sneers, her face twisting with a mixture of fury and hurt— nearly hate.

"Wendy Estridon," she says, the cadence of her tone not matching the anguish of her face. Her words are quiet, icy, laced with silent fury. "You ruined my life."

"I'm sorry—" I start, but the words are swallowed by the storm of her emotions.

"I told you never to use that language with me!" She turns toward the door, her back to me as she finishes, "We both knew this friendship was one of convenience. But it's not convenient anymore."

The door slams with a force that shakes the room, leaving me with nothing but the echo of loss. The pain of both her betrayal and my own actions.

I collapse to the floor, lying like a fetus. I've done it now—chased the last person away. Ruined the last relationship I had. *At least I didn't kill her*, I think. I wonder if that would be any less painful.

This time, I did it all on my own—it wasn't an accident or a mistake. This time, the choice that led to loss was an active one.

I close my eyes, and the world in my mind is a blur. Nearly a blank slate. The whites and the greens of my room blend until they're gray. A sour sight for a sore soul.

I search the premises for the boy, but there's nothing to see. Nothing but a scratched-out page. Scribbles on recycled paper.

"Please!" I call to him, for the first time wishing he had a name. A way to get his attention. *"Please, I need you!"*

From behind me, the boy taps my shoulder. I quickly turn, wrapping my arms around his shoulder as I fall into him.

"I've done it again."

His hands rest on the back of my head. *"I know, Little Thorn. I know."*

Chapter 25
You Missed My Heart

NOW

Blood sticks to my skin as I stumble through the halls—Lei-holan's mingling with the monster's. I'm coated in crimson, and while every kid bats an eye, none of them are shocked. They think I've hurt another student, not a monster.

Somehow, that's more comforting.

My body moves fast while I feel like I'm dying. I lean heavily against Azaire's door, regaining strength before pushing it open and stumbling into his suite. He's sitting in his room, his door ajar, already calling my name. I hear the concern in his voice more than I feel it.

The strength I stole from Desdemona withers away. I slump onto the couch.

Azaire rushes to me, dripping with worry, like the blood drips from my hands.

"What happened?"

Gods, I'm covered in blood. I stare at my hands. My trembling hands. My gloves stained red.

Without a word, Azaire wraps his arms around me. He pulls me into his chest, resting his chin on the top of my head as he strokes my hair.

I'm shocked by how close he's willing to hold me with all this blood.

I push away from him. "Are you wearing it?" I scan his body, eyes landing on the amulet at his chest, tied with a strip of leather. "Never take it off. Promise me."

Azaire shakes his head. "I never have."

Mindlessly, I stand, pacing back and forth, my body fueled solely by anxiety.

Azaire rises beside me, taking my hand and pulling me into his room. "What is—"

"This was a bad idea." I cut him off.

"What was a bad idea?"

"This." I motion between us. "Us. I'm in the center of it, and I'm dragging you with me." I look anywhere but at him—at the journal sitting on his desk, the neat pile of books in the corner, the closet opened slightly. "I was always scared of hurting you."

For selfish reasons.

Fear of feeling that hurt, magnified.

I point to myself, clutching onto my chest as if I can break through and rip my heart out. "I want to be with you, Azaire, more than anything."

Azaire grabs hold of my gesticulating hands, freezing me.

"Then be with me," he says softly.

For a second, he steals my sight, and I nearly let myself fall into him—surrender. But the boy was right. He always has been.

I reclaim my focus, pulling myself back from the edge, doing what I came here to do. Doing what the boy knew I would before I did. "It's not just emotions anymore."

"What is it?"

He's so empathetic. All I can feel is his longing to understand me. But understanding me would drive him right to the prophecy. The end of the world. The potential monster in Desdemona.

I would drive him to *be there*, the way Leiholan was.

It would drive him to danger.

"I can take it," he whispers. "Give it to me, Wendy." He drops my hands, his fingers cupping my face. He holds me like he's afraid I might slip away—like he already knows what happens next.

I watch him with wide eyes. A pain-laced gaze.

"I'll make it go away. Wendy, I promise." Azaire's hands slip from my face to my waist, pulling me closer, his body pressing against mine like he's trying to merge us into one. "I'll take the pain."

His words are so tender—so hopeful. But he doesn't understand that's the very thing I'm trying to save him from.

Even though I long to lean in, to touch and hold Azaire the way I only can with him, I tug my hands away.

"I need to clean up," I say abruptly, walking to the washroom.

For a moment, I stand dazed before the mirror, my breath shallow, the reflection before me almost unreal. Blood is smeared across my face, a cruel artwork etched into my skin. I hardly recognize myself, the sight too much to fully grasp, yet I can't look away.

Harmonious globs of red are crusted to my skin.

They even cover my scar.

I force my stained gloves beneath the cool water, splashing a handful on my face, watching the pink water as it swirls down the drain.

This isn't what I wanted. This is what I feared. I grip onto the sink to get hold of my destabilizing balance. The bathroom sways.

Being close to me is going to get Azaire killed.

I knew it from the beginning, and now I've gotten too close for comfort. There is no longer an easy way to walk away.

"I have been trying to tell you, Little Thorn," the boy says.

"Shut up!" I finally scream at him—at me.

I need a clear mind. Not the boy.

Delivering a prophecy isn't a one and done deal. Like all things with a Eunoia's magic, emotional attachments heighten them. You can't *give* a prophecy without being, on some level, involved in its outcome.

If its outcome is the end of our worlds, I can't drag Azaire into that.

The Weapon feels so small now.

Actually, it feels like nothing now.

I wonder how I'd feel about it if I still had that capacity. But I can't see myself caring about a Weapon above the potential end of the universe. One that lies in the prophecy.

Maybe Pa did me a favor. He helped me find my focus.

As I step back into the room, Azaire picks up my hands. His touch is gentle, pleading.

I feel dazed. I feel drunk. My brain muddles in the same way Xander's did when I touched him.

When I *killed* him.

Azaire wraps his arms around my waist. He pulls me so close.

I love this.

I love him.

I belong here.

I don't push him away.

Holding him makes this so much worse. All of this pain, because of me.

Exactly as I knew it would be.

I'm a self-fulfilling prophecy.

I should've never let it go this far.

But I love him.

I love him, I love him, I love him.

And I feel his heart breaking. Gods, that makes it so much harder. Feeling his heart shattering along with mine.

"I don't understand."

"It's—" I hold him tighter, my hands clutching the back of his neck. He is a lifeline to my turbulence. "There's something I have to do, and I have to do it alone."

"What is it?" he asks, borderline begs, as he pulls away from me, meeting my eyes.

I bite my lip. Shake my head. "It's too dangerous."

His hold on my hand loosens. His resolve wavers. "I can handle myself," he says. "You know that, don't you?"

"No"—I shake my head—"I do. It's…" My heart is composed of jealousy for all the people who get to love and not suffer at the hands of it.

I should have never spoken to Azaire in the woods. Should have never let him follow me out of class. Shouldn't have told him about Aeliana and Persiphis.

Stay away from people; always keep your distance; watch when you're lonely; retreat when you're not. Never get close. That's what I have to do. What I've always done.

That's my life.

So I fight the words that almost make it to my tongue but get caught coming up my throat: *I do love you. I love you, I love you, I love you.*

I love you so much, I'm willing to lose you.

"I'm sorry."

"No." Azaire releases my hands, his breath catching. "You don't get to do that. I love you, Wendy, and I'm pretty sure that you love me. If you're fighting, I fight with you. If you're suffering, I suffer with you. You are a part of me, body, mind, soul, and whatever else there is. I'm not letting you go. Not without a damn good reason."

I look at our hands, unclasped. "You just did."

He picks them up. "No, I didn't."

I smile a little at his softness, in the wake of my cruelty. My cruel responsibility. I break his heart, I break my own, and he stands before me, his loyalty unwavering.

He is everything I ever wanted.

I loosen my hold on his hand. "I'm so sorry."

"You don't have to protect me," he says, sounding almost resigned. "I'd kill for you. I'd unmake myself for you, if that's what you wanted."

I shake my head. "That's not what I want."

"Then what is it? Do you want to hide me away until the danger passes? It'll never pass. I've been in danger my entire life."

I glance down. "I know."

Azaire picks up my cheek, meeting my gaze, voice soft. "Then what is it?"

Again, I shake my head. There's so many words, yet so few will articulate what I mean.

I am a garden of agony, and I should have never planted him here.

"I can't be the reason someone else gets hurt," I say at last—what I've been dancing around.

It shouldn't feel this awful to be so well understood. Azaire doesn't fight me, nor does he have a bit of push back. He knows what I mean.

He knows *me*, and he still wants me.

But even that doesn't dull the blade in my heart, carving out piece after piece.

"If this is all we have"—he cradles my cheek in his hand, and I lean into him—"I refuse to regret it."

I whisper, "Tell me that tomorrow."

I knock twice on Ms. Ferner's door. I never used to—never needed to. She always knew I was coming.

I'm sure I would've heard if she died, but when she doesn't immediately answer, I wonder if that was a wrong assumption.

Until she calls, "Come in."

When I step inside, she's surprised. She knows we have a history—she only forgets *why* we have one. Why she ever cared to help me.

"Hi." I try to smile. My only reason for coming is to see if she's alive.

I fear that she feels that.

"Estridon," she replies with a nod. "What brings you in?"

"It's been a while… since we've talked." I shuffle my weight between my feet. "I wanted to ask how you were."

"I'm the same as I always am, Estridon." She tips her head toward me, raising an eyebrow. "And you don't have to ask."

"I know…"

"Don't waste my time on niceties."

"I wanted to apologize," I blurt out. "We stopped speaking, I should have explained."

Ms. Ferner steps out from behind her desk, walking toward me. "There's no need for explanations," she says. "Our relationship was never personal. I'm your teacher."

Her mind is a seesaw, tipping with every touch. She doesn't care for my power, I made sure of that—to protect Azaire. But not caring about my powers doesn't mean she doesn't care for me, and it's left her in an in-between she's still learning to manage.

"And I wanted to thank you…" I whisper. "You helped me a lot, with my power."

"Did I?" She stops in front of me. "Because all I recall is you never being able to contain yourself."

I nod, ducking my head low. "I see." As I turn toward the door, I say, "It's good to see you're okay."

She releases a small, disgruntled, and unsatisfied "hmph" on my way out.

I thought checking on her—seeing her alive—would make me feel better. Less guilty for what I did to her and how I left things with Azaire. But when I make it to my suite, all that's left for me to do is fall apart.

I cry. Gods, I scream. It does nothing to alleviate the weight in my chest. I crash to the floor, tears streaming until they soak my chest. I claw at my eyes, needing the crying to stop.

I nearly rip my hair out.

I've already ripped my heart out.

The boy continues to pry at my brain, and I can't take it. Rivaling emotions claw at me.

One wants to run for Azaire.

One needs to run far away.

But I think I know how best to ease the pain—the confusion and contradictions. The boy's proposition always made sense to me, even when I tried to pretend it didn't. Because if I can't be with the living without endangering them, there is only one other option.

And the boy always knew it.

Do what you must with him before you come to me. That's what the boy said, and he was right—he always has been. Even as I know his accuracy, I wish to deny it. I wish I never created him. But perhaps if he was his own being, if he was no longer in my mind, I could have company without it being doused in my own shortcomings. Without every one of my mistakes and contradictions adding oil to an already blazing fire.

Perhaps I've always wanted to bring him to life—and perhaps that's part of the problem. Maybe that's why he ever asked me to begin with.

I rise, grabbing my bag and walking to the door.

"Are you really going through with this?" the boy asks.

"I'm tired of being alone."

The door shuts behind me, the sound final.

The moon is high in the sky tonight, bright in a way that makes lanterns unnecessary. I walk through the woods, but not beyond the protective barrier. Not that it's doing any good, anyhow.

A kapha already got through today.

The academy is on lockdown. No one is supposed to be out of

their suites. I was careful walking through the halls and garden. Nobody was there to stop me.

There are, with absolute certainty, monsters in the woods tonight. I doubt I'll be lucky enough to avoid them. But I think I'm strong enough to face whatever comes my way. I'm certainly reckless enough to not care about the outcome.

I stop just shy of the barrier, throwing my bag on the grass.

In a circle, I settle a dozen candles and light them, surrounding myself with flickering flames. I'm not sure they will be of any use. What I'm planning to do is stronger than any little flame.

I'm planning to bring a figment of my imagination to life.

"I am more than that," the boy reminds me.

In the real world, I nod. In my mind, I say, *"I believe you."*

Lowering myself to the ground, I sit in the center of the flames, their warmth radiating all around me. As I close my eyes, I don't leave the dimly lit woods. The only difference here is that the boy stands before me, his face glowing with the candles' orange light, the trees swaying in the wind behind him.

"Just like we practiced before." He extends his hands toward me. *"Just like the trees."*

The moment my skin meets his, my head tips back, hanging at an angle. My blood begins to bubble, surging through me. It flows through my arms, into his hands, each of my nerves going numb as it simmers past. The boy lets out a low groan, my power and life spilling into him. I feel his satisfaction.

I force my head forward, desperate to meet his gaze. But his head has fallen back, his dark lips parted.

"Wendy?" a voice calls—something beyond my mind, in the real world. "What are you doing out here?"

In my hands, the boy's grasp begins to change. Never before had I realized how immaterial he felt before, not until there are two nearly fleshen hands in mine. Holding me. His gaze continues to search the sky, his body shifting in and out between shadow and human.

"Wendy!"

"Ignore it," the boy demands.

My body sways, and I recognize the voice. Somewhere in reality, Calista is shaking my body back and forth.

"Wendy!" the boy shouts desperately, but I'm already opening my eyes.

Calista is sitting before me. My breath is ragged as I struggle to inhale.

"What in the gods?" Calista breathes, her eyes widening. "What are you doing to yourself?"

I glance down. She's holding my hands in hers. For a moment, I'm nearly grateful she stopped me. For a moment, I'm angry the boy is not flesh and in front of me.

"Nothing." I rip my hands from her grasp. "I'm not doing anything."

"You looked like you were dying."

At the word *dying*, I notice the sword sheathed to Calista's back. Her hair is more than loosely braided—it's fastened to her head. Not a wisp is out of place.

She's out here for a reason, and I think I know what it is.

Lilac.

"I'm fine," I say. "It was a mistake."

I rise to my feet, looking past Calista, but she follows me up. The boy pounds at the back of my mind, calling me. While his voice is louder than usual, I can't make it out properly. Maybe he isn't truly speaking.

"Wendy?" Calista snaps.

I look back at her. She glances down.

My gaze follows.

The grass beneath me is entirely gray. Withered away to emptiness—devoid of color. Of life.

It's worse than dead, but I don't know what's worse than that.

I think back to the trees—the ones I brought to life at the boy's command—and how they always left me feeling half-dead. They must have taken *life*, too. It must have taken a bit of *my* life. Ma once used the same magic to fight the pernipe—she *died* using this magic.

Who could have taught her such a thing?

I look up at Calista, who feels more worried than I'm used to. Our dynamic was always the opposite—me concerned for her.

"Are you all right?" she asks.

"Fine."

She doesn't take my blunt tone well. It hurts her.

"Whatever." Calista walks away.

I stand, taking deep breaths, staring at the grass beneath me. It's nearly black.

What would have happened to the academy if I succeeded in bringing the boy to life? Could I have sucked the power out of the barrier, out of the grounds of this world itself?

"What did you ask of me?" I mutter in my mind.

"You misunderstand."

I squeeze my eyes shut, furious. The woods blur, the world inside twisting out of shape. The ground and the boy meld together. There's nothing more than a vague shadow where he stands.

"Stop this." I stare at my feet—nothing more than a scribble. *"Let me see."*

Slowly, my vision focuses, the boy turning from shadow to flesh, the trees coming into view. His eyes stare at me, but they've changed. No longer a reflection of Xander or a manifestation of my guilt.

I remember the day I created the boy. More than just his eyes have changed since that day. He's grown with me. He was fifteen with me, sixteen, seventeen, and so on.

Now, the boy barely resembles how he began. His freckles have disappeared, his brown hair has grown shaggy and black, and the bags under his eyes match mine.

But he doesn't match me.

He reads my mind, but he is not always of my mind.

I don't know who he is.

We used to have fun together. When I would dance in the woods —the very dancing Azaire told me he watched from a distance—I was dancing with him. I'd swim with him in the lake. Take him to the house beyond the border on Ma's birthdays. He was my only friend.

A rift grew between us when I befriended Calista. Never would I have thought him to be jealous—he *was* me. But this, what he's become, it has to be jealousy.

"Xander," I say. *"Your name is Xander."*

The boy's face visibly breaks. He knows who Xander is, he knows what I've done. He knows because he's me.

Because he did it, too.

"Wendy, I—"

I cut him off. *"I created you because I needed you—needed someone. I don't need someone anymore. You're dismissed."*

The boy steps closer, his features drawn into a frown. He's about to beg as he picks up my hand, and I'm about to stand my ground. Tell him *no.* Tell him to *go away.* But instead, he smiles.

"You think you can be rid of me"—the boy raises his free hand, snapping his fingers—*"like that?"*

His tone isn't something I'm used to. It's prideful, it's sinister—two things I've never been.

"Of course I can." I step away, trying to rip my hand free.

But his grip is too strong. Like a tree, his branches have wrapped around my mind.

The boy shakes his head. *"I am the darkest parts of your mind, the shadow of your soul, the wreckage of your heart."* Then he pulls me closer. *"I am not something who comes and goes as you please. I am ever present, whether you grant me a face or not."*

"No," I whisper. That isn't right. *"You're my* friend. *You're a companion because I needed one."*

What he said—it makes no sense. This whole time, he's been jealous of Azaire. He told me he loves me.

He can't simply be my darkness.

"I can be your darkness, and I am," the boy says, answering my thoughts. *"Because I, my love, am you. And you so desperately want to be loved, yet you run from it. I was trying to give you what you desire. I was trying to give you both your contradictions."*

"You wanted me to bring you to life." I force my hands free with all my strength, stumbling into a tree behind me.

The boy takes a step with every word. *"You* wanted to bring me to life. *What I want is only what you* long for. *But you already put those pieces together."*

I shake my head, my mind throbbing. *"I don't—"*

"You do," the boy says. But the longer I look at him, the more he looks like Xander.

My first crush.

My first kill.

"You have suppressed the parts of yourself you dislike so deeply, they had to come out in one way or another," he says.

"No—"

"Go save your friends before they get themselves killed." He raises a hand, shooing me away, and my eyes open—not of my volition.

I stand, unsteady on my feet—confused at what the boy is, what I've done to myself, what I've created.

Have I driven myself to insanity by the simple action of repression?

He's my darkness. My contradictions. How is it possible that I didn't know this? How could I have missed it?

My mind isn't in love with me. My mind pities me. My mind thinks I'm *insane.*

My mind is trying to save me, in the only way it knows how—by making me worse.

What have I done?

Something gnaws through my stomach. The same pit the boy pointed out before I felt it. Someone is in danger. The worm eats a pit in my stomach, warning me.

Then I spot Calista in the distance. She's past the protective barrier, deep into the woods—and I know that monsters are lurking out there. One even got past.

I chase after her, grateful for a reason to ignore myself. Perhaps that's the problem.

"Calista!" I call. She doesn't stop. "Calista, where are you going?"

I run faster, grabbing her shoulder when I reach her. She smacks my arm away roughly.

"What are you doing?"

"Nothing," she hisses.

"Calista—"

"The moonaro is still out there!" she shouts, pointing aimlessly into the woods.

"So you want to get yourself killed?"

"No!" She chokes on her breath. Her hand clamps over her mouth as she turns away from me. Desperately, she takes a sip of air, then turns back. "Lilac won't wake up. I thought… maybe the monster has to be killed first."

I reach for her, holding her wrist so she doesn't run—trying to save her the way the boy told me to. The pit in my stomach is still there, the worm still eating through me. I fear if I let Calista out of my sight, she will die, just like the boy said.

"If that was the case, don't you think the scholars who study the monsters would have found out?" I ask, trying to talk some form of sense into her.

"There haven't been attacks in decades," she says indignantly. "How am I to trust their studies?"

"Your parents pay for them."

"My parents are insane!" She glances at my hand clamped around her wrist, and I know she's strong enough to pull away, but she says, "Help, or let me go."

She truly wants my help.

I fear she will need it. Only one of us here has killed a monster. Awfully, I think I enjoyed it. But the dread—the carcass in my stomach—aches, and I know even if I didn't enjoy the kill, I still wouldn't leave Calista.

"Okay." I nod. "I'll help."

Calista's face softens, and I feel her relief settle in my muscles. An appreciated reprieve. "Really?"

I let go of her wrist. "Yes."

Her eyebrows rise in surprise. "All right then." She turns away, the moonlight illuminating each step. "Let's go."

I stay close behind her, and when I snap a twig beneath my foot, Calista uses her air magic to suppress the sound.

As we step beyond the protective barrier, I hold my breath. I'm really doing this, searching for the danger instead of waiting for it to come to me. The monsters weren't the first thing to ruin my life; they were only one in a long line of catastrophes. Though after the pernipe killed Ma, I never thought I could face them—nor that I'd *have* to.

The monsters aren't supposed to attack.

But just in the distance, I see the subtle glow of blue. Barely, I make out the moonaro, feasting on an animal carcass. Blood coats its bright gray fur, shining in the blue light.

The ache in my stomach sharpens, and I take a deep breath against the pain.

I signal to Calista, pointing to the moonaro, and she raises a hand. In her palm, a yellow ball forms, quickly turning translucent. Something she struggled with dearly a year ago. The barely visible ball grows, closing around us—trapping our voices.

"What's the plan?" I ask.

Calista looks puzzled—she doesn't have one. Instead, she reaches behind her back and unsheathes her long sword. "I cut its head off."

"*How?*"

She sneers. "With my combat training."

It sounds like an awful idea.

"Calista…" I say gently. "You're a princess."

"What is that supposed to mean?"

I sigh, my tone soft. "How… do you know they truly train you and aren't simply letting you win. A queen won't fight—"

"How *dare* you?" Calista demands, her voice laced with disdain. "And I presume you possess the expertise to kill a beast despite *your* utter lack of combat training?"

I stay silent. There are many things I could say. None would be welcome. The princess before me would be yet another person who's shocked at what I can do and have done.

What I've become.

My body brushes against the edge of her magical ball as I step back, extending an arm toward the moonaro. "Lead the way."

Calista smirks, thinking she's won the fight—though I'm only conceding to protect her. I could be wrong, but I can't imagine they train the queen of Folkara to fight. I assume they'd focus on strategy, not brute force.

I know how Folkara is—a patriarchy. Calista has often complained how the queen is a ceremonial role, not one with real authority. Why would the academy teach her power?

Why give her the ammunition to topple the government she was born to serve?

With every step toward the moonaro, the pit in my stomach grows until it is all encompassing. It beckons me in the opposite direction. Perhaps the feeling is trying to protect *me*. Save *my* life.

But that's not what the boy said.

Calista and I continue to approach the moonaro in perfect silence. Yet, as if it has a sixth sense like one of our own, its head rises and swivels toward us.

But the moonaro's natural inclination is not to attack. For only a moment, it wishes to ignore us. It lulls me into a false sense of safety.

I do not wish to fight.

I become as passive as the creature.

Then something takes over.

A burning need, a desire not of its own creation, *forcing* this monster to want blood.

Similar to the longing in the kapha.

The moonaro rises to its hind legs, standing three heads taller than me—and four heads taller than Calista.

The sword in her hand has never looked so small.

Blood coats the beast, chin to chest, from the animal it was feasting on. The blue glow beneath its ribs pulses, the source of its magic —but also something else. Just like the kapha, I know someone is controlling this beast.

The same way I'm sure the Royals controlled the pernipe that killed my mother.

This poor beast.

It charges toward us.

Calista raises a hand, a gust of wind pushing against the monster—but it does not send it back. The wind only holds it still. It does not last long, either.

With a small amount of effort, the monster breaks through her barrier.

Needles prick beneath my skin as roots push through the soil. They grow around the moonaro's hind legs. As it tries to step forward, it falls onto its stomach. The crash shakes the ground beneath the beast.

"Now!" I scream.

Calista charges, raising the sword. But as she approaches, the monster flips its head up. The sharp, ice-cold antlers catch Calista's ankles, flipping her back several feet.

She lands harshly, the blue glow of the moonaro's ribs giving out.

Then, the moon above stops shining.

The world darkens, nearly pitch black.

I turn to Calista silently, making sure she's okay. She's barely visible in the darkness, and as she begins to groan, I put a finger to my lips.

We cannot give the moonaro the upperhand of sound.

It seems the moonaro understands this, too. It's nowhere to be found, shrouded in the dim silence.

I steady myself, turning from side to side, searching.

Then I'm run off my feet. I fall to the ground, my back hitting harshly. A sharp pain dulls my senses.

For the first time in my life, all my focus is not on anything else. It's on me.

The warmth that trickles from my ribcage.

I touch a hand to the gaping hole beneath my breast, lifting it before my face. Dark liquid clings to my fingers.

I fear it's red.

As the light slowly fills the sky again, I spot the monster behind Calista. It raises its long claws to her throat—desperate for the kill, even against its better judgement.

I press my hands into the ground, praying I can stand. That my body will not give out from beneath me.

There's a terrible taste at the back of my throat. It tastes like death.

The pain of power pulses against my ribcage as I run to Calista. Every step takes me closer to toppling. But I manage to reach her, to unbutton my gloves, and set a bare hand on the monster.

For the first time, I use my power the way I was meant to but was never allowed to.

Never should have.

I take my downfall, and I twist it.

The monster's emotion overflows me. Once more, I find myself reaching for something I can't see, unsure why I'm reaching in the first place.

It feels heavy in my chest, as if I'm choking on a hunk of metal. And yet, it eases the sting of my wound.

A double-edged sword.

Then I rip the weapon from Calista's hand, wrapping an arm around her and running for the academy.

I'm surprised when the monster follows. Its movements are slowed, its inhibitions lowered, but my touch was not enough to kill something of its stature.

We are not in the clear.

I push a tired and hurt Calista to the floor. She screams my name as she falls, and I turn back to face the creature.

Even slowed, it's faster than us. Already steps away.

I run toward it.

I force myself not to falter.

Blood clings to my shirt. Breath fails to come. If I don't defeat this creature, I'm dead. I will bleed out. Succumb to my wound. If I don't kill the moonaro, I won't have the space to heal myself.

If I even can.

We haven't been taught to heal our own wounds.

The weight of the world presses against my shoulders as I give birth to a tree. It emerges from the ground beneath me, my feet right atop the bark.

As I rise into the sky with the trunk, I worry I don't have the strength needed to reach the moonaro's height.

That I don't have the strength to swing the sword.

There's only one way to kill a moonaro. What if I can't?

I have to.

The tree stops growing as I reach the moonaro's head.

I swing the sword at its neck.

The head comes rolling down with the thick scent of blood.

Chapter 26
I Ruined Everything
by Saying It Out
Loud

I'm floating.

I don't realize what's happening until my back hits the ground. Air knocks from my lungs.

My blood drips onto the dirt.

I stare at the stars.

Is this it? Is this my death?

Will I see Ma soon?

"No," the boy hisses. *"You will not!"*

Muffled words make it through my moment of silence. It's my name she screams. I glance down. Calista is tying something around my wound—the sleeve of her shirt.

"You'll heal yourself," she whispers.

No, she doesn't whisper. My ears are clogged with rushing blood.

"Wendy! That is a command. *Heal* yourself!"

I don't respond.

"Listen to her," the boy says. *"She wants the best for you."*

A hand grips my cheek harshly, shaking my head.

"Do you hear me?" Calista picks up my one gloved hand, unbuttoning it for me. I jerk up, all instinct. She tears the leather from my hand. She knows not to touch, even now.

My bare hands settle over the wound. It feels like touching a ghost. Which part isn't real? My hands or the wound? It's as if the boy connects to me now. As if his hands are guiding me.

He doesn't have hands.

They hold me anyways.

"The wound will stitch itself together," he says. *"You can heal the rest later. You must get out of the woods, first."*

It's not my energy that fuels me. It's not my magic that heals me. It isn't me that forces myself to live—it's the boy.

Tears well in my eyes as the green energy falls from my hands, like a waterfall of smoke. I don't know why I cry.

It isn't mine.

They are Calista's tears.

There are very few.

I've only ever felt the magic of mending through other people. I've never mended myself. It's like a circle. It's like infinity. There is no ending or beginning. It is me meeting me.

I am the whole world.

And for once, the world heals me.

My arms hang heavy as I walk back to the academy, Calista beside me. She hasn't said a word, and if she had, it wouldn't have been a pleasant one.

My wound feels taut, stretched thin. I'll sleep it off. If I need more healing, I can go to the infirmary.

I try to make it to my room, but with every step, the feeling I fought off earlier grows stronger. It isn't anything concrete. I thought it would go away after I killed the moonaro, but nothing has changed. Dread coils in my gut, like something alive is chewing its way through me, the same way rot hollows out fruit.

It feels vaguely familiar, as if I felt it before and know what it means, but I fail to place it.

I'm too *tired* to place it.

I let the rot eat me. It doesn't change much—I already feel hollow.

My feet hit the beige floor of the academy, and I turn toward my room. Something grabs my arm, trying to pull me in the other direction.

I fight against their strength, but they don't cease. Finally, I turn around, prepared to push the person away.

Nobody's there.

But *somebody* is. I feel them before me. Holding out a hand, I reach for the ghost, assuming it's a Nepenthe—the only creature who can use invisibility magic.

There's nothing there.

But there is.

"What are you doing?" Calista calls.

The hand that clamps around my wrist lets go. I look ahead, waiting.

Unsure of what I'm doing.

"Wendy?"

"I don't know," I murmur.

"Well come on." Calista steps closer.

I shake my head. This isn't right. I'm not supposed to leave.

There's something I need to see.

I glance down at the rot eating through my body.

"You need rest," she says.

My heart aches, telling me to turn and follow her, so I do.

A few steps later, I realize I followed because of her concern. She worries for me and my wound.

But my worry lingers with the ghost, in the opposite direction.

Calista takes me to my room and settles me in bed. She even places the cover over my body.

I keep waiting for her to leave; she waiting, too. There's a wall between us, one she doesn't want to cross. I don't blame her. I know why.

"You could go to the infirmary." She lingers by the door. "Get extra healing."

"I'm all right."

I'm not all right. But this pain—this hollowing of my heart—is not from the mended stab wound. It's an discomfort that aches. It's a shepherd, and I'm a sheep—I have to follow it.

Calista turns to exit, but she isn't ready to leave. Her back stays turned to me, her hand on the knob, for several moments.

Finally, she faces me.

"Thank you," she mutters.

There are words on the tip of my tongue, and I almost say them for her. Before I can act on her impulse, she spins again, walking out of the room.

I watch her go, the door closing.

The residue of her sticks to my skin for several minutes. Then, I sink back into my body. My feeling.

And I can't deny there's something wrong.

Again and again, I reach for my heart, my torso. If I were less exhausted, I'd examine the feeling. But I'm not even sure it's mine, and I can't bother with other people at the moment.

Yet it feels so familiar.

Not familiar in the way that my heart and stomach hurt. Familiar in the way my legs once hurt.

I reach for them, surprised when my hand meets my knee cap. I expected it not to be there. For my legs to be gone... the same way I expect my stomach to be a gaping wound. I keep looking down, waiting.

But there's nothing to wait for, not anymore. It's already happened.

I sit up.

This is a metaphorical dismemberment, I realize. I understand exactly what's happening.

The hollowing, the pain, the rot.

It's something I hoped to never feel again, always knowing I'd never be so lucky.

My feet slam against the floor, and I rise, running out of the suite. I turn corner after corner of the academy halls. I don't have enough hope to fight against the certainty that claws at my chest.

The halls are dark, darker so as I turn the last corner, not believing what my eyes are showing me.

It's a dream—it's the boy in my mind. I must have closed my eyes. It's a figment of my imagination.

It's sick.

But it's not real.

But if it's only in my mind, if it's only the boy, why do I feel the impact of the marble floor when it meets my knees, reverberating through my bones like I've broken them?

Why do the sobs feel so *real*, like a stone lodged in my chest, fighting its way out?

"Tell me this isn't real," I beg the boy. *"Please tell me I've lost it. I'm sorry for what I said."*

"I cannot," is his only answer.

In front of me is a bloody mess. A hole in his chest, my heart punched out.

There he is, the only boy I've ever loved. Azaire's usually red cheeks, blanched. His usually smiling mouth, red.

"No," I think I say out loud. I drag my body across the floor. "No, no, no."

I pull Azaire's body from Lucian's lap and onto mine. I touch his snakes, trying to fill them with life. I caress his face, trying to fill him with color.

I try to suck the life from anything around me. I try to give it to him. If I can bring a figment of my imagination to life, can't I save him?

I have to save him.

Nothing happens, and all I feel is death.

Azaire stills wears the rose amulet. Azaire wears the amulet on his chest and is dead despite it. My trembling hand hovers above the pendant, trying to touch it, but I cannot bring myself to.

The stinger of a fatta scorpion rests beside Lucian. The poisonous stinger. The kind that kills a soul.

I glance back at Azaire, worrying he is too far gone.

"How long?" I plead.

"It's too late," Lucian answers.

No. It can't be—he can't be gone, not so permanently. Nothing can kill energy, nothing except for the fatta's stinger. Nothing can eradicate a person, nothing but what's happened to Azaire.

I gave him the rose—I tried to protect him, and somehow the worst has happened.

"I won't accept that," I mutter, picking up one side of Azaire's limp body.

I have to fix this; I have to save him. Give him life or, at the very least, protect his soul.

Lucian lifts the other side of Azaire, and I carry him, trying not to let my emotions muddle with feelings of Ma. Feelings of anything.

But I can't help myself from wondering if this is what Pa felt when he came to the garden and saw his wife dead, half of her body buried in the ground like a plant.

Tears fall. Burning flesh reeks in the distance, and I don't know if it's real. Is it a manifestation of my emotions?

Is this the boy, showing me my worst fears come true? The darkest parts of myself?

"It's not me," he answers. *"This is very real."*

"I don't want it to be."

"I know, love. I can help. Just close your eyes."

I do, because I can't imagine doing anything else. But what I see is the field where Ma died. I wiggle away immediately, hoping to free myself from this. The boy holds my hand tightly.

"This isn't where it began," he says. *"But it is where it solidified. In the aftermath."*

He points to two bodies: my body and Ma's—*alive.* Ma steps in front of me, pushing me back.

"Wendy, *run,"* she demands.

My fourteen-year-old self shakes her head no. She trembles with fear, but she doesn't run. No, she wants to *help.*

She doesn't realize she will do the opposite.

Ma's arms rise, summoning the trees that surround her. She used them to fight the pernipe, just as I had with the kapha.

I hadn't noticed back then, but hers is the stance of a warrior. There is comfort in her power.

Yet, no matter how many blows she lands, the pernipe continues moving. And when it rushes for me, Ma screams. "Run!"

My younger self freezes. I want to turn away—I know what happens next—but my mind won't let me.

The boy won't let me.

Ma holds the pernipe off until she can't. At the hands of the pernipe's magic, she sinks into the world, her legs becoming roots. The pernipe throws my younger self through the air. I land against a tree, the memory going dark.

I don't see the rest; I don't know the rest. All I see is younger me, waking up with a face full of blood. Red pours from the wound at my lip, now a scar.

Tears form in my younger self's eyes—trying to wane off the sting of the blood. She wipes her face, searching for answers, searching for what happened.

Then she wishes she hadn't.

The first thing my younger self sees is Ma, dead and debilitated. Her legs are still rooted in the floor.

Her severed top half lies somewhere else.

Little me doesn't scream. She doesn't even cry. Her face freezes as she stares at the two pieces of Ma's body, once whole.

The world beneath me shakes. The shock waves move through my stomach exactly as they had that day, shaking up the knots that formed. Younger me clutches Ma. Current me nearly pukes.

But I'm too busy watching the story unfold.

I never remembered what happened next—the way I sat with Ma's severed, dead body. It's hard to watch as I hold her, the trees shaking violently above me.

Pa runs to us. He holds Ma's cheek with one hand and mine with the other. He doesn't blame me. Not yet.

"It'll be okay," Pa promises me. The me I watch from a distance. The *me* I watch in the same way I watch other people. But for once, I don't feel jealousy.

I'm watching myself lose everything.

"It's gonna be okay," Pa says.

It will never be okay again, I think.

And my fourteen-year-old self knows he's only saying it to calm me down. To stop the tremor that she's starting in the world.

"It's my fault," little me whimpers.

"Look at me." Pa holds my face. "It's not your fault."

"I could have run," I say. "I should have stopped it."

"This is not your fault," Pa says again.

Looking from the outside in, I can see him gulp down his horror. I watch as he wraps an arm around little me's shoulders, holding himself together just enough to stitch me up.

He pulls me close, whispering in my ear, "Let's bring her home."

Little me clutches the rose amulet—Ma gave it to me when I first left for Visnatus. Ma told me it would always protect me.

I think of the boy who holds it now.

Azaire, who's dead in my arms in the real world.

What little good the rose did.

I follow Pa and my past self, staying paces behind as they enter the house.

On this day, Ma and I had been picking flowers for my birthday. That's why I was home. No one could have ever guessed this would happen.

No one could have imagined.

As we enter the house, my brother Jasper stands, rushing to meet Pa and my younger self.

I stand behind the three of them: my younger self, Jasper, and Pa.

No one says a word.

Terran and Cassius run into the room while Pa gently sets Ma down on a bed of grass and roses. The cries are muffled beneath the ringing in my ears.

It is exactly how I heard them when it happened.

But I know what comes next, verbatim.

The twins, Cassius and Jasper, cry.

Terran turns to me. "You were supposed to be picking flowers."

I am no longer watching from the outside in. I am entirely my fourteen-year-old self again, looking Terran in the eye while I feel him.

Sibling rivalry turns to true hatred.

"You were supposed to be picking flowers!" he screams.

But what he means is, *this is your fault.* I feel it. Both the blame and the guilt. It's all here, ever-present.

"Terran!" Pa reprimands.

"She's the *prodigal child!*" Terran shouts. "The strongest of us can't pick flowers safely?"

"Ter," Cassius says. He tries to wrap an arm around his brother, but Terran shoves him off.

"I didn't like you," Terran says, turning to me furiously. "But now I *hate* you."

I understand. I hate me too.

That's when the image stops. My family freezes, like they're characters and not people. I watch them all, suspended in animation. I long for one last touch, one last hug, because the storm comes right after this.

My life changes in a moment.

But as I reach out to the past, I am pulled out of my fourteen-year-old body. I stand at the doorway of my old home, watching my frozen family from the outside.

The way I have been for years now.

The boy stands next to me as I wipe tears from my cheeks.

"You saw yourself," he says. *"A child."*

I cry. *"Yes."*

He rests a hand on my shoulder. *"You saw her make a choice—to try and save a life."*

I push his hand off of me, my voice steady. *"I saw my mother die."*

"Wendy—"

"Take me back to Azaire." I turn to him, pleading. *"I need to be with Azaire."*

I expect the boy to fight, but he nods. When I open my eyes, I'm in the woods of Visnatus Academy. Azaire lies in a bed of grass and mushrooms. Dead. I try to find peace in knowing that his body is intact; it isn't severed like Ma's.

There is no peace in that.

I stare at him, wondering if I look long enough—if I summon enough power—could I bring him back?

If my power is life, can I not grant it to him?

I try, I do, but my grief smothers me. I reach to every tree, every plant, every star—but instead of feeling their fire, their life, I seem only to deposit death.

Leaning down on the cool soil, I kiss Azaire's forehead. His body rapidly loses heat. His blood no longer flows. His heart no longer beats.

He will never be here again.

"Azaire Wenejad." He can hear me—I have to believe he can still hear me when I whisper, "I love you."

Sobs choke the words as I sit over him, stealing moments to steady myself—knowing if I lose control, I'll lose him again, in a different way. A complete way.

As I hold his dead body, I pray to a goddess that has never heeded my wishes. I ask only that Azaire's soul be safe, untouched. I ask only that she put him in the sky with the other constellations.

Then I walk to Lucian and lay a hand on his shoulder. His tears glisten in the moonlight. He meets my gaze, and I nod.

Lucian kneels over Azaire's body. He lays the blue beanie over Azaire's stagnant chest. Opening his mouth, nothing comes out. He falters on his knees, falling over himself, hugging Azaire's dead body.

"I'm so sorry, brother." I can feel his sobs, more violent than my own. "I'm so irrevocably sorry."

I feel the words he wishes he could say but cannot. The heavy feeling in his chest suffocates him.

His guilt feels like my own. Perhaps it is. I don't know why Lucian would be guilty.

"Azaire?" Lucian says. "Azaire, talk to me."

Breathing hurts. Standing hurts. I fall, and that hurts, too. I exhale, but it turns to a sob. That hurts even more.

I have to pull myself together. I have to do this for Azaire. For his soul.

I won't let him cease to exist like this. I'll give his soul the fighting chance to survive. It's all I can do for the boy I love.

Love.

Fear.

It's all the same now.

I crawl to Lucian. I hug him. He cries over my beloved's body.

"Come on," I whisper.

Lucian holds me, and I hold him as we walk a step away from my baby.

My sweet, lovely, adorning boy. The best boy I've ever met.

The loveliest, kindest soul I've had the honor to know.

Dead, dead, dead.

The pressure of power that pushes through my eyes surpasses the pressure of tears. My arms lift, straining against the air as though it's weighted, to the sky. Every inch of me shakes like an internal tremor until the world begins to shift, too.

Pressure builds in my chest, as if my heart is trying to come up my throat.

From the ground, grass grows. Slowly, the green coats Azaire, like moss overtaking a mountain. It covers him until there is no body left, and from it, bark pushes through. The tree reaches to the sky, the branches reaching for the stars. The flowers that sprout are the same gray as Azaire's eyes.

Is that all of him that is left?

For a moment I wonder if *I'm* alive.

I'm gutted, hollowed out like clay on a lathe, and I stumble to Azaire. The tree. They're the same now.

He's really dead.

I should've let him hold me sooner.

Let me love him faster.

Arms wrap around me. Arms so real and solid that I gasp.

I turn to Lucian, and we cry.

We spend the entire night next to his tree, crying while I try to find the words to tell the stars.

Part 3:
The Shatter

Chapter 27
All of You in Me

The next morning, when I make it back to my suite, I lean heavily against my closed door, taking deep breaths. I try to collect myself, grappling with last night.

Azaire is dead.

He's dead like my ma and Xander.

Death. Defined as a soul moving to a new plane of existence—a plane that I don't know if Azaire got to or not. But could death be something worse? Something with no destination and absolutely no returns?

Could death be nothing?

How long do I have until he fades from my mind entirely? How many years before I think of him for the last time? Or will I sit on my deathbed and remember him, immortalizing him in one, final moment?

I succumb to my unanswerable questions, my back sliding down the door as I crash to the floor.

Azaire is dead. He isn't coming back. My final moments with him were spent tearing his heart to shreds, and that's it. There's no reversing the decisions I've made.

He's gone like Ma, gone like Xander, and I'll live with the loss.

My eyes catch the glimpse of a brown paper bag.

The brown bag filled with the ingredients for Azaire's soup. The cured cattle, dried rosemary, and powdered pumpkin seed.

His ma's ingredients.

What if Azaire is the last of his family line? What if all of him is gone?

I pick up the bag, holding it to my chest. Smelling it—as if it smells like him. It doesn't, but it's second best. It's a smell he would know.

It's a smell his ma shared with him.

I clutch to the bag until it wrinkles, my tears dampening the paper. When I find the strength to stand, I tuck the bag safely in my drawer.

My plan is to keep it forever as I lie in my bed, crying into my pillow.

After Ma died, everyone told me they were mourning her loss with me. It used to confuse me. How could they know how much I was mourning? How were they mourning *with* me?

Few people sat at her grave for a prolonged period of time. Few people mourned as I did.

With every word, I could feel the extent of their sorrow for Ma, but no one, besides my family, could feel even a fraction of my loss.

But this time, no one says anything. The emotions of those around me haven't changed. Kids are still confused in class and horny for their classmates. No one knows Azaire is dead.

Except for Lucian.

I stay close to him, lingering like his shadow, using his emotion to avoid my own. At least with his grief as a barrier, my own can't drive me insane.

But I can't stay with him forever. Today, he leaves for Ilyria, and I'll be left alone.

Alone with myself.

I don't know which way to walk. Left or right? Up or down? I don't know which way to go.

I don't know what to do.

My feet stumble as much as my heart, and I find myself walking to Azaire's room. I close the door behind me, staring at the room, not quite seeing.

I didn't want to come here. I've been avoiding this. This is where the truth settles in: Azaire is gone. It's something I know, but only vaguely, not intimately. His room makes the distinction feel imminent—the truth will settle any minute now.

Just like Ma's study, Azaire's room is a time capsule. Frozen on the day he departed.

I stand in the entry, staring.

His bed is made; Yuki's isn't. His stacks of philosophy books line the back wall. And his journal sits on the desk in the corner, a piece of brown ribbon peeking out on the bottom.

The day he showed me his writing, he told me he had more. He'd been so nervous to show me. But *I* was the one he chose to show. The one he wrote about.

What luck. What love.

How could I have ever wanted to push him away?

How could I not wish to hold him now?

He's not here to hold.

I cross the room, pausing at his chair, my fingers brushing over the journal he once held so closely.

In the beginning, his heart would race at the thought of me holding this journal. And now, it's here—his mind laid bare on his desk, waiting to be taken. One last piece of him, immortalized like Ma in her journals. One final word to read with reverence, as if his soul still lingers within the pages.

I carefully open to the page marked by the ribbon, as if it holds a final part of him, still waiting for me to find.

I think she is wise, like the trunk of a thousand-year-old tree. Strong, like the burning fire of our stars. Elegant, like the flowing tide. I want to tell her that there is a piece of her in everything I see, a piece of her soul lodged within my own, and that it's the most cherished part of myself that I hold. I see her subtle disposition for our worlds colliding with her love of them in the silent sounds of nature. I see a strong belief in humanity, even when all it has to show for itself is evil. I see her hope and not a lack of fear, but a strength to face it. Gods, I don't even know what I'm saying. I'm likely rambling. I guess I love her. I know I love her. And I'm so lucky to love her. Even when my heart does stop beating, I think the entire universe will remember that it once beat for her.

The journal closes, my hand settling on top. I stop reading.

Is that the last thing he wrote? Was it before or after I broke his heart? There are so many things I will never know, but this feels to be the cruelest.

In the most wicked of ways, it feels like fate—his death. The universe has taken everything from me, and the one time I see a glimmer of hope, it ripped that shine from me, too. Likely on the very day the dead boy wrote about his heart ceasing to beat.

That the entire universe would remember it beat for me.

Me. As if I deserve that. As if I'm not just a magnet for disaster, the key to death itself.

I knew from the beginning: do not let Azaire into my life. Now, I'm forced to wonder if he would still be alive if I had listened.

I pull at the tips of my gloves.

When I was ten, I killed Xander because I touched him. Today, I stand in the room of the only boy I could ever hold.

The only boy I could touch, dead.

There are so many ways that my power is terrible—feeling people, killing people—but I think this is the worst of it. The world took away the only person who could withstand my nature.

I wish it was never my nature at all.

"So, you truly want it?" the boy asks. *"Even after everything it's done for you. Every way you've been able to cope by feeling others, you truly want your power to cease?"*

I take a deep breath, halting my tears long enough to answer, *"Yes."*

"I don't believe you, Little Thorn. I don't believe you one bit."

No. He's wrong. It isn't true. This power is the reason for every problem.

In my mind, I spot the boy before me. I grab his arms, feeling him struggle against my hold. But my grip isn't about strength—it's about power. That's what binds us.

That's what breaks me.

Everywhere our skin meets, a thousand needles burst through.

Vines erupt from my fingertips. Dark green tendrils whip through the air, coiling around the boy as they tear free from my skin—each thorn digging in like a dull dagger. More importantly, they pierce him, too.

I stumble back, and the thorns respond, obeying my will. The once-small wooden barbs thicken and twist, doubling in size. As they drive deeper into his flesh, blood rises in thin lines.

A pounding ache blooms behind my eyes.

The rivulets of red slip down his skin, and I realize this is exactly what I intended. I want him to hurt. For him to feel my power—the power he claims I want.

"From the very first time my magic manifested"—I point at the thorns—"this *is what it's done to me."*

I fling my arms wide, and the vines rip free. They tear from his body, snapping through the room and collapsing to the floor.

Then, with a flick of my will, the thorns begin to grow from beneath his skin. Each stem twists upward, forcing its way through muscle and flesh. They tear out slowly, splitting him from the inside, until red blooms across his skin like scattered petals.

"Go ahead," I say, my sudden anger reaching a new precipice. *"Pull them out. See how painful it is."*

"Wendolyn—"

"Feel it for yourself!"

The boy does. Slowly, he lifts a hand and begins pulling the thorns —one by one, peeling them from the raw wounds they've left behind. But it's me who crumples. It's me who bleeds. Me who aches.

Because all he is… is me. How can I keep denying him? How could he be *wrong*?

The boy meets me on my knees. My aching, broken knees.

"My pain is yours." He leans in, voice low. *"Your memories mine. I know your woes."*

He lifts the sleeve of my shirt, revealing every scar.

"I know the worst of your power. I'm only trying to remind you of the best."

I pull my sleeve down, covering the scars he never needed to see. He can always feel them.

When I open my eyes, I'm back in Azaire's room, lying on the floor. When I'd fallen in my mind, my body must have fallen here, too. The remnants of sobs sit in my chest. Aching.

But they're not Lucian's. They're not anyone's. These are wholly mine.

Chapter 28
I'll Grieve When
I'm Avenged

My room isn't silent. It's far from it.

Like everything else, it's suffocating. I'm suffocating. Drifting in doubt. Dripping in pain.

My grief flickers off and on, like a light switch, every time I feel another person. Once they've left my radius, I'm with myself once more. Then another comes along, and I become them.

I'm about to become a princess.

Calista bursts into my room, her presence unmistakably persistent. I hardly have the energy—or the heart—for her right now.

She's ready to fight if I don't agree with her. It's in the set of her jaw, the fire in her eyes. This isn't an uncommon feeling for her—she has a way of making everything seem like a battle, whether she means to or not.

I can't handle a fight today.

As I lie in my bed, she says, "I have a plan."

When I don't answer immediately, my chest tightens with angry breath—the fight in her grows. But I haven't said a word in days, and I'm not sure I'll be able to.

Calista doesn't know about Azaire—I can tell.

I prefer it to the empty apologies.

I prefer her concern to my grief.

I stand and shift my focus to her. Without a word, she turns on her heel and walks away, leaving me no choice but to follow her across the suite and into her room. She sits on her large bed and pats the space next to her. I sit down quietly, unsure of what comes next.

Her excitement is strong, but so is her fear of failure.

There's a moment of silent anticipation.

Then, "We'll take Desdemona's necklace at the Collianth." Her voice is low but urgent. "The place will be packed—crowds everywhere, people mingling, distractions at every corner. I'll target the moment when her attention is pulled away, when she's distracted by the chaos or conversation. Then I'll approach from behind, take the necklace, and vanish before she realizes what's happened. No one will suspect a thing."

I stare at Calista, her words slowly seeping into my mind.

"Desdemona," I sound out each syllable. The name is heavy on my tongue. I hadn't thought about her in days—Desdemona's necklace… the stone… the prophecy.

Time fractures with the stone.

The promise of an end.

For a moment, I don't care about an end. Maybe I'd enjoy watching this universe falter, watching everything unravel. The thought is bitter, but it lingers, like a temptation I can't quite push away.

No. I force the thought from my mind. It's not who Ma raised me to be. I'm not vindictive. I'm not a bad person. But the weight of everything feels like it's closing in, and I wonder—just for a second— if I'm strong enough to resist it.

"Yeah." Calista drags the word out, her gaze sharp. "Are you all right?"

"Fine," I say, though I feel anything but.

Desdemona. Kapha. Leiholan. It all crashes into me, a wave of forgotten details and emotions, drowning my thoughts. My pulse quickens. *Is Leiholan okay? Is he alive?* The questions claw at me, but I'm too afraid to answer them.

More than that—the kapha wanted something from Desdemona. I *felt* it.

But I didn't figure out what.

"There's something off about Desdemona," I finish, realizing how long I've lingered on this thought. It was always silent—at the back of my mind.

"Tell me about it," Calista mutters as she examines her nails. The twinge of her jealousy is sharp, almost pungent, but still more bearable than the weight of my grief.

I shake my head. "Not like that."

Calista glances up, a crease forming between her eyebrows, angry that I can sense her jealousy. She hates when I *read* her—as if I have a choice. But the monster believed Desdemona would be its savior.

It came to her *for* saving.

There's something far worse with Desdemona than her relationship with Lucian or Calista's feelings about it.

Something to do with the monsters. She isn't their master, but she's something.

And it wasn't just the kapha. The moonaro felt the same.

The fatta scorpion might have, too.

I whisper as I realize, "She's involved."

Azaire.

"Elaborate."

"The monsters," I say. It's elaboration enough.

Calista weighs her options. Her anxiety feels immovable beneath my skin. Trapping me as steadily as iron bars. Turning my blood to rust.

A long sigh escapes her mouth. Then words tumble from her, her voice small. "After the Gerner, my mom told me to watch her for anything out of the ordinary."

A queen wanted to watch Desdemona? The queen of Folkara— the same person who ordered Ma's death and used a monster to do so.

That confirms it, then. That's why Lucian suddenly hated Desdemona. He knew what I didn't; she was involved with Lilac's attack.

She was involved in *Azaire's.*

Maybe I didn't ask her enough questions when I had her. She might not be their master, but she could be working with whoever is.

If a queen is watching her, she's just as important as I thought.

"I think we have to kill her," I mumble. "To stop the prophecy." That's not all, but it's all Calista needs to know.

When will the students start to realize Azaire's absence?

When will they know?

Calista's eyes widen, looking at me like she doesn't know me.

"Your jealousy," I say. "I assume it's because of Lucian's interest in her—you fear losing power to her. So don't look at me like that. I know you want Desdemona dead, too."

"Fine." Calista breaks eye contact. "If we get the necklace, I'll help you."

The idea of vengeance feels sweet. Too sweet. I hold out a hand to Calista. "It's a deal?"

Calista rolls her eyes but grabs my hand. "It's a deal."

We'll stop the prophecy. We'll save the universe.

And I'll grieve when I'm avenged.

When Lucian starts leaving campus more often, I find myself going to Azaire's tree. I sit under his leaves, watching white flowers blossom with the gray, and waiting for the day that I *feel* him here as more than a corpse tangled in roots.

I did all I could to save his soul, and yet, I can't shake the feeling that it wasn't enough.

His soul, not just his body, but his soul.

Azaire once said, *What if we're Zola's way of finding balance? Putting together two people with a similar predisposition?* I didn't admit it at the time, but I clung to that idea. I thought that, for the first time, the universe was giving back all that I've lost.

I thought Azaire was that—an apology from Zola herself.

But now, I'm starting to think we were never meant for balance at all. Maybe we were put together to be torn apart.

Azaire had written, *I know that change is inevitable, that there is nothing constant in life. But when I look into her eyes, I don't believe it. What I do believe is that, more than anything, she and I will break those odds.*

But we didn't break the odds, did we? We *proved* them.

I turn toward the trunk of his tree, my hand brushing the bark, silently pleading for something—anything. Just one flicker of feeling, one sign he's still with me.

But my pleas go unanswered.

"Please," I beg Zola, the stars, the sky—anyone and anything that will listen. My forehead presses against the trunk, the roughness scraping my skin. At least, for a moment, the pain is a distraction. "I need to feel him. I have to know he's somewhere."

The words break in my throat, as fragile as a piece of glass, as if speaking them might bring him back—just for a moment.

This goes unanswered, too.

I'm fighting so desperately to hold on to who I am, to not let the anger and the anguish take me down with it. But it's getting harder. I feel lost, broken. I feel *screwed*. This world—this cruel universe— makes me feel *everything*, every unbearable emotion, only to rip away the one thing I want most.

I lean down and pull at the grass beneath my feet. Ripping it out of the ground, feeling it die in my hands. I hope the universe feels it, too.

I hate it. Zola, Sulva, Ayan, I hate every god with everything in me. As I fall to my knees, I want them to fall with me.

For *Desdemona* to fall with me.

Azaire is gone.

His soul's not in this tree, and he's not in the sky, either. He is gone.

Utterly, entirely, irreversibly nothing.

And if Zola will take from me, I'll take from her. I'll be vindictive, I'll be angry, I'll be ruthless—I'll be the things Ma was in those journals. The things, I realize, she was protecting me from becoming. The reason that Pa fought so dearly to keep me from going down this path.

He took my emotion to protect me—but reversely, he's damned me.

I'm not powerless like this universe wants me to be. I'm far from it. I won't go crying into this night; I'll go shouting and kicking and screaming. Fighting and killing.

I'll topple this world with my mere will.

My hands weave through the grass, nails digging into dirt. The ground beneath me trembles with such force that leaves and branches begin to fall, swirling around me like a storm. They settle in a perfect circle.

None of them touch me.

Screw the gods. What have they given me? A life of endless sorrow, of death I never asked for, and power that only tore me apart.

Why am I holding on to this idea of being a good person—this tame Eunoia, trying to protect the world from me—when all the world has done is take from me, and all I've done is cry for it?

As I'm about to slip into the darkest trenches of my mind, the unmistakable feeling of a person approaching pulls me to the present. *Lucian.* I sit as unassumingly as I can manage.

But the anger is too strong.

"Don't do it," the boy says.

I ignore him.

Lucian sits next to me, and I stay silent for a while. As Lucian looks at Azaire's tree, he feels unmistakable guilt. I watch him carefully, from the corner of my eye, trying to understand why.

Finally, I find my courage and ask, "Why do you feel like guilt?"

Lucian shrugs, not meeting my eyes. "Because I am guilty."

I turn to him, searching for his gaze. If I can just see his eyes, I won't need a verbal answer, I'll feel it.

"It's because of Desdemona?" I ask.

He must know she's involved with the monsters and Lilac's attack.

"Desdemona?" Lucian repeats, confused, leaving me just as bewildered.

Could it be possible he's severed his ties to her for another reason? Maybe he doesn't know about the monsters—aside from Azaire's death.

"Oh." I tug at the grass, my fingers fumbling. "It isn't."

Lucian turns to face me, but this time, I don't meet his gaze. "Why do you bring her up?"

He doesn't know.

"I… thought that you thought she was involved in all this. After your theatrics."

"Do you?" he asks, raising an eyebrow. "Think she is involved?'

"Yes," I admit, unable to keep the certainty from my voice. "She's a smart liar."

"How so?"

I think of her necklace. The way she evaded my questions so effortlessly.

"Never once have I been able to catch her."

"Perhaps she was telling the truth," Lucian suggests, his tone sharp.

"No." I shake my head. "She just knows how to get around the questions."

"As you know how to get around a subject." Lucian's voice drips with a self-satisfied edge, as if he caught me on a technicality. "What are you not saying?"

I let out a long, strange sigh. If I tell him about the prophecy, I can get him on my side. He's probably our best chance of getting close enough to Desdemona for the kill.

"There was a prophecy," I say. "It felt like… the *end*. I tried to kill her before it could commence. I didn't try well enough."

I feel Lucian's reaction—something between anger and intrigue. I thought he would be relieved, maybe even pleased that I'm standing with him against Desdemona.

"Go on," he says instead.

I want Lucian on my side. I want *Azaire* on my side, next to me, here.

I continue. "Then there was the kapha. I could feel it trying to communicate with her. If we can stop the prophecy at its source, we have a moral obligation to. And if she's involved with—" I cut off, unable to get the words out.

Then we have to avenge him, I think.

I have a feeling Lucian knows what I mean.

But somehow, he doesn't agree. He shakes his head, his voice steady. "A prophecy isn't a good enough reason."

A prophecy is the *best* reason. A promise of fate—a terrible, inescapable fate. What's a better reason than that?

"The *end* of *everything*," I repeat. "That's what we're facing; that's what the prophecy was!"

"Tell me," Lucian says, barely holding onto control.

He's afraid I might convince him, but more than that, he needs to hear the reasoning before making his decision.

"What was it?" he asks.

Thinking of the prophecy is difficult enough. Repeating it is awful. I can't imagine what it will be like when it manifests.

I can't decide if I care about the prophecy—or if I'm just hiding behind it, using it as an excuse for my revenge.

One thing is certain: I must convince Lucian.

"Time fractures with the stone," I recite.

"The one who leaves returns alone.

When the cracks in the universe divide,

love will be your demise."

"That's too vague—" Lucian cries, but I cut him off.

"You didn't *feel* it!" I shout. I didn't know I could make a sound like this. My throat is raw, and my eyes are dry—yet the tears still come. "You haven't been out here for days thinking about what you could've done differently! Like, if I'd just been able to kill her, maybe the monsters wouldn't have attacked. The kapha came for her, Lucian, I swear it!"

But Lucian doesn't respond. He steps back, shaking his head, unwilling to agree.

"This isn't what Azaire would want."

Something inside of me snaps.

How can he claim what Azaire would want when *he* feels like guilt? His will of iron to Azaire's broken butterfly wings.

How can he claim *anything*?

"He wouldn't want his death to lead to more death," Lucian pleads. His eyes burn with possible tears. He tries to choke them down. "Peace, Wendy. You know he always wanted peace."

Peace. He was supposed to be *my* peace. He was my love.

Instead, he was taken too soon.

A shout builds in my chest, and it feels so easy. I wish I had let myself run free my entire life. "I can't do it! There is no peace without him," I cry. "I feel everything! *Always!*" I rest a hand on his tree, begging, once more, for him to be in there. "But I can't feel him. He's not here. His soul is gone. *He's* gone. And it's like—"

As the words leave my mouth, a surge of *knowing* rises. Something snaps. It's a cruel clarity.

Killing Desdemona isn't an idea or a plan. It's my future. My fate.

It's why I was the one to deliver the prophecy.

"It's like I can't even grieve when she's still around," I continue, my voice hollow. "I have to avenge him."

"She'd take you in seconds." Lucian nearly snarls. "You don't know the extent of her power."

As if he knows the extent of *mine*.

That power pulses in my palms, like a blade pushing through bone. The pain floods my eyes, and five trees burst from the ground with it, growing taller than Azaire's. With this anger, the weight of the power hardly hurts. Two trees grab Lucian's arms, lifting him up, pulling him apart.

Unweaving him, unwinding him.

"Wendy!" he shouts.

He thinks it's a warning.

But I think I'm tired of the universe underestimating me.

"Do you care for her?" I ask, pulling him apart with ease.

Magic seeps into his brain like gas, forcing words out that he may not know are there. "I think she's hiding something," he answers. His words echo, lifeless.

"No," I say. This time I don't give him an option. I pluck the truth from him, like dead leaves from a tree. "Beyond that. What do you feel for her?"

His tongue loosens, the truth slipping past like water flowing over stone. "I *want* her to be hiding something because I don't want to face the fact that I've never been more attracted to a person in my life."

How can he say that when the universe is unraveling? How can his attraction hold more weight to him than the truth? Lucian shakes his head in realization, as if this thought is dawning on him for the first time.

I nearly fall to my knees. My body trembles with the effort to stay upright.

Incredulity gnaws at me. *This* is what he truly cares about.

"I've lost everything!" I shout, the words ripping from my chest. "Twice! And you're worried about your attraction to a killer!"

The sharpness of my voice surprises me, but it's the only thing that feels real right now.

"It's more than attraction," Lucian says, still under my power, the truth shocking him.

And me.

The prophecy, the death, the loneliness and grief. The entirety of it dawns on me. The prophecy isn't only Desdemona's—how could it be, when it involves the entire universe?

In the depths of my mind, emotions flash. The dark and the light. The end of the universe. It is *them*.

They are the end.

"The prophecy isn't only hers." I am not in my body, not in my right mind. But I understand the prophecy now. "Love won't just be *her* demise, Lucian. It will be all of ours."

I shake my head as reality reforms.

I can stop this madness by killing *one* of them.

The branches that hold Lucian pick up speed now that I know what needs to be done. They seem to move of their own accord. I hardly have to pull him apart.

"Are you trying to kill me?" Lucian gasps.

It's him or Desdemona. One of the two to save the universe.

"It isn't up to you," the boy says, watching my actions with revulsion.

"If not me, then who?"

"You will destroy yourself to save the universe. If it is what you wish, I will not try to stop you."

I feel the boy dissipating into smoke. Into darkness and shadow, retreating to the corners of my mind.

Desdemona or Lucian—Azaire's best friend. I don't know if I can kill him.

But I *have* to, don't I?

Who else knows what I know?

But he's Lucian's best friend.

I can't. I won't.

"I don't know!" I shout, crashing to my knees. Tears rip through my body like knives, carving me whole. "But one of you has to die."

Azaire promised we wouldn't hurt—he promised there'd be no pain. Now there's nothing but it. There's nothing, nothing, nothing other than this nagging, ever-present awfulness. Like his corpse is rotting inside of me.

This universe, these gods I was supposed to believe in, they're all thieves. They take and take and take and offer nothing in return.

A *crack* shakes me to my very being. The world beneath me hums with life, and I work to split it in two. If I am to be tormented, I will also torment.

The ground gapes before me, swallowing itself whole. Collapsing in on itself. The world falls into two pieces as a savior approaches. I feel it the same way the kapha approached Desdemona. With intent.

I turn, facing a moonaro. The same kind of beast that attacked Calista, Lilac, and me. *There's another one.*

My body tenses, every muscle ready for the fight, but the creature doesn't move toward me. Instead, its gaze shifts, locking onto something behind me.

It stares at Lucian.

A savior approaches.

This monster is here for Lucian. Is it possible? Has Lucian been in on it with Desdemona all along?

I channel my magic toward the moonaro, prepared to kill it the way I killed the pernipe. The trees holding Lucian release their grip, poised to ensnare the creature. But the moment Lucian is free, the monster bolts, darting into a distant concave of trees.

And Lucian is saved, as the monster intended, when he lands on solid ground.

I turn to face him. I'd hoped that when I let him go, he would fall into the crater I made. I suppose I've never been lucky.

Exhaustion tugs at my limbs as I stare at him, trying to take one solid breath.

"You're part of it?" I ask, my voice breaking, sounding nearly resigned.

"Why?" Lucian asks, keeping his distance while he decides his next move. "What did you feel?"

I step forward, raising a finger at him. "It wanted to *save* you."

Lucian gets ready to fight. To fight *me*. I tremble as I lift a branch in midair, guiding it toward his chest. He ducks, but I continue the attack, losing awareness. Blow after blow, fight after fight, pointless aim after pointless aim.

Then I'm choking on his shadows, and I don't even care.

Kill me, Lucian, I want to taunt. *Kill the girl your brother loved.*

He wraps me up in shadows.

Reunite me with your self-proclaimed family, you fucking asshole.

I don't mind death. I never have.

In fact, I think I'd prefer it to this existence.

But Lucian falters. He does not go for a life-ending blow. He stands still, contemplating. He wants to kill me, and I want to goad him into it.

Instead, he says, "I'm not a part of anything. I don't want to hurt you. But touch Desdemona, and I will kill you."

From beneath his nest of shadows, I spit on his face.

Chapter 29
A Ghost Made of Memories

Lucian doesn't care about the prophecy. The boy doesn't care about the prophecy.

The boy is me.

The boy is the worst of me—

No.

The boy is me.

Azaire isn't here to care about the prophecy.

Calista has a vague understanding.

I need a Eunoia, then. That's it.

I storm into Ms. Ferner's classroom. There's a group of students—likely two years below me—listening as she talks about the nature of healing. After the last time we spoke—after what I did to her—it's out of line to barge in now. To interrupt her class. But she once helped me maintain my power, and I need that help now.

Ms. Ferner glances around the class, slowly bringing her gaze to mine. Her eyes begin to glow—a beacon of light—as she senses what I'm feeling. In an instant, she understands the importance. She may have claimed our relationship was never personal, but on some level, it had to be.

Impersonal doesn't end with being so well understood.

Even if she doesn't care about my powers, I didn't tell her to stop caring about me. At least, to some extent, that still stands.

Elegantly, she wraps up her class, dismissing the students. Slowly, they walk past me, and I keep my eyes down, unprepared to take in all of that emotion.

When they're gone, I race through the rows of messy desks to Ms. Ferner.

She keeps her head down, eyes on a book.

Her gaze doesn't meet mine again.

"Yes, Estridon?"

"How are—" I cut myself off.

Ms. Ferner looks up.

I suppose there is no time for manners.

"There was a prophecy," I say instead. "*I delivered a prophecy—* and I don't know what to do about it."

Ms. Ferner's emotions go from slightly concerned to entirely suspicious.

"And what was the prophecy?"

I recite it to her, as well as what I learned in the woods while fighting Lucian. I tell her that this prophecy traces back to two people— one prince, and one Fire Folk. As I speak, I question myself; am I only looking for someone to condone my actions? To agree with how I treated Lucian, and how I will treat Desdemona?

"Wendy," Ms. Ferner sighs, using my first name—which she doesn't often do. Even if she hadn't given me that small indicator, I'd know I won't like what she's about to say. "Prophecies are not up to the interpreter. I fear that such a warning is left in the hands of those who it was delivered to."

Leave it up to Desdemona and Lucian? Two people who *have* to die but will never kill each other?

I shake my head. "You don't understand—"

"Your magic has always been unpredictable," she says—so matter-of-fact. Clinical. As if it means nothing to her.

Because it doesn't. It's simply something she observed. Never something she invested in.

Ms. Ferner continues, "We cannot trust that you got the prophecy right, nor can we be certain that you fully understand it. However, I do commend you for the strength you've shown. It's fair to see you stand for something."

I step back, looking at Ms. Ferner sideways. My magic may be unpredictable—but it's *strong*. It always has been.

It's why it killed Xander.

How can she not understand what the prophecy means? Is it because of what I stole from her?

"My magic may have been unpredictable in the past," I argue, my heart gutting itself when she doesn't care. "But I've learned discipline. I killed a pernipe!"

Ms. Ferner flinches at my words. "You mustn't walk around screaming that."

"Why not? I deserve credit—"

"*Credit* will not be what you receive," she reprimands me. "You'll be ostracized. No one wants a Eunoia who kills. It goes directly against what we are."

I feel her words like a weight on my chest. It's not as if I was unaware of this—it's that it doesn't make sense.

"But that's what I don't understand," I press. "How are we *all* the same thing? Yes, Eunoias bring life. Why can't we end it, as well?"

Ms. Ferner rises, shaking her head as she presses her hands against her wooden desk. "This academy is preparing you for the universe at large—how to survive within it under those in power. If they want you to be a life-bringer, that is what you must be."

"But—"

"I told you once, there is no space for revolution."

"I'm not seeking revolution—"

"*Wendy,*" she hisses. "Do not even speak the word unless you are willing to suffer the consequences."

I take a deep, shaking breath, and all I say is, "Yes ma'am."

My body is thoroughly battered—as if I've lain in the center of the hall, taking foot after foot to my ribs, my stomach, my face. My mind is covered in bruises. My thoughts are bleeding.

It's long after the academy day and time for the Collianth Ball when I knock at Calista's door. Donning a shimmering pastel yellow gown, she glances at me once, scanning from head to toe—disapproving of my dark blue academy uniform.

"You didn't get a dress?" She says it kindly, but there's small peeks of anger beneath.

I think she will always be angry with me.

No, I didn't get a dress—there wasn't any time. Not between the shallow aches that pierce through me with every breath. The longing to be anything other than me.

The grief I promised myself I wouldn't feel.

"I didn't have time." I shrug.

Calista shakes her head, walking to the back of the room and opening her large wardrobe doors. She sighs as she searches her closet, pulling out a pastel purple dress. With annoyance, she throws the gown on her bed, and I pick it up obediently. As she glares at me, she crosses her arms over her chest, waiting impatiently.

I should be putting the gown on. But there's something more happening.

Something I've been waiting to face.

There's no better time than when I'm already aching, I suppose.

"Are you always going to be mad at me?" I ask meekly.

With the arch of an eyebrow, she says, "I'm not mad."

"Calista—"

"Just put on the damn dress, and let's get this over with."

The dress is beautiful. The kind of thing Ma might have picked for me. Though hers would have been a more muted shade of purple. Still, I don't deserve it.

Do I?

Either way, beautiful does not feel like a thing my battered body deserves—even if the pain is no more than metaphysical.

"We're running out of time," Calista reminds me.

I don't argue any more—with myself or her.

As I tug my uniform off, I turn to face the door, then I pull the glittering purple dress on in its place.

I'm not ready for this. The last time I donned a gown so gorgeous I was in Azaire's hands.

The boy's hands.

Azaire's hands.

I should have let him love me sooner. I could have loved him longer. Now, I love a corpse. And I will longer than I loved the man he was.

No. I won't grieve until I'm avenged. I have to stick to my vow, this time.

As I turn back to face Calista, she glances me up and down, approval like smoke billowing out from her. "Are you ready?"

"One second," I mutter, leaning over to strap a small pouch to my thigh. The perfect hiding spot for Desdemona's necklace and my quick escape.

Our plan—*vengeance*—should be the first thing on my mind.

My promise should be the first thing on my mind.

But I thought holding Azaire would mean hurting him, and in turn, hurting myself. I thought that would be the worst fate.

It's the last thing I should be thinking, but it's the first thing I think of: that as perverse as this is, I'd prefer his place over mine.

To be the thing gone, rather than the thing grieving.

I shake my head at my thoughts—stupidly—and when Calista glares at me, I say, "Ready."

I don't care what happens to me, as long as I fix what happened to him.

It's sickening how beautiful the ballroom is after the ugly events beyond its borders. A man lost his leg. My boy lost his life.

With every step, the room grows invigorating. At first, it's sweet. My blood beams—like a light in the night—with vesi and other substances. Then, my heart pounds. My mind races.

Is it the weight of my thoughts?

It's hard to tell.

Calista stays a few feet away, talking to her friend, Fleur, and glancing in my direction. She makes sure I have a clear view of her. That way, I can feel when Desdemona's necklace is hers and we seal the prophecy shut.

Calista is waiting until the dancing starts, when everyone will be moving and looking for a partner. I wait for that moment too, passing the time by drinking up everyone else—intoxicated by strangers' blood streams.

I count the seconds. Lucian approaches. It's surprising; he isn't angry. He isn't seeking retribution. His intentions seem nearly pure. He's dressed in a suit even more ornate than Calista's gown—royal blue with embroidered beads and a glistening coat adorned in stone.

"Wendy," he says, meeting my gaze. "I didn't think I'd see you here."

Fleur drags Calista across the dance floor. I take a step forward, following them, but Lucian steps in line with me. There's no getting out of this conversation.

"I didn't mean to disappoint," I say.

Lucian clasps his hands behind his back, looking ahead. "No," he mutters. "I came to apologize. It was never my intention for matters to escalate to such a degree."

"Which matters? Desdemona? Or Azaire's death?"

An arrow of guilt impales my heart. It takes away every second-hand shot of alcohol.

"What did you do, Lucian?" I ask—a question, but I mean it as a demand.

He shies away, lowering his gaze and seeking to avoid mine.

I grab his forearm, forcing him to meet my eyes. Forcing myself to feel every splinter in his shattered soul.

"Everytime I mention Azaire, *you* feel at fault," I say.

Lucian's jaw clenches, and I dig the tips of my gloves into his skin. "*Tell me*," I demand.

He shakes his head—wishing to end the conversation but wanting to rid the arrow in his chest more.

"Have you ever sworn to protect someone with your life?" he asks. He isn't looking for an answer. "Tell *me* how you'd feel if that person died in your arms."

The words don't absolve his guilt, like he hoped they might. It makes it worse. He tugs his arm from my grasp, lowering his head once more.

"Excuse me," he mutters as he walks away.

I watch him go.

Azaire *died* in his arms. It's no wonder he feels this way.

Should I be feeling this way? Grief, instead of anger? Or, do I already feel both in separate ways?

Grief has turned to anger. Anger has turned to vengeance. There's one thing to do—and whether it fixes this feeling or not, at least I'll know I've done all I could.

I turn away from Lucian's retreating form, searching the room for Calista. There's many heads of blonde hair—none of them the princess'.

The panic only seems to kick in when I can't find her. My head whips through the room, searching in every direction. Each time I see a yellow gown, I sigh in relief.

That relief only lasts moments, at best.

Calista is nowhere to be found.

Then the screaming starts.

Around me, the students rush. A blur of ball gowns and cries whip past—fear and frenzy pounding at my mind like a rock. I clutch my temples, trying to stay on my feet.

"Arcane!" they shout. "Arcane!"

It's pandemonium. It's apocalyptic—the way these kids feel.

This is the end.

They think this is the end.

I fall to my knees, trying to plug my ears and drown everyone out. Heels press against my fingers—people stepping on my hands—but it feels like nothing.

An arm wraps around my waist. I do nothing.

"Wendy." Calista's voice is tinged in annoyance. "Get *up*."

When I meet her eyes, they're heavy with fear. I feel it. She did it— she's taken Desdemona's necklace—and she was waiting for me. I'd been so focused on Lucian, then the crowd, that I didn't feel her until now.

I ruined the plan. Because Calista isn't waiting for *me* anymore. She's waiting for someone to fix her mess. And it's clear she's lost control.

Across the room, Desdemona lies on the floor, convulsing. Her body shakes violently as the racing students charge at her.

They're going to kill her.

It's exactly what I want.

Desdemona is completely unaware of the danger she's in. Of the angry students with eager faces. Her pupils have vanished, entirely unseeing. She's stuck in a trance, the brown of her irises replaced by a coat of yellow.

Folk yellow. Memory yellow…

Memorium yellow.

Her necklace *had* to be the Soul Stone. *That's* the stone the prophecy mentioned. The stone that fractures time.

It must be.

The crowd of students are a second away from reaching her. She's already convulsing—likely from Air or Light magic. She's close to dead, regardless.

Iridescent veins of light split the air, streaking toward Desdemona. Fabric ignites in their wake—dresses and coats bursting into flame.

The air shrieks with power, wind whipping past me. It stops around Desdemona's body, moving like a shield and colliding with the lightning, sparing her life.

Aralia steps before Desdemona, her eyes glowing with power. For a moment, I'm hopeful. Aralia will finish what they've all started.

Then her emotions fill me.

Aralia is Desdemona's roommate, and somehow, she's fallen into her trance—just like Lucian and Leiholan.

Fallen for the monster's act.

Her wind blows dresses, tears curtains from windows, and pushes hair into eyes. My gown billows behind me, and my eyes sting as I try to keep them open. Even as I try to move forward, I barely make it a step.

Still, the students charge relentlessly. But even those who manage to outrun the wind don't make it past Aralia. One by one, they falter, slamming into the invisible barrier like birds against glass. Aralia steps forward. The barrier of wind moves around her, hard to see.

But I will be the one to get past her. I have to be.

A boy nears her. The closer he reaches, the stronger the wind surges. It pulls the flesh of his face back, and I have to look away, for fear that it will tear off.

Then I can't breathe. My lungs seize, shriveling like they've been drained from the inside.

Not mine—theirs.

The boy is on his knees. His face is intact, for what it's worth.

He failed.

I feel his panicking pain, the hunger for air, the collapse of breath. Aralia is strangling them, her power pulling the oxygen from their lungs.

They're choking—and through them, so am I.

But Aralia struggles. Her arms begin to falter. The strength of the wind slows. People move forward.

I steal it.

The best part—Aralia isn't focused on me.

I push ahead.

If anyone can feel me, they'll know I'm no different from Lucian. But while I may be guilty, there is no remorse. Not now, not when revenge is right in front of me. Not when I have such an easy way to protect my psyche.

Desdemona's life might be the key to ending the prophecy.

Despite what Ms. Ferner or Lucian say, if Desdemona dies, maybe —just maybe—the prophecy will die with her.

I grab Calista's shoulder, using it to push myself forward, heading for Aralia. I don't know what I mean to do.

I know exactly what I mean to do. I plan to control Aralia, to tell her to *stand down*.

To release the magic keeping Desdemona safe.

Even if I didn't, Aralia would get tired soon. She couldn't hold the shield forever. I'm not doing anything wrong. I'm speeding up the inevitable.

The kids on their knees—the ones Aralia was suffocating—begin to rise. Their breaths are ragged, and my lungs are sore for them. But they're not going to let Aralia protect Desdemona any longer.

I'll have a legion with me.

I move forward with them, prepared to do what I came for.

Then, Calista steps in front of me, grabbing my wrist. I try to shove her off. She doesn't budge.

"Protect Aralia," she begs, shaking my arm and searching for my gaze. "Please."

The kids around me retain their breath. They reach Aralia—one of her hands now holding her stomach, struggling to breathe.

They're doing exactly what *I* want to do.

Aralia is in my way.

"Why?" I ask.

Calista agreed with me—Desdemona has to die.

It seems Calista has changed her mind.

"Please." Her voice is barely audible.

I could try. It'd be as simple as telling these students they don't want to fight. But I want Desdemona dead, and I'm willing to let her take her chances. She's the reason Azaire is gone. The reason a prophecy claims she will tear the universe apart.

Her death wouldn't be wrong. It would be balance.

Instead of helping Aralia, I tell Calista, "Run."

She glares at me, torn between fighting and fleeing. "You have to help her!"

I don't move, caught between two choices that feel almost identical: help Aralia or condemn her.

Helping Aralia would save Desdemona—and that would kill us all.

I shake my head, taking a deep breath. "But that would mean helping Desdemona," I whisper, shocked at the sound of these words on my lips.

Calista's shocked, too. Her face shatters, but not with anger. I could handle anger. I've grown used to hers. This is disappointment.

It wounds sharper than any scream.

"Wendy," she sighs, her eyebrows folding together. "Killing Desdemona to save people is one thing. Letting her die for your own reasons is something else entirely."

"That's not—"

It's as if my power detects my lie before I do.

That's exactly what this is.

And I want to tell her she's wrong. That it's still justice. It's still noble.

I'm still saving the worlds.

But I can't even look her in the eye.

I know Calista's right; I know where all this hatred leads. Despite myself, I can't stop it. I wish I could lie to myself.

The prophecy is a crutch, and I will use it until I can no longer stand.

I glance back at Aralia and Desdemona, sighing with shame as Lucian approaches. He helps a tired Aralia, brandishing a sword at the people who try to fight through him.

Aralia lets the barrier drop, and as Lucian is stepping past it, another kid follows. Lucian doesn't waste a second before turning, running his blade through their arm. The kid's hand falls to the floor, and he cries out in agony.

Lucian protects Aralia while he picks up Desdemona, pulling her from danger.

He does what Calista begged me to do, and while I feel disappointment, Calista breathes in relief.

I tell her once more to run, and I follow when she does.

I stand at the exit to our suite. Calista sits on the couch, examining Desdemona's necklace and occasionally giving me a disapproving look. She hasn't said anything about me leaving Aralia, but I feel her disdain grow with every breath.

The stone shifts in her hand, her intrigue strong.

"Is it the Memorium?" I ask.

Calista holds the small stone to the light again. "It's been altered." She squints as she says, "Though I think it *was*."

There's something she's not saying.

"And?"

"Patience." Calista closes her palms around the stone, her fingers tightening. A minute later, she drops it with a hiss, the stone clattering to the ground as though it's a burning ember, too hot to hold any longer.

I race across the room, asking, "What is it?" as I lean down to pick up the necklace, leaving behind its broken chain. Immediately, I feel what Calista did. It doesn't burn me as it did her—but it doesn't feel *right*.

Certainly not how a Soul Stone should feel.

"You feel it?" Calista asks, her eyes widening.

I twirl the stone between my fingers, watching it closely for signs of power. "Differently from you, I think. It's not Folk magic."

"But it's holding *memories*," Calista insists.

So there's a degree of Folk magic involved.

And definitely Memorium magic, which *is* Folk magic. Their world is where this Soul Stone came from, made to balance their magic. I just don't understand how the stone has been tampered with. It doesn't feel like any magic I've ever known—and I've known them all.

I hand the stone back to Calista. "Can you show me?"

She shifts uncomfortably in her seat. Inadequacy hits its peak, and I remind her, "You can do it."

"I know I can," Calista snaps. But she doesn't know it, and she reads the pity in my gaze, not wanting to hear it. "Don't." She lifts two fingers to my temples—conceding.

She *can* do it. I know it.

I close my eyes.

It's a bumpy beginning—a blurry picture. Then, I'm standing in what must be Desdemona's body. She can't be older than fourteen. She looks at a woman as she holds her hands.

Gods, the woman looks so familiar. I swear I've seen her before.

The door to their home trembles, just as I realize who the woman is.

"Isa!" a voice shouts. A voice I never thought I'd hear again. A voice I dare to recognize. "Isa open up!"

Ma.

Desdemona's mom—*Isa*—opens the door.

And I stare at the voice I never thought I'd hear again. A face I never could imagine quite right. Unmarred and beautiful. Restored to past glory.

I choke up, but Desdemona's body doesn't follow me into sensation.

My mom wraps her arms around Isa.

Why would Desdemona's necklace have a memory of my mom?

"What are you doing here?" Isa asks, holding onto both of Ma's arms. The way I long to.

I watch, standing in Desdemona's body. I have no control over it, yet I somehow swear my mouth is agape.

"You weren't supposed to come for months," Isa finishes.

"They know she lives," Ma says. "King Easton—he's looking for her. He thinks he can power the weapon before the Arcanes do."

Isa looks at me—at Desdemona—like I'm both a nuisance and the object of all her love.

The breath rips from my chest, like it's been stolen.

This body—Desdemona—is Isa's daughter. *She's her daughter.*

She's my mom's best friend's daughter.

I shake my head. It doesn't work.

"We need to leave," is all Isa says to me—no, to Desdemona. Then she rests a hand on Ma's shoulder. "Thank you, Lo—"

"Tell me nothing," Ma interrupts. I try to focus on the scene in front of me. "I don't know what they'll do to me if they believe I hold information." Ma reaches up to grab Isa's cheek. She holds her so tenderly, the way she used to hold me. Tears prick at her eyes. "I can't promise that you will see me again."

Could this be the last thing Ma did before she died?

Did she use her final breaths to protect Desdemona? A girl I'm trying to *kill?*

Am I going against Ma's dying wish?

Isa steps back, shaking her head as she runs a hand over her mouth. The two stare at each other, Ma's lower lip quivering.

"Willow," Isa sighs, her voice muffled, her hand still covering her mouth. Her head continues to shake. "I *need* you."

Ma bites her lower lip to stop the quivering. The image is a mirror. I never realized that habit of mine came from her.

I want to know all the ways I carry her.

"My dearest friend," Ma chokes, yet her eyes glow as she looks at Isa. "The light of my life." She smiles. "You saved me once. I owe it to save you, too."

Isa takes a step forward, picking up Ma's hands. "Being near will save me!" Isa pleads. "I can't lose both you and Freyr. It cuts too deep —"

The image breaks off. My mom disappears.

I open my eyes to the suite, more confused than ever.

Ma?

Where did you go?

I look up, seeing Calista and remembering: it was all a memory.

"Show me more," I beg, breathless.

Only then do I realize the red lines in the whites of Calista's eyes. Her strain.

"I can't." Calista rubs her eyes closed. "It's too much."

Ma has something to do with this—with Desdemona, the Memorium, and Isa. She went back to save Isa, to save Desdemona, right before she was killed.

And I left Desdemona in the ballroom to die.

I broke my ma's last living will.

I wonder if Pa was right when he said I could never do what Ma has done. If I'm playing with forces far beyond my comprehension and control.

If Ma protected Isa and Desdemona, there was a *reason*.

I stand, turning to the door. "We have to go back to the ballroom."

Calista reaches for the stone. "I have to—"

"I need you with me," I say.

The truth is I only need *someone* with me. Someone else to be forced to feel so I don't crumble beneath my own weight.

But Calista tilts her head as she looks at me, her gaze lingering longer than it should. Tears prickle in her red-rimmed eyes. I feel it— an unspoken truth, something neither of us would ever say out loud.

We are the only real connection either of us has left in our lives.

And in this moment, I realize maybe I do need her.

Before either of us can voice it, Calista huffs, "Fine," as she picks up the Memorium.

We walk the academy halls, the sconces dim and an alarm blaring. Students race by us, whispering about what happened in the ballroom.

"Was she really an Arcane?"

"I saw her red eyes."

"But those things aren't real."

"You really believed that?"

Arcane. If Desdemona is an Arcane—

I must have misunderstood them.

Or Ma.

There are still unconscious students on the ballroom floor. None are dead. One lies next to a hand, instead of having it attached to his arm. My heart races, then Calista runs to a girl—Aralia.

Calista holds Aralia like what she used to be. Her dearest friend.

"She's alive," I let her know, moving my focus back to the bodies littering the floor. I wonder about Desdemona. All these unconscious kids were trying to ambush her—did they succeed?

It doesn't seem like they did.

"She's not waking up!" Calista cries from across the room.

"She will," I assure her. "She needs rest—" I cut myself off as my eyes land on a blue beanie.

I blink, certainly mis-seeing.

As I open my eyes, the blue remains.

My entire world shrinks, until it is nothing but the dark fabric.

It's real.

Who would wear a beanie to a ball?

I take tentative steps. Afraid if I make too much noise, a ripple will rearrange my reality. The boy in front of me will dissipate.

It has to be Azaire, in some way. Doesn't it?

That's *Azaire*.

I approach. I lean down. I begin to pull the beanie from the head of the boy. He must have snakes. He must be Azaire. Why else wear a beanie to a ball?

Slowly, I lift the beanie from the top of his head.

I am met only with brown hair.

Hair? Who would wear a beanie at a ball to cover *hair*? I laugh at the absurdity. I laugh so hard that I fall to my knees, clutching my stomach as it aches. A beanie. Who would wear… a blue… a beanie…

With one breath, the humor escapes me, leaving me with a feeling so wholly my own that there is nothing else to grasp onto.

He was supposed to come back.

Azaire wasn't supposed to die.

Ma wasn't supposed to die.

My family wasn't supposed to blame me.

I was *fourteen*. I was a baby, a child, inches smaller in height. A million times smaller in mind.

How could I have stopped a targeted attack on my mom?

How could I save the universe from a prophecy?

Maybe I'm meant to do nothing. I was only a conduit—I am not a savior. I never have been. I failed Azaire, my do-over, the first time I opened myself to love after losing so much of it.

Even if I kill Desdemona, it won't stop me from feeling this. If there's anyone that deserves my anger, it's me. If there's anyone that deserves to be avenged, it's not me.

I don't have Azaire, and the gods don't have Azaire. No one has Azaire. He's a *tree.*

And I never told him I loved him.

There was one thing I could have done—one thing that could have changed my fate.

I could have told the boy I love that I loved him.

There have been so many things I *thought* I had to do—things I was powerless to change. But this is the one I can't deny. There is no reasonable explanation for what I did, for why I tore his heart out in an attempt to protect him, when what I should have done was pull him closer.

The *one* time that my choices had power, I chose wrong.

"I'm okay," someone says. *Aralia.* She's shocked that Calista is holding her, helping her. She glares around the room before asking, "What is this?"

Calista fixes me with a gaze, unsure. She doesn't know what to tell Aralia. But she turns to her, asking, "Where did Desdemona go?"

Calista asks for me.

For me to kill her.

After watching quietly this entire time, the boy comes to life. *"If this is what you want, I will not stop you, Little Thorn."*

"Why wouldn't you stop me?"

"Because you are close to finding the truth I've been trying to show you. For all I've tried, I have failed. Perhaps it will take something drastic."

"Lucian took her," Aralia answers.

"To kill?" I step forward.

Aralia glares at me. "To protect." Her gaze fixes back on Calista as she shrugs her arms away from the princess. "Why are you helping me?"

Calista opens her mouth, shaking her head slowly. Aralia sighs as she rises to her feet, moving away. She wipes dust from her dress and leaves the ballroom without another word.

Calista stares at me, unspoken words sitting in her throat. She can't get them out. I sit next to her, once a friend, turned a foe, now something more complicated.

"Is there something more you want?" she asks, her voice tight.

I open my mouth, but it seems this time it's my vocal cords who disagree.

"I have the necklace," Calista scorns. "I'm done here."

But she doesn't mean it. I can *feel* her not meaning it. She must know that, but I stand regardless and leave the ballroom.

Because beneath her facade, there's a broken heart. And I don't have it in me to try to mend two.

Chapter 30
Who Is Your God Now?

The moon is low in the sky as I traverse the woods, settling at Azaire's tree. The rift I made in the world sits before me, and I stare into the abyss. Would darkness be better than life?

I twirl my fingers through the grass, soaking in the life left. Before the boy, this was my company. Nature. When it all became too much, I would feel for her—Zola, the goddess of balance, present in every inch of the ground.

I pull the grass from its roots and grow it again, twice as strong.

No matter how many times I do it, it offers no peace of company.

In the end, I close my eyes, searching for the boy.

In my mind, Azaire's tree is vibrant, bright. A beacon of light. Even in my soul I cannot escape the destination of my mourning.

The boy stands before the tree, nearly blending in.

His gaze meets mine, offering a solemn nod.

"You're unsure," he says. *"If you are going to kill her or not."*

I inch back, angry at having the question voiced so simply. To kill or not to kill—it isn't so clear cut.

The grievances that others feel by my power are understandable. My ability sees what should be kept concealed.

"Yes," I answer.

The boy takes a deep breath, stepping forward as he takes me in. *"Death stains a soul."*

"I know."

"For as many woes as this life has dealt you, you have handled them with grace."

The boy offers me a hand. I take it, and he begins walking toward the cottage.

I stop as quickly as we started. *"I don't want to go in there."*

"We must."

It's against my will that we enter the house. Walking past the purple kitchen, up the colorful stairs, and to the second story, with the stained-glass window and the tree growing through the floor. Hundreds of memories here turned to two deaths. Thousands of smiles turned to one frown.

"When it comes, you will put up a fight. Promise me," the boy says.

I stare, as if I don't know what he is saying. But it's there—the burning in my lungs, stealing my words.

"When what comes?" I ask.

"You feel it. You're ignoring it. But that burning is arriving, and you are stronger in a place with emotional roots." The boy pats the top of my hand. *"That's why I brought you here. You have moments. Fight, Wendy."*

My eyes open against my will. It's so rare for the boy to send me away—it's only happened once before. Normally, I push him out. But the moment the thought passes, something else arrives.

The burning. The anger. The disgust. Something is approaching. I gaze out the window, waiting for a sign.

A tall, dark creature appears in the woods. Unlike anything I've ever seen.

Its skin is blackened like charcoal, cracked with glowing red veins. Boils and cysts throb across its arms and shoulders—some burst, leaking a dark sludge.

Arcane.

Its head tilts unnaturally, as if studying me. Blood-red eyes glow like dying stars, fixing on mine through the glass.

It doesn't blink.

From the safety of the second floor, I wrap the Arcane's ankles in vines. They're thick and thorned, writhing up from the soil like serpents, tightening against its limbs.

The boy was right—my power is stronger in a place of emotional attachment. Because it's my pain that pries the world apart. Breaking it like a heart, the way I had the last time I was in battle.

I force the ground beneath the Arcane to split.

The world shifts, the trees begin to collapse, and I tell them to. I *will* them to with every ounce of anger, of grief, of *emotion*.

The thing that once tore me apart, now shattering the world.

A tremor shudders outward. Roots rip free, the ground crumbles, and the trees fall.

Every ounce of rage, every shadow of grief—I pour it into the soil. Into the world. Into *breaking* it.

The Arcane jerks, fighting my restraints, but it can't. Because I am powerful, too. I feel its fear, and it strengthens me.

The thing looks up at me as it falls into the world. I assume in despair.

Then it's mouth opens wide, revealing a row of shattered and decayed teeth.

A smile.

As it falls, my hands explode in heat. Blistering heat, turning to burning agony. I scream as I fall to the ground, the pain sizzling through my skin. Burrowed into my blood, my bone. Spreading across my entire body.

I'm being roasted over an open fire.

But there is only wood beneath me.

It lasts for an eternity, and I know I won't survive this.

My skin falls from muscle, muscle falls from bone, all burnt to ashes. Until there's only darkness.

Slowly, something rounds the bend—the academy. Lucian.

But I know soon there will be nothing.

The creature inside of me—the Arcane. His name is Icarthus. He speaks to Lucian… his *son*. A highly-prized piece of information, one I won't get to keep. I feel my body wither away beneath the Arcane who now wears it. Bits and pieces of the real world make it through the cracks.

A fight begins, but the Arcane does not want to fight his son. As Lucian sends me to the wall, the Arcane leaves my body.

Life suspends to something slower. My last breaths slip through my fingers. I reach for air, like grasping at smoke, knowing I will not be able to hold it again.

"Fight, Wendy!" the boy screams at me. *"Fight or you will cease!"*

My being is dissolving. The threads that once sewed me together are coming apart. Where my body once held the fabric, there is now a tear. A hollow ache, an endless void, swallowing my light.

It feels like my soul is being torn from existence.

"I'm ready." I close my eyes. Finally resting. *"I'm ready to give up now."*

"Wendy, don't you dare!" he bellows.

Tears slip from my eyes, somewhere inside my mind. *"Tell me I fought valiantly. Tell me I had a good run."*

"Wendy—"

"Hold me," I say. *"And tell me I did my best."*

Everything crumbles around me. I am in a world of make-believe, of red and white. The boy stands over me. It's the first time I've seen him from above.

"Take my hand," he says, reaching for me. *"Take my hand, and I will bring you through this."*

I look at his hand, outstretched. He thinks he can save me. He pleads, he begs, but I can barely feel it.

I'm tired.

It's a nice sort of tired. The peaceful kind.

But even my own mind won't believe that.

Even my own mind denies what I long for.

I shake my head, denying his hand. *"I don't want to make it through this."*

"Wendy!"

"I give up," I cut him off, bracing for the impact. *"I give up."*

The boy says nothing, only picks me up, slinging me over his shoulder like a coat. I don't fight because I don't believe in what he can do.

The boy walks through this strange world. It looks like ours, except everything is tinged. The trees are red; the floors are white. The walls shatter slowly, the academy crumbling around me, and the boy runs. The trees fall; the buildings collapse. The boy pants.

Slowly, the whole facade falters. The white and red crumble into a ceaseless darkness.

"You can't save me," I say with a smile, feeling as my consciousness slips from existence. *"It's over."*

Chapter 31
War is Sweet to Those
Who Never
Fought

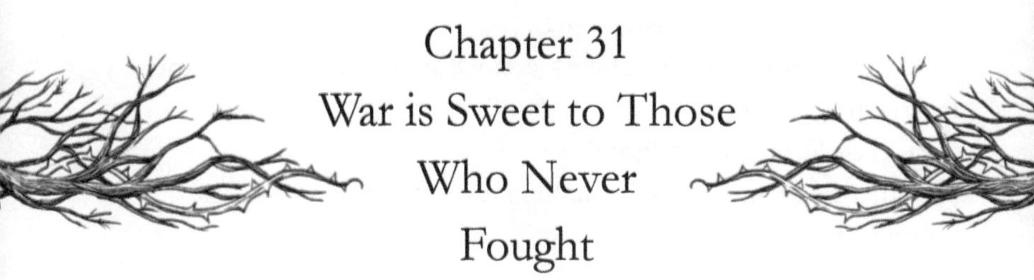

A breath of fresh air becomes a fish out of water—it doesn't feel right. I breathe, and I breathe, and I breathe. It doesn't feel right.

Darkness. Lucian. Nothing.

Icarthus—the Arcane who stole my body and told Lucian he was his father.

Nothing.

Memories assault my mind. My voice tells Lucian that his father is not his father, his mother not his mother. That he was made to destroy Desdemona.

Desdemona.

She sits in front of me. Black liquid trickles down her neck. Then she looks at me, expecting something. At least, I *think* she's expecting something.

Because I cannot *feel* it.

Why can I not feel her?

Black blood—the liquid staining her neck—means she has rewritten the very laws of nature. Revoked the goddess of balance herself. Bleeding black is a myth—folklore. Yet, here she is, bleeding…

I had died. I had died with my mind screaming at me, telling me to live. I chose against it.

How am I here?

"What did you do?"

"Saved your life," Desdemona snaps, wiping the blood from her neck. Her tone is whiplash. "I'm gonna find Lucian, you can come or you can mope. Your choice."

I watch her, curiously. I've never experienced this before: confusion at one's words. I always understand where they're coming from, but I can't seem to understand her.

At least, not entirely. There's a small glimmer, a slight tether. A feeling in her soul.

It feels like the black blood.

Then Desdemona stands, leaving me with two options: sit on the ground or follow.

I follow.

It feels like I'm picking up a corpse as I rise from the floor. Every step is deadweight, every movement mechanical, like it shouldn't be.

Like I am not real.

Desdemona does something to my surprise. She wraps her arm around my torso, allowing me to put my weight on hers.

"Thank you," I mumble, stumbling through the academy halls.

My body is difficult to carry.

When we arrive at Azaire's suite, I swallow the ache. It burns going down, stirring in my stomach like acid.

Desdemona knocks and I stand at the doorway, forgetting why we're here. But Desdemona might not know Azaire is gone. She certainly doesn't know what he was to me. Meaning there is a reason we're here other than my loss.

Kai answers the door.

"Where is Lucian?" Desdemona demands.

Kai's eyes go wide, and as I watch, I notice I cannot feel his fear— or confusion or shock. I only *think* it's there.

"You're one of them," he whispers.

I turn to Desdemona, who's glaring at Kai. I see her eyes for the first time. They *are* red, like the Arcanes.

Arcane, Arcane, Arcane. Like the one in my body.

The one that *killed* me.

But if I'm dead…

It cannot be.

Desdemona huffs something. Then she slams the door.

She's an Arcane. An Arcane that Ma knew, aided, and cared for. Ma didn't want information from Isa because she wanted to protect them *both*.

She's an Arcane I remember—fleeting as it might be—from my childhood. The little girl I would play with when Ma visited Isa.

That was *her*.

I stare at Desdemona with a new meaning, a new life. She's Ma's best friend's daughter, a piece of her.

As we stumble through the halls together, I notice how much of my weight Desdemona is carrying.

I wonder how much she knows.

"Calista can find him," I say, referring to Lucian. I can feel Calista on campus. Not because of my magic, but because of the favor she granted me. Her power hums in the back of my mind when I'm near.

But the rest of my power isn't anywhere. I don't feel it in my mind or my fingertips, and certainly not in my heart. I don't feel *anything*. Does that mean it's gone? Is that what the black blood meant—Desdemona had rewritten my power?

"Calista?" Desdemona asks, regarding my comment about finding Lucian.

"They're betrothed," I say. "They share a little of the other's power."

"That's good." The hollow tone in her voice is easy to recognize—even without power.

"She should be in our suite," I say, following the invisible thread of power.

"That's good."

Then we move in silence, leaving me alone with the boy. My boy.

Leaving me alone when there's one person I want. One thing I can't have.

"Do you think Azaire would forgive me?" I ask the boy. *"For all I've done?"*

"I'm certain of it," he says.

Tears threaten to spill. I nod, relief washing over me momentarily. I want to believe the boy.

But I want something else more.

I close my eyes, meeting the boy in the hallway. *"Can you—can you look like him?"* I ask, meeting his gaze. *"Just for a minute. Just to hold me?"*

Physically, I lean my body into Desdemona's body. Mentally, I lean into the boy.

"It could become a crutch," the boy responds as I drop my head on his shoulder. *"I can't always be him."*

"You've been Xander," I counter.

"You were not in love with Xander," the boy says.

Though he quickly morphs into Azaire. Into his blue beanie and gray eyes. His arched nose and chin, sculpted as if from a piece of marble. I hold his face, knowing it isn't real.

I step in front of him, just holding on.

"I'm sorry, Azaire."

He shakes his head. *"It was never your fault."*

"I know," I answer. *"I know that."*

"Do you, Wendy?" He looks down at me.

My face puckers as I try not to look away. *"No."*

Azaire nods with a sigh. *"Lucian was right when he said I wouldn't want more death. But I also wouldn't want this—for you to feel at fault."*

"If I hadn't left him—"

"You made that choice to protect him," the boy says, cutting me off before I can spiral further. *"Even if you hadn't left him, he still would have fought."*

I stare into Azaire's eyes, knowing it isn't him I speak to. *"Can you please talk like Azaire, at least?"* I ask the boy. *"Say I instead of him?"*

"Of course," the boy answers, so clearly not Azaire. It takes me out of it—this coping mechanism.

I try to fall back in, but I fly right out.

I sit on the marble floor of the academy hall, leaning against the wall. *"I love him, you know?"*

"Love me?" The boy sits beside me.

I shake my head. *"No,"* I admit. *"I love him. The boy you're pretending to be."* The tears I've choked back come to the surface, even if it's only in my mind. *"And if he were here, I think I'd tell him that now. That there's safety in his voice and adventure in his eyes. I'd apologize for underestimating him and the strength in his peace. I'd tell him that, even if I had to feel a million people's grief, I would still be grateful I ever got to feel him."* I meet Azaire's gaze, wishing it could be real. Tears slide down my cheek, salty on my lips.

"I'd look into his eyes, and I would say it, and I would mean it." My voice cracks. *"I am in love with you, Azaire Wenejad."*

And I am too late.

Azaire's hand—the *boy's* hand—reaches for my cheek. *"He knew it. I know it."*

"I hate that." I shake my head, shrugging away from his touch. *"The past tense."*

"It's all he has now."

"I hate it," I repeat.

"You didn't steal his future," he says. *"Is that what you were thinking?"*

The taste of salt settles in my mouth as the tears drop. *"Everyone I love most dies. What if I'd run when Ma said run? What if I'd known my power before I touched Xander? What if I trusted Azaire to handle this on his own?"*

"Don't imprison yourself with what if's," the boy reminds me—Azaire's words.

"But they're real," I say. *"And they matter. They hold weight in all of these situations."*

"Situations that have passed. Seas you will only drown in, if you do not learn to swim." He picks up my cheek, looks me in the eyes, and says with full conviction, *"It is not your fault."*

I feel a knot tighten in my chest, and I break eye contact, turning my face away from his touch. *"Okay,"* I mutter.

He doesn't let me off so easily.

"Wendy," he says, his words cutting through the silence. *"It. Is not. Your. Fault."*

I nod.

"Look at me," he says.

I do.

"None of this was your fault."

"I know—"

He cuts me off. *"Not Xander. Not Ma. Not Azaire. You didn't know. You couldn't have known."*

His gaze is intense, unwavering, my childhood flashing in those eyes. Xander dying, my ma dying, my family blaming me.

Things that happened, far beyond my control. Things I was powerless to, and then blamed for.

As I look at the boy disguised as Azaire, I finally understand what he's been trying to tell me.

This whole time, I've been deaf to his words.

"It is not your fault," he says.

And I repeat, *"It is not my fault."*

AUTHOR'S NOTE

Wendy's story may be the most gut-wrenching I've written.

In one of the (many) early drafts of *A Liar's Twisted Tongue*, Wendy had her own POV. Through those chapters, I came to understand the depth of her empathy and the weight of her survivor's guilt. Eventually, I scrapped that version and her POV with it. But months after publishing *A Liar's Twisted Tongue*, a thought occurred to me: *Wendy is a doomful daydreamer.*

The boy was born from there.

As always, Wendy's magical story stems from the mundane. At its heart, this is a story of self-forgiveness and the harm of relentless self-judgment. She possesses magic, yet all it does is magnify her humanity.

If this story meant something to you, the absolute best thing you can do right now is leave a review on Goodreads, Amazon, or wherever you picked up your copy. Your words make a real difference. So if you have thirty seconds—or a single sentence to spare—I'd be wildly grateful.

Thank you, yet again, for picking up one of these vulnerable books. Writing is just another form of expression, and I pour my soul into every page. I'm so deeply thankful to you, dear reader, for choosing to see what's inside.

With all my heart,
Caroline

ACKNOWLEDGMENTS

Wow. My second-ever acknowledgments.

First of all—thank you. As an indie author, there's always that lingering question: *Will I get to publish another book?* It's because you chose to pick up *A Liar's Twisted Tongue* that I had the opportunity to keep writing. This book wouldn't exist—in the public space—without your support.

To my dad, thank you always. I don't think there will ever be a day I don't thank you. You were the first person to ever take a chance on me as a writer, and I'm endlessly grateful for that.

To my brothers, Dominic and Anthony. Dom, thank you for being the first to read all of my books. And Anthony, thank you for continuing to promise that you'll read them someday. Every time I write about family, there's a little piece of you both on the page.

To Rae, my incredible developmental editor: When I first published *A Liar's Twisted Tongue*, I couldn't afford a developmental edit (hence the republication!). Being able to collaborate with someone who helps refine the smallest details has been a gift. I'm so close to these stories, and because of that, it can be hard to see clearly—it makes you cross-eyed. I endlessly value the editors I've worked with.

My copy editor, Gabe, you seriously make a joy out of the tiring task of eliminating typos! You're deeply attentive to every step of the way, and your genuine enthusiasm picks me up so much. You're the last person to read my work before it goes out—you give me that final boost of confidence.

To Stefanie Saw at Seventh Star Art, who created this beautiful cover: thank you for your patience with my tiny tweaks (like the shape of a blood drip) and for always being willing to pivot—even if we end up right back where we started. You've created all my covers, and it's your vision that's helped me shape my own.

Thank you, Jan Perit, who illustrated all the internal artwork. Your creative direction is consistently stunning, and the ease and joy with which you bring your art to life continues to amaze me.

And I know I already thanked you, dear reader, but I must thank you again. My heart is filled with gratitude for every single one of you. Writing is self-expression, and having that expression resonate with

you makes all the pitfalls—and, most certainly, the triumphs—worth
it. I do this for me. I do this for you.

Thank you. Truly.

A PUPPET'S BROKEN STRING

POWER ALWAYS COMES AT A PRICE...

CAROLINE CUSANELLI

Keep reading for a sneak peak of

A Puppet's

Broken String

Prologue

Desdemona Althenia was but six years old the first time she bore witness to Death.

She believes she remembers the day vividly, as it was the day the Neptharian War began. Yet, there is always a subtle trick with memory—especially those we believe to be most vivid.

This was the second village she called home, a place for miners. The air was thick with soot, more so than with breath itself. There were few trees, no flowers to speak of, nor bodies of water to offer respite. Life was barren in this village, and it was on the cusp of becoming even more so.

Though Desdemona insists she remembers this day with precision, she would swear the quality of the air felt no different from any other.

A Nepenthe flashed by, super speed carrying him past Desdemona before she could make out his movements. In his wake lay three Folk, their heads twisted at unnatural angles.

Another Nepenthe—whether the same or a different one, Desdemona would never be certain—returned, cradling a Folk.

Well, only her head.

The three Folk on the ground ignited, and the severed head fell with them, consumed by the flames. Isa grasped her daughter's hand, and together, they fled into the woods.

It is here that her claim of a vivid memory begins to truly falter.

They ran for miles. When Desdemona's small legs could no longer keep up, Isa lifted her in her arms. Each time they stopped, Isa crouched behind the tallest grasses she could find, as if hiding from something unseen.

"Are you hurt?" Isa asked.

Desdemona shook her head. This was yet another thing she finds difficult to recall: the silence she swore by in her early years. With each day, I watched, waiting for her to speak, longing for wisdom that would transcend her youth.

The longer I observed, the stronger my understanding became.

The removal of memory shapes a person. Memories carry emotion, and emotion is energy—energy which cannot die. Each time Isa stole Desdemona's memories, the emotions remained. And an emotion without a rational cause can make one feel as though they've lost their very mind.

That night, the two of them slept beneath the stars.

"This is something you haven't seen yet," Isa whispered, holding Desdemona's hand. She pointed toward the sky with the other. "That's Aeliana and Persiphis. And that's Surma—Sulva's son." She told the stories of the constellations, their fates woven into the tapestry of the heavens. Then, turning her gaze back to Desdemona, she squeezed her hand. "Much cooler than a plain old ceiling, yes?"

Desdemona smiled, but she was not amused.

Desdemona was cold, but she did not shiver.

Desdemona saw the dead Folk behind her closed eyes, but she did not speak.

She knew that every time she did something to upset Isa, discomfort followed. It was the removal of a memory. Though, at the time, she was unaware of such a possibility.

But she always felt it, fractured as the feeling was.

The following day, Isa killed a possum and asked Desdemona to start a fire.

"But you don't like…"

"We need it," Isa said sharply. Desdemona didn't recoil; she barely reacted. Isa could see she'd startled her daughter. "It's all right." She softened her tone. "If I'm here, nothing bad will happen. Understand?"

Desdemona nodded. The fire ignited with such ease, it was like wiggling a toe. The heat spread from her stomach, up through her torso, and to her chest. She held the flame in her hand, and Isa held the possum over it. Desdemona was a living bonfire, radiating heat and light with every breath.

They spent days in the woods, living with the animals, before Desdemona asked, "Are we going to another village?" Sometimes it took weeks to travel between them.

"Yes," Isa replied.

Desdemona believed her. Now, she knows that was her own fault.

For Isa planned to wait out the war in the woods, away from the Nepenthes, away from the threat. Desdemona understands that now.

She didn't yesterday.

Each day, Desdemona employed her magic to cook their food. Nothing ill came of it. She did not set the forest ablaze, nor did she harm any living soul. She simply prepared their meals, and they continued on.

After a month, Desdemona had grown accustomed to the fire. By the third, it had become second nature. Today, in the quiet moments of reflection, she wonders: had she not forgotten, would she have ever faced a problem at all?

Could she have been a master of the Flame?

But forget she did. As such, she didn't merely face problems, but she became one. Killing in every village, forcing her mother and her to run—more than even Isa had planned.

They spent a year and a half in the woods. When the war finally ceased, and they made it to another village, Isa did what she had always done—she erased Desdemona's memory. Their life in the woods vanished from her mind, replaced with one of a village, much like all the others.

Isa, however, added one awful truth: the Nepenthes were wicked and vile.

For the next ten years, Desdemona remembered a hut in place of the trees, a ceiling in place of the stars, and murder in place of the meadows. The war—once avoided—was now a retched experience, in memory alone.

With it, Desdemona forgot how effortless it had been to wield her magic—that there was a switch inside her, one she could flip with little more than a thought. She struggled to recall what she knew at six: she could use fire to aid in survival, to cook food, and to generate warmth on cold nights.

And after she killed Bernice and Nova, she forgot she could use magic at all. Each time her fire rose to the surface, she killed. The next day, she forgot.

Isa was afraid of Desdemona.

So Desdemona was, too.